Scheming for Love

Scheming for Love

Blake Karrington

www.urbanbooks.net

Urban Books, LLC
300 Farmingdale Road, NY-Route 109
Farmingdale, NY 11735

Scheming for Love Copyright © 2018 Blake Karrington

ISBN 13: 978-1-945855-71-9
ISBN 10: 1-945855-71-1

First Trade Paperback Printing October 2018
Printed in the United States of America

10 9 8 7 6 5 4 3 2 1

*This is a work of fiction. Any references or similarities
to actual events, real people, living or dead, or to real
locales are intended to give the novel a sense of reality.
Any similarity in other names, characters, places, and
incidents is entirely coincidental.*

Distributed by Kensington Publishing Corp.
Submit Orders to:
Customer Service
400 Hahn Road
Westminster, MD 21157-4627
Phone: 1-800-733-3000
Fax: 1-800-659-2436

Scheming for Love

by

Blake Karrington

Prologue

Gloria made her way through the jam-packed club and fought the urge to push everybody that bumped into her. On average, Sparkles rolled in at least 300 people each day of the weekend, including Sundays. All types of people occupied the club—the second largest in Charlotte—and everybody came for the same reason, which was to get drunk, dance the night away, and hopefully get laid. Everybody but Gloria had come out with that intent in mind.

"Can I have a double shot of Hennessy?" Gloria asked, holding up a twenty-dollar bill for the bartender. She put her back against the bar and scanned the club, mentally noticing things like the exit doors, bathrooms, and the number of people who were in the VIP sections, both downstairs and upstairs. She looked for the security and noticed how they were spread out throughout the club. Right at the moment she was about to turn around and grab her drink, she laid her eyes on the man of the night, making his way through the crowd with two security guards walking closely behind him.

"Can I buy you a drink?" a guy sitting at the bar offered, snapping Gloria out of her thoughts. She was irritated by the man but was also expecting for someone to hit on her. Gorgeous was an understatement when it came to Gloria. She was half black, half Puerto Rican, and her caramel complexion complemented her cute face. She had 34B breasts, long curly hair, and a petite frame. Tonight she had on a black Dolce and Gabanna fitted dress, and on her feet were a pair of black Saint Laurent heels. A Prada clutch was in her hand.

"I'll pass," she yelled back. She threw back the double shot and walked off on the guy before he could say another word. Other pressing issues needed to be attended to, and Gloria didn't have that much time to waste. She made her way through the crowd of dancers on the floor and walked down the short hallway to where the owner's office was. One guard stood outside, stopping Gloria when she walked up to the door.

"Take it back downstairs." The tall, brolic man spoke with force.

"Tell Dion that Missy is out here," Gloria continued.

The guard wasn't familiar with who she was and wasn't too thrilled about bothering the boss.

"Trust me, he wants to see me," she added.

The guard shook his head. "Wait right here," he told her, then went into the office and closed the door behind him. Gloria quickly reached under her dress and grabbed the compact 9 mm off her inner thigh, taking the safety off just as the office door was opening up. Without hesitation, she raised the gun, aimed it at the center of his forehead, and pulled the trigger. *POP!*

Dion, who was sitting behind his desk, froze up after hearing the shot. By the time the second guard, who was standing next to Dion, pulled his weapon, Gloria turned her gun on him. *POP! POP!*

He, too, took a bullet off the side of his head and one in his chest. Dion was in shock, watching Gloria step over his guard's body and walk right into his office. Her gun was now pointed at him. He tried to say something, but Gloria wasn't there to talk or try to negotiate for his life. She walked up to him and fired a bullet into his face. *POP!*

Dion fell out of his chair, and to be sure that he wouldn't recover from this one, she walked up, stood over him, and squeezed another bullet into his head. The music was so loud in the club that nobody heard the shots. Gloria tucked the gun into her bag, then pulled out her phone and took a picture of Dion's lifeless body bleeding out on the ground.

Not wanting to press her luck, she then put her phone in her bag and walked out of the office, stepping over the bodies and using a handkerchief to wipe off and close the door behind her.

Chapter 1

Raymond looked around the mall from his seat in the food court, waiting for Amanda, one of his clients, to show up. His private investigating business was starting to pick up, and the more clients on his caseload, the more strained his time was.

"I know I know. Sorry I'm late," Amanda pleaded, walking up and taking a seat at the table with him. "The kids wouldn't let me go, and my husband is here."

"Come on, Amanda, you know being on time is important. Next time I'm gonna have to charge you for that," Raymond told her as he looked around to make sure her husband wasn't in their vicinity.

"Just show me what you got," she said, just wanting to get to the business.

Raymond reached into his bag and pulled out a gold folder, passing it to her. This was the moment Amanda dreaded. She only wished that Raymond hadn't found anything on her husband, but that quickly went out the door.

"He's definitely seeing someone else," he told her. The pictures inside the folder spoke for themselves. Amanda and Doug had been married for six years, but from the looks of the photos, Doug seemed to be single. There were pictures of him and a cute white, blonde female hugged up on a park bench. Other pictures showed the two hand in hand, walking into a restaurant, and then there were a few of Doug and this mystery woman heading into a Holiday Inn. He even had the nerve to be hugging and kissing in public like he was having the time of his life.

"How long?" Amanda could barely get out, looking down at the photos.

"I really can't tell. It has to be at least a few months. He has keys to her place," Raymond informed, reaching in and grabbing another folder. "It wouldn't be right if you didn't know everything," he said, passing it to her.

Amanda looked into the folder and almost had a panic attack. Other photos showed Doug and the blonde female having sex in his car. Amanda was hurt, and it showed as the tears began to fall from her eyes. She quickly got it together, wiping the tears from her face. Sadness turned into anger within seconds, and now thoughts of killing Doug entered her mind. Her head was spinning, thinking about the constant lies and betrayal and the few nights he didn't come home due to "overtime" at his job. That was all bullshit. She felt more stupid than she could have imagined, but now, the truth had been revealed.

"I can keep these, right?" Amanda asked, stuffing the pictures back into the folder.

Raymond affirmed with a nod of his head. He hated this part of the job and actually felt sorry for her. He couldn't see why Doug would want to cheat on Amanda when she was the better-looking blonde in the first place. It didn't make sense, but nothing in the private investigation business did. At this point, there was nothing else Raymond could do. He was paid to do a job, and now that this job was done, it was time for him to move on to the next job, which was calling his phone at that moment.

Gloria woke up to Alisha, her ten-month-old daughter, laughing hysterically next to her. Her husband, Dillon, was the culprit, making funny faces at Alisha until she pissed her Pampers. Gloria wanted in on the fun, rolling over only to have a sippy cup smacked up against her head.

"Rough night?" Dillon asked, looking over at the wig sitting on the nightstand. Gloria smiled, rubbing her forehead where the cup hit her.

"Yeah, fifty grand richer type of night," she replied. She was happy for a minute, thinking about the money, but then her thoughts shifted to how she felt last night after she did what she did. She didn't understand why, but for some reason, things seemed off. Out of the eighteen people she'd killed under contract, none of her hits made her feel the way she felt right now. Of course, this wasn't something she could explain to Dillon, seeing as how he was always worried about the line of work she was in. For the past five years, he had begged her to get out of the contract killing business and spend more time with the family, but Gloria just couldn't let it go. At times, even Dillon had to admit that the money was good. Her safety was his only problem.

"You know I would love to be home playing housewife," she replied, cradling Alisha.

"Yeah, I wish you could too. If I had the ability to . . ."

"I know, I know, baby," Gloria cut in, stopping before he started talking about his job and how he wished he could be making more money. Hearing how unpredictable the construction business was and how work was hard to find at times always made her feel bad. She could see in his eyes how bad he wanted to work. It was days like today when he didn't have any work that depressed him, and having Gloria go out every day risking her life to provide for the family stressed him out even more. Gloria didn't mind, though.

"So, look, I got some running around to do today, but I was thinking that we could all go out for dinner tonight," she said.

Dillon glanced over at Gloria and said with a hint of frustration, "Anthony's football game is tonight. We were supposed to be taking the team out for pizza afterward."

Gloria flopped back onto the pillow with the baby still in her arms. "Damn, I forgot. At what time is the—"

"The game starts at four o'clock," Dillon said, cutting her off.

Gloria could hear the attitude in his voice, and he had every right to be mad considering the fact that she'd missed four home games this season already. Every time she didn't show up, Dillon was left to explain to Anthony why his mom didn't show up to his games. It was something he'd become accustomed to doing.

"I gotta get Alisha ready for daycare," Dillon said in a low tone. Gloria had messed up the perfectly good morning they were having—another thing she often did.

"We're outside North Lake Mall, where police have identified Amanda Carpenter as the primary suspect in the killing at Sneaker Mania, here inside the mall," a female news anchor from KCB News reported. "The victim is a forty-year-old white male, who sources say was the shooter's husband."

Tamika walked into Gwen's office with a serious look on her face. Gwen was so caught up in the news, she didn't realize what was going on.

"Would you look at this. . . ." Gwen said, pointing at the TV with the remote in her hand. "She needs to get down with—"

"G, somebody killed Dion last night," Tamika said, finally getting Gwen's attention.

Dion was a reliable ally to the MHB crew. Years ago, the all-female clique took Charlotte by surprise, eliminating the male competition at an alarming rate. The war between MHB and the men of Charlotte was bitter and nasty. A lot of lives were lost on both sides, and it wasn't over until Dion came forth and ended the war through vigorous negotiations and compromises. For two years straight, both the men of Charlotte and MHB lived in peace, but not without a few bumps along the way.

"Do they know who did it?" Gwen asked, turning the TV off.

"No, but people in the club seem to think that it was a female who did it."

Gwen could already see how bad things would look to Dion's crew, and it just as easy for them to start pointing their fingers at MHB.

"Look, I want you and Tiana to go over to Malvern street and let Tank know that we didn't have anything to do with that," Gwen instructed.

Tank was Dion's uncle, and he had a short fuse. If he had any information that MHB had anything to do with Dion's death, the war would be back on in no time, a situation Gwen didn't want to occur.

"Let me find out what the hell is going on," Gwen concluded, getting up and walking out of her office.

Carmine got out of his car and looked around the cemetery where he and Gloria were to meet. The place looked empty, minus a couple of gravediggers preparing a plot. He didn't know it, but he was being watched and had been ever since he drove into the cemetery. Gloria stood behind a ten-foot tombstone, watching and waiting to see if he came alone as she'd told him to. Carmine was with the mob and worked for Emilio Castellano, the man who had put the hit out on Dion. He was one of the last of a dying breed, and he did what it took to keep his kind around. "His kind" meant the culture of the Italian Mob, which was beginning to fade into a mere memory.

"I would say that you're late, but something tells me that wasn't the case," Carmine said as Gloria approached. He couldn't help but notice the semi-automatic handgun she clutched in her hand, down by her side. Carmine didn't feel threatened, but more so aware.

"Is that my money?" Gloria asked, looking down at the manila envelope in his hand.

He smiled, passing her the envelope, but also unable to take his eyes off of her. Her beauty was a thing of perfection, even in the eyes of somebody like Carmine. Italians were big on their lineage and not mixing with other races, but for Gloria, Carmine was willing to make an exception.

"You should let me take you to dinner," Carmine offered, just trying his hand. She wasn't having any of it and wasn't going to entertain his comment. Gloria was about business and business only, and it was clear from the look that she gave him. It was a look that told Carmine to beat it.

"Tell Emilio to be expecting a call from Agnis sometime today. It would be in his best interest to have what she wanted from him. I would hate for him to be on the other end of this," she said, tapping the gun on her thigh. She stood there, waiting for Carmine to even think about making a move on her for what she had said. He would have met his end right there in the cemetery. Carmine was far from stupid and knew that she had the drop on him. Gloria stuffed the envelope into her back pocket, turned around, and started heading back from the way she came.

"Aren't you gonna count the money?" Carmine asked, watching her ass switch side to side as she walked away.

"If it's not all here, I'll know where to find you," she yelled back without even turning around.

Carmine watched as she dipped in and out of the tombstones until she eventually disappeared like a ghost. Aside from her being gorgeous, Carmine knew that she was a stone-cold killer and for that, he planned on taking her a little more seriously in the near future. Her threats were duly noted.

Rev. Index was the second largest distribution company on the east coast. They sold and traded products all over the country, ranging from car engines to smaller things like household products, such as soap and toilet paper. The owner's name was Jennifer Green. She had started the company with her husband when he was alive, with nothing but a vision. Now the company was worth more than a billion dollars, and it was getting to the point where Jennifer was thinking about giving the company over to her son, Raymond Green. The only problem with that was Raymond could never be found.

"Raymond, call me back as soon as you get this message," Jennifer spoke into the phone.

In about an hour, a crucial business meeting was about to take place with some potential investors from China. As the vice president of Rev. Index, Raymond didn't look as though he was going to be there, which was a little embarrassing.

"You might wanna think about finding a new vice president," Jennifer's brother James said, walking behind her toward the conference room. "The boy just got so much growing up to do."

Jennifer had heard these words from her brother many, many times before. If it weren't for Raymond being her only child, James would have been in line to be the vice president.

A knock on the door grabbed both of their attention, and when Jennifer looked up and saw that it was Raymond standing there, she was relieved. "I been trying to call you," she said, getting up to hug him.

James stayed seated with an attitude, only waving his hand at Raymond.

"I know, Mom. I'm just caught up with this new case right now."

"Case? What case? Raymond, are you still spying on people?"

Raymond chuckled. "No, Mom, I'm not spying. I'm a private investigator."

"Hell, that sounds like spying to me. And I thought you were going to stop."

Raymond did promise to put his P.I. business on hold once he became VP, but business started to pick up, and he was focused. There just weren't enough hours in the day. "James, can you step out for a second so I can talk to my mom?" Raymond requested. He didn't want his uncle hearing about his personal issues. James got up and left the room, even though he didn't want to.

"Mom, you know I love you and I would do anything for you, but you can't expect for me to put all of my time into this company."

"What, like I had to do? You know, me and ya father built this company with our own blood, sweat, and tears."

"Yeah, I know, Mom, and that's what I'm trying to do with my company. It's not as big as yours, but it's mine, and if I learned anything from you, it's to never give up on what you want out of life."

Jennifer became sad, taking a seat in one of the chairs. "So, you're gonna leave your feeble old mother out to dry?" she panted.

"That's not what I'm saying. I'm still your VP, but I have my own company to run, too. I'm not gonna be able to make it to every meeting you set up. Just know that when you need me for the important stuff, I'll be here for you."

Raymond was sincere with his words, and Jennifer understood how he felt. She, too, was once in his shoes, and now she was the boss. At this point, all she could do was hope that Raymond would find enough drive to want to take over the family business. This was her legacy, and she didn't want it to go to waste, or go to her alcoholic brother, for that matter.

Gloria walked into Agnis's Beauty Salon and was put right into the middle of the latest gossip.

"Now, G, don't lie. Last week, when that girl came through that door, what did she smell like?" Agnis asked, putting her on the spot.

The whole shop got quiet, and all eyes were on Gloria.

"Come on, Aggy. Don't make me say it," Gloria pleaded.

"Oh no, girl, tell them. They think I'm lying," Agnis egged on. Everyone waited for the answer. Gloria tried to mumble the word, but that didn't work.

"Fish?" a woman yelled out from the hairdryer.

"Yeah, girl, fish. I don't know if the girl wanted a perm or a pap smear," Agnis yelled out. The whole shop went up in arms. "Bitch smelled like an all-you-can-eat sushi bar. Smelled like she rode a dolphin to get over here," Agnis continued. The whole shop was laughing at her jokes. "I knew it was something fishy about that girl."

Gloria put her head down, but she couldn't hold it back. She, too, started laughing and shaking her head.

"I wouldn't do that in her pussy!" Agnis yelled out, pointing to Gloria shaking her head side to side. "Ya damn face fuck around and fall off."

Agnis and the whole shop laughed so hard their stomachs started hurting. It took every bit of ten minutes for order to be restored, and then after that, it was time to take a break.

"Let me see you in my office, mamacita," Agnis told Gloria, nodding for her to follow her. In public, Agnis was different than she was behind closed doors. There, she was focused and serious. It was like night and day, but it came with the business. A half black, half Italian female only made it out the ghetto one of two ways. She did it by either hitting the books or dealing with the crooks. Agnis chose the latter, and over the years, she'd become connected to some major players.

"Did Emilio call you?

"Yeah, one of his people dropped the rest of the money off about twenty minutes ago. Thanks," Agnis said, taking a seat in her chair. "I got something else lined up. Just came in today."

Agnis swirled around in her chair, grabbed the bag off the floor behind her, and swirled back, placing the bag on the table. It was always Gloria's choice whether to accept a contract on somebody's life, and it was important in her eyes that she never became personally involved with the reason why she was killing that person. This was why she rarely asked any questions. All she needed was the name, the address, and the money—all of which Agnis provided.

"Now, be careful with this guy. He's handsome as hell and probably could talk you out of your panties if you let him."

"What do you mean by that? Who is he?" Gloria asked with a curious look on her face.

"He's the mark, and that's all you need to know, G," Agnis shot back. "Just don't get too comfortable with this guy." Agnis warned Gloria about him because she knew this new target was a good guy; innocent beyond all measures. If Gloria actually got to know this guy, he was the type that would make it hard for anybody to kill him. He was just that likable.

"You know after this one we'll be taking a break for a while," Agnis began. "Not permanently. Just for about a year so I can take care of a few things."

Agnis didn't want to worry Gloria with the real reasons why she needed to take some time off, at least not right now while she was still considering treatment options for the small lump that doctors found occupying her left breast. This kind of information on Gloria's mind could prove to be detrimental. Agnis needed her to be sharp on her toes with this hit, seeing as how this particular hit was on the sophisticated side of things.

Tamika and Tirana felt tension the moment they walked through the doors of Club Sparkle.

"We here to see Tank," Tamika said.

"Tank don't wanna talk to you. Now get da fuck up out of here while you still can," the guy told her. He flashed the chrome .45 just to let her know that he was serious.

Tamika tapped Tiana for them to leave, but when she turned to head for the door, Tiana didn't move.

"Nah, we ain't goin' nowhere until Tank bring his ass out here," Tiana snapped. She and the guy who pulled the gun had a stare-off. Tiana wasn't easily intimidated, and that was why Gwen had sent her with Tamika. "Stop acting like y'all don't know who the fuck we are," Tiana went on. By this time, everybody in Charlotte knew who MHB was, and for some of the thugs that had been around for a while, they knew what the female clique was capable of.

"Everybody cool tha fuck out," Tank yelled from the top of the steps. "You right, we know who da fuck y'all are," he continued as he came down the steps. "So you should understand why my boys feel some type of way. It was a bitch that came up in here and killed my nephew," Tank said, walking up to Tiana and Tamika.

Tank was one of the ones that was around when MHB first popped off, and he was also one of the few that stuck around when Dion squashed the beef.

"I give you my word that MHB didn't have anything to do with this," Tamika explained. "You know we run a tight ship, and nobody in our circle make this type of move without Gwen's approval."

Tank reached into his back pocket and pulled out a photo and passed it to Tamika. "So, you saying she's not one of y'all?" Tank asked.

Tamika looked at the picture, and so did Tiana, but neither one of them recognized her. Tank wasn't so sure of it, and before he excluded them as suspects, he was going to need a better explanation to bite down on. If not, then everything Dion did to bring this city peace was going to go clean out the window.

"Look, to show you that MHB is still committed to our treaties, I'm asking you to allow us to help you find out who did this to Dion. If she's from Charlotte, we'll know before the week is out."

Tank stood there, thinking about it for a moment. This was a generous offer considering MHB's shooters were the prime suspects. In any event, Tank was going to entertain the offer and give Gwen the opportunity to prove that she and her clique didn't have anything to do with it. It was the bare minimum he could do, given the relationship Dion had with Gwen over the years.

"You got one week," he told Tamika, then turned around and walked off.

***

Gloria sped through traffic like a mad woman, trying her best to make it to Anthony's football game. The whole thing slipped her mind while she was in the process of following up on the intel she had gotten on Raymond. She was actually in the midst of telling Dillon she'd be there when he texted her.

"Come on, Gloria, you gotta stop doing this," she mumbled to herself as she switched back and forth through the highway lanes. She didn't even care about being pulled over at this point. She pulled her phone out of the center console and tried to call Dillon's phone. It went straight to voicemail. Her clock showed six twenty-five, and it killed her that she had forgotten what time Dillon said the game would start. As she was getting off the highway, her heart sank to her stomach. The football field was empty. A few cars were still left in the parking lot, but none of them belonged to Dillon. It was one of the worst feelings in the world, especially since this game meant so much to Anthony. It was one of those times Gloria didn't want to go home and face the music, but she had to. It brought tears to her eyes.

"Damn," Raymond said out loud, looking over at the clock on the wall. It was five o'clock, and his desk was still packed with paperwork that he needed to get through. He had so much to do, with little time to do it. That evening, he was supposed to be meeting up with a new client and then checking up on some intel he had to get to close another case. It was possible he could close one case and then open up another all in the same night, but that just didn't seem like the case on this time crunch. Reality set in, and to avoid hearing his mother's mouth, Raymond decided that he would stay and finish the work he had. He had given his mother his word, and this was something he planned on seeing through.

Chapter 2

Raymond sat in the train station, waiting on his new client to show up. He was a little excited this time around because, for the first time since he started this P.I. business, it was a man asking for his help. Women were the main sex checking to see if their significant others were having an affair, and most of the times, they were right.

"Mr. Harding?" a short, chubby Spanish man asked, walking up to Raymond, who got up to greet him with a handshake and a smile.

"I have to admit, you're the first male client I've ever had," he said, taking a seat. "So, before we begin, let me inform you of the services I can provide," Raymond began. "My hourly rate is two hundred dollars. If I have to tail your wife outside of the city, you're responsible for gas, tolls, and anything else I need in order to monitor her behavior. I will provide photos, audio surveillance if possible, and upon request, I can let you know in real time where she and the other person may be at. I'm not a divorce lawyer, nor am I a marriage counselor. If she's cheating on you, I'll make sure you know. I'm not responsible for any violence that may occur due to my investigation. That's it in a nutshell, so if you wish to continue, I'm going to need you to sign these forms," Raymond said, reaching in and pulling out a folder.

The man, Jesus, looked down at the paperwork. He was a little hesitant about signing it. He knew that once he did, the answers to all his questions were going to be answered. He wasn't sure how he would react to his wife of eight years if she were caught cheating.

"If you need some more time to think about it, I can give you—"

"Nah, that's okay," Jesus said, cutting him off. "I need to know, and it doesn't matter how much money it will cost."

Jesus pulled a pen out of his jacket pocket and signed the papers. This, along with the fifteen hundred dollar down payment, were enough for Raymond to get started, which he was enthused to do.

Gloria knocked on Anthony's bedroom's door before she walked in. He was so caught up in Call of Duty he didn't even see her standing behind him. Gloria didn't interrupt right away, but rather looked at the content of the game he was playing: guns, bomb, and people being shot to death. The game was violent and graphic, and looking further, it looked as though Anthony was really good at it. He was running through the stage he was on, shooting up everything. He dropped behind cars and used sniper-like techniques to kill his opponents. Gloria stood there for about five minutes watching him play. Then she cleared her throat to get his attention.

"I see you really like this game," she said, breaking the ice. Anthony didn't respond, and only gave her a quick glance before getting back to his game. Gloria took a seat on the edge of the bed above him while he sat on the floor. The tension was obvious.

"So, how about you turn the game off so we can talk?" Gloria felt bad seeing his body language, which made it clear that he didn't want to talk. "I know that you're mad at me because I missed your game last night," she said, pulling him up to the bed with her. She didn't know it, but the football game was only half of Anthony's pain.

"Are you really my mom?"

"Of course I'm your mother. Why would you ask something like that?"

"All of my friends' moms do stuff with them. They pick them up from school; they take them out, go on trips, and Brian's mom even helps him with his homework. You don't do none of that stuff with me."

Anthony wasn't telling a lie, neither. Gloria couldn't remember the last time she picked him up from school or took him out anywhere. Over the past couple of years, Gloria hadn't done too much of anything with him.

"Anthony, you do know that I love you, right?"

Anthony didn't respond.

"Anthony, look at me," she said, turning his face toward hers. "You really don't think that I love you?" she asked. Gloria's stomach flared into knots. He didn't answer, but only put his head down. It brought tears to her eyes. She didn't know the extent of her neglect, and up until now, she thought that she was a good mother.

"Anthony, baby, I want you to look at me," she said, turning his face toward hers again. "I messed up big time, and I'm sorry. I'm asking you to give me a chance to make it up to you," Gloria pleaded. "I give you my word that from this day forward, I won't miss another one of your games. I don't care if it's a home game or an away game. I will be there. I promise I will spend more time with you and be a better mom for you." She couldn't control tears from falling from her eyes. "Can you give me another chance? Can you please forgive me?" she begged.

Anthony did love his mother and didn't like to see her cry. At the same time, he did want to be loved himself, and for her to show it. This was something Gloria understood now.

"Don't cry, Mommy," Anthony said, wrapping his arms around her.

They both sat there holding each other, and it was at that very moment that Gloria knew she had to make some changes in her life that would bring her family closer together.

After Raymond had been following Carmen the whole day, something interesting finally happened. The Gomez case was one that Raymond wanted to close before he moved on to the next. Pulling up to a building in Center City, Carmen waited, and then a nice young man entered her car. Raymond sat in his car about a block away, looking through a pair of binoculars at what was going on.

"That's not Mr. Gomez," Raymond said, watching Carmen opening the door for her companion.

When they pulled off, so did Raymond, tailing them at a good distance. To Raymond's surprise, they didn't go that far, only a few blocks away to an underground garage. The young man got out of the car and headed for the garage. In the P.I. business, Raymond had found that everything was not always what it seemed, so he wasn't ready to rule anything out yet. This piece of information wasn't enough to take back to Jesus, but the night was still young. So, instead of wrapping it up for the night, Raymond decided to tail Carmen for a little while longer, just to see what else she had going on. Hopefully, she had other plans.

Gwen had allies in every part of the city, and on the north side, it just so happened to be Agnis. Anything that went down in this part of the city, she would know about.

"Well, look what the cat dragged in," Agnis said when Gwen walked into the salon. She wasn't MHB, but she respected the female movement and often had dealings with them. "So, what can I do for you, boss lady?" Agnis asked as she continued to curl a client's hair. Gwen wanted to speak in private, so she gave Agnis a slight nod to walk with her outside.

"This better not be no setup," Agnis joked, stepping outside. Gwen smiled at her words.

"A club owner named Dion was killed the other night by a female. Have you heard anything?" Gwen asked, looking off down the street.

"Nah, I haven't heard anything about that. You know I'm out the loop these days. Why? What's going on? Is that your people?" Agnis asked, only to check Gwen's temperature.

"He's not my people, but I gotta make sure that the female who did it isn't one of my people. That rumor is in the air. You already know how that go."

"Yeah, I do. If I hear anything about it, I'll hit you up," Agnis assured.

Gwen wanted to stay and kick it, but she had a lot of running around to do. Helping Tank find the murderer had become a priority. Because of the manner in which the killing happened, that task could prove to be impossible. Gwen and Tank didn't know what Dion had going on on the side, nor were they aware of the many females he had in his life. One thing Gwen knew for sure was that the truth about what happened would reveal itself. It always did in Charlotte.

"Detective, I think you might wanna check this out," the forensic unit officer said, walking into Detective Santiago's office. "Another partial print came back from the scene of the club."

"Do we have a match?" Santiago asked, lifting his head from the computer.

"Yeah, it's a match, but only to another partial print we got off a steering wheel in that Johnson murder," the officer explained.

"Let me take a look at that," Santiago said, reaching out for the plastic bag with an empty clip inside of it.

Detective Santiago was still working the Johnson case, in which a sex offender named Barry Johnson was murdered coming out of the courthouse after rape charges were dropped against him. The car that was used in the bold daylight shooting was found a couple of blocks away with the engine still running. The only evidence that was found in the car was a partial print that wasn't matched to anybody in the criminal system.

"Sir, that's not it," the officer continued. "The partial print dates back to two other homicides that had taken place in the city within the last two years. It's the same thumbprint that was found on magazines at the scene," the officer explained.

Santiago sat there listening. "So, what are you telling me? You think we have some type of serial killer out there?" Santiago said, curiously raising one of his eyebrows. Charlotte wasn't known to birth serial killers. Most of the murders that had taken place came from territorial disputes or some type of gang activity. Never just random killings.

"I took the liberty of sending my findings to Richard, the behavior analyst, and he told me that by the way each victim was killed, it looked as though this was a hitman."

"A hitman?"

This was a shocking twist Santiago didn't foresee, but the more he looked at the evidence collected at the scenes, the more he was able to see Richard's theory. It was more than enough for Santiago to go back to his superiors and ask to be put on the case. If anybody were qualified to take on this type of case, it would be Santiago, the city's most feared detective, and its most valuable cop.

Dillon looked down at his dick sliding in and out of Gloria as he pounded away, doggy-style. A thin, clear layer of her cum covered his dick, making his long brown pole look shiny. Dillon already came once, and was now working on number two. The way he was fucking Gloria tonight was like no other.

"Ssshhhhhh," she whispered, not wanting to wake the kids by screaming like she wanted to. "*Duro*, papi, *duro*," she said, feeling herself about to cum again. "Oh God, yes."

"Dis daddy pussy?" Dillon asked, smacking the top of her ass. She looked back at him, watching him smack it again.

"Sí, papi, it's yours," she moaned.

Dillon took his thumbs and spread her ass cheeks apart so he could go deeper inside of her tunnel. It drove Gloria crazy feeling him that deep inside of her, and within a few seconds, she was at her peak. The sweat from Dillon's chest dripped down onto her ass, causing a clapping sound to echo throughout the room.

"I'm cumming, papi," she moaned. "*Duro*," she yelled out, throwing her ass back at him. "Don't stop, don't stop."

"Come all over daddy dick," Dillon encouraged, feeling himself about to blow as well. He could feel her walls tightening up around his dick. Her face balled up as her cum squirted out of her pussy and onto Dillon's dick. He came inside of her at the same time. The combination of her wet, warm cum and his thick, creamy cum inside of her only intensified the orgasm and made it last longer than usual. Gloria didn't even have the energy to turn over onto her back. She just flopped down onto her stomach and laid there in a paralyzed state.

Dillon was beat, too, flopping down onto the bed right beside her. He was exhausted from his performance. This was something that they both needed at this point, especially in Gloria's case. It would not be long before she had to get up and leave for work.

Tamika looked over at Gwen while she was driving. She could see the frustration on her face when she came up with nothing concerning the female that killed Dion.

"Who da hell is this?" Tamika said, looking in the rearview mirror at somebody flashing their headlights.

Gwen didn't have a clue who it was and was not about to pull over. She reached under her seat and grabbed the black Glock .40 and placed it on her lap. Tamika followed suit, reaching into her Gucci bag and pulling out a 9 mm Ruger. The lights behind them kept flashing, and when the opportunity presented itself, Gwen turned off onto a smaller street. The car that was following them came to a stop behind them. Gwen and Tamika got out of the car with guns in hand, ready to shoot anybody who attempted to show a morsel of aggression.

"Hold on—I'm MHB. I'm MHB!" a female voice yelled out, holding her hands out the window. The female got out of the car, and Gwen immediately recognized her from the shop. "Gwen, I really need to talk to you," the female said, walking up. "My name is Tish, and I'm from the north side. I was in the salon earlier when you came in. I work there."

"Yeah, I remember you. So, what's going on? What's this all about?"

"I overheard some of the conversation you and Agnis had earlier. That female you were describing to her sounds just like a female that be coming into the shop. She's Agnis's friend."

Gwen walked back to her car while Tamika kept talking to Tish. She grabbed a surveillance photo from out of her car and walked back over. "Do she look like this?" Gwen asked, passing her the picture.

The female in the photo held a striking resemblance, but Tish couldn't confirm one hundred percent whether it was the same woman. "If you want, I can book you in my chair for Friday, and you can see for yourself," Tish suggested. It didn't sound like a bad idea. At that point, Gwen didn't have anything to take back to Tank.

"Well, how often do she be there?" Gwen asked.

"She comes in at least two times a week. Agnis normally does her hair on Fridays."

Gwen looked over at Tamika, who simply shrugged her shoulders. It was a good observation on Tish's part, and these were the times Gwen appreciated having someone from MHB in every part of the city. In any event, Gwen's plans for Friday were now canceled, and Agnis's Salon was going to be the place to be.

"Can I ask you something?" Dillon asked, looking down at Gloria curled up under his arms. "I know it might sound crazy, me asking you this, but how in the world did you and Agnis meet? I mean, what's the story behind that?" Dillon had always been curious as to how Gloria became the person she was. She never really told him the whole story.

"Let me tell you something about Agnis," Gloria said, looking back up at him. "I remember one day when I was a kid, no more than fifteen years old at the time, a boy named Robert tried to rape me at a party she threw for her niece. Robert was twenty-eight at the time. Anyway,

Agnis found out about it a few days later. She called me over to her house, and when I got there, she had Robert strapped into a chair with plastic on the floor beneath him."

Dillon sat there listening to the story, picturing it as it was happening.

"Her niece, Capri, was sitting on the couch, crying. On the coffee table in front of her was a 9 mm. It came out that Robert had managed to rape Capri two times successfully. It was crazy," Gloria said, thinking about the horrible details.

"Damn, that's fucked up," Dillon said, looking up at the ceiling.

"Capri wouldn't shoot him, though. No matter how many times Agnis told her to do it, she just couldn't bring herself to do it. Then Agnis looked at me. I was scared to death , hoping that she wouldn't ask me to do the same thing. That hope was short-lived. I can remember her words clearly: *Shoot 'im*. I almost shit my pants.

"I looked at Robert, and all the thoughts of what he tried to do to me came rushing in. I could remember him pinning me up against the wall in the basement, trying to pull my pants down. I must have said stop a hundred times. He was a real asshole. Even though he wasn't able to penetrate me that night, those thoughts alone gave me the courage to walk over and grab the gun from off the table. I'd never held a gun in my hands before, let alone shot somebody.

"When I walked over to Robert, I could tell that he was pleading through the tape that covered his mouth. He started squirming in his chair as though he knew I was about to shoot him. Agnis just sat there looking on, and so did Capri. I thought that Agnis was going to stop me when I raised the gun up and pointed it to his head. I thought that it was going to be some sort of test, and it was, just not the kind of test I hoped for. This was a test to see if I would go through with it. Agnis looked at me and nodded her head. I never blinked. I looked Robert in his eyes and pulled the trigger."

Dillon laid there in silence for a moment. He had never known how deep the relationship between her and Agnis was, until today. It was at this very moment he understood why she trusted Agnis the way she did.

"Thank you," Dillon told her.

Gloria sat up in the bed, looking into his eyes. She wanted to see his reaction to everything she had told him, and just as she had hoped, Dillon was understanding. This was the reason why Gloria loved him so much. No matter what was going on in her life, never once did he judge or complain. The only issues he ever took up with Gloria was the ones about their children, something she respected.

"I love you, Dillon."

"I love you too," he replied, grabbing her cheeks and slowly pulling her down to his face to kiss her. Secretly, all this talk about killing was turning Gloria on, but not in a sexual manner. It had made her want to get back to doing what she did best, and the one thing that was on her mind was Raymond, her next big paycheck.

Gloria

I know I told Agnis that I was going to chill out for a couple of weeks before I started on the next job, but I really didn't feel like playing the good housewife right now. I messed with the kids for a bit, had some great sex with my husband, and now it was time to get back to work. It was around ten o'clock at night, and I thought this was the perfect time for me to do some recon work over at the Rev. Index building. The first things that I noticed right off the bat were the two security guards who patrolled the building, and one guard who sat in a booth by the parking garage. Surprisingly, none of the guards had a gun, but they did have Taser guns, which could sometimes be even worse than being shot with a bullet. The next thing that I noticed were several exit doors, including the front door and an emergency door by the loading docks. In case any of these exit points didn't work, there were hundreds of windows on the first and second floor that I could climb out of.

Damn, this job was going to be difficult, especially since I couldn't just walk up and put a bullet in his head. I had to be creative with this skill. I had to think about this a little longer and calculate his every move if I wanted to get the job done right. One thing I knew for sure was that his death wasn't about to take place at this building. Too much had to go into it, and I wasn't about to be on my James Bond 007 thing.

Chapter 3

Gwen pulled into the Texaco gas station on Broad Street to fill up her tank before she headed over to the north side. The young African American male gas attendant walked over and stood off to the side, waiting for Gwen.

"Ma'am, can you turn your car off?" the man asked when she rolled her window down.

Gwen did as she was asked and then passed him a hundred-dollar bill. "Keep the change," she told him, then rolled her window back up. Her phone began to ring in the center console, and when she looked down at the screen, it was Tamika. "Yeah, wassup, Meek?"

"Why did you leave me? I wanted to come with you," Tamika said.

"I know you did, but I wanted to be incognito. I don't want to draw any unnecessary attention. Us rolling up in there together wouldn't look good. Besides, I'm just checking it out. I'm not gonna move on it until I know for sure."

Gwen paused, hearing something on the top of her car. It sounded like rain for a second, but then brownish-looking fluids rolled down her windshield.

"I don't want my car washed!" she yelled at the attendant. Gwen took a closer look at her windshield and could see that this wasn't water. Then the strong scent of gas came through her vents. "Shit," she said, attempting to start her car.

Before she could get the car started, a tap on her window got her attention. A black male stood there with a gun in his hand, waving for her to roll down the window.

"I'm not gonna tell you again," the man yelled out.

Gwen thought about it. If the guy really wanted to kill her, he would have done it by now. She complied, rolling her window down. A cell phone was thrown into her car. The guy waved his gun, telling her to talk. She could tell by the way he was dressed, who he was working for.

"Wassup, Tank?" Gwen said, putting the phone on speaker.

"You must think this shit is a fuckin' game," Tank spoke into the phone. "Give me a good reason why I shouldn't let my boy set ya car on fire with you in it."

The guy outside the car still had the pump in his hand.

"You don't wanna do that, Tank. You know good and well who I am—"

"*Fuck* who you think you are," Tank snapped.

Gwen stayed calm. She didn't want to give him a reason to go through with it, but at the same time, she didn't want to seem like a pushover. "Look, Tank, I'm doing this as a courtesy for Dion. I already told you that my crew didn't have anything to do with it. As a matter of fact, right before your boy poured gas all over my car, I was on my way to check up on something that was brought to me the other day."

Tank got quiet on the other end of the phone. Not only was he still mourning his nephew's death, but he was also still angry that he hadn't found the person who had done it yet. That had been his main focus since the news of Dion's death popped up.

"Find out who da bitch is, or next time I'm gonna light the match myself," he said, then hung up.

The gunman took the phone back from her, stuffed the gun back into his pants pocket, and walked off. Gwen didn't waste a moment's time, starting her car and pulling out of the gas station, smelling like premium gas and all. She definitely wasn't about to be late for her appointment.

Raymond could feel it. Tonight was going to be different than the other nights with Carmen. For about two weeks straight, she'd become a master at eluding Raymond, losing him several times. It was almost as if she knew she was being followed.

"Ray, I need you to take care of something for me," Jennifer said, walking into his office. I need you to run a check on our financials. I want to be sure that getting in bed with the Chinese is the best thing for us."

"Mom, we got people in positions to do this type of stuff."

"I know, but when it comes to my money, the only person I trust is you," she said, slamming the papers on his desk. "It shouldn't take that long, and after you're done, you can take off for the rest of the day."

This was actually the break Raymond was looking for. He looked on the wall and saw that it was two o'clock. That left him more than enough time to get the investigation started on Carmen.

As Jennifer was exiting the office, she stopped at the door. "Honey, I know I been working you to the max, but I assure you that it's for a good cause. You just have to trust me and know that everything that I'm doing is to better your life and the life of your children one day." Jennifer smiled.

"Come on, Mom, you know I'm not ready to have any kids right now. And the last time I checked, I'm supposed to be married in order to do that. I don't see me putting a ring on anybody's finger any time soon."

"I know, I know. I was just hoping you would make me a grandmother before I die. You know your mother is getting old."

"Okay, Mom. Can we have this conversation later? I really don't feel like hearing you talking about death. You're not gonna die any time soon. One thing that you taught me was to never give up in life. I know the boss lady ain't contradicting herself right now," he said, walking over and giving her a kiss on the forehead.

Jennifer couldn't do anything but shake her head. Raymond was so ahead of his time, and had been like that for years. When it came down to it, there was nobody better in her eyes to take the reins of the family company. As long as she was alive, she wasn't going to have it any other way.

Gwen couldn't afford to be running late, so she drove all the way to the north side in a gas-scented Range Rover. She kept all the windows rolled down the whole way there, not wanting the gas fumes to make her drowsy. A further and more in-depth conversation was going to take place between her and Tank over this. When Gwen finally got to the salon, it was four o'clock, ten minutes before her appointment. The shop looked a little crowded.

"Twice in one week," Agnis yelled out when Gwen walked through the door. "Don't be coming over here to the north side tryna recruit," she joked.

If only Agnis really knew how far MHB's hand reached. "Never that, sis. I keep hearing about this spot, so I figured I'd bring you some business. I hope I'm welcomed. You know one order from me and every chick in my clique would be up in here." Gwen smiled.

Agnis really didn't want her there, but she didn't want Gwen to feel that way. It could cause suspicion.

"Nah, girl, you're always welcomed to stop by," Agnis assured her. "You got an appointment?"

"Yeah, I booked her," Tish spoke up. "Just give me a couple minutes."

As soon as Gwen sat in the waiting chair, Gloria walked through the door. For the first time, Agnis didn't have any loud outburst for her customers. Instead, she nodded slightly for Gloria to go to the back. She did, without a second thought, feeling that something was going on. It was way too quiet for it to be a Friday.

Tish made eye contact with Gwen, but it wasn't necessary. Gwen had already gotten a good look at Gloria and put two and two together. Gwen had looked at the surveillance photos numerous times and had the image locked into her memory.

"I'm done. You can come over here," Tish said to Gwen, taking the cape off of her client.

Gwen kept her Louis Vuitton bag in her hand while Tish put a fresh cape over her. The awkward silence made Gwen feel a little uncomfortable. She became even more uncomfortable when Agnis dropped what she was doing and headed straight to the back where Gloria went. Gwen pulled a silver .45 automatic from her bag and set it on her lap. She wasn't sure how this was going to play out, but she wanted to be prepared for whatever came out from behind those doors.

"So, do you think she knows who I am?" Gloria asked, pulling the black Glock .40 from her waist. "You know I'm not going to jail."

"I don't know why she's looking for you, but one thing I'm sure of is that she's not a cop, and she wouldn't be working with them. She's the head of MHB."

Gloria looked over at Agnis. She was well aware of what MHB stood for. About a year ago, Gloria's cousin became a member and tried to get Gloria to do the same. It never happened, though. Gloria was in her own world then, just as she was now.

Gloria cocked the gun back slightly to make sure she had a bullet in the chamber, then she walked over to the door. She cracked it open about an inch and checked the surroundings. It was a full house with people still coming in.

"Not here," Agnis said, reading Gloria's body language. There were way too many people in the salon, most of whom knew who Gloria was. This type of heat in the salon would cause more problems. "Listen to me," Agnis said, getting Gloria's attention. "Just go out the back, and if she asks any questions about you, I'll find out what she wants."

Gloria wasn't the type of person who ran away from her problems, and running out the back door made her feel like a coward. The only reason why she was going to do it was because of Agnis. She didn't want to bring the police into her life, not in this manner.

Dillon thought to himself as he was leaving the construction site that this was going to be another one of those lonely nights, ending with him probably masturbating to porn before going to bed. He never really told Gloria this, but this wasn't the type of life he was hoping to live after they got married. As of late, she was hardly home, and when she was there, she spent most of it sleeping.

"Cab!" Dillon yelled out while standing curbside. His truck was parked a couple of blocks away, but he really didn't feel like walking after this hard day. He was being more lazy than anything.

As he was getting into the cab, Dillon's phone began to ring. It was Gloria.

"Hey," he answered. "How was your day?"

"It was okay," Gloria replied, coming from behind Agnis's building. "I'm really calling you to let you know that I'll be home a little late today."

"Whoa, Gloria, did you forget that we had parent-teacher meeting tonight at Anthony's school?" Dillon asked in frustration.

Gloria had completely forgotten about it and had made plans to catch up with Raymond that night. The job required some level of sophistication, so proper preparation would prevent poor performance.

"Just let the teachers know that I had to work late. I'll make the next one for sure."

Dillon gritted his teeth as he looked out the cab's window. His frustration turned into anger in a matter of seconds. He wanted to snap, but he knew that it wouldn't get him far.

"Gloria, we really need to talk," he said, shaking his head.

"Well whatever it is, we'll talk about it when I get home," she said, then hung up the phone before Dillon could protest.

This was exactly what Dillon was talking about. He looked down at his phone and was about to call her back, but had second thoughts. It was more than likely that she wouldn't answer, knowing that it was him. However, a phone call was going to be made, and Dillon knew for sure that the person on the other end was going to answer it. Men cheated on their wives every day, and in Dillon's eyes, he was well justified to do so. Whether Gloria would kill him if she found out was the real issue.

***

"Girl, if you bought it, it's yours," Agnis yelled out to a client that was getting some weave put into her hair. "Just don't let ya man pull on it too hard when he hit it from the back. He messed around and pulled out a track or two," Agnis joked.

She had the whole salon laughing. All except Gwen, who was still trying to figure out where Gloria went. She never came out from the back room with Agnis, and that was about an hour ago. At times, Agnis would cut her eyes over at Gwen to see her reactions. Gwen wasn't new to the game and played it just how she was supposed to. Gwen didn't seem bothered at all, nor did she inquire about Gloria's whereabouts. It was as if she didn't care or even know who Gloria was, for that matter.

As Tish put the finishing touches on Gwen's hair, Gwen tucked her gun back in her bag and was ready to leave. Pure curiosity made Gwen want to know what was really going on and what was the connection between Agnis, Gloria, and Dion. Before she went back to Tank with what she knew, she wanted to be sure that she had the full story, and not just parts of one.

Chapter 4

Gloria rushed through traffic, trying her best to make it to Rev. Index before Raymond got off work. As she pulled up and waited across the street, Gloria couldn't help but think about Dillon and how mad he was. He didn't show it much, but Gloria knew that he was upset about her not making it to their parent-teacher conference. Anything involving the kids that Gloria dropped the ball on made him mad.

After about fifteen minutes of her sitting there in her car, Gloria's thoughts were interrupted when an all-white Camaro peeled out of the parking garage. It was Raymond's car for sure. Same make and model, and the license plate number matched.

Gloria was driving a grey 2016 Mustang, so it was nothing for her to keep up with the muscle car. She kept a good distance, weaving through traffic while catching every light Raymond went through. He stopped on the corner of 8th and Market Street and just sat there. Gloria was at the top of 9th Street, looking on. She was a little confused but sat there and waited anyway. Only about a minute went by before Raymond pulled off again. Gloria pulled off with him. She didn't have a clue what was happening, but she took note of every move he was making.

After tailing Carmen from Center City, Raymond was shocked that she was heading toward her house with a man in the car. This was odd, considering she usually took the male to the other side of town before she eventually lost Raymond. This prompted Raymond to call her husband.

"How are you, Mr. Gomez? If you don't mind, I want to ask you a few questions," Raymond said as he continued to follow behind Carmen.

"Sure. Go ahead," he replied, willing and ready to answer.

"I'm following your wife, and it seems as though she has another man in the car with her. Do you know if she picks up a neighbor, or maybe someone in your family?"

"No, Carmen don't have any business having another man in my car."

As he was explaining, Carmen was pulling over about a block away from their home. The young male got out and stood by the bus stop, while Carmen continued on. Raymond stopped at the same corner and was able to get a good look at the man. He was an African American with a nice build and good looks.

"Mr. Gomez, are you still there?" Raymond asked.

"Yeah, and Carmen just pulled into our driveway. There's no man with her," he snapped, hoping that the guy would have still been in the car.

"No, that's because she just dropped him off up the street. Tell me, what is she doing now?"

Carmen walked through the front door and headed straight for the bedroom, barely even speaking to her husband.

"I didn't have plans on going anywhere, but it seems that she does," Jesus stated, walking into their bedroom and seeing her clothes laid out on the bed. She had jumped in the shower and had the nerve to be singing.

"She's up to something. Please let me know everything she does tonight and everybody she's with," Jesus said.

Raymond wasn't in the position to be complaining about the overtime he would have to put in, just as long as Jesus was paying the tab.

Raymond

Last year I bought a 1996 Chevy Caprice so I could get around the city without drawing any attention to myself. It was too risky to use my personal car when investigating someone. It was a little too flashy.

I thought about that this morning, when Jesus called to check on his wife's status. As I was following behind her, I kept my distance, not wanting to be made by her. That could ruin the whole night. I had been driving for about a half hour before Carmen pulled into a quiet suburban area. Beautiful houses, nice cars, and peaceful was the only way I could describe the neighborhood.

Instead of pulling over when she pulled into a driveway, I decided to circle the block. Once I turned the corner, I punched the gas, hoping that I could get a couple of pictures of her and her male companion going into the house. By the time I got back around the corner, the same man from earlier had gotten out of Carmen's SUV and made his way up the driveway. Carmen got out and followed behind him. I quickly snapped a couple of pictures and took down the license plate numbers of both cars in the driveway. I'm telling you, Joey from the show Cheaters *don't have nothing on me.*

Just when I thought that they were going to stay in the house, they both emerged, got into the Audi R8, and pulled out of the driveway. I had no idea where they were going.

***

"What the hell is he up to?" Gloria mumbled to herself, following Raymond from a block away. She looked around, not really knowing what street she was on. This whole night was starting to throw Gloria off. She was clueless why Raymond would stop here, then stop there, but never get out of the car. He looked like he was up to something, and Gloria was curious as to what. At the same time, an opportunity could present itself so she could get the job done that night. She surely would be ready if one did.

Raymond

The two drove miles outside of the city until they pulled into the parking lot of Hibachi's, a popular restaurant only a few people from Charlotte went to. I couldn't believe Carmen told Jesus she had a work-related dinner to go to with a client. For a minute, it looked like the story may have checked out; that is, until I saw her hugging and kissing the gentleman when they got out of the car.

I sat and watched them enjoy themselves in the restaurant for about an hour, and aside from the hugs and kisses they shared earlier, it seemed like there was much more affection between the two. They smiled and gazed into each other's eyes while sitting across from each other. He held her hands in his, periodically kissing them during the intense conversation.

I had to admit, the guy Carmen had with her was charming. He was a six feet tall, with an athletic build, strong facial features, and jet black, wavy hair. He dressed nice, too, wearing a fitted polo shirt, some Dolce and Gabanna slacks, and a pair of brown Tom Ford dress shoes. I could only guess whether he knew that he was dealing with a married woman.

"Fuck it," Gloria said, grabbing the gun from under her seat.

Her thoughts went into overdrive, thinking about ways she could kill Raymond without it looking like a murder. The only thing that she could come up with was making it look like a suicide: get low behind the other parked car, creep up, and stuff a rag in his exhaust pipe and hold him in the car at gunpoint. Carbon monoxide would have him dead in a few minutes. Whether he would stay in the car at gunpoint was another story. As soon as Gloria was about to get out of the car, her phone started ringing on the passenger's seat. She wasn't about to answer it, but then Anthony's picture popped up on the screen. Seeing that, she immediately answered.

"Hey, sweetie. What's going on?" she asked while keeping an eye on Raymond's car.

"Mommy, I been trying to call you for the past hour," Anthony said.

"Why? Is everything okay? Where's your dad?" she asked with concern.

"I don't know where Daddy's at. He didn't come back, and Alisha keeps crying. I don't know what's wrong with her," he explained.

Gloria was pissed because she could hear Alisha crying in the background. "Listen, baby, go into the refrigerator and grab your sister's sippy cup and give it to her."

She could hear Anthony doing just that, and within a minute, she could hear that Alisha had stopped crying. "Now, what I want you to do is change her Pull-up. Can you do that for Mommy?"

Gloria was close to calling it a night and going back home to the kids, but then there was some action happening. Raymond's brake lights had come on, indicating that he was about to pull off. She stayed on the phone with Anthony, but pulled off right behind Raymond, trying her best not to lose him. She kept Anthony cool, calm, and collected on the other end of the phone, and once she saw that the kids were settled down, she hung up the phone. Her focus was back on Raymond, and she promised that she would do her best to get this over with that night.

After dinner, Carmen and her male friend headed for the expressway and went back to the same house where they had previously switched cars. Raymond thought that the night was coming to an end, but he was wrong. Instead of her getting back into the car and leaving, she followed her male friend into the house. It only took a few seconds for the living room lights to go out, and then moments later, a light came on in one of the bedrooms upstairs. At this point, Raymond knew what was going on, and as he sat there snapping a couple of pictures, the lights in that room went out too.

"To hell with it," Raymond mumbled to himself as he was turning the key in the ignition. A set of headlights from an oncoming car made Raymond lift his head up. The car was coming down the street at a high rate of speed, and it looked as though it was heading straight for him. Tires screeched as the car tried to come to a stop, but the closer it got, Raymond knew that it was going to hit him. All he could do was brace for impact at this point.

WWWHHHHAAAAAMMM!!! The car crashed into the front passenger's side and pretty much tore the bumper off. Raymond was dazed from the airbag bursting in his face. When his eyes finally adjusted, a familiar face rolled out of the car that had hit him. It was Doug, husband pf his former client Amanda, and he had a 12-gauge shotgun in his hands. Raymond didn't even have time to grab his 357 SIG Sauer from out of his glove compartment before Doug let off a buckshot. *BOOOOM!* The small pellets ripped a large hole into the front windshield.

"You dumb muthafucka. You ruined my marriage!" Doug yelled out, firing another buckshot into Raymond's car. He staggered across the street to get closer. Raymond managed to fall out of the passenger's side door to avoid the pellet, but Doug kept coming. He was drunk and had been crying up a storm.

"I'ma kill you," Doug yelled, walking over to the side of the car where Raymond was still trying to get himself together. Doug came from behind the car and had nothing but hatred in his eyes. He raised the shotgun, cocking another round into the chamber.

"Come on, man, don't shoot me," Raymond pleaded, holding his hand out in front of his face.

Right before Doug was about to pull the trigger, he looked up at an image coming toward him. He started to aim his gun at the image but fell short as the bullets began to fly in his direction. *POP! POP! POP! POP!* Every single bullet hit Doug in his chest.

Raymond watched as Doug's body fell to the ground. When he turned to see where the shots had come from, his eyes locked onto a woman who was standing about fifteen feet away from him. He was still a little groggy from the crash, so it was hard for him to make out the face clearly.

"Get in your car and leave before the cops come," Gloria told him, walking over to Doug's car and getting in. She threw the car in reverse and backed it off of Raymond's car.

Raymond still couldn't see Gloria' face, but he knew
for sure that it was a female. He didn't ask any questions,
nor was he going to stick around for when the cops came.
He knew that it would be nearly impossible for him to
explain everything that went on tonight without being
arrested. At this point, all he wanted to do was get the hell
out of there, and that's precisely what he did, jumping in
his car and pulling out of the parking space.

As he was pulling off, he could see Gloria getting into
her car. He tried to get her license plate number, but it
was way too dark.

Chapter 5

Rolling into the West Side Diner, Gwen was stopped by an armed man almost immediately. She was by herself. A couple of heads turned, hearing her heels click- clack through the diner. Her skin-tight jeans showed off her thick thighs and plump ass. Several men and a few females who were in the restaurant looked on. Gwen was sexy as hell, wearing a white V-neck Polo T-shirt that showed off her flat stomach, and on her feet were a pair of Christian Louboutin heels. With all eyes on her, she smiled inwardly, seeing that she still had it.

"I hope you came here with some good news. My patience is running thin," Tank said, not once lifting his head up from the newspaper he was reading. Gwen was getting tired of subjecting herself to his aggressive tone. She was trying to be patient. Before anything, she wanted to address that.

"Tank, don't let my kind gesture of me helping you out confuse you about who I am," Gwen said with a serious look on her face. "I'm not scared of you, and I will never be scared of you. I'm quite sure Dion told you what I'm capable of doing to this city. Just look around you. I own Charlotte," she snapped, smacking Tank's newspaper.

When he looked up, every female that was in the diner, including one of the cooks, was now on their feet in support of Gwen. A couple of the women looked like they were armed, and the rest were simply ready for whatever. It took Tank by surprise. He looked around and could see that Gwen wasn't messing around. The stories he heard about MHB, along with what he saw with his own eyes today, was enough for him to tone it down a bit. Out of respect, he folded his paper up and set it to the side.

"What you got for me?" he asked, still trying to keep his face.

Gwen could see that she had humbled him somewhat. With that, she gave a wave of her hand, and the females who were standing took a seat and went back to doing what they were doing.

"Listen, the female that you're looking for isn't MHB, like I told you. I think she might be a shooter for some chick named Agnis."

When Tank heard the name Agnis, his face lit up but then quickly turned into a frown.

"I take it you know who she is," Gwen inquired.

"Yeah, her and my nephew had some dealings before."

When Tank mentioned "some dealings," he was referring to Dion going to her to get somebody clipped. He could recall Dion using her once or twice before.

"I'ma kill dis bitch," he snapped, clenching his teeth.

"Yeah, well, before you do that, you might wanna get to the core reason why Dion was killed," Gwen said, reaching into her bag and grabbing some photos.

Tank slowly looked at the pictures while Gwen explained the content of them.

"Emilio Castellano," Gwen said.

"Why would Emilio want my nephew dead?" he asked, looking at a picture of Emilio standing with Agnis outside of her shop.

"Take one wild guess. It makes perfect sense," she said. "Emilio owns just about every building on Delaware Ave. What building would you kill for if you wanted to corner the market?"

Tank picked his head up from the pictures. "The club," Tank said, shaking his head.

Gwen could see the anger in Tank's eyes. "So, how do you wanna play this? Do I have to get my people out of the way?" Gwen asked, knowing the possibility of a war.

"Nah, you good. I'ma take care of this personally," he said, tossing the pictures onto the table.

Gwen got up from her seat, leaving the photos there. As she was leaving, Tank stopped her. He looked Gwen in her eyes and thanked her for her help. She smiled then walked out of the diner.

"Boss, I just got off the phone with the Cubans, and they wanna know if we're still on for next week," Carmine said, walking up on Emilio's back patio.

"Why wouldn't we still be on? Am I still freaking breathing?"

"I just assumed that we would keep our heads down until Dion's death—"

"You're right, but we still gotta eat," Emilio cut in. "If you think that I would let his death slow me down, you're not as smart as I thought you were. Besides, nobody even knows I had anything to do with that."

"I understand, boss. I was just looking out for our best interests. War and money never lived under the same roof. It's bad for business."

Emilio sat there in thought for a moment. He always liked listening to Carmine's advice, despite the fact that, at times, Carmine could be a little too aggressive. In all reality, he was probably the only one in his crew that Emilio had a deep love for, and that wasn't just because Carmine was seeing his daughter. Carmine reminded Emilio of himself many years ago. He was a thinker, unlike most of the hotheads in the organization. That was a quality that could go a long way in the mob, and with Emilio nearing the end of his reign, there was no one

more perfect than Carmine to head the family. He was
definitely Emilio's number one guy.

"Can we really afford to go to war?" Butch asked Tank,
pulling out a chair and taking a seat next to him at the
table. "I mean, we already got money problems, and we
really don't know if Emilio had anything to do with it. Do
you trust those MHB chicks?"

"I don't think Gwen would lie to me. She knows the
consequences."

"I think you should be sure of it just in case," Butch said.
His complaints didn't stop there. "Don't get me wrong,
we got guns and bullets for days. Hell, we got a small
army. The thing that's missing is money, something we
can't afford to go to war without."

Tank sat there listening to everything Butch had said.
He was right about finding out whether Gwen's story
checked out. If they were to go to war over a false accusa-
tion coming from MHB, Tank would lose a lot of love and
respect from the people around him. In war, lives are lost,
people go to jail, innocent people get hurt, and it's like
the money on the streets comes to a screeching halt. This
was the kind of thing that tore apart families and made it
unsafe for people to walk the streets. This was something
Tank didn't want to put his people through, especially
over some false intel.

"We gotta pay Emilio a visit," Tank said, finishing his
glass of juice.

"And what about Dion? Who's gonna take care of the
funeral?"

Tank hadn't even thought about it yet. The reality of
Dion's death hadn't hit him just yet, and it was like that
for a lot of people. "Get with my sister and take care of it.
I really don't feel like dealing with it right now."

Butch nodded his head, understanding how his friend felt at that moment. On the inside, Butch secretly hoped that Emilio had something to do with it so he would have somebody to kill. Like Tank, Butch was also close to Dion and had an enormous amount of love for him. If he didn't do anything else with the remaining time he had in this world, Butch was going to help find out who had something to do with Dion's death and take it upon himself to kill every last person involved.

Chapter 6

Raymond didn't get a wink of sleep the previous night. He was still very much confused about the events that had taken place on Monday night with Doug trying to kill him. What was even more confusing was the mystery woman that saved his life. It all unfolded so fast, and there was still much to register. Raymond thought about calling the cops and reporting what happened, but thought against it. Too much time had passed since the time Doug was killed. It just wouldn't look good on Raymond's behalf.

"Mom, I'll be there as soon as I can," Raymond spoke into the phone while walking over to his bedroom window. As he was talking to Jennifer and looking out the window, something had caught his attention. "I'll be there in a few," he said, then hung up.

Every morning before Raymond left the house, he checked outside to make sure he wasn't followed home by somebody like Doug.

"Now, what do we have here?" he said, grabbing the binoculars off the dresser.

At the end of the street, a silver Mustang was sitting there with the engine still running. It looked much like the Mustang he saw the shooter pulling off in the other night. Raymond couldn't see if anybody was in the car, but this time he was able to get the license plate number. He had a few connections at the police station, and before he left the house, he was going to see who the car belonged to.

***

"Emilio, you got a call," Carmine announced, walking into Emilio's office. Emilio picked his head up from the plate of food he was devouring.

"You can't see that I'm eating?" he snapped. "Take a message."

"Boss, this guy sounds black," Carmine said with a confused look on his face.

This was a call Emilio didn't want to miss. He tossed his fork onto the plate with an attitude, then reached for the phone.

"Who am I speaking to?" Emilio said into the phone.

Before the voice on the other end of the phone could say anything, Bruno, the head of security, walked into the office with a small brown shopping bag in his hand.

"I found this outside in the lobby," he said, walking over to Emilio's desk and showing him the severed head that was inside.

"Killing Dion was the worst thing you could have done," a voice spoke on the other end of the phone.

Emilio knew exactly who he was talking to now.

"So, you send me a freakin' head in a bag? See, that's the problem with Blacks. You guys are so overdramatic."

"You might wanna take a closer look at the head before you start talking reckless to me," Tank said.

Emilio snapped his fingers for Bruno to bring the head back over to him.

"Next time, it will be your wife's head, or maybe even your daughter's," Tank said while Emilio looked at the head. "While I was at your home, I could have done just that."

Emilio was becoming furious now, seeing that the head belonged to Sally, a man he kept around his family for protection at all times. It was proof that Tank had gotten too close to his family.

"You know, you're playing a dangerous game, kid." Emilio motioned for Carmine to go and check on his family while he continued to entertain Tank. He was as gangster as they came, but when it came down to his family, he was soft.

"Look, kid, I don't know what you think you might know, but I didn't have anything to do with Dion's death," Emilio lied.

Tank didn't believe him but needed a little more proof aside from what Gwen had told him. "I got a reliable source that your hands were all over this."

"Yeah? Well, your source is a freakin' liar," Emilio snapped.

Just then, Carmine came back into the office and gave him the thumbs up that his family was safe and secure.

"For your sake and the sake of your family, you better be right. If not, I'm killing you, ya faggot-ass boyfriend Carmine, and ya family."

"Oh, yeah? Well, you can go fuck yourself, you black piece of shit," Emilio snapped then hung up the phone. "This freakin' guy's got some balls," he said to Carmine and Bruno.

"What do you want me to do with this?" Bruno asked, holding up the bag with Sally's head in it.

Before Emilio could answer the question, a bullet came crashing through the window behind Emilio's desk. It grazed Emilio's ear, then hit Bruno in the chest. Several more shots were fired through the window, causing Emilio to roll out of his chair and crawl under his desk.

Carmine dropped to the floor, too, pulling out his gun and firing wildly out the window. Emilio grabbed the gun that was strapped under his desk and started shooting alongside Carmine. Gun smoke filled the room, and after a vicious exchange of bullets, the room became silent.

Emilio looked over and could see a small red dot moving back and forth across the wall of his office. Then the phone began to ring. Emilio didn't want to run the risk of lifting his head above desk level and getting it taken off by a bullet. Instead, he yanked the cord, toppling the phone down to the floor where he was.

"You fucking *muli*. You know you just killed yourself, right?" Emilio hissed into the phone.

"My nephew was killed in his club, which is in your section of the city. If you didn't kill him, then I know for sure that you can find out who did. That's your mission now. Find the bitch that pulled the trigger, or I'm holding you responsible for Dion's death."

The red dot continued moving around the room until it reached Bruno's lifeless body. Another bullet came through the window, hitting Bruno in his head. Both Carmine and Emilio turned their heads in anguish, seeing the bullet knock a chunk out of Bruno's head.

Emilio went to say something, but Tank cut him off.

"Call me when you get a name," Tank said.

The red dot disappeared, and to be sure, Emilio made Carmine get up first. Nothing happened, but what Tank left behind was a message that said he wasn't playing any games. At the same time, it was at that very moment Emilio knew that this attack was a declaration of war. There was no way he could go to sleep comfortably at night until Tank bit the bullet. In Emilio's eyes, he'd gone too far, and there was no coming back.

"I want you to give our friends in Jamaica a call. Put them on the next flight. I'll explain everything to them when they get here," Emilio said, then walked out of his office.

Gloria

The sound of a garbage truck woke me from my sleep. When I opened my eyes, I was sick to see that I was still in my car. I couldn't believe I fell asleep last night. I'd never slipped like this before.

When I picked up my head to look around, I immediately noticed something on my windshield wiper. I grabbed my binoculars to look down the street at Raymond's house. His car wasn't in the driveway, which was another problem I had to deal with. I was never this careless, and those were the type of mistakes that could cost me my life. Lord knows I couldn't afford that right now.

Before I pulled off, I grabbed what I thought was a ticket. It wasn't a ticket; it was an envelope. Inside it was a note that read: Meet me at the Ridge Street Diner, third booth from the exit door in the back, at noon sharp. Don't be late, and make sure you come alone.

I was in awe reading this. My heart almost jumped out of my chest. Was this Raymond? Did somebody else spot me? Was this Agnis? If it was her, I knew I was not gonna hear the end of it. So many thoughts ran through my mind. Who was it, and what did they want? I had to find out, and if push came to shove, I would put a bullet in whoever's head it was at the slightest act of aggression.

"I know for sure that this was personal," Detective Santiago said to his female partner, Detective Cruz, as they both looked down at the body of a black male. He had been shot in his face multiple times, and his money and jewelry were still on his person.

"It might've been personal, but it was definitely two shooters," Cruz said, squatting down and moving some leaves away from a couple of shell casings. This wasn't Cruz's or Santiago's jurisdiction, so they had to be careful with the evidence.

"Come on. Let's get out of here before they start getting in their feelings about us doing their job," Santiago said as he took one more look around the scene.

Just as he was heading back to his car, his phone started to vibrate in his pocket. He paused to answer it.

"This is Detective Santiago."

"Good morning, Detective. This is Detective Johnson from the Logan Police Department. I was down here investigating a murder this morning, and we got a full fingerprint off a shell casing."

"Okay, and what's that got to do with me?" Santiago asked, wanting to get to the real reason behind this call.

"The partial prints you entered into the system matched the full print I got off the scene of my homicide case."

Now Johnson really had Santiago's attention. The partial prints Johnson referred to were those from the recent club shooting and a homicide from three years prior.

"Wait a minute. Where did this murder happen?" Santiago asked out of curiosity.

Detective Johnson began to explain everything he knew about Doug's murder. This could have been the break in the case he needed, especially if he had a match on the partial print. He wasn't about to waste another minute thinking about it.

"I'll be at your office in twenty minutes."

***

Gloria stopped by her friend Rodney's house to pick up a few things. Bullets, extra clips, and a couple of handguns were just a few of the items she took. Rodney and Gloria went way back and had been good friends since middle school. As they got older and started their careers, their jobs complemented one another. Rodney was a gun wizard, while Gloria used them daily in her contracts. Rodney was like the James Bond of the hood when it came to his gadgets, and most people didn't even know he existed. Gloria wanted to keep it that way if she could.

Gloria pulled up to her house, knowing what was about to transpire between her and her husband. It was as if he didn't even care when she walked through the front door. He only glanced at her on his way up the stairs, coming from the kitchen. It had Gloria thinking for a moment. She really didn't feel like the drama that morning, but she had to know why the kids were in the house all by themselves for part of the night.

"Where were you last night? And why do you have an attitude?" Gloria asked, following him up the steps.

"Keep ya voice down. The kids are in the other room 'sleep."

"'Sleep? Why isn't Anthony in school?"

Dillon walked into the bedroom, put his coffee on the table, then turned the TV on.

"Hello? Am I talking to myself?" Gloria asked.

Dillon looked at her, and all he could do was shake his head. "Are you serious? Are you going to stand there and tell me that you forgot that I had to be at the new site today to get my schedule?"

Gloria did forget. She had been so fixed on catching up with Raymond that it totally slipped her mind. "I'm so sorry baby. I really am. You know—"

"You ain't trying hard enough," Dillon snapped, having heard this excuse one too many times. Today, he was just fed up with it. The only way he was going to work on the new project downtown was if he went to get his schedule today. If he didn't, he would have to wait until the next project came along before he was able to work again.

"You know, if you were more focused on our family instead of taking contracts, we wouldn't be having this conversation right now."

His words struck a nerve, one that opened the door for Gloria to say how she'd been feeling. "You know who I was when you met me. All this—" Gloria said, waving her hand around the room. "All this is what you wanted. This was the life you wanted."

"And you agreed to it!" Dillon yelled at her.

"I told you I didn't want kids right now. You did this."

Anthony, unfortunately, walked up to Gloria's bedroom door the moment she said that she hadn't wanted kids. He had heard her loud and clear, which was evident from the look he had on his face when Gloria turned around and saw him standing there. Her heart sank to her stomach, and at that moment, she wished she could have taken back her words.

"Aw, buddy, we woke you?" Dillon said, walking over and hugging him. "Come on. Let's get you something to eat."

Anthony didn't move and started crying right there on the spot. Hearing those words coming from his mother hurt his feelings. He cried hysterically, to the point where he fell to the floor. Dillon had to pick him up and take him to his room. His cries cut through the house and through Gloria's heart. She wanted to go and comfort him but didn't, knowing that she couldn't be the one to console him after such harsh words.

***

Detective Santiago looked into the computer screen at the fingerprints that were found in the Darby murder case. After comparing the partial prints, they matched the fingerprint from the Darby case. The issue now was linking the print to somebody. He was hoping that somebody's prints were already in the system.

"Whoever this guy is, he's never been arrested," Cruz said, walking over to Santiago's desk.

"No match?" he asked with a disappointed look on his face. Santiago turned back and looked into the computer screen. He looked closer at the prints and saw what he thought were some differences. "What if we're looking in the wrong place?" he asked Cruz.

"What do you mean by that?'

Santiago pointed to the computer screen. "These prints look a little thin, don't you think?"

Cruz looked at the screen and had to agree. "So, you think we might be looking for a female?"

"Yeah, and while we're at it, let's see if we can get a warrant for the print itself."

The warrant was so that in the event someone were to get arrested and had these prints, they would automatically be detained. Santiago had a gut instinct that the person he was now looking for was a female, one whom he'd treat just like a man once she was in custody.

Gloria left the house around 11:25, only having enough time to take a quick shower and grab a bite to eat. As she dipped in and out of traffic, the only person she could think about was Anthony. She never even got a chance to get to the bottom of the reason Dillon wasn't home last night. That was an argument for another time.

When Gloria pulled up to the diner, she parked her car in a manner that would give her easy access for a speedy exit. She also took a good look around, noticing a couple of exit doors in the diner. She wished she could see who was sitting in the booth, but she couldn't, which also made her nervous. Whoever this was had picked a good place to sit, whether they did it on purpose or by coincidence. Either way, it concerned Gloria.

She got out of the car and tucked the Glock 9 mm into her back waistband. The diner was semi-crowded, and when Gloria looked to the back door where the booth was, she couldn't believe Raymond was sitting there looking right at her.

Gloria

Damn, this man looked good. Handsome would be an understatement. This couldn't be the same guy from the night before. Don't get me wrong; I loved my husband, but hell, Raymond had it going on. He looked like something right out of GQ Magazine, *and I could tell that he worked out from his build. Just how I liked it.*

Damn, what was I talking about? I had to tighten up. He was my mark, and that was it.

Stay focused, Gloria.

"Good afternoon," Raymond greeted with a smile on his face when he stood up.

He couldn't help but to take in the sight. Her Seven jeans showed off her curves. Long, curly hair dropped behind her shoulders, complementing her sexy green eyes, and in her hand was a Gucci tote bag. She was a sight for sore eyes.

"I thought that the least I could do for you for saving my life the other night was buy you lunch."

"Is that what you summoned me for?" Gloria shot back.

Raymond smiled, looking into her eyes. He held his stare, and without Gloria even noticing, he grabbed hold of a .38 snub nose under the table, cocked it back, and held it by his lap.

"So, what is your name?" Gloria asked, looking him back in his eyes.

"Ray," he replied, gazing back into her eyes. "And what's yours?"

Gloria smiled but hesitated. She damn near gave him her real name. "Shooter. You can call me Shooter," Gloria shot back.

"Well, you know what, Shooter? I think I know who you are," Raymond said, taking a swallow of his orange juice.

His words took Gloria by surprise, and she was seconds away from reaching for her gun, thinking that he might have made her.

"My mom must have hired you. Didn't she?"

"And what would make you think something like that?"

"First off, I know my mother is overprotective."

Gloria wasted no time capitalizing on his mistake, nodding in the affirmative. It was smart thinking, because it was true that Jennifer always told Raymond that she had eyes on him at all times. Raymond never thought that she was serious when she said it, so he never really paid it any mind.

"I have been assigned to look after you. I have been doing it for a couple of weeks now," Gloria lied. "I'm still a little confused as to why that guy was trying to kill you."

"That's another story, but I'm also curious as to why you're watching over me."

"It's because of people like that. I'm here to make sure you get around safely."

That was another bald-faced lie. The only reason why Gloria protected Raymond last night was because she wanted to be the one to get the job done. It would have looked funny if Doug had gotten away with it, and the money that Gloria had already received for the hit would have had to be returned. Gloria wasn't about to let that happen. The way Raymond died had to be on Gloria's terms only.

"So, you're like my li'l guardian angel," Raymond replied.

"Yeah, but I need you to do me a big favor. Can you please not tell your mother that you found me out? She will fire me on the spot, and I really need the job."

"I'll tell you what. If you ride along with me tomorrow, I'll keep this between me and you."

Raymond felt, since his mother wanted someone to look over him, he might as well put them to work. It didn't bother Gloria at all. Being this close to him would probably present a better opportunity for her to finish the job.

"That sounds like a deal." Gloria nodded.

Raymond sat there, continuing to eat his food with his right hand, with his left hand on his lap. At this point, he didn't feel like Gloria was a threat. He de-cocked the gun and loosened up. Gloria was also feeling a little more comfortable, relaxing her grip and putting the safety back on. For a moment, things had almost gotten ugly.

Amanda was in bed, curled up in the fetal position when Detectives Cruz and Santiago rang the doorbell. She was sick about Doug's death, and even though he had cheated on her, she didn't want him to die behind it.

"Yes, can I help you?" Amanda asked when she opened the door.

Santiago flashed his badge and identified himself before asking permission to enter the house. She agreed, hoping someone could give her some answers about what happened.

"Can you tell me why anyone would want to kill your husband?" Santiago asked, looking around the house before taking a seat on the couch.

Cruz stayed standing, looking at the many pictures Amanda had hanging up on the wall.

"That's what I don't understand. Doug didn't have any enemies that I know of. Aside from him cheating on me, he was a pretty decent guy," Amanda answered.

"Cheating on you?" Cruz asked. "With who?"

Amanda broke down the whole situation and how she had hired a private investigator to follow Doug around. She explained this was done when their marriage had gone through some rough patches. Amanda told Cruz about the time that she caught him cheating and about the pending case she had open for shooting Doug in the leg at the mall. "I'm out on bail for that right now," Amanda said.

Cruz and Santiago looked at each other. "I'm sorry, Amanda, but I have to ask you, where were you the night Doug was killed?"

She pulled up her pajama leg and showed Santiago the court-ordered ankle monitor. "I'm under house arrest. I can't leave the house unless it's to see my lawyer and to go to work," she told him. "I was here all night. You can check."

"That won't be necessary, ma'am, but what I do need is the phone number to the private investigator who you hired to follow your husband. If possible, I would like to ask him a few questions."

"You don't think he had something to do with it?" Amanda asked, looking from Cruz to Santiago.

"We just wanna rule out all potential suspects, and if possible, we would like to speak to the woman Doug was cheating with."

"Yeah, good luck with that," Amanda said, getting up from the couch. She walked upstairs to retrieve Raymond's number for the officers.

In Santiago's eyes, everybody was a suspect until he cleared them. In this particular case, Santiago was looking for someone specific: someone with small hands, that of a woman. For him, it was playing one big game of connect-the-dots, and from his experience, one good lead always led to another. He only hoped that Raymond could shed a little light on Doug's personal life.

Chapter 7

"Was there anyone following you, and did you take the route I told you to take?" Emilio asked when Carmine got out of his car.

"No one was following me. I made sure of it."

"Good, because today is the day that we clean up this mess we made. First things first, we need to get rid of Agnis and the bitch. I don't want Dion's death coming back to haunt me later on down the line."

"Agnis? You wanna kill Agnis?" Carmine asked with a confused look on his face. "Isn't she protected by the elders?"

When Carmine spoke of the elders, he was referring to higher officials from the few remaining families in the Mob. Agnis had put in some serious work for some very important people, not to mention that she was half Italian and half black. On her Italian side, her father was a made man from the Gambino family, and though she was a child conceived out of wedlock, Agnis always had the protection of her father's name.

"Don't worry about the elders; I'll take care of it. Just grab a couple of the boys and head down to the church for now. Make sure you take some flowers to Bruno's mother for me and send her my condolences. Let her know that she'll be taken care of for the rest of her life. Bruno had a little boy, and I'm going to make sure that he's well off." Emilio got serious with his next words. "We're family, and family gotta stick together."

"No problem, boss. I'll take care of it," Carmine assured.
Emilio couldn't make it to Bruno's funeral today because he had a very important meeting to attend with the Jamaicans, and their flight was about to touch down. The other reason was that he wasn't trying to be out in public while a war was brewing. Low key was the best way to be right now. With somebody like Tank running around the city, anything was liable to happen.

Gloria sat in her car outside of Agnis's Salon, thinking about everything she had planned for today. It was a must that she had a sit-down with Agnis to see if she could terminate the contract on Raymond's head. She felt like her cover was blown, and she didn't want to risk either the police getting involved or Raymond doing something stupid that would make her want to kill him prematurely.

Anthony also had a football game this evening, and to make up for her harsh words pertaining to her not wanting children, she thought that she would surprise him by showing up at the game. To tell the truth, she knew that tonight was going to either make or break her relationship with her son.

"Hey, Kim, is Agnis in?" Gloria asked when she walked into the shop.

"No, mamacita. She hasn't been here all day," Kim replied.

Gloria looked around the salon at the few people that were there. It was quiet, which made the atmosphere a little unusual.

"Is everything all right?" Kim asked.

Gloria pulled her phone from her bag. "Yeah, everything's good. I just need to talk to her about something."

Gloria tried calling Agnis's phone, but it went straight to voicemail. Gloria left the shop, wondering where she could be. It wasn't like Agnis to just go MIA. She was a grown woman and all, and she did her thing with the fellas, but never did Agnis tell Gloria to meet her at a certain time and didn't show up. Maybe Gloria was looking into it too hard. Hopefully it was nothing, but for now, Gloria had to rush over to Rev. Index to try to get an early start on Raymond before he took his lunch break.

On his way to the funeral, Carmine stopped by the Billiard to grab a couple of guys to attend the funeral with him. These were nothing less than some shooters who wouldn't hesitate to kill anyone for Emilio. They drove back to back in three Cadillac Escalades with the Italian flag flapping on the antennas. Bruno was 100% Italian, and Emilio was going to make sure he was buried like one.

When Carmine made it to the church, he noticed a fair amount of people outside. For it to have been a private viewing, there were a lot of people inside as well. Maybe a little more than 100 were in attendance.

"Hi, how are you, Mrs. Viola?" Carmine greeted, walking up and taking a seat next to Bruno's mother in the front row.

Carmine probably knew Bruno's family better than anybody else, as he and Bruno had grown up together. Mrs. Viola had a lot of respect for Carmine and his family, but she hated the fact that the Mob took hold of her boy.

"I'm sorry about Bruno. I'ma make sure the person who did this—"

Carmine couldn't finish his statement before Mrs. Viola cut him off. "I told you boys to stay out of this way of life," she said, dabbing her eyes with her handkerchief.

"You two were so damn hard-headed," she said, staring at her son in a casket in front of her.

Carmine kept his gaze on the floor out of shame. He remembered all the talks she used to have with him and Bruno, about how the Mob was overrated in these times. Sometimes Carmine wished that he and Bruno had listened to her.

"And where's Emilio? I thought he would have been here," Mrs. Viola said, digging into her bag.

"He's out getting to the bottom of this. He sends his deepest condolences. Here," Carmine said, reaching into his jacket and pulling out a small but puffy manila envelope and passing it to her.

She looked down at the envelope but didn't take it. "You tell Emilio I can pay for my own son's funeral. I don't need nothing from him, not even his guilt money."

Mrs. Viola got up and walked over to Bruno's casket, leaving Carmine sitting there. He understood how she felt right now, so time and space would be granted to her.

Carmine walked over and said, "Again, I'm sorry for your loss." He took one last look at Bruno, then turned around to leave the church. He couldn't stand to be in Mrs. Viola's presence right now.

"I'ma step outside for a minute," Carmine told his men. As he was making his way up the aisle, he noticed two black men with full beards entering the church. Right from the start, he knew that something was wrong with this picture. The hairs on the back of Carmine's neck stood up, and in the blink of an eye, the two bearded men came from behind his back with twin AR-15s. This wasn't a social call, nor was there going to be any talking. Carmine drew his weapon, but before he could get off a shot, the two men opened fire.

"Everybody get down!" Carmine yelled over the loud gunfire coming from the back of the church.

The large assault rifles showed no mercy. Bullets tore through the pews and the walls with ease, hitting people as they tried to get out of the way. Bullets hit Bruno's casket, the piano, the pulpit, and the door that led to the priest's chambers. Bruno's family members scrambled around on the floor, looking for something to hide behind.

Mrs. Viola was Carmine's only concern. He crawled over to her, grabbing her and pulling her over to where he was, all the while firing several shots into the direction of the gunmen. The bullets from the AR-15 just kept sounding off. Carmine thought that it would never stop.

"Keep ya head down!" he yelled out to Mrs. Viola, shielding her with his body.

The gunfire finally stopped, and the only thing that could be heard in the church was the gunmen reloading their rifles. This gave Carmine and his boys the opportunity to return fire, which they did with everything that they had. *POP! BOOM! POP! POP! POW! POW! BOOM!* Bullets flew all over the church.

Carmine got a good shot off, hitting one of the shooters in his chest. He stumbled backward out of the door with the AR-15 still firing into the church. The second gunman kept Carmine and his men at bay. The bullets continued to whiz by Carmine's head. Then, out of nowhere, the gunfire stopped again. The church became quiet again, and this time when Carmine came from behind his cover, the two gunmen were gone. Carmine darted toward the door, hoping to catch the one he had shot. By the time he made it outside, a gold Jeep Cherokee was speeding off.

Loud cries began to sound off in the church. So many people were injured. Lifeless bodies were littering the floor of the church. The gun battle was over, but the carnage those gunmen left behind was vicious. The priest was hit in the leg, Bruno's mother dislocated her shoulder when she fell to the ground, and the church was in ruins.

This was the by far the harshest blow the Italians took thus far, and sadly, probably wasn't going to be the last one of this magnitude.

"Raymond, there are two detectives here to see you," his secretary said, knocking on Raymond's door.

He picked his head up from the paperwork he had on his desk. He was shocked to hear that, and the first thing that came to his mind was that he was on his way to jail. Visions of Doug's body hitting the ground right in front of him flashed in and out of his thoughts. He had no idea whatsoever what he planned to say.

"Tell them to come in," Raymond told her, moving the paperwork to the side.

Detectives Santiago and Cruz entered his office, introducing themselves with pleasant smiles.

"How can I be of some assistance to Charlotte's finest?" Raymond asked, crossing his hands on the desk.

"We're investigating the murder of Douglas Carpenter," Santiago began.

"Murder?" Raymond shot back as though he didn't know what was going on. "When? Why?" he asked. He hadn't known it until then, but he was a natural, award-winning actor. Cruz was even convinced by his initial reaction that Raymond didn't have anything to do with it.

"His wife told us that you were hired to investigate him and provided her information on his infidelities," Cruz stated.

Raymond nodded in the affirmative, still playing the part of being shocked by the news.

The detective continued, "I know these things are confidential, but we really need to know who is the woman he was cheating on Amanda with."

"I'm sorry, sir, but I can't release that information without Amanda's consent. People depend on confidentiality, and that's what I provide. That's why business is good."

Santiago whipped out his phone and had Amanda confirm that it was okay for Raymond to discuss any and all of the information he had on Doug. Raymond still didn't want to, but he had no other choice. He didn't seem suspicious in the detectives' eyes, so the best thing for him to do was cooperate.

"Her name is Vivian Smith. She works with Doug at the factory," Raymond explained, getting up and going into his file cabinet to retrieve Doug's file. "I really hope that you find the person who did this. He wasn't a bad guy, and I think that he and Amanda could have worked out their problems."

Aside from having a mound of paperwork to go through, Raymond had some other things he needed to be attending to. "I'm sorry that I don't have more time, but I do have to get back to work," Raymond told Santiago. "Everything I have on Doug is right there. If you need to ask any further questions, you can always call me. Here's my office and home number," Raymond said, passing him and Cruz a card.

As they were on their way out the door, Detective Cruz stopped. "I just had two more questions for you if you don't mind," she said.

"Shoot," Raymond replied.

"Did Vivian give you any indication that she was capable of murder?"

Raymond capitalized on the question, hoping to divert even more attention away from him. "No, not really. But there was this one time that Vivian and Doug got into a heated argument one night. I don't know what it was about, but what I do know is that it ended with Doug getting smacked pretty hard." Raymond chuckled.

Cruz smiled and was about to leave, but then Raymond stopped her.

"Detective, you said you had two questions. What was the other?"

Cruz turned to face him. "Well, if you don't mind me asking, where were you Thursday night around midnight?"

Emilio walked into his office, only to see Carmine sitting behind his desk. A half bottle of whiskey was clutched in his hands, and by the looks of things, Emilio knew that he was having a bad day. There were blood stains on his shirt from helping the wounded, bloodshot red eyes from drinking and crying for the past hour, and the only thing on his mind was murder. Emilio didn't even want to ask what had happened. Instead, he took a seat on the couch and patiently waited for Carmine to tell him everything.

Chapter 8

Gloria walked around to the back of Raymond's house, periodically looking around to see if any of his neighbors were out. His house was nice, sitting on a couple acres of land just outside of Charlotte. It was nothing for her to disable his alarm system, and once inside, she drew her 9 mm Glock and held it down by her side. She wasn't sure if Raymond or somebody else was in the house, or if a huge dog might come barreling toward her from another room. The deeper she went into his house, the more she admired his taste. The house was decadent and plush.

The downstairs was decorated with a long leather sectional couch, a 65-inch plasma TV on the wall, and oak hardwood floors throughout. When Gloria went upstairs, things got even better. She knew from the minute she walked into the bedroom in the front of the house that it had to be the master suite. A huge California king bed sat directly in the middle of the room. It was mounted up off the floor a whole foot, which made the bed look even bigger.

"You got it going on," Gloria mumbled to herself.

A noise coming from downstairs caught her attention. She stopped mid-stride on her way down the hallway, listening closely. The first thought that went through her mind was that the house was settling, but then it started to sound like somebody was walking. Gloria kept her hand wrapped around her gun, raising it and pointing it toward the steps.

"You know you don't have to keep following me. . . . I mean, breaking into my house, disabling my alarm system. It's really not that deep," Raymond shouted from downstairs.

Gloria's heart began to race, knowing exactly who it was now. She remained quiet, kicking herself in the ass.

"How about I make you a deal? If you ease up a little bit, I'll pay you double what my mother is paying you," he offered, his voice still amplified from downstairs.

Gloria stuffed the gun into her back pocket and made her way down the steps. Raymond was leaned up against the partition, unarmed and with a smile on his face.

"You don't have to do that. I was just checking on you, and ya back door looked like it was tampered with. I wasn't sure, so I—"

"Are you really worried about me to the extent that you would go this far to protect me?"

"I would protect you with my own life if I had to." Gloria sounded so sincere she almost convinced herself of it.

They stood there, sharing yet another awkward moment with each other.

"Damn, I see something better in your future," Raymond said, breaking the silence.

"Tell me what might that be," Gloria shot back.

"I could see you living a life where you could be completely happy. A life where you wouldn't have a worry in the world."

"And are you in the picture in this premonition of yours?"

"Fortunately for you, I am."

They stood there staring at each other for what seemed like hours. Gloria's phone vibrated in her pocket, snapping her out of her trance. She pulled the phone out and looked at the screen. It was a reminder alert, telling her that Anthony's game was today. She didn't say another word to Raymond and headed for the door.

"You owe me a new alarm system!" Raymond yelled out with a smile on his face. All he got in return was the front door slamming in his face.

Detectives Santiago and Cruz walked up and knocked on Vivian's door. They stood there and waited for someone to answer. When the door opened, a beautiful Hispanic female poked her head out of the door.

"Hi, is Vivian home?" Cruz asked.

"I'm Vivian. How can I help you?"

In comparing Vivian to Amanda, Santiago could see why Doug had cheated. Vivian had an innocent look to her, and she also had a body out of this world. Detective Cruz couldn't see how somebody like Doug snagged her in the first place.

"I need to ask you a few questions about Doug," Santiago said.

The alarmed look on Vivian's face said it all. She didn't understand how—or why—the cops would know about her and Doug. As it turned out, she hadn't known that Doug was dead until the detectives sat her down and told her. Santiago questioned her about the argument that they had had, and she denied it fully.

"When was the last time you saw Doug?"

"Two nights ago. We went to a hotel, but we ended up talking about his wife. He said that she found out about us and was talking about getting a divorce. I was bummed out, so I ended up going home."

"Is that all? Did he tell you where he was going after he left you?"

Vivian had to think about it for a minute. "He did snap about the private investigator that was watching him. He said that he was going to kill him. I just thought he was blowing off some steam."

Santiago and Cruz looked at each other in a curious manner. These were the little dots Santiago loved to connect, and being that Doug had good reasons for wanting to kill Raymond for messing up his marriage, Detective Santiago didn't rule out the possibility of Raymond turning around and killing Doug in order to protect himself. The more Santiago thought about it, the more things were starting to come together.

Gloria pulled into the Allentown Recreation Center parking lot and could see that Anthony's game had already started. Dillon was surprised to see her walking up the bleachers, but smiled and was happy that she made it. Alisha was happy, too, reaching out for her mother from Dillon's arms.

She looked out into the field and didn't know which player was Anthony. Gloria didn't even know what team he was on until Dillon pointed him out. She felt so embarrassed. Anthony was a little tall for his age, so he played wide receiver.

"How is he doing?" she asked while bouncing Alisha in her arms.

"I know this might not be the right time, but we need to talk when we get home," Dillon said to Gloria as he continued to watch the game. It came out of nowhere, which made Gloria concerned about what it may have been about.

"Something you can't say now?" she replied, turning to face him.

Dillon kept his eyes on the game. "We just gotta figure out what we're going to do."

"What are we going to do?" Gloria asked, turning her face up. "What's that supposed to—"

"It means that we just need to talk," he said, cutting her off.

"I'm here, aren't I? Damn!" she yelled.

Some spectators who were watching the game turned to see what all the noise was about. Gloria snapped on them as well, telling them to mind their business. When she turned back to say something to Dillon, he had walked off and was making his way to the sidelines to talk to Anthony.

He was right when he said that this wasn't the time and the place for their conversation, but Gloria was already hot. She thought that she had done the right thing by making it to Anthony's game, but she was now starting to regret it, because what she believed to be the beginning of a good night was turning into something tragic.

Chapter 9

Gloria

Dillon had me pissed off all night, and then he had the nerve to leave the house before we got a chance to talk like he suggested. I swear, if he wasn't the father of my children, I might have hired myself to kill him. His mother had the kids for the weekend, so hopefully we'd have time to clean up this mess.

It was already 4 p.m., and Gloria couldn't find Raymond anywhere. He wasn't at home, nor at Rev. Index like she thought he would be. There was only one more place to check, and that was Raymond's P.I. firm. The office was in downtown Charlotte, a place where Gloria hated to drive. Traffic would be at a standstill around this time.

Gloria sat in her car contemplating for a moment, and just when she was about to put the car in drive, there was a tap on the passenger's side window. When she looked over, Raymond was leaning over, looking in with a smile on his face.

"Let me in. I need to talk to you," he said, seeing that she was about to pull off on him. "Give me one minute of your time."

Gloria didn't want to. This was going against her better judgment, but she did it anyway.

"What do you want, Raymond?"

"I just wanted to show you my life and what it is that I really do," he said.

"That's not how this works. I'm really not supposed to be getting close to you. I'm here to protect you, not to get personal." Gloria sat there staring at him.

"It's like you don't have an emotional bone in your body," Raymond said, looking into her eyes.

"I do have emotions, but at the same time, I have a job to do. This is how I pay the bills."

"A job? You call this a job? You crazy as hell. I could have blown your head clean off your shoulders when you broke into my house, or I could have called the cops on you when you killed Doug right in front of me. But I didn't. You wanna know why I didn't do it?"

Gloria didn't have to say anything, because Raymond was going to tell her anyway.

"Because I know you got people that depend on you right now. A mother, father, children, or maybe even a man," Raymond said. The truth behind his statement made Gloria think. Raymond could see that he had hit a nerve.

"So, what do you want, Raymond?

"I just want you to ride with me for 48 hours. See what it is that I do, and if you feel like you're not interested in it, I'll leave you alone. You can watch me from a distance, and I won't bother you one bit. I'll even double the salary my mother is paying you."

Raymond laid it on thick. Though Gloria wasn't supposed to be getting close to her mark, Raymond was making it hard. Gloria could see that he was going to be a problem, one that she wasn't sure how to deal with.

Gloria had considered Raymond's proposal. She felt that it was the least she could do for him since he spared her life. Gloria had to step out of her car so she could try to call Agnis again. She hadn't answered her phone in days, and nobody in the salon had heard from her. This was unusual for Agnis to go MIA like this, and not let Gloria know what was going on.

"Where the hell are you?" Gloria mumbled to herself when Agnis didn't answer the phone again. She couldn't stress about it too much, because the issue at hand needed all of Gloria's attention.

"Let's get on with it," she said, getting back into the car. Raymond looked at her and smiled, holding his stare. It was a little uncomfortable.

"Are you okay?" Gloria asked, still feeling his eyes all over her.

"I have to honest with you. I've never seen a woman as beautiful as you before, and it's mind-boggling that you do what you do for a living."

His comments made Gloria blush a little, but she quickly got it together.

"So, where are we going?" she asked, hoping that he didn't see the effect he was having on her.

"Before we pull off, I have to ask you something. Do you feel bad about killing Doug? I mean, do you ever think about—"

"Thought you already established that I don't have an emotional bone in my body. But let me ask you something. Do you ever think about all the marriages you destroy from all the investigating that you do? Tomato, tomatoh. We both ruin lives no matter how you look at it, so don't be so fast to point the finger at me. I only kill the body, but you, you kill the heart, and in my eyes, that's far worse."

Raymond wanted to respond, but he didn't know how to. What she said did make sense, but there was more to what Raymond did as a P.I., and the only way he was going to get that across to Gloria was by showing her.

Instead of taking Gloria's car, Raymond convinced her to ride in his and be the driver, so he could review his notes on Carmen while they followed her.

"So, who exactly are we looking for?" Gloria asked, looking over at Raymond.

"Her name is Carmen, and her husband hired me about a week ago"

"A guy hired you? I thought it would be the other way around."

"Yeah, well, men aren't the only ones who cheat. This is the first time I've had to watch a woman, and from what I've seen thus far, y'all cheat better than anybody."

Raymond kept his eyes on the road and cautioned Gloria to do the same, because Carmen was dipping in and out of traffic like she knew she was being followed.

"You're gonna end up losing her." Raymond smiled.

"I got her," Gloria said, maneuvering through traffic with ease.

While Gloria was watching what was in front of her, Raymond was paying attention to what was going on behind them. "It looks like we might have somebody following us," Raymond said.

Gloria looked in her rearview mirror and could see a dark-colored Crown Victoria pulling in behind them. She let out a frustrated sigh as the red-and-blue lights began to flash.

"Yup, we're definitely being followed." Raymond chuckled.

Raymond immediately began to retrieve his license and registration as they were pulling over. Carmen's tail lights got smaller and smaller until her car entirely disappeared into traffic.

When the two detectives got out of their cars, Raymond knew exactly who they were. Gloria rolled down her window, and before Raymond could say anything, Detective

Santiago started talking. Cruz walked up and stood at the passenger's side window, looking down at Raymond. Raymond passed Gloria his license and registration to give to the officer, but when she rolled her window down and held it out for him to grab, Santiago asked Raymond to step out of the car.

Raymond was walked back toward the Crown Victoria while Cruz kept a sharp eye on Gloria. The only thing Gloria could think about was what would happen if they asked her for her license. It would have been a problem, because Gloria would have had to reveal her true identity, which was something that she really didn't want to do in front of Raymond, or to the cops. That, and the fact that she was carrying a unregistered gun in her bag, had her worried. Had the detectives acted like they were going to take her into custody, she wasn't going without a fight. Jail wasn't something Gloria saw in her future, and before she would allow herself to be one with a six-by-nine cell, she would go out in a blaze of glory.

After about a minute, Raymond came back to the car.

"They want me to follow them down to the police station," Raymond said. "They want to ask me some questions about Doug."

"So, what did you tell them?" Gloria asked with concern.

"I told them that I would follow them. It's not that serious. All I got is the same answers I gave them before. Relax, I got this."

The whole way down to the police station, there was total silence in the car. They both were at loss for words, and at just about every red light, Gloria thought about getting out of the car. She wasn't sure if this was a set-up or not, and if it were, Raymond was going to be the first person who caught a bullet from her gun.

When Raymond pulled into the 18th Precinct, Santiago and Cruz got out of the car and waited in front

of Raymond's car like wolves. Raymond looked over at
Gloria and placed his hand over hers.

"Look at me, Shooter," he said, tapping her hand until
she turned to him. "I'm not gonna tell on you, so if that's
what you're thinking, you need to get that out of your
head."

He looked out of the window at the detectives standing
there waiting. As he was about to get out of the car,
Gloria grabbed his arm. "Keep all of your answers short
and sweet. The more lies you tell, the more you'll have to
keep up with."

"I'll do that. Now, I gotta do this for show, so don't
freak out," Raymond said, then leaned in and kissed
Gloria. She knew how important it was to play along and
not give the detectives anything to be suspicious of. His
lips up against hers were something else. A small peck
felt like a full-blown makeout session. She didn't open
her eyes until Raymond was out of the car. She watched
as they took Raymond into the police station, and right
before the double doors had closed, Detective Cruz
turned around and gave Gloria a hard stare, one that was
quite intimidating.

For security purposes, Dion's funeral wasn't spoken
about to anyone that wasn't immediate family. The
funeral was so low key it happened at night outside of city
lines, and attendees had to be recognized at the door by
Tank himself.

"Yo, everything's good out front. Won't nobody be
running up in here," Butch said, walking up and standing
next to Tank.

"And what about the cemetery? Do everybody know
what to do?"

Even the drive to the burial site was strategically planned out. Everyone at the church had to leave at a separate time and take separate routes to meet up at the cemetery. There could be no following one another back-to-back like normal funeral processions.

"Yeah, and we already got people waiting there. We got the whole cemetery on lockdown. Trust me, bro, our family is safe."

Tank had started the war and was going to do everything in his power to remain at the head of it. He knew beyond a shadow of a doubt that Emilio was going to strike back, and strike back hard. The Bruno funeral shooting was a low blow, but Tank had more tricks up his sleeve and was going to use them just as soon as he buried Dion.

"Li'l sis is coming," Butch said, seeing Johanne get up from her seat and walk their way. "I'll leave you two alone."

Tank exhaled deeply, knowing that he was about to hear it from his sister. Johanne was the oldest out of two boys and two girls, and she was also the most violent of them all. Sometimes she overdid it, but that was her style.

"I hear that you're going to war with the Italians. Are you being safe? Are we safe right now?" she asked, looking at Tank.

"Of course we're safe, big sis. That's the last thing you need to worry about."

There was a pause for a minute. They both looked up at the white-with-gold-trim casket sitting in the front of the church.

"Look, Tank. I don't care who you go to war with, just bring me the person who killed my son. It don't matter if he's dead or alive, just as long as the body is sitting in my living room. Do you think you can do that for me?" Johanne asked, wiping the tear that fell down her cheek.

He hated to see his sister cry, but he also felt her pain. Losing someone that close was hard, and Tank could only imagine how it would feel to lose a child.

"I got you, sis," he said, leaning in and kissing her head.

Tank was going to do anything and everything in his power to make that happen. On that, he got up and walked to the front of the church without saying another word. Butch and Johanne followed behind him, all standing before Dion's casket.

Chapter 10

Raymond

Damn, I had to get out of there. I couldn't believe those crazy detectives had me in there for almost eight hours questioning me. As I expected, Shooter was gone by the time I got back to my car. I didn't blame her, though I did want to talk to her about what was said in the interrogation room.

As soon as I walked into the room, they'd hit me hard with question after question. They asked me about my P.I. firm; they asked me where was I the night Doug was murdered; and they also asked me about Gloria, wanting to know her relationship to me. I kept the answers short and sweet, just like Shooter told me to. Her strategy worked, too; that is, until Detective Cruz started asking me about the second car I registered in my name. I was nervous as hell because that was the only piece of evidence that could put me at the scene of the crime. Not only that, but the car was still sitting in my garage. I lied and told them that the car had caught fire so I had it demolished. It didn't seem like they believed me, but they left it alone.

***

"Tish, do you have somebody in your chair right now?" Agnis yelled from the back. She needed help with the new shipment of weave that had come in the other day.

"No, but there's a guy here who wanna see you. I think he wants his dreads done," Tish yelled back.

"Well, tell him we're closed right now. He can make an appointment for tomorrow."

Tish stopped what she was doing and stepped to the back with Agnis. Tish sort of felt bad for the guy, especially since he had offered to pay extra for an appointment this evening.

"Oh, and call Gloria and tell her to come and pick me up," Agnis instructed.

She could see by the many missed phone calls that Gloria was trying to get in touch with her. Agnis didn't want to tell her, but she had been going through some personal issues, one being that during a routine check-up, her doctor found a small lump under her right breast. For the past couple of days, Agnis had taken some time out for herself, wanting to be alone to register the possibility of her having breast cancer. Her next doctor's appointment was for tomorrow, when she would get the final results from her blood tests. It was going to show exactly what was wrong with her.

"And when do you plan on telling me about the new man in ya life?" Tish joked.

Agnis smiled. "Girl, please. I wish there was a Mr. Right I could cuddle up to," Agnis joked. "Hell, girl, I got bigger problems." Agnis caught herself, not wanting to put her business out there just yet. At the same time, she really didn't trust Tish that much, ever since Gwen came back snooping around. She wasn't sure, but Agnis thought that Tish was either MHB or was trying to pledge. In any event, Agnis's personal life was going to remain personal. Didn't need her running back and telling Gwen her business.

"And what about the guy? He's still out there waiting," Tish said.

"Tell him to come back tomorrow. I'm so tired right now. Hell, if you wanna stay here and do it, you can."

"Shit, I'm not staying here. I got a party to go to tonight," Tish said. When she walked back into the front of the salon, the guy was still there.

"I'm sorry, but we're closed for the day. You can come back in the morning, and we'll take care of you."

The man got up to leave, but when Tish started walking toward the door to let him out, the guy pulled a black .45 from his hip. He grabbed a handful of Tish's hair and pointed the gun at her face. The gun was huge, and it had a silencer on it, along with a beam. He didn't even give Tish time to scream. A bullet was sent from the large gun, almost knocking Tish's head off. The impact from the blast pushed Tish backward. The noise from her body falling got a hold of Agnis's attention in the back.

"What in the world is going on out there?" Agnis said, stepping out of the back. When she walked out and saw the guy standing over Tish's body with the gun in his hand, she darted for her office. The man raised his gun and started shooting at Agnis, tearing holes in the sheetrock wall behind every stride she took.

She practically dove into her office, grabbing hold of a Mossberg pump that was strapped under her desk. The man couldn't see right away that Agnis was armed, but he quickly realized it when she came out firing.

BOOM!

The guy dipped behind the partition in the nick of time.

"You gon' die today!" Agnis yelled out as she stepped over Tish's body. She was a mere ten feet away from the partition the shooter had ducked behind. Out of nowhere, several bullets crashed through the window, one hitting Agnis in her leg.

Agnis fired out of the front door window but didn't hit anything. The man came from behind the partition, rapidly firing at the same time Agnis fired off the last bullet in her weapon. She missed, but the guy hit Agnis in the same leg that had just been hit, causing her to fall back into the check-in desk.

The man walked up with his gun pointed at her face. His long dread locs were draped over his shoulder. "Bloodclaat pussy girl. You can't kill me. I'm Jamaican," the guy yelled with the gun clutched tightly.

"Take whatever you want. The money is in the office in the top right drawer," Agnis pleaded.

"We don't want money," he replied in his thick Jamaican accent.

Right then, another male Jamaican walked through the front door, stepping through glass and standing next to his partner. "I wanna know who you use to kill Dion," the second shooter chimed in.

"Now, think about what you gon' say before it get ugly in here," the other Jamaican said.

"I don't know who you're talking about, or who the hell Dion is."

Without warning, one of the Jamaicans stepped on Agnis's leg, right at the entry wound. It hurt like hell, but Agnis handled the pain. It was going to take an awful lot more to get her to talk. While one stood on her leg, the other slammed his gun into Agnis's mouth, knocking two of her teeth out in the process. Agnis still managed to laugh with the gun in her mouth. They knew she wasn't about to talk right then and there, and there wouldn't be much longer until the cops showed up. The only other option they had was taking Agnis somewhere secluded so they could extract the information they wanted, as one Jamaican suggested to the other.

Chapter 11

"She's slowing up. What do you want me to do?" Gloria asked Raymond as she kept her eyes glued to the road. She hated being on driving duty, but Raymond convinced her, due to the lack of sleep he had gotten the night prior.

"Just take it slow," Raymond said in a somewhat seductive manner.

Gloria caught that and couldn't help but to smile. Raymond was a big flirt, and it amused Gloria at times.

"You really need to get some sleep tonight."

"Hell, if I keep up with this type of business, I'm gonna be doing a lot of sleep in my grave," Raymond joked.

They both smiled, but they got right back to business. Carmen had pulled into a gas station, but it didn't appear as though she was getting any gas. Instead, a man jumped out of an SUV and got into Carmen's car.

"Did you see that?" Raymond asked. It was fairly dark, so he couldn't get a good look at the guy. "Shooter, where did he just come from?" Raymond asked, looking around the parking lot.

Gloria picked her head up, having not been paying attention in the slightest. "That looks like a Tahoe, but I'm not sure of the year." She knew the make and model because she used to own a Tahoe. Dillon wrecked it one night, and they ended up giving it away to a family member a while back.

"Keep up with them, Shooter," Raymond encouraged.

Gloria noticed Raymond was well prepared that night, aside from his inability to drive. He really took care of business, and even though Gloria wasn't too enthused about what he did, she had to admit, it was beginning to be a little fun chasing people around.

"Okay, I just got off the phone with her husband, and he said that he doesn't have a clue where Carmen is going tonight."

"It looks like they're going over the bridge," Gloria pointed out.

"You got plans for tonight?" Raymond asked, looking over at Gloria. He could tell that it was going to be a long night.

Gloria thought about it, and since Dillon walked out on her the other night, she wasn't in a rush to get back home. She definitely didn't feel like another night of sleeping in her bed by herself while Dillon either slept in Anthony's room or on the couch. Whatever the case may have been, Gloria was free for the night, and with any luck, she was going to clip Raymond tonight and get it over with. That would be a win-win.

Detective Santiago sat on his porch and cracked open a nice cold beer. He promised himself that he would never bring his work home with him, but for some odd reason, he couldn't seem to get Raymond's interview out of his head. He could tell that he was hiding something pertaining to Doug's death, but he just couldn't pinpoint it. It was burning him up, too, because if Raymond did know something about Doug's death, more than likely he would know something about the person who killed him.

"Papi, the kids are sleep, and I'm about to take a shower," Rosa, Santiago's wife said when she came out onto the porch.

Santiago grabbed her arm before she went back into the house, pulling her down onto his lap. "Come, mami." He smiled. "You know that I love you, right?" he said, wrapping his arms around her.

"Of course I do, papi. What's gotten into you?"

Santiago thought about the interview he had with Amanda, and how she had to hire somebody to see if her husband was cheating. He assured Rosa that he would never put her through such a scandal. Hearing and seeing the outcome of this type of behavior was a reminder, and having a wife as beautiful as Rosa was all the reason why being unfaithful wasn't an option.

They both sat on the porch and spent some much-needed quality time together. This was something they both were going to need, because after tonight, Santiago was going to be extra busy trying to crack the case of Charlotte's contract killer.

Raymond was perplexed as they followed Carmen's car into an Indian reservation just outside of Charlotte. Gloria, however, put two and two together almost immediately.

"It looks like they're going to the casino," Gloria said after seeing Carmen get off at that exit.

Before long, Carmen's car pulled into the Cherokee Casino parking lot. Unbeknownst to her, she was being followed. Gloria kept her distance, circling the casino before parking in the same garage. She parked on the same level, but by the time Gloria and Raymond were getting out of the car, Carmen and her friend were already on the elevator heading for the lobby. Raymond was hoping that they wouldn't check into the hotel, because he would be forced to do the same, or wait out in the parking lot until Carmen and her friend left.

"Let me ask you something," Raymond asked Gloria as they got onto the elevator. "What would you do if your significant other—"

"I would kill him," Gloria said, cutting him off. She had a smile on her face, but she was dead serious about what she would do if Dillon cheated on her.

"Hell, anybody that cheats on you deserves to die." He smiled, looking over at Gloria as they walked off.

The elevator doors opened up, and out walked Carmen—alone. Raymond looked at Gloria and mouthed the words *That's her*. He had a confused look on his face, because he knew that she had just had a man with her, and they should've already been in the lobby. Where he had gone was anyone's guess. Gloria shrugged her shoulders, not knowing what to do.

Carmen's cell ringing broke the silence. "No, baby, it's okay. Take your time. I'll check us into the room," Carmen said before hanging up the phone.

Gloria and Raymond followed behind her as she headed toward the check-in counter. They heard her request a room that she claimed to have had a couple of nights ago. Raymond and Gloria stood behind her in line, and once Raymond heard the desk attendant tell her the room number, he was hoping he could get a room on the same floor.

"Can I help you, sir?" the clerk asked Raymond after he finished up with Carmen. Raymond tried to convince him to give them a room on the same floor as Carmen, but the clerk seemed skeptical. That's when Gloria stepped in with her fake bubbly personality. She began speaking in Spanish, telling the clerk that Carmen had taken their special room. A cute face and some nice tits always did the trick. Obviously, the clerk couldn't give them the same room, but he gave them the room right next door to Carmen's.

"I gotta take this," Raymond said, stepping away from the counter. It was Jesus, calling to check on the status of his wife.

"Well, it seems as though your wife is at the casino in Raleigh with another man. Nothing much has happened yet, but they did check into a hotel only about a minute ago. Now, you have two options. I can check into the hotel and see what else I can come up with, or I can head over to you and show you what I got so far."

"No, check into the hotel. I want you to know everything you can," Jesus said. "Don't worry about the cost. I don't care how much you spend or how long you gotta be down there. Just get me the pictures, the name of the man she's with, the room number they're in, and anything else you can come up with."

Jesus was furious, but this was the information he sought out. He just didn't know that it was going to hurt this much.

Gwen had gotten a call a few hours ago from a friend who just so happened to be a cop, telling her that a female with an MHB tattoo had been killed. Gwen and Tamika rushed to Agnis's Salon, where police and detectives were combing the scene for evidence.

"There she go right there," Tamika said, pointing to the young rookie cop coming over to them.

The police officer, April, had pledged MHB and had been a member for a couple of years.

"Thanks for calling me," Gwen said to her. "Do you have any idea who could have done this?"

"Nah, the detectives are still processing the scene. A witness said that they saw two men with dread locs coming out of the shop with Agnis and throwing her into the back seat of a car. There's a lot of blood in there, too," April replied.

"Two black men with dreads?" Gwen asked with a confused look on her face. She could count on two hands how
many Jamaicans she dealt with, none of whom displayed
characteristics like this.

"You think it was Tank and his boys?" Tamika asked,
thinking about their last encounter in the diner.

"No, it wasn't him. Me and him had an understanding.
Besides, he's all the way on the other side of town. He
wouldn't come all the way out to the north in broad
daylight to kill one of us. This has to be somebody else's
work."

All three girls watched as the coroner brought Tish's
body out. It only made Gwen even more angry than she
already was. Since Gwen started this bold female movement, only four members had lost their lives in the streets
of Charlotte, and the reason for that low number was
because of the way Gwen ran her clique. It wasn't about
running around the city playing cowgirls and Indians
with local dope boys like when MHB started. Now, it was
about empowering women in all aspects of life, whether
it be in corporate America, or all the way down to the
labor field. The organization was on another level and
had little to do with the street life. Tish's death raised a
lot of questions as to what this was all about—questions
Gwen planned on getting answers to in the near future.

"April, thanks for everything. If you hear anything else,
hit me up," Gwen said, then tapped Tamika so they could
leave. "Yo, get the word out about these two rastas. As
soon as we find them, let me know," she told Tamika.

"So, what do you wanna do after we find them?"

"We're gonna do what we do best, then get back to our
daily routine."

After making love, Detective Santiago and Rosa laid
in bed, cuddled up next to each other. When his phone

started vibrating on the nightstand, he knew that it had to be something important.

"Yeah," Santiago answered, sitting up on the edge of the bed.

"Get up, sunshine. I got a major break in the case," Detective Cruz said in an excited voice. "Get dressed. I'm sitting out front right now."

During the interview they had with Raymond, Cruz had taken Raymond's license and lifted several finger-prints off of it, just to see if it matched the fingerprints they already had. There were two sets of prints lifted, and when the results came back, one set of prints was a positive match to the print taken from the Darby murder scene. The other print didn't match at all.

When Santiago finally got dressed and went out to the car, Cruz explained everything.

"So, you're telling me that Raymond Harding is the hitman?" Santiago asked, looking down at the prints and comparing them.

"If it's not him, then it has to be somebody close to him," Cruz replied. Judging by what he was looking at, Cruz was right. The prints were a match. Santiago just wasn't sure if he was going to be able to get a search warrant with this evidence. Cruz may have needed a warrant to lift the prints off the license, and since Raymond hadn't given her permission to do so, it was likely illegal. That wasn't going to stop Santiago from trying his hand anyway, and he knew just the judge who might grant the search warrant. It was 12:25 a.m., and if Santiago could get that warrant, he'd be kicking down Raymond's door within the next couple of hours.

Gloria

Damn, I was not even sure that I was supposed to be feeling this way about Raymond. I was definitely not

*supposed to be getting this close to him. It was like each
day that I was around him, he was breaking down the
wall between me and my mark. It's kind of hard for
me to explain the feeling I got when I was around him.
As much as I kept telling myself to stay focused, there
were times when his compliments and concern for my
well-being were a turn on—not to mention that he was
sexy as hell. I should have listened to Agnis. Temptation
was a bitch, and she was knocking at my door.*

"Yo, I really appreciate you chilling with me tonight,"
Raymond said, walking back over to the bed from the
mini bar. So far, Raymond had snapped several pictures
of Carmen and the male that she was with on their trips
between the casino and their room. Gloria didn't do any
of the surveillance, though she thought it looked fun
from Raymond's perspective. She herself kept trying to
reach Agnis, who was still MIA.

"Did you get everything that you need?" Gloria asked,
lying back on the bed.

"Yeah, I think I got enough. You wanna see my pictures?"

"Nah, I don't wanna see that crap." Gloria smiled,
pushing his camera away.

"Why? The guy is handsome. Maybe not as handsome as me, but he's a good-looking guy," Raymond
said, continuing to scroll through the pictures. "You
know, Shooter, you're a nice-looking woman, and often I
wonder if you have someone special in ya life. You can't
cook for shit, can you?" he joked. "Or maybe you're the
Beyoncé type, who just lays in bed and don't put in work."

"Boy, please. You wouldn't know what to do with this,"
Gloria shot back in a sassy tone.

Raymond could only imagine. He refused to comment on that, at least for right now.

"Oh, and while you're here, I wanted to give you something," Raymond said, getting off the bed so he could reach in his back pocket.

The small white envelope he pulled out caused Gloria to raise one eyebrow. Inside was a diamond necklace with a matching diamond bracelet. Gloria didn't know the worth of it, but the price tag was in the range of 27K for the both of them.

"What? Why?" Gloria stuttered, looking down at the set.

"You saved my life, and I appreciate you for that," he said as he put the bracelet on her wrist. "I don't know what it is about you, Shooter, but you're special," he said, putting the necklace around her neck.

Gloria didn't know what to say. She was taken aback by the generous gesture. Before she could say anything, Raymond stopped her. Something else caught his attention.

"Shhh," Raymond said, reaching for the remote control. "Do you hear that?" he asked, turning off the TV. He shushed Gloria again, then stood up on the bed.

"Hear what?" she asked, looking at him like he was crazy.

They both were still and listening attentively. Raymond quickly pulled out his phone, pressed a couple of buttons, and pressed it up against the wall. Now Gloria could hear it. She stood up on the bed and pressed her ear up against the wall.

"Oooooh, papi, yes. Right there," the female yelled out.

Raymond and Gloria looked at each other then busted out in snickers as the moans continued through the wall. Gloria covered her mouth, shocked at the turn of events.

"I'm ready to get out of here," she said, walking over to the mini bar and grabbing a bottle of tequila.

Raymond jumped off the bed with the same attitude. He didn't think that there was anything else he needed to get for Jesus. He was almost tempted to call him so he could hear Carmen himself, but that was too over the top. The evidence Raymond had was more than enough, and Jesus would agree once he got a hold of it.

"Come on, Shooter. Let's get out of here."

Chapter 12

"Too many of our boys are being killed, and if not killed, then put in the hospital," Emilio said, sitting at the head of the table in his man cave. "I buried about six people in the past week, and I can't afford to bury another."

The war that Emilio thought he had in the bag had turned out to be a disaster on the battlefield. Emilio did what he said he would do, which was slow up all money being made in Tank's part of the city, but what he didn't expect was for the same thing to happen to him. Tank's crew came on the north side every day and night, trashing the neighborhood and shooting up just about every last one of Emilio's businesses. It put a dent in his money flow, and it didn't look like Tank was going to be letting up any time soon.

"I really don't have time to be playing tit for tat with these people. If you cut off the head, the rest of the body will fall."

Tank had twenty-four-hour protection around him, so it was hard for anybody to get even remotely close to him without taking a bullet.

"Have you heard from the Jamaicans yet?" Carmine asked.

"Not since yesterday, but I'm more than one hundred percent sure that they got Agnis already. Once you send those crazy-ass Jamaicans after somebody, it's gonna get done. I should have used them to kill that dumb fuck Dion."

"You know there's another problem brewing," Carmine said. "I got the word that Tank's brother is coming home, and that guy's supposed to be a problem. He's gonna want blood, so this war might last longer than what we expected."

"Fuck Larue," Emilio snapped. "I'll bury him right next to Dion."

"Hey, don't we still got people upstate that could touch him before he even gets out?" Carmine asked.

"Now that you mention it, I still got a few good men upstate who owe me favors. I'll make a few calls to see what I can do. In the meantime, that kid Tank is a dead man walking. Fuck allying pressure. I want you to finish this stupid war once and for all."

"So, how do you want me to play it?" Carmine asked.

Emilio sat there in thought for a few seconds, then he looked over at Carmine. "Burn this fuckin'" city to the ground. I'll rebuild it when the smoke clears."

Carmine looked at Emilio and began to laugh. He thought Emilio was just joking around. Emilio wasn't laughing, though. Carmine could see that he was serious, so he voiced his concerns. "Boss, you really think that's a good idea? We got a lot to lose if we go that route."

"I want every bar on the south side shot up and burned to the ground. I want every known drug corner shot up and shut down. Number houses, crack houses, whore houses, and corner stores. I want them all burned to the ground. I want innocent bystanders to get shot. I want blood on the streets, and I want everybody scared to come out of their homes," Emilio yelled, hitting the table with his index finger.

Carmine had a confused look on his face. "Innocent bystanders, boss?"

Emilio got out of his chair, walked over to Carmine, and leaned in. "I wouldn't give a fuck if the Pope was walking across the street with a Bible in his hand. If he gets in the line of fire, you better blow his fuckin' head off. You got me?"

Carmine nodded his head.

"You better start listening to me when I tell you to do something. Being soft in this way of life doesn't get you anything but taken advantage of. You're business minded, Carmine, I give you that, but when the war is on, you gotta be able to kill with no remorse. Now, maybe I was a little too hard with killing the Pope, but if the average priest comes strolling across the street, then you better shoot him," Emilio joked, smacking Carmine on his back before walking back over to his seat. "No, seriously, kid, out here you can either be the prey or the predator. You gotta ask yourself: Which one are you? Me, I choose to kill instead of being killed." On that note, Emilio grabbed his cigar from the ashtray and walked out.

It was nine thirty in the morning and Dillon's car was just now pulling into the driveway. Gloria watched from the living room window and could tell that he'd had a long night. As he got out of the car, he was sluggish and didn't look to be in a good mood. When he walked into the house, he paused when he saw Gloria, then proceeded to the kitchen without saying anything.

"Here we go again," Gloria mumbled to herself, following behind him. "So, now we're not even speaking to each other?" Gloria said, standing by the entrance.

Dillon went into the refrigerator and pulled out some leftovers. "Good morning. Is that what you're looking for?" he asked, tossing the plate of food into the microwave.

Gloria wanted so bad to just flip out on him. She was Puerto Rican, so the urge to grab one of the kitchen

knives and cut him ate at her. Instead, this time she
stayed calm. "If you don't mind me asking, where were
you at last night?"

"That's the question I should be asking you. And why
was your phone off?"

Gloria bit down on her bottom lip, trying her best to
keep her composure. She couldn't believe that he was
trying to change this around on her.

"Let's try this again, Dillon. Where da hell was you at
last night?" she snapped, pulling the 9 mm Glock from
her back pocket. Dillon didn't even see the gun until
Gloria walked over and took a seat at the table right in
front of him. She put the gun on the table so he could see
it.

"So, what, you gon' kill me too?" Dillon chuckled.

"I'm really starting to consider it," she replied with a
fake smile. "Are you cheating on me?"

"You're losing your mind, Gloria. Why would you even
ask me a stupid question like that? Cheating on you . . ."
he said, shaking his head.

"So, why can't you answer my question?" Gloria shot
back.

"Just like I told you the other day: I'm tired of being
in this house by myself. I'm tired of being the only one
who's raising our kids. You're not holding up your end
of the bargain. You said that you wouldn't let your work
come in between us. You said that you would always
put this family first. You lied to me. You lied to our kids.
What kind of woman does that?"

Gloria sat there listening to what Dillon had to say, and
it was sad to say that most of what he said had some truth
to it. Gloria didn't want to see it that way, though.

"You think this way of life we live is free. I'm the one
bringing in all the money. *Me*, not you. You think this
big-ass house was free? You think the clothes on ya

back was free? You think that Audi sitting out there in the driveway was free? You think that jewelry you wear is free? You think those luxury vacations we took as a family was free? News flash, Dillon, this shit ain't free!" Gloria yelled.

"Money isn't everything, Gloria," Dillon said, trying to speak over her.

"You have a baby alligator in the basement. What kind of woman buys her husband exotic pets, Dillon?" She had gotten off topic for a minute, but got right back to the business. "So, where were you at last night, Dillon?"

Dillon got tired of her asking him. "You really wanna know, Gloria? When you turned ya phone off last night, I went to my brother's house. We hit the strip club then went to Max's to get something to eat. Mind you, the whole time I was out, ya phone was off. I figured you wasn't coming home. I went back to Jay's house, smoked some weed, drank a bottle of Patron, and I was done. I woke up about an hour ago, and here I am. If for some reason you don't believe me, you can call Jay's wife. She knew exactly where her husband was last night and who he was with," Dillon said with an attitude.

Gloria could tell by the tone in his voice that Dillon was hurt too. She could see it in his eyes and hear it in his speech. Gloria actually started to feel bad.

"So, what now?" Gloria asked, wanting to know the outcome of all of this. "Where do we go from here?"

Dillon raised both his hands as though they were scales. "You gotta weigh what's more important to you. In one hand, you have your contract, and in the other, you have me and our children. This is your choice, and let me be clear: if you choose ya contracts over us, I'm gonna leave you. Me and our kids are going to get as far away from you as possible, because the only thing that's gonna come out of you living the way you are is pain. I don't want to be the one who has to tell our kids that Mommy's not coming home, or worse—that Mommy is dead. I really don't want to bear that burden," Dillon said, getting up from the table. As he was leaving the kitchen, he stopped next to Gloria. "And if you ever pull a gun on me again, I'm gonna forget that you were my wife. I give you my word, you're gonna have to use it," he said then walked off.

Raymond was running late, and he knew that his mother was going to give him an earful, especially since he hadn't finished the paperwork concerning the deal with the Chinese. Raymond was so busy with the Carmen case that it totally slipped his mind. As soon as Raymond got into the building, Jennifer was waiting for him in the lobby. She had a look in her eyes that broke Raymond's heart.

"Sorry, I'm late. I had a long night," Raymond said, leaning in to kiss her forehead.

Jennifer blasted Raymond for being late some days, and for not coming in at all on others. Not only was the Chinese paperwork not done, neither was the budget report for the quarter.

"Raymond, when I die, this company is going to you to do whatever you please with it. I worked hard to build this company with your father, God rest his soul, and it seems to me that you're just gonna let it go down the drain. It's like you don't even care what we sacrificed over these years."

She was making Raymond feel like the most ungrateful child alive. He'd never seen his mother this upset before, and he was now beginning to see why. There was a multi-million-dollar company at stake, and Jennifer wanted to see the company get passed down to her only child. The only other alternative was James, her brother, someone she knew would drive the company to the ground.

"Mom, I need a little bit more time to get my affairs in order. After that I'll give this company all of my time. I promise you that," he assured her before making his way to his office.

As soon as Raymond got to his office, he called his buddy Sally down at the police station. He wanted her to run the license plate number he got from the Tahoe the other night. Today Raymond was going to present all of his findings concerning Carmen to Jesus and finally close the case. Before he did that, he wanted to make sure all his facts were right.

"Sally, hey, beautiful," Raymond said, buttering her up first. "I need you to run a plate for me."

"Now, you know that's gonna cost you, and I'm not talking about dinner and a movie," Sally joked.

She was an older white woman with a good heart and was also a good friend of the family. Any time Raymond needed some assistance, she was always there for him.

"Sally, you better stop flirting with me before I take you up on your offer one day. I'll show you what a young bull could do to you," Raymond joked.

Sally broke out into laughter, just thinking about how she knew she wouldn't be able to handle somebody with vigor like Raymond. "Give me the numbers, Mr. Nasty man," she chuckled.

"NC tags CT-106. It's a Tahoe," he explained.

Sally tapped on her computer, and within a few seconds, she had the information. "That car is registered to a Dillon Jones," Sally told him, giving him the address.

Raymond mumbled the name to himself. Just to be sure, he asked for the name again, then wrote it down. "Thanks, Sally, I owe you one."

"Oh, no, you owe me more than one, so be at my house around eleven. I'm going to wear my good lingerie and bring a tub of lube too. The plumbing is a little rusty," Sally joked.

All Raymond could do was laugh at Sally before he hung up.

"Dillon Parker. I wonder what kind of skeletons you have hidden in your closet."

Raymond thought about calling Jesus, but decided not to after receiving this information from Sally. He wanted to find out a little more information on Dillon before he did. The one person he did end up calling was Gloria.

"You miss me already?" Gloria answered.

"I was wondering if you wanted to help me complete my investigation," he asked.

"Sure, let's get it done."

Chapter 13

"Wake up, you dumb bitch!" Jamaican Travis yelled, smacking Agnis in her face. "Wake up!" he yelled again, smacking her a second time. "You can't sleep forever," he snapped, grabbing a fistful of her hair and yanking at it.

It woke Agnis right up. "Agghhhhhhh!" she screamed, almost falling out of the chair she was strapped to.

It took a minute for her eyes to adjust, and when they did, she took a look around the room. She could see the bloody towels on the bed from them patching up the two bullet wounds to her leg.

"What da fuck do y'all want?" Agnis snapped.

"I just want the name of the girl," Travis said, taking a seat on the bed next to Agnis.

"What girl? I don't know what girl you're talking about," Agnis replied.

"I know every ting. You hear me. Don't play no games wit' me."

"I don't know what you're talking about."

Jamaican Sam came up from behind her and punched Agnis in the back of her head. It almost knocked her out.

"I'm not gonna ask you again," Travis said, pulling a gun from his waist and cocking it back. Agnis looked at Travis with a straight face.

"You might as well kill me, 'cause I'm not telling you shit," Agnis said with conviction.

Travis looked over at Sam and began to laugh.

"You two muthafuckas are dead. Do you know who I am? Do you know the power I got in this city?" she asked, looking Travis in his eyes.

"Yeah, Agnis, we know who you are. Do I care? I don't give a fuck who you are. All I know is that if you don't give me the information that I'm looking for, you gonna die in the worst way." Travis snapped his fingers at Sam for him to go and retrieve his duffle bag. He did just that, setting it on the floor right in front of Agnis and Travis.

"Are you sure you wanna go through with this?" Travis asked, leaning over and unzipping the bag. "This is gonna get messy, and I don't think that the person that you're protecting is worth it."

It was going to take more than Travis's threats to get Agnis to talk. She wasn't going to tell on Gloria no matter what Travis had in his bag. Her loyalty to Gloria was deep, and just as important to her as her own life. Travis was seriously about to figure that out.

"Go fuck yourself, you stupid-ass Jamaican."

"Last chance," Travis offered, pulling out a blow torch and a sewing kit.

Agnis chuckled at the torture device and still showed no signs of fear. "Let's get this show on the road," she said, then coughed up a glob and spit it in Travis's face.

"Tank, we got a problem out there," Butch said, walking into Tank's living room where Tank was feeding his fish. "I just got back from down the way, and it looks like a war zone. It's the fuckin' Italians, and it's like they know all our spots," Butch explained.

Emilio held to his word, and Carmine executed the order just as he was supposed to. Tank wanted a war, and that's precisely what he was getting.

"Oh, and they burned down ya mom's bar . . ." Butch continued in a low tone, not wanting to be the one who told him.

Tank picked his head up from the fish tank after hearing that."I'ma kill Emilio."

"Yeah, and the Narc is having a field day out there with our people. Like five of our workers got locked up in one night."

Tank went back to feeding his fish. "So, is the product still moving?"

"It's barely moving. The streets look like a ghost town. Hardly anybody wants to be out there."

Before Tank could reply to Butch, his house phone started to ring. Only a few people had his landline, so whoever it was had to be of importance. He walked over and grabbed the cordless phone off the wall.

"Yeah," he answered.

"Good afternoon sir, this is Captain Mill calling from Smithville State Prison. Can I please speak to Tavares Grant?"

"Yeah, this is him. Is something wrong with my brother?" Tank asked.

"He was involved in a stabbing yesterday. He's currently in the hospital in critical condition."

"Critical condition?" Tank snapped. His blood began to boil.

"He was stabbed multiple times in his upper body."

Tank stood there listening to the captain explain as much as he could. From the tone of his voice, Tank could see that it wasn't looking good for Larue, his brother.

"Tank, what da hell is going on?" Butch asked, hearing something was going on with Larue.

Tank got all the information pertaining to what hospital Larue was in and how visitation was going to be set up. After that, he hung up the phone. Tank didn't say a word at first, walking over and taking a seat on the couch. He stared off into space with a blank look on his face. It was the kind of look Butch was all too familiar with. It was a look to say that somebody was going to die. Butch wasn't sure what happened, seeing as how Tank shut down, but what he did know was that whatever it was, it wasn't good.

Tank continued sitting there, and the only person he could think of being responsible for this was Emilio. Even if Emilio didn't have anything to do with it, Tank was going to blame him for it anyway.

"He's a dead man," were the last words that came out of Tank's mouth before he headed for the stairs. He needed and wanted to be alone , and then, after getting his thoughts together, he was going to call the rest of his family to let them know what was going on.

Agnis screamed out in pain as Travis took the blow torch and melted her skin over the two bullet wounds. They both had to sit on top of her to keep her still. Sam shoved a sock in her mouth to muffle the screams.

"Don't cry now. This is what you wanted, right?" Travis said, smacking her across the face. He nodded for Sam to bandage up her leg, which he did.

"Come on, Agnis, do you really wanna die like this?" he said, removing the gag in her mouth. "I don't understand why you would take this type of pain for somebody who wouldn't do the same for you. I can help you, though. I can stop the pain," he said, grabbing the mini blow torch.

Agnis looked Travis in his eyes and began to laugh. "You can do whatever you want. Fuck you!" she snapped, trying to spit in his face again.

He didn't like that one bit. "I'm gonna seal ya mouth up now." Travis went to turn on the blow torch and pointed the hot blue flame at her face. He started easing it closer and closer to her eye. Sam held her face still.

"Aaaahhhhh!" Agnis yelled out as the fire made contact with her eyelid. Just the tip of the fire caused severe damage to her eye, melting it shut and completely taking its ability to see again.

"I can do this shit all night," Travis said through her screams.

"Fuck you! Fuck you! Fuck you!" she yelled out and then began to shake. She was in so much pain, and was so exhausted, she almost passed out.

"Agnis, did you know our friend Sam here is a registered nurse back home in Jamaica? So, if you think about dying on me, he's gonna bring you back to life so I can continue to make you suffer."

As Travis was talking, Sam was preparing the IV to rehydrate her. Agnis was playing, and in his own little way, Travis respected it. She wasn't breaking for nothing. Most men who had been in her shoes before had started talking before the blowtorch was even lit. Though he did respect her, he still had a job to do and wasn't going to let up.

"After Sam cleans you up, we're gonna play another game."

Detectives Santiago and Cruz had spent the entire day before trying to get a warrant so they could search Raymond's house for possible evidence of Doug' murder. However, the magistrate judge wasn't inclined to do so, for fear that Raymond's constitutional rights had been violated when Detective Cruz took it upon herself to lift the prints off the license without his permission or without getting a warrant. The judge struck down their application for a warrant, but he instructed Cruz and

Santiago to find an independent source of probable cause or to simply get Raymond's permission to search his home.

"You think we should try the consent route?" Cruz asked Santiago as they were heading back to their car.

"Nah, if he did have something to do with these murders, he's not just gonna let us walk into his house. We gotta wait 'til he slip up. Trust me; he'll fuck up."

They both sat in the car in silence for a moment. Cruz looked out of the window at the patrol cars pulling into the station. She thought about the chain of events that led up to this moment. It was as if a light bulb clicked on in her head that made her almost jump out of her seat in excitement.

"Question: Do you remember the other day when we pulled Raymond over?"

"Yeah, why? Where are going at with this?"

"There was a female driving his car, and she was the one who passed him the license and registration to give to you," Cruz explained.

"Oh, shit."

Santiago now shared the same excitement that Cruz did. Instead of sitting in the car, they both got out for some much-needed air.

"How many sets of prints were on his license when you checked?" Santiago asked, wanting to be sure.

Cruz smiled, telling him that it was only two.

"Damn it! We had that son of a bitch," Santiago said, resting his hands on the top of his head. It was like getting hit by a Mack truck, feeling like the murderer they were looking for had slipped right through their fingers. Chances like this happened less than often with homicide detectives. Nine times out of ten, if a murderer got away clean, chances of catching back up to them were slim to none, especially for someone like Gloria, who Santiago and Cruz knew nothing about.

"Let's go find our friend Raymond. See if he can give us what we're looking for," Santiago said as they both got back into their car.

Chapter 14

Gloria

It was almost time for me to meet up with Raymond, but first I had to stop at my house and have a conversation with Dillon. After driving around all day, I had had time to think and realize that I was wrong and had more to own up to than what I'd been able to admit thus far. Reality had set in, and I could now understand how Dillon felt and why he felt that way. It was a must that I try to fix things between us.

When I got back home, no one was there, and that was strange, because normally Dillon and Alisha would be there.

"Dillon!" I yelled out, hoping he would answer me from somewhere in the house, but he didn't. Where the hell could he be, and where was the baby? I pulled my phone out to call my sister, but before I could, the phone started ringing. It was Raymond calling me.

"Are you still at work?" Gloria asked, looking down at her watch. It was only twelve o'clock.

"Yeah, but I'm about to get out of here. I was thinking that we could do lunch."

Gloria thought about it, debating whether she should look for Dillon. Then Gloria came to the realization that it was time to get it over with. No more games. No more putting it off. No more feeling bad for Raymond. The quicker she got this job done, the quicker Gloria thought she could get back to her family.

"No, lunch sounds good. I'm on my way to you," Gloria said, then hung up the phone. She had her mind made up, and today was going to be the day that Raymond checked out.

"Mr. Harding," the secretary yelled through the intercom. "Those two detectives are back again. I left them in the lobby this time. Do you wanna see them?" she asked.

"No, Candice. Tell them that I left for the day," Raymond said in an irritated voice. Raymond really didn't have anything else to say to them about Doug's murder, and if they weren't coming to arrest him, he was done with dealing with the matter.

"Damn, Agnis, they really fucked you up," Emilio teased, smacking the side of her face to wake her up.

She was lying in bed with her wrists handcuffed to the headboard and her ankles shackled to the bed frame. Travis and Sam stood to the side, while Emilio took a seat on the bed. Agnis slowly opened her eyes, resting them on Emilio. She was furious but didn't even have the energy to frown up her face.

"Look at you, Agnis," Emilio said, looking at her then up to the IV bag that was attached to her. "It's a war going on right now between the Italians and the Blacks, and I think you have the ability to end it if you just give up your shooter," he said in a calm voice, hoping he could get through to her.

Agnis had to clear her throat before she could talk. "You know me, Emilio. I would die before I betray a friend," she whispered.

Agnis started to chuckle through her pain. He couldn't believe it.

"You laugh while looking death in the face? Is the girl really worth it?"

Agnis stopped chuckling, then looked Emilio in his eyes. "If you think this is something, then wait 'til she gets her hands on you. She's not gonna be merciful; I can promise you that," Agnis warned.

Agnis started laughing again, and it burned Emilio up to know that what Agnis said may have had truth to it. Once Gloria found out that Emilio had brought Agnis harm or even death, she wouldn't stop until Emilio died in the worst way. A part of him knew that and understood how important it was for him to find and kill Gloria first. Just the thought of having to face a killer like her scared the hell out of him.

"Who da fuck is she? Where da hell can I find her?" he yelled, grabbing hold of Agnis's face and squeezing it. Agnis spit on him, which only made Emilio smack her.

He looked over at Travis. "Did she have a phone?" he asked.

Travis grabbed it off the table and tossed it to him. Travis and Sam hadn't bothered to look through it, but Emilio knew that Agnis had to have the shooter's number in her phone. Emilio got up from the bed and started to scroll through the phone. There were a few names that stuck out, but there was one that really got his attention. It said, MY CHILD. Emilio knew that Agnis didn't have any children. His gut was telling him that this was the number he was looking for, and from the suspicious look Agnis had on her beat-up face right now, it was almost like a confirmation of what he was feeling.

"I'll be right back," Emilio told the Jamaicans then headed for the door with Agnis's phone in hand.

***

When Raymond pulled into the driveway, Gloria looked around, wondering whose house this was. It had to be at least 5,000 square feet and sitting on five acres of land. The landscaping was beautiful, and the many trees surrounding the property made for good fresh air.

"Come in for a minute," Raymond said as he was getting out of the car.

When Gloria stepped out of the car, she could smell the forestry around her. The aroma of pine, lumber, and freshly cut grass filled the atmosphere.

"Whose house is this?" she asked, following him into the house.

"This is my dad's house. When he died, he left it to me because he knew that my mother wouldn't have been able to live here after his death. Too many good memories, you know."

"It sounds like they were in love," Gloria replied, looking around the huge house: beautiful marble floors, a massive fireplace in the living room area, stainless steel appliances in the kitchen with granite countertops throughout, and in the backyard there was a large mahogany deck that overlooked a beautiful pond. This house was way better than his house in Charlotte.

"Gimme fifteen minutes," Raymond said then ran upstairs to take a quick shower.

The whole time he was upstairs, Gloria stood on the back deck, taking in some fresh air and enjoying the magnificent view. It took Raymond exactly fifteen minutes before he was back downstairs.

"Now, if I were a female like yourself, I'd probably still be laying out my clothes," Raymond teased, stepping out onto the deck with Gloria.

She turned around just as he was walking up on her. He looked rather handsome for a quick fifteen-minute changeup. He wore a gray Dior T-shirt, blue Louis Vuitton jeans, and some black Louis Vuitton sneakers. On his wrist was a diamond bezel-set Audemars Piguet watch. The scent of Acqua Di Gio coming from his skin tickled Gloria's nose hairs. She was shocked at how attracted she felt to him in that moment, and she was even more surprised by how close she allowed him to get to her.

He was about a foot away, and all he had to do was grab her by the waist, and Gloria probably would have melted in his arms. Raymond looked into her eyes and seized the moment, moving in closer and taking hold of her hand.

"Forgive me," he said, leaning in and pressing his lips up against hers.

Gloria's brain was screaming out no, but her body was telling her something different. She didn't know what came over her, and it took Raymond pulling away for her lips to stop moving.

"Dillon Parker," Raymond said, ruining the moment.

When Gloria heard him say her husband's name, her heart dropped into her stomach. She had to be sure she'd heard it correctly.

"What did you just say?" she asked. Her natural instinct was to reach for her gun, thinking that Raymond had figured her out.

"Dillon Parker. He's the mystery man Carmen's been cheating on her husband with. I had a friend of mine run the plate to the Tahoe, and it was registered to a Dillon Parker," Raymond explained.

Gloria didn't even know where to begin with processing this information. She merely sat there in a trance while Raymond continued explaining how he knew where Dillon lived and he wanted to take a peek before he reported all his findings to Jesus.

Gloria barely heard anything, and could only see red from how mad she was. She didn't want Raymond to see her reaction, so she quickly pulled herself together.

"So, let's go see if this guy has a girlfriend or a wife," Gloria said and then headed back to the car, Raymond in tow.

"I can almost guarantee that he's in that building," Detective Cruz said, referring to the possibility of Raymond being at Rev. Index. Though the secretary told them that he wasn't there, Santiago had a feeling that she was lying. He didn't want to force his way into the building without a warrant, so he decided to wait until the end of the workday to see if Raymond came out then.

Cruz thought that Raymond was there when they had first arrived, but dipped out shortly thereafter, sometime in the past two hours.

Santiago was thirsty for the arrest, and it was right within his grasp. He felt like a professional hitman was one of the hardest criminals to catch, and if he managed to apprehend one, it would be his greatest accomplishment since he had joined the force. At the same time, apprehending someone who killed people for a living wasn't going to be easy by a long shot. This type of sharp-minded criminal never even considered prison an option, leaving whoever was trying to put them there in a very dangerous situation. A hitman wasn't going to surrender willingly. Ten times out of ten, there was going to be a vicious shootout. The million-dollar question was: Who's going to be left standing after it's all said and done?

Gloria almost swerved off the road several times thinking about Dillon and how hurtful it was to find out about him cheating. She couldn't believe how bold he had been, knowing what Gloria was capable of doing to him.

"So, how long has Carmen been cheating with this guy?" Gloria asked, wanting to get some clarity.

"I'm not sure, but it had to be for a couple of months now," Raymond explained as he scrolled through his phone. "Here he is," Raymond said, holding up his phone to show her the photos he had taken of the adulterous couple.

Gloria looked over, and there was Dillon, sitting in the restaurant with Carmen. Gloria damn near crashed into the back of the car in front of her. There was no doubt that this was Dillon. Gloria started sweating, and her throat was getting dry. Her stomach was getting queasy as well. She remembered listening to Carmen having sex at the hotel at the Casino and could now visualize Dillon being the one who had her screaming. Other events started coming to mind, like when he left the kids in the house by themselves, or when he lied about staying the night at his brother's house. It was all a lie. Gloria wanted to throw up, and the look of disgust on her face got Raymond's attention.

"Are you okay, Shooter?" Raymond asked with one eyebrow lifted to the sky. "You look upset."

"Yeah, I'm fine. I just hate when people do dumb shit like cheat. It makes me so mad. Maybe it's because I have been cheated on before," Gloria lied, trying to clean it up. "Look, his house should be coming up on the next street," she said, pointing at the numbers on the houses.

She pulled over at the top of her street and parked. Gloria didn't think that Dillon was home, but he was, and he was stepping out of the house right as they approached. He was dressed to impress, too.

"It looks like he's leaving out," Raymond said, looking through the binoculars. "He's not driving the Tahoe neither."

When Dillon pulled out of the driveway and pulled off, Gloria took off behind him. Raymond noticed the conviction in Gloria's behavior. "I like you, Shooter, but I really don't know much about you, except for what you told me."

Gloria wasn't trying to hear anything Raymond was talking about. She was too focused on keeping up with Dillon. The more she followed behind Dillon, the more anxious she got and wanted to confront him. Dillon pulled into a TGI Friday's parking lot. He was so pressed about getting inside he didn't notice Gloria pulling up and parking a couple of cars away from his.

Gloria reached for her Gucci bag in the back seat, from which she pulled out a 9 mm Glock.

"I don't think we're gonna need that," Raymond said with a confused look on his face.

Gloria was zoned out at this point and was already out of the cart and heading for the establishment. Raymond got out of the car but didn't follow her right away, feeling like something was wrong. From where he stood, he could see Dillon and Carmen sitting in a booth by the window.

Not paying attention to the hostess who was trying to give her a vibrating pager, Gloria walked right past her and went straight for the booths in the rear of the restaurant. Carmen was so mesmerized by Dillon's elegant speech she didn't even notice Gloria walking up to them, standing right behind Dillon. Gloria stood there looking at Carmen smile at Dillon, and as she was digging in her bag to retrieve her gun, a hand reached out from behind and grabbed Gloria's wrist. When she turned to see who it was, Raymond could see the tears and pain in her eyes.

"Come on, it's not worth it," he said in a low tone, lightly pulling at her. Gloria stood there for a second then started to walk away with Raymond.

Right when she was near the door, Gloria stopped. She thought about it, and it was pure jealousy that took over her body. She snatched away from Raymond and headed back toward the booths, this time not hesitating to draw the gun from her bag.

Dillon didn't see Gloria yet, but he could see the fear of God in Carmen's eyes. She started to scream as Gloria raised the gun, but those screams were muffled by a single shot. *POP!*

The bullet hit Carmen in the center of her forehead, knocking her back into the booth. Dillon didn't have to turn around to know who it was that pulled the trigger. Customers ran out of the restaurant after hearing the first shot. There was terror and panic in the restaurant. People were screaming and scrambling to get out. Dillon didn't move, but instead just sat there and watched several more bullets enter Carmen's lifeless body.

Raymond couldn't believe what had just happened. He could see the whole thing unfolding from where he stood. Through the crowd of people screaming and tripping over each other coming out the door, Gloria emerged, walking out slowly and calmly, with the gun still clutched in her hand. She got back into the car like nothing ever happened, and if it weren't for Raymond being a little fast on his feet, Gloria would have pulled off without him in the car.

Dillon, who was still in shock, looked over at Carmen's bullet-riddled body slumped over on the table. He knew who the shooter was. It had Gloria's name written all over it.

Chapter 15

Only immediate family was allowed to visit Larue while he was in the hospital. Tank was among them, watching as his brother struggled to breathe on the machine. Larue had been about to be released to a halfway house in a couple of weeks, and nobody could have predicted what Larue was going to do once he was home. Everyone that knew him personally was sure that life with him out on the streets was going to be better. It was a tough blow for the second time around, and Tank was so mad he couldn't even think straight.

Larue's doctor walked into the room with two nurses by his side, causing Tank and his sister to look up. Aside from the three prison guards that were in the room, two local police officers stood outside the room. Tank knew that it was time. The injuries Larue sustained were far too serious, and the chances of him waking up from this coma were below five percent. And even if he did wake up, he wouldn't be the same and would more than likely suffer for the rest of his life. The only reason he was still alive was the breathing tubes he had coming out of his mouth. This was actually his only sign of life. After the doctor explained all of this, the only thing to discuss was who would pull the plug on Larue.

"You do it," Johanne yelled, pushing Tank over to the doctor.

For the first time in decades, Tank began to cry. First Dion, and now Larue. There was no way he could hold back his tears. This was his family, and after today, both of them would be gone. The walk across the room toward Larue felt just like walking the green mile, and as Tank stood over Larue, he could feel another piece of his heart being chipped away. Johanne wasn't making it any easier.

"Look what you did. Look at him," Tank's sister cried out. She had to turn her head. The closer Tank got to pushing the button, the louder her cries got. She was right. This was all his fault, and something Tank would have to live with for the rest of his life.

"I love you, brother. Sleep well," he mumbled, reaching up and pushing the button. "We'll be together soon."

The machine stopped, but miraculously, Larue kept breathing. Everyone was anticipating for him to stop breathing pretty quickly, but he didn't. Even Johanne stopped crying for a moment to look in closely at his chest slowly rising up and down. Tank looked at Johanne, and she looked at the nurse, and then, breaking the silence with an urgent tone, the doctor told everybody to clear the room.

After the shooting at TGI Friday's yesterday, Raymond and Gloria found themselves staying in a hotel out near the airport. Neither one of them wanted to go back home after what had happened, fearing that the police were going to be looking for them all over the city. For the past twenty-four hours, Raymond and Gloria had been isolated from the world, only listening to their thoughts.

"I gotta make a call," Raymond said, getting up and walking toward the bathroom.

He wanted to call Sally to check up on the shooting that had taken place yesterday. He thought that his face, along with Gloria's, would be all over the news by now, wanted for murder. Lucky for him, it wasn't.

Sally explained that the footage that the detectives had was from inside the restaurant. None of the cameras outside were operable during the time of the shooting. She told Raymond to go to NBC News to see pictures of the suspect they were looking for.

Walking back into the room, Raymond said, "They got a couple of pictures of us in the restaurant, though you really can't tell that it's us. It's on the news website."

It was blowing Raymond's mind that he was hiding out in a hotel with a woman who he had seen kill not just one, but two people in the short time he'd known her. The first he could understand to a certain extent, but murdering a woman in cold blood was something different.

"Are you ready to talk now?" Raymond asked, taking a seat next to Gloria on the bed. There were a few things he needed to get clarity on.

Gloria was at the point where she was getting tired of lying to Raymond about the reasons why she had truly come into his life. Within the last twenty-four hours, she had made up her mind that she wasn't going to kill Raymond, and as soon as she got in touch with Agnis, she was going to give her the money back. Gloria couldn't explain it, but for some crazy reason, she was attracted to Raymond, and not just in the physical sense.

"Before I say anything, I need you to give your word that you'll believe every word that comes out of my mouth," Gloria said, turning to face him.

Gloria was hesitant at first, but Raymond looked her in the eyes with sincerity. "You can trust me, Shooter," he told her, placing his hand over the top of hers.

"Dillon is my husband," she began.

Raymond wasn't shocked at all about that piece of information. When Raymond first told her that Dillon was the guy Carmen was cheating with, it was obvious she knew him and felt some type of way about it.

"That's not all, Raymond."

Gloria became silent for a minute, looking into his eyes. She felt that it was time to tell him everything.

"I was paid by your uncle to kill you."

Raymond twisted his face up in confusion.

"What did you just say to me?" he asked, looking at Gloria like she was crazy. She tried to move in closer to him, but he jumped up off the bed.

"Nah, nah, nah, say it again."

"Raymond, I'm sorr—" She was cut off before she could finish.

"Say it again. Let me hear you say it again!" he yelled. He was mad beyond words, so much so he walked over and grabbed a gun off the dresser. He turned around and pointed it at her with his finger on the trigger.

Tears formed in Raymond's eyes, thinking about his uncle's betrayal. "Why?" he asked, still holding the gun up to Gloria's head.

She remained calm. "I'm a contract killer, Raymond. I don't get into the specifics. I just do what I'm paid to do."

Raymond clutched the gun even tighter, but Gloria showed no sign of fear. She stood up from the bed with her hands up. "Put the gun down, Raymond," she said in a relaxed voice.

"Give me one good reason why I shouldn't shoot you in the face. Just one," he snapped, clutching the gun in both hands.

Gloria lowered her hands down to her side. "Think about it Raymond. If I wanted to hurt you, I could have. I've had a million opportunities, but every time I was getting ready to, I just couldn't do it," Gloria said, inching closer to him.

Even she couldn't explain why. She'd looked into the eyes of many men before, killing them and not once hesitating, but when it came down to killing Raymond, things were different. Falling for him was truly unexpected.

"Raymond, I'm truly sorry for everything."

The sound of Gloria's phone vibrating on the bed caught her attention. She looked at Raymond, who had the gun still pointed at her. She didn't even ask for permission to turn around and answer it.

"Where the hell have you been?" Gloria answered, excited that it was Agnis's phone number popping up on her screen. It wasn't who she thought it was, though.

"Hello, kiddo," Emilio said into the phone.

Gloria looked down at the phone. "Who is this? And where da fuck is Agnis?"

"Calm down. Agnis is still alive for now, but how long she stays this way is totally up to you." Gloria listened attentively. "You see, kiddo, we got a little problem. I put a hit out on Dion, and Agnis sent you to do it, which makes her my accomplice. In return, she sent you, so that also makes you a part of the conspiracy. Bottom line, Dion's family wants blood money to fix the problem. We pay it, and they'll drop it. Other than that, we'll be hunted like dogs until all of us are dead."

"How much do they want?" Agnis asked, anger overtaking the look on her face.

Emilio had to come up with a number that would be realistic, because the last thing he wanted Gloria to figure out was that this was a setup and he was actually trying to kill her. That wouldn't end well for him, and he was well aware of it.

"They want a million dollars, cash, and I'm not paying that tab alone," Emilio told her.

"What do you want from me?" Gloria asked, looking at Raymond, who still kept the gun pointed at her.

"You need to come up with half. I tried to get it from Agnis, but she's . . . Well, you know Agnis."

"Put Agnis on the phone. I wanna talk to her," Gloria requested, only wanting to make sure that she was alive.

Emilio walked over and put the phone up to Agnis's mouth.

"Say something," he demanded, plucking Agnis's head several times.

Agnis was drained, but she mustered up enough energy to say two words. Two words Gloria heard loud and clear.

"Kill him," Agnis whispered.

Her faint voice crushed Gloria. She knew Agnis had to be beaten pretty badly.

"Meet me at the Plateau at eight o'clock tonight. Put the money in a clear bag so I can see it. You got one time to do something stupid. I'm killing Agnis, and then I'm killing you," Emilio threatened. "I'll call you before the drop to make sure we don't have any problems," he said, then hung up the phone.

Gloria wanted to throw her phone up against the wall but quickly realized that she was going to need it. Raymond was still standing there, but he had lowered his gun at the sight of how upset Gloria looked.

"My friend is in trouble. If you're gonna shoot me, then do it. Otherwise, get out of my way," Gloria said, walking past Raymond. He stood there for a couple of seconds, watching Gloria grab her things and head for the door.

"You're not getting rid of me that easy," Raymond said, following behind her to the car.

Gloria didn't say a word. She simply pulled out of the parking lot and made a dash for the expressway in hopes of making it home to get the money then meet up with Agnis's abductors at the Plateau in Fairmount Park by eight o'clock that night.

"I can't lie, she's bold," Detective Santiago said, looking at the footage from TGI Friday's on his computer. Seeing as how Gloria didn't wear a mask or any type of disguise, it was easy for Cruz to identify her. She recognized her immediately. They weren't too sure about the guy she was with, because he had a bucket hat on and the front of it was covering his face. Santiago's gut was telling him that it was Raymond, but there wasn't enough to prove it.

"Do we know what kind of car she was driving?" Cruz asked, looking at the scene.

"The cameras outside weren't working, but witnesses seem to think that she was in a new model vehicle. Some say it was a dark blue, while others say that the car was black," Santiago explained. "But this guy is the key," Santiago said, pointing to the screen at Dillon sitting in the booth with Carmen. "That's Dillon Parker sitting there having lunch with the girl. If you look closely, he didn't even budge when that woman came from behind him and started shooting. It's like he knew this was going to happen."

"So, where's Mr. Parker at now?" Cruz asked.

Santiago began looking through some police reports on his desk. This report says that he was treated at the hospital for minor injuries and then was released."

Before the police could thoroughly interview Dillon, he left the hospital, avoiding the many questions he would face about the event that had taken place. Detective Cruz wasn't about to let him off that easy.

"I think we should visit Mr. Parker. Hopefully, he can provide us with some type of reason why he's still alive, and why Carmen is dead."

Chapter 16

"Can I trust you?" Gloria asked, breaking the silence in the car.

Raymond really didn't know what to say to the woman who was being paid to kill him. The whole situation was still fresh to him and a lot to process. All this time he was under the impression that she was there to protect him, but he was blinded by her beauty and never thought to verify her story. Then there was his uncle, a snake in the form of a weak man, waiting for the perfect opportunity to show his fangs. Raymond knew that he wanted parts of the family business, but never did he think James would take his life for it.

"I'm not gonna lie, Shooter. I really don't know what to think right now. I'm actually confused," he told her. "After all this time we spent together and all the opportunities you had to kill me, why didn't you just get it over with? Why go through all of this?"

"You probably wouldn't believe me if I told you the truth."

"Try me," Raymond said, looking over at her as she was driving.

Gloria looked over at Raymond and cracked a little smile before turning her focus back on the road. The reason why Gloria didn't kill him was beyond her own understanding. This had never happened before, and Agnis had warned her about him from the start. She should have listened to her.

"We're here," Gloria said, happy to have a reason to end the conversation for now. Gloria parked a ways up the street from her house. She sat in the car for about five minutes, looking up and down the street for anything out of whack. The coast looked clear. "He's probably in there," she said, noticing Raymond's car in the driveway. "I'll be a couple of minutes, so stay put."

Tank stood on the balcony at the rear of his house, tipping a bottle of Moscato to his lips. He was contemplating his next move and what the future may hold for him after this war. Emilio had Tank's part of the city on lockdown, and for now, there wasn't a dollar being made on either side. Both were starting to feel the effects of the war, but Tank was determined to finish it and see every last Italian removed from Charlotte. It he didn't, everything that he'd done up until now would have been in vain.

A knock at the door caused Tank to lift his head. It was Morrisa, his girlfriend, coming by to check on him. She could only imagine what he was going through. She walked up to him and wrapped her arms around his waist, placing her head on his chest.

"Just give me the green light," she said, looking up at him. "You hear me?" she said, nudging him to get a response.

Tank looked down at her and kissed her forehead. Morrisa was the best-kept secret in Charlotte, and Tank loved her. She was loyal and had been since the day he met her, and though she was MHB, she never had a problem putting Tank first. She was the first one that would get her hands dirty for him. The only reason he didn't dispatch her out into the war zone was he feared losing her. Another death this close to him wouldn't sit well with Tank right now. For that reason alone, Morrisa was going to be sitting this one out.

Gloria eased through the house with her gun out and down by her side. When she got to her bedroom, Dillon was sitting on the edge of the bed as though he'd been waiting for her.

"Did you really have to kill her?" he asked, only to be ignored by Gloria. She went straight for the safe in her walk-in closet and began to count out a half million dollars. She really wasn't in the mood to talk, but Dillon pressed the issue.

"Did you know that she was married with children?" he snapped, walking into the closet. Gloria grabbed her gun off the floor. She didn't want to kill the father of her children, but he was asking for it. "Do you have a conscience? Are you really that heartless?"

Gloria had enough. She jumped up, grabbed Dillon by his throat, and pushed him up against the wall. The gun in her hand was pointed at his face.

"What about me? I was married with children. Did you ever think about that? Did she have a heart when she was screwing my husband? Did you have a conscience when you left our kids in the house by themselves while you took that bitch out on a date? Did you?" Gloria yelled, pressing the gun up against his cheek.

She looked into his eyes, and all Dillon could see was emptiness.

"Was it worth it?" she asked. She shook her head and let his neck go so she could grab the money and leave. Before she left the closet, she stopped at the threshold, turned around, and looked at Dillon. He had the nerve to look angry.

"You told me that the next time I pull a gun out on you, you was going to forget that I was your wife," Gloria said.

Without warning, she let off a single shot, hitting Dillon in his knee. He fell backwards, grabbing his knee as he slid down the wall. Gloria stood over him and pointed the gun at his head.

"I'm not your wife, and if I even get the slightest feeling that you're gonna retaliate against this, next time I'ma kill you," she said, then turned around and walked out.

Before Gloria left the house, she went behind the China cabinet in the dining room and retrieved her favorite gun, a Glock .40, along with two magazines. Rising up, she looked at two pictures of her two kids through the glass of the China cabinet. Not wanting to get emotional, she headed for the door.

"Shit," she mumbled, stepping out onto the porch and seeing a black Crown Victoria pulling into her driveway. She recognized the car from when the detectives pulled her and Raymond over the other night.

Detective Cruz knew exactly who it was when Gloria came walking down the steps. She and Santiago got out of the car and for a moment, they all stopped and stared at each other. Santiago looked over at Cruz, who was easing her hand toward her gun. Santiago began to do the same. Before either one of them had a chance to do anything, Gloria drew the Glock .40 from her back pocket and didn't hesitate to let the bullets fly. *POP! POP! POP!*

The first bullet hit Cruz in her chest, spinning her around 180 degrees before she even had the chance to pull her gun out. Santiago drew his weapon and returned fire, nearly hitting Gloria in her head as she backpedaled up onto the porch. The bag of money she had in her hand dropped, and it was too dangerous for her to get it back.

POP! POP! POP! Gloria continued firing, taking cover behind the thick wooden beam holding up her porch.

Santiago took cover behind his car. *POP! POP! POP!* He returned fire again, knocking large chunks of wood out of the beam right by Gloria's head.

Looking over, Santiago could see Cruz lying still in the driveway, with her white shirt covered in blood. He went around to the back of the car, grabbed her hand, and pulled her to cover. He wasn't even worried about Gloria anymore, ripping off his shirt and pressing it up against her wound.

Gloria saw the opportunity and thought about getting the money, but she didn't want to risk it. Instead, she darted down the steps, all the while aiming her gun out in front of her. She ran to the back of the house, hopped over two fences, and came out onto the next street over.

"Officer down! Officer down!" Santiago yelled into the phone at the dispatcher. Santiago desperately wanted to chase behind Gloria, but he couldn't for fear that Cruz would end up bleeding to death if he eased up the pressure on her wound.

Gloria got to the top of the block when out of nowhere, Raymond pulled up in his car.

"Get in!" he yelled, unlocking the door.

Detective Santiago just sat there, holding his shirt up against Cruz's chest, listening as the sirens blared in the distance.

"Come on, Angela, stay with me. Breathe, kid," he yelled.

Her body went into shock. Cruz started shaking and choking on her own blood. The wound was fatal, and despite him trying his best to keep her alive, Santiago could feel Cruz's soul slowly leaving her body. Santiago didn't even attempt to give her CPR as he watched Cruz take her final breath, then die with her eyes open.

"You better hope this bloodclaat bitch show up. If she don't, I'm gonna do something real nasty with you," Travis threatened, taking Agnis's finger and bending it backwards in an attempt to break it. Agnis yelled out in pain through her gag, so badly so that Emilio started to feel bad for her.

"Leave the freaking girl alone," Emilio snapped. "She may be a half breed, but she still has Italy running through her veins. It's bad enough I gotta kill her, for crying out loud."

If the right family got wind that Emilio killed Agnis, he would be killed a million different ways. Her biological father was still loved by many in the Italian Mob. Even Emilio felt the weight of guilt on his shoulders in doing what he was doing. That's the reason why he refused to allow the Jamaicans be the ones who took the life of an Italian. If anybody was going to kill her, it was going to be him and him alone. The Jamaicans could do whatever they wanted with Gloria.

"You're bleeding," Raymond said, looking over at Gloria when they stopped at a red light.

"I lost the money. I lost the money," she agonized.

Gloria looked down at her shirt and could see the blood running down her left sleeve. Almost immediately after, a burning sensation came on. When she lifted her shirt, it was apparent that a bullet had grazed her. It was somewhat deep and needed to be tended to.

"Damn it! I let him shoot me," Gloria said, digging into her Gucci bag. Detective Santiago did manage to get off a good shot during the gun battle. If the bullet hadn't hit the wooden beam before it grazed Gloria, the damage would have been a lot worse.

"There's a shopping center coming up. I'll grab a few things from Rite-Aid so we can get you cleaned up," Raymond told her.

He instructed Gloria to reach into the back seat and grab one of his sweatshirts to wrap around her arm, which she did. At the next red light, he put the car into park, then helped her. The whole time he was tying the ripped shirt around her wound, Gloria had a blank look on her face. It was as if she didn't even care about what had just transpired less than ten minutes before. The was no sign of emotion, nor did it seem like she was in pain.

"Are you okay?" Raymond asked after finishing the knot.

Gloria looked at him. "You know my husband . . . I mean my ex-husband, said that I was heartless. He said that I don't have a conscience, and I'm starting to believe it," Gloria said with a hint of sadness in her tone.

Raymond actually felt bad for her. "You're not a bad person. Don't listen to your ex," Raymond told her. "You wanna know how I know that what he said isn't accurate? Because I'm still alive and sitting here with you, instead of being dead."

Gloria found some comfort in his words and thanked him for them. She felt humbled to have somebody like Raymond, who wasn't judging her for the line of work she was into. Even when she admitted to being paid to kill him, Raymond stuck around as opposed to getting as far away from her as he could. To Gloria, that spoke volumes, and it was at that very moment she knew the reason why she felt the way she felt about him.

"Let's go get you patched up."

***

Detective Cruz died in Gloria's driveway, but her body was transported to a local hospital so detectives could comb the area for evidence without becoming emotional over seeing one of their own lying dead right in front of them. It would have been too hard for everybody to do their jobs.

"We have another safe down here," a detective yelled out from Gloria's basement. No longer needing a warrant to search her home, Detective Santiago tore the place apart, and he had plenty of help doing it. Within a couple of hours, Santiago found out just about everything there was to know about Gloria. He found her secret stash of guns and ammunition behind the China cabinet, and a safe in the floor of the master bedroom's walk-in closet, which contained a little more than $100,000 and a 10 mm gun. The safe that was discovered in the basement was the holy grail of evidence.

"I can't believe it," Santiago mumbled to himself, looking at the contents that were pulled from the safe. It was the files from her last three hits, including Raymond Parker, whose case was still ongoing. The file contained pictures, addresses, phone numbers, photocopied credit cards, and more. It was one thing to assume they were dealing with a hitman, but it was another to actually find undisputed evidence that supported his assumption.

"Listen up, everyone," Santiago yelled out when he got back upstairs to the living room.

"I want us to be thorough in this investigation, so make sure you bag and tag everything, and nothing leaves this house without me seeing it first."

For Detective Santiago, this was personal. Cruz wasn't just his partner; she was like family, and it was for that reason alone, his intentions were no longer to arrest Gloria for murder, but to kill her.

Chapter 17

Carmine and his boys pulled off onto Broad Street, two cars deep, heading for Old York Road. They were on their way to a new house Emilio had rented for his family until the war was over. Emilio needed them out of harm's way because, at this point, Tank didn't have any picks on who or when he was going to strike.

"Let's pick up Alice and the kids and get them home safe. Then we're going to get back to the city," Angelo said to Carmine, who was driving.

When Carmine pulled up to the red light, Angelo looked over and saw a red Dodge Challenger. The driver of the Challenger looked over and smiled at Angelo, to which Angelo grabbed hold of the gun that was on his lap.

"Check it out," Angelo told Carmine, nodding his head at the window. The driver of the Mustang smiled at Carmine too. Out of nowhere, a female picked her head up from out of the lap of the driver of the Mustang. She looked over and blew Carmine and Angelo a kiss, then went back to what she was doing.

Carmine and Angelo shared a laugh. When Angelo turned to give the driver some props, the female had lifted her head back up, but this time she had a gun in her hand. It was Morrisa, Tank's girl, and she didn't hesitate to let the bullets fly.

"Oh, *shit!*" Angelo yelled, ducking his head below the window.

POP! POP! POP! Bullets exited the driver's side window of the Mustang and crashed through the passenger's side of Carmine's Escalade. Carmine got hit in his shoulder but managed to throw the truck in park and roll out of the driver's side door. Angelo wasn't that fortunate. As he attempted to crawl out of the passenger door, Morrisa shot him in the top of the head.

Carmine returned fire on the Mustang but hit nothing but the hood. The second Escalade that was with Carmine was a couple of cars back, but his two men jumped out anyway, guns blazing. Morrisa got out of the Mustang and took cover behind the rear of the car. Her driver, Cologne, did the same while returning fire.

Carmine's men had MP5s, so it was hard for Morrisa to get off a good shot. Good thing she wasn't alone. G and Rell pulled up in a Chevy Trailblazer, blocking off the intersection. Rell got out of the passenger's side with a Tavor X95 assault rifle, fully automatic. When he opened fire, it sounded like a hail storm. Carmine's men immediately took cover behind the Escalade. The X95 .300 AAC projectiles knocked golf ball–size holes in everything that it hit.

"Get in the car!" G yelled, wanting to get Morrisa to safety.

She walked backward toward the Trailblazer but kept firing at Carmine's car. Carmine reached around the back of the truck and fired several shots in her direction, hitting Morrisa in her chest as she fell backward into the back seat. Her vest saved her, but the bullet knocked the wind out of her.

Seeing Morrisa get hit, Cologne walked across the street, firing his weapon at Carmine. He was so fixed on killing him he didn't even care about his own life. Rell followed suit, walking down to the two SUVs with his assault rifle hollering.

Fearing for his life, Carmine took off running down Old York Road. One of Carmine's boys tried to take off running with him but was hit in his back by Rell. The bullet exited his stomach, taking stomach particles with it. Carmine's other shooter played dead, falling to the ground like he had been shot. He didn't want any parts of the gun Rell was toting. Cologne wanted Carmine bad, and was about to take off behind him, but a cop car sped down Old York Road right toward him.

The cops saw some of the shootout and jumped right into action. Cologne wasn't going out in handcuffs. He spun around and fired several shots into the windshield of the cruiser.

Rell reloaded, shoving another sixty clips into the rifle. As the cops exited their cars, Rell let them have it too.

"Let's go, let's go!" G yelled out from the Blazer. Rell and Cologne darted toward the jeep, and right before Cologne jumped into the back seat, one of the officers shot him in his back. Morrisa still pulled him into the car.

Rell got back out of his car and fired every last bullet he had in his gun at the cops. He jumped back into the Trailblazer, and G sped off down the street, trying to get as far away from the scene as possible.

Raymond really didn't feel like going to work today, but he had to in order to present his research on expanding the company overseas to his mother. He also wanted to confront his uncle about his treacherous plan to kill him. Despite their differences, Raymond had been under the impression that his uncle did love him. He was wrong in so many ways.

Once in the conference room, Raymond and his mother sat at the heads of the long rectangular table. James sat somewhere in the middle of the table, looking unimportant as usual. Several other board members were there, as well as a representative from China.

"Okay, since we're all here, let's begin," Raymond said, pulling out a folder that contained all of his documentation. "As you all know, me and my mother have been planning to expand the company overseas. China is—"

"I don't think China would be a good place to expand to," James said, cutting Raymond off. "I think the move would be a little premature, seeing as how we're not ready for this type of commitment."

"To be honest with you, Uncle, your opinion doesn't matter here."

"We're stronger in the United States. If we're gonna expand—"

"Again, James, it doesn't matter what you think. And since you have so much to say, have you been over the financials? Do you know how much money we made last quarter, or how many contracts we have with companies across the United States? Do you even know how much this company is worth?"

Raymond was making a mockery out of James, knowing he didn't have knowledge of that type of information pertaining to the company. It had been years since he'd been involved with the day to day operations, so he was lost. Raymond walked around the room, dropping off a copy of his findings to everybody.

When he got around to his uncle, he leaned in and whispered, "You won't even have a job when I take over this company."

James was hot under the collar. Raymond went on, discussing the particulars. Expansions, along with a few other proposals, were some of the things he talked about, and from the looks on everyone's faces, other than James's, it looked as though he knocked the ball out of the park.

"Okay, this meeting is adjourned for today. I expect for everyone here to have a report on my desk by the end of the week, with your opposition or agreement letter to the plan Raymond just handed out," Jennifer concluded.

As everyone was leaving, Jennifer stopped James and Raymond. "I need to see you two in my office in ten minutes," she said, then walked out of the office.

Raymond had a feeling his mother was going to have something to say about him and James's feud in the meeting. He really wanted to tell her about James's attempt to have him killed, but Raymond didn't want to put that kind of stress on her heart, which was already bad. James wasn't going to do anything but lie about it anyway, something he was good at. Raymond had plans for dealing with him personally, and before it was all said and done, James was going to learn his place.

After Dillon was released from the hospital with a gunshot wound to his knee, he was immediately taken to the police station and interrogated for sixteen hours straight. Detective Santiago put him in the meat grinder, but not once did he confess to knowing what his wife did for a living. He told Santiago that he was shot by her because he charged at her during a heated argument about him cheating on her. Dillon sat there with his kneecap shot, and not once did he even consider telling on Gloria, or making her look bad, for that matter. At the end of the day, he still loved her, even though he knew that it was over between them.

Santiago wasn't buying his story, but that was the only thing he had to go off of at the time. At this point in the investigation, Dillon couldn't be charged with anything.

"I want a twenty-four-hour tail on him," Santiago told another detective as he watched Dillon leave on crutches.

"He knows more than what he's telling me, and if my hunch is right, he's gonna lead me right to her."

Santiago was on his way back to his office when somebody yelled out his name. It was a uniformed officer, walking up to him with a man behind him.

"This is Jesus Gomez. Carmen Gomez's husband," the officer introduced.

This was exactly who Santiago wanted to talk to. He needed to know everything about Carmen's life and how it led up to her being brutally murdered. Santiago had a mountain of questions, and the answers he was about to get were going to be mind-blowing.

"What's going on between you two?" Jennifer asked, slamming her office door behind her. "Raymond, what was that all about?"

Raymond looked at James. "I don't know, Mother. Maybe you should ask your brother. He seems to have his own plans for the future of this company," Raymond replied.

"I don't have a clue what he's talking about, Jennifer. I think Raymond has something else he wants to get off his chest," James said, daring Raymond to say what he thought he knew. It was almost as if he wanted to give Jennifer a heart attack, and Raymond almost fell for it.

He looked at his mother and smiled. "It's nothing, Mother. Me and Uncle just have a few differences, that's all. I'm sure we'll clean this mess up."

"Yeah, because I can't have my only son and my only brother fighting over this company. You two are going to have to learn how to work together."

Raymond didn't have anything else to say and decided to excuse himself.

"James, what did you do to my son?" Jennifer asked once Raymond was gone.

"Jen, he's just too young to run this business. I love my nephew, and yeah, we bump heads, but this is your company we're talking about. You and your husband built this company from scratch. I really don't want to see all that hard work go to waste if something were to happen to you and he had to take over as president."

"I hope you're not anticipating my death any time soon, little brother," she said, with one eyebrow raised.

"Wow. I really can't believe you just said that to me. Do you really look at me that low? Why would I want my only sibling to die? Did you forget that I was here before all of this?" James said, twirling his finger around the office. He was actually starting to make Jennifer feel bad.

"Raymond is a hard worker."

"And I understand that, but he's not ready. Hell, he pays more attention to his P.I. business than yours."

Jennifer thought about it.

"And since you brought up your own possible death, let's talk about it. I'm not gonna sugarcoat this, because you're my sister and I love you, but the truth of the matter is, you need a heart, and if we don't find one for you soon, you are going to die. If and when that time comes, you need to make sure that this company is passed down from generation to generation. All I'm asking is that in the event something were to happen to you, that you allow me to step up and run the company until Raymond is responsible enough to do it himself. Believe me—when he's ready, I'll be glad to pass the reins over to him."

Jennifer took a seat in her chair and went into deep thought when James walked out of her office. In a sense, Jennifer did feel like James was right in some aspects of the conversation, but at the same time, she wasn't ready to turn her business over to her brother either. She knew

James meant well, but he wasn't prepared to run the company by himself. He thought that he could hide his drinking and gambling problems from Jennifer, but she was well aware of them. Until James gained control over those two vicious addictions, he was going to remain in the same position that he was in, which was on the sidelines.

Raymond sat at his desk, looking at a blank computer screen. His body was there physically, but his mind was somewhere else. He wondered how Gloria was doing and whether she was safe. He had put her up in one of his mother's condos for the time being but really didn't have time to check up on her all day. Raymond's thoughts were rudely interrupted when James walked into his office. Raymond looked up as James was closing the door.

"Look here, you li'l mama's boy. I've been with this company for as long as you were alive, and if you think that for one second I'm gonna let you come in and take all of this away from me, you really don't know your uncle," James said in a low voice.

Raymond got out of his chair and walked over to him. He stood toe to toe with James, looking him right in the eyes. "You don't scare me, James, and if you think you're gonna have something to do with this company and live to talk about it, you really don't know your nephew. I'll die before I let you run my mother's company to the ground," Raymond shot back.

"Well, as you already know, dying can be arranged. This is a grown man's game. It would be a shame to hear that you were in a bad car accident, or that you broke your neck falling down a flight of steps. You never know what might happen," James threatened.

Raymond smiled. "Are you threatening me, Uncle?" Raymond asked, looking into James's eyes. He couldn't believe that his uncle was being so blunt about his intent to kill him.

"No, this isn't a threat, nephew. Why would I do that to my sister's only child?" James had a crooked smile on his face, only pissing Raymond off more. The tension in Raymond's office was getting thicker by the second, and it was just a matter of time before fists started flying.

"You know, Uncle, I'm glad that we had this conversation. Now that I know you're trying to kill me, I'll be a little more careful," Raymond said, smacking the side of James's arm, letting him know that it was time for him to leave.

When James turned to walk out of the office, Raymond stopped him at the door. "Before you leave, Uncle, I want you to know that there's a flip side to the coin. You could easily die from a heroin overdose, or die in a house fire that you accidentally set yourself. Smoking cigars while lying in bed can be very dangerous."

"Raymond, you're making big threats for a child. To be honest with you, I really don't think you know what you're up against. I'ma give you a piece of advice, and it would be in your best interest to take me seriously. Tell my sister that you think that it's in the best interest of this company that you make me the new VP. Do it, or I'll kill you and then speed up the death of your mother at the same time."

On hearing that, Raymond snapped, throwing a right hook. The punch landed right on James's chin, knocking him to the ground. He stood over James and was about to stomp his face in, but then a loud commotion in the lobby got his attention. He could hear Barbra, the main secretary, yelling at someone. A couple of seconds later, Detective Santiago came walking up the hallway with a piece of paper in his hand.

"Raymond Harding, I have a warrant for your arrest," Santiago said, walking up to him.

He was so fixed on Raymond; he didn't care James was getting up from the ground with a bruised jaw. Santiago was aggressive when slapping his cuffs on Raymond.

James stood to the side, holding his jaw with a smile on his face. He watched as Raymond was being led down the hallway, and for a minute, James felt a sense of victory. That was until Jennifer and Dorothy, from legal, came rushing down the hall. He knew from experience that his sister wasn't about to let Raymond sit in jail for even one day, as long as she had something to do with it.

Chapter 18

Tank walked into his bedroom, where Morrisa was standing up, looking at herself in the mirror. She lightly rubbed the bruise on her chest from where she was shot, thinking about what could have happened had she not had a vest on. Tank walked up and wrapped his arms around her waist.

"Why are you so hardheaded?" he asked, kissing her on the top of her head. "I told you not to do anything. My boys—"

"I know, bae, but I'm not about to let anything happen to you. I will kill every last one of them if I have to," she said, turning around to face him.

He loved Morrisa for this reason and more. "Are you okay?" Tank asked, looking down at the purple-and-black bruise on her chest.

"Yeah, I'm good. I'ma go finish this," she said, reaching for the vest sitting on the edge of the bed.

Tank grabbed the vest out of her hand before she could put it over her head. She was true to Tank and would go to hell and back for him without hesitation. That was the reason why he didn't want her out there on the battlefield.

"You've done enough. I need you here with me," Tank said, looking into her eyes.

Before he could get out another word, Butch knocked on his door. He had a phone in his hand, passing it to Tank.

"It's the Italian dude," Butch told him.

Tank looked in shock, taking the phone. "Wassup, Emilio? Did you get that name yet?" Tank said, walking to the other side of the room.

"You and I both know that this isn't about me giving you a name—but for kicks, her name is Gloria Parker, born and raised in Raleigh. She does hits, and she's on the run right now for killing a cop. It's been all over the news," Emilio explained. "Now, look, this war isn't getting neither of us anywhere, and the attention that it's bringing to the city doesn't look good. It's costing us thousands of dollars every day. So, how about we call it a truce?"

"Come on, Emilio. Beef like this just doesn't go away with a simple phone call. We need to have a sit-down. Things need to be hashed out, and my family needs to be compensated for my nephew's and my brother's death. And please don't try to convince me that you didn't have anything to do with the stabbing at the jail," Tank said, looking over the balcony into the swimming pool.

Emilio refuted having anything to do with Larue's death, but he failed to mention Dion's.

"So, look, Emilio, we can bring this war to an end, but it's gonna cost you."

Emilio looked at the phone as though he was being humiliated. "Cost me?"

"Yeah, I said it. It's gonna cost you, muthafucka. Did I stutter? You started all this shit anyway. Now, if you wanna keep this war going, we can do that too. All I got left is guns and bullets," Tank warned.

Emilio became quiet on the phone, thinking about what Tank said. Sometimes the cost of ending a war was better in the long run than the cost of going through with it. Emilio had a lot more to lose than Tank did on the financial side of things, and with moving his family from house to house, along with looking over his shoulder day and night, the good of this proposal far outweighed the bad. At the same time, if in fact Emilio did entertain Tank's meeting, the location had to be somewhere neutral. He didn't trust Tank as far as he could throw him.

"I'll give you a call back to figure out a time and a location. In the meantime, call your men off."

"I can do that. Oh, and before you hang up, I want you to bring the bitch with you. She killed my nephew, and my sister wants her dead. This is the most important factor, so if you can't handle that, then we'll go back to—"

"No, no, no. I think I can manage that," Emilio said as he looked down at Agnis's battered face. "I'll let you know when I have her."

The call was then dropped. Tank walked back over and tossed Butch his phone. Morrisa watched as Tank flopped back onto the bed and began staring at the ceiling. Both Morrisa and Butch looked confused, but Tank wasn't.

Gloria woke up, and the first person she thought about was Agnis. After the incident that happened at her house with the detectives, she wasn't able to make it to do the exchange with the Jamaicans. Gloria honestly didn't know if Agnis was dead or alive, and seeing as how she had to get rid of her phone, there wasn't any way for the Jamaicans to get in touch with her.

"Damn!" Gloria blurted out, sitting up in the bed. Her face was all over the news for being a cop killer. There weren't many places she could go at this point. It was a sheer act of God that Raymond managed to get her out of the city with all of the roadblocks and random stops.

Gloria got out of bed and walked out of the master bedroom and headed straight for the mini bar in the living room. Looking around the huge condo, she had to admit that it was plush, with white walls and cream marble floors that complemented the long white sectional couch wrapped around the square coffee table. Above the mantle was a 70-inch plasma TV with a surround sound system that gave the room the feel of a movie theater. The kitchen had all stainless steel appliances, and the cream marble countertop island sat directly in the center of the kitchen.

"Must be nice," she mumbled to herself, looking around the condo.

She walked over to the window with a glass of whiskey in her hand. Gloria was in awe. The 180-degree view of Charlotte was breathtaking, and also somewhat therapeutic. Gloria began to think about her next move. She figured by now the Feds had joined the local police in the manhunt, making it even harder for Gloria to move around. She needed Agnis's number, but the only way that she would be able to get it would be if Dillon gave it to her. He had Agnis's number in case of an emergency, but getting to him was the problem. If his phone was on, it was more than likely tapped, and it was a guarantee that law enforcement was watching her house. Gloria didn't know how she was going to make it happen, but one thing she did know was she wasn't about to be cooped up for much longer.

The company's legal team followed Raymond down to the police station, along with Jennifer. Fortunately for Raymond, he was only wanted for questioning, and not for the actual crime of murder. In the 18th District, that could change in the blink of an eye, especially in the case of a cop killing.

"Now, explain to me one more time: Where were you last Wednesday? And don't lie to me," Detective Santiago said in a frustrated tone. The interrogation was in full effect and had been for the past two hours. Raymond was standing his ground well.

"Like I said, I got off of work early that day. Maybe around eleven thirty. I went for a jog in the park, and then went home to work on my presentation," Raymond told the detective.

Even with a lawyer present, Santiago interrogated Raymond as though he were a suspect. He was more than positive that Raymond was going to mess up during this line of questioning. But Raymond kept his cool and made sure his answers were short and sweet, just like Gloria told him to.

"So, what's your relationship to Gloria Parker?" Santiago asked, taking a seat on the desk in front of Raymond.

"Who da hell is Gloria Parker?" Raymond asked with a curious and sincere look on his face.

"Don't play dumb with me, Raymond. You know exactly who I'm talking about. The girl that you had in the car with you when we pulled you over. She's the same girl that was at your house when we stopped by."

"Gloria. Well, that's not the name she gave me. I thought her name was Pamela."

Raymond pulled out his phone in an attempt to call her. He actually scrolled through, then called Gloria's old phone, knowing that it would be off.

Raymond tried to turn it all around and play the victim, as if he were going to be killed next. The show that he put on only infuriated Santiago more, because he felt in his gut that Raymond was full of shit. No matter what Raymond said, or how good a liar he was, the fact still remained that people had ended up dead, and Raymond was too closely connected to the victims to be this oblivious.

"Well, if you don't have anything further to discuss with my client, we'll be leaving," Dorothy said, getting up from her seat.

With the limited information Santiago had on Raymond, there wasn't enough concrete evidence to bring formal charges against him for murder or conspiracy to commit murder. Until Santiago got more, the only thing he could do was watch as Raymond walked out of the police station, just as he had to watch Dillon be let go. But just like with Dillon, Santiago was going to keep a sharp eye on Raymond. Out of the two, someone had to slip up and lead Santiago straight to Gloria. At least that's what Santiago was hoping for.

Dillon could feel someone following him ever since he left the house. Looking in his rearview, he noticed a dark-colored unmarked car behind him. It was changing lanes just as he was. When Dillon got off at the exit, so did the car. Right at that moment, Dillon concluded that it was the cops, and it was obvious why they were following him.

By the time Dillon pulled into his brother's driveway, Anthony and the other kids were outside playing dodgeball. It was amazing to Dillon as he looked at his kids and could see that they were the only ones innocent in all of this mess. They had no idea that their mother was a cop killer and on the run.

"Dad!" Anthony yelled out, being the first one to see him. He, along with two of Terry's kids, ran up to Dillon. He struggled to stay on his feet, still not used to his crutches.

"Dad, what happened to you?" Anthony asked, pointing to Dillon's knee.

"I had a bad day at work, son. I'll be all right," he lied.

Terry walked out of the house and passed Dillon baby Alisha, who couldn't stop smiling at the sight of her father.

"Come in for a minute, brah," Terry said, nodding toward the house.

"Nah, bro. I'm just trying to get my kids home. Plus, I'm tired as hell."

"No, bro. I think you should come in for a minute," Terry insisted, tapping Dillon's arm and giving him a serious look. He didn't want it to be obvious to the kids what was going on inside the house.

Dillon was so distraught about what had been happening the past few days that it took him a minute to catch on. Terry instructed the kids to keep playing while he and Dillon disappeared into the house. The two detectives who were following Dillon weren't really worried about Dillon being inside of Terry's house, so they just sat back and waited.

"Bro, ya wife is downstairs," Terry whispered, pointing to the basement door.

Dillon looked at the door and then back at Terry with a shocked look on his face. He got up and hobbled down the stairs on one leg, and sure enough, sitting on top of the dryer was Gloria. She looked like hell. Before he got a chance to say anything, she got to the main reason why she was there. She jumped down off the dryer and grabbed her Louis Vuitton bag off the chair.

"There's enough money in here for you and the kids to start a new life," she said, passing him the bag.

Dillon looked into the bag and saw that it was filled to the brim with wads of money. He didn't like where this was going.

"I'll call Jackie today to see if she can get a good sale for the house."

"And where do you think I'm about to go?" Dillon asked, cutting her off with his face twisted up.

"If you want our kids to have anything resembling a normal life, you need to get them as far away from Charlotte as possible."

"Come with us. We can start—"

"There's no more 'we,' Dillon," Gloria asserted.

Dillon threw the bag of money to her feet. "You really think it's over between us? You must have lost ya motherfuckin' mind. It's *never* gonna be over between me and you. 'Til death do us part. Do you remember that?" Dillon snapped. "The only way out of this relationship is if one of us dies."

Gloria pulled a compact .45 from her back pocket and pointed it at the center of his forehead, shutting him up. She looked Dillon in his eyes. "I don't love you anymore. And I will never forgive you for what you did. I can never see myself—"

"Shoot me then. Go ahead. Shoot me," he said, looking her in the eyes.

"Is this what you really want?" she asked, pressing the gun up against his head.

Dillon wasn't backing down. "Pull the fucking trigger," he yelled again with his eyes filling up with tears. "I'm as good as dead without you in my life anyway."

The first time Gloria had ever seen a tear fall down Dillon's face was in that moment, and though she never actually planned on killing him, his reaction softened her heart. Gloria did have love for him, but it wasn't the kind of love Dillon wanted or could accept. Gloria wasn't the type of woman who could forgive once her heart was broken. With Gloria, it was a one-shot deal when it came to her love, and once Dillon betrayed her, it pushed her away for good.

"Take care of yourself, Dillon, and don't let our kids grow up to be anything like me," Gloria said, lowering the gun and then walking past him and heading for the steps. Leaving her family behind was the hardest thing she ever had to do, but it was necessary, because the mission she was on right now didn't guarantee that she would be alive tomorrow.

As Gloria was heading up the stairs, she stopped and turned back around. "Oh, I almost forgot: I'm gonna need Agnis's phone number."

"Your friend not coming for you," Travis said to Agnis. "After I kill you, I'm gonna kill her too" he said, pointing to Agnis, who looked half dead.

She was still tied to the bed and was in excruciating pain. Travis and Sam had seen Gloria's face all over the news for the past few days and knew for sure she was out of town by now. Agnis was starting to become dead weight and worthless to them. The only thing left to do at this point was put a bullet in her head, something Travis was ready to do, despite Emilio's orders.

"It looks like ya time is up," Travis said, grabbing the .50-cal from off the dresser. He cocked a bullet into the chamber, walked over, and pointed the gun at Agnis's head.

Before he pulled the trigger, Agnis's cell started ringing on the bed right in front of Travis. He wanted to pull the trigger and get it over with, but Sam gave him a look to say that it might be Gloria. Travis reached down and grabbed the phone but kept his gun pointed at her head.

"Yo," he answered, looking down at Agnis.

"For your sake, she better still be alive," Gloria spoke into the phone. She sat in her rental car, looking straight ahead at the cars driving by her.

"She must got God on her side, 'cause I was just about to put a bullet in her head," Travis replied. "You better be calling to tell me that you're ready to meet up and that you got the money."

"Yeah, I got ya damn money. Now let me talk to Agnis," Gloria lied. She was well short of the cash to pay the tab. She wasn't about to let Travis know that, though.

Travis put the phone up to Agnis's mouth and tried to make her say something, but the only thing he could get out of her was a couple of grunts and some broken up words. It was enough for Gloria to recognize her friend. She could also tell that Agnis was hurt pretty bad. Gloria looked down at her watch, then up at the street sign to see where she was at.

"Be at the Plateau tonight at twelve o'clock and make sure you bring Agnis with you. We make the trade and everybody gets home safely. But if you try to do something stupid, I give you my word that I'm gonna kill you," Gloria promised, then hung up the phone.

Travis looked down at Agnis with a smile on his face. If she only knew how close to death she was. "You live to see another day, but if ya girlfriend doesn't show up tonight, it's lights out for you."

Chapter 19

"Emilio, are you ready to go?" Carmine yelled out from the other room

Emilio came walking out of the kitchen with a plate of spaghetti in his hand. "Carmine, you freakin' cock sucker," he said, setting his food on the dining room table with an attitude. "Do I at least got enough time to eat my freakin' food?"

"We gotta go if we want to get there on time."

Emilio took a seat at the table and started eating his food anyway. "And explain to me why I have to go with you. The last time I checked, I was paying you to make these runs for me."

Ever since the price of cocaine skyrocketed, Emilio began making new friends with people in other drug businesses. There was a war going on outside, but Emilio couldn't let that stop the money train from rolling. A friend of Emilio introduced him to some Cubans, who had exactly what he wanted for the best prices.

"These aren't our regular guys we're dealing with," Carmine said. "They know you, boss, not me. So eat ya food in the car so we can get this over with."

Emilio looked at Carmine like he was crazy. He threw his utensil on his plate and walked over to Carmine. He smacked Carmine so hard across his face it busted his upper lip. He then grabbed Carmine by the throat and pushed him up against the wall.

"You better watch how you freakin' talk to me. Don't forget that you work for me," Emilio snapped, looking into Carmine's eyes with anger.

No one ever talked to Emilio in that fashion, and if it weren't for Carmine's daughter, the consequences would have been more severe.

"Now go get the freaking money and put it in the car," Emilio ordered.

Carmine did what he was told. Emilio was like family, but he was the boss first. Carmine had no other choice but to respect it.

It took Raymond every bit of an hour to get to his mother's condo, a drive that usually only took twenty minutes from anywhere in the city. The police were on his tail, and the last thing he wanted to do was lead them back to Gloria, so he sacrificed a little extra time for the purpose of shaking them.

Raymond walked into the condo and tossed his keys onto the table by the door, then called out for Gloria. She came out of the bedroom with a tank top and some boy shorts on. Even with a bullet wound to her arm, she still looked sexy as hell.

"I tried to call you," Gloria said, walking across the room toward the bar. Raymond was so caught up in how her ass fit in her boy shorts, he barely heard a word she said. "I had to get Agnis's number. . . ."

"Here," Raymond said when Gloria turned around to face him. He took the book bag off his shoulders and passed it to her.

"What's this?" she asked with a curious look on her face.

"It's the half million dollars. Use it to get ya kid's father back. I know ya money is kinda low right now, so I figured I'd help out."

Gloria looked down at the money. She couldn't believe he would do something like this, especially considering the circumstances and what the money was being used for. Raymond never ceased to amaze her.

"Thank you," she said.

"Oh, and I was at the police station," Raymond said. "They tried their best, but you know I didn't say a word." He walked over to the bar to join her. Gloria poured herself a shot of scotch and threw it back. She jumped when Raymond came from behind her and wrapped his arms around her waist.

He then whispered in her ear, "You're safe. I will never let you go to jail."

"Why? Why are you doing all this for me?" she turned around and asked him.

Raymond looked down at the diamond necklace he bought her that she still wore around her neck. "You wouldn't believe me if I told you."

"Well, tell me anyway. I need help understanding."

Raymond leaned in and pressed his lips up against hers. The kiss was very intimate, so much that Gloria had to pull away.

"What are you doing?" she asked, looking into his eyes.

Raymond didn't say a word, but leaned in for another kiss. This time the kiss was a little more passionate. His full lips covered hers as he lightly slid his tongue across hers. By now, Gloria had submitted, locking her arms around his neck.

Raymond thought about her bullet wound, pulled back, and looked at it. He wondered if he had irritated it. Obviously, that wasn't the case, because she pulled his face back down to her, kissing him again.

"Are you sure about this?" Raymond asked, moving a few strands of hair from her face. Gloria nodded her head, taking his hand and walking him back toward the bedroom.

Raymond began peeling off his Brooks Brothers suit as he followed behind her. Gloria was mesmerized by how handsome he was and how tight his body was.

"Be gentle," Gloria said once she got to the bed.

Raymond didn't hesitate, pulling her tank top over her head, then tying it around her arm to put a little more pressure on the wound. She laid back on the bed, squirming her way to the middle. He helped with her bra and then her boy shorts. He looked down at her, only to take a mental picture of her beauty. In a flash, his pants were down and his boxers were off. As bad as he wanted to indulge in some foreplay, the time wouldn't permit him to. He needed to feel his dick inside of her, and he needed it now.

Gloria hissed, feeling Raymond slide the head of his dick up and down her crease before pushing himself inside of her. The deeper he went into her, the more Gloria bit down on his shoulder. Once all eight inches were inside of her, he held it there and then looked into her eyes. He could feel her walls tightening up around his dick, and then a warm surge of fluids lubed her canal. She planted her head in his chest and moaned loudly as the orgasm made its way through her body.

"Raymond," she whispered, gyrating her hips to get him to start stroking.

Her box was so warm and wet, Raymond had to slow down, take in a couple deep breaths, and think about some poor African kids starving so that he wouldn't explode prematurely. Every stroke he took was long and deep, exploring spots inside of her that Gloria didn't know existed.

"You're mine now," Raymond whispered as he sped up his strokes. "Cum all over this dick."

He took his pole out and rolled her onto her stomach. When he went back in, he knew he wasn't going to last much longer. He started pounding away, slamming his dick in and out, causing her ass to clap up against his abs.

"Oh, shit, I'm cumming," Gloria yelled out, pulling the sheets off the bed.

Raymond wasn't playing with it neither. He was fucking Gloria like he was a porn star. The clapping got louder as Gloria squirted her cum all over the place. Raymond pounded harder and harder, feeling himself about to cum as well. There was no way he could pull out now; Gloria's insides were too good, plus he was caught up in the moment. His thick, warm, creamy cum splashed inside of her, and it was right then and there Gloria was brought to yet another orgasm. This was by far the best dick she ever had, and by the way Raymond collapsed onto the bed, she knew that it was definitely good for him as well. They both lay in bed, hugged up next to each other, until they fell asleep from exhaustion

"I just got off the phone with Pedro, and he wants to meet at Sixty-ninth Street, behind the old movie theater," Carmine said, getting into the car with Emilio. "I got two million in Joey's car and another million in the trunk."

Emilio looked at Carmine like he was crazy. "So, you got me riding around with a million dollars in my car?" Emilio asked rhetorically. "You're a freakin' genius."

Emilio had been in the game long enough to know the things that got the federal government's attention. A million dollars cash would surely raise their eyebrows. Trying to explain where he got the money to a federal agent was a conversation Emilio didn't want to have.

"I got a few guys here already," Carmine said, pulling into the empty car garage in the back of the movie theater. "Here, I brought this for you." He reached under the seat and pulled out a .50-cal Desert Eagle.

"Now, what in the hell am I supposed to do with that?" Emilio snapped, almost ready to backhand Carmine. "Do I look like a goddamn shooter? You know what, Carmine?"

Emilio clenched his teeth and got out of the car, shaking his head. After waiting for his boys to lock and load their weapons, he made his way up to the second floor of the garage. The Cubans were already waiting there with heavy security. Pedro was sitting on top of a BMW 850, surrounded by his men.

"And you must be Emilio," Pedro greeted, getting down from the car and extending his hand. Getting straight to the point, he asked, "I don't want to hold you gentlemen up too long, so what's the order for today?"

"I need about two hundred kilos, and I need them for about ten thousand a pop. Just like the good ol' days," Emilio said.

"Ahhh. As much as I would like to accommodate you on that, the price of coke ain't what it used to be. I thought Giovanni told you that. My kilos go for fifteen a pop, easy."

"Yeah, but who's buying two hundred of them at a time? Come on. Giovanni did tell me you were a reasonable man."

Pedro looked into the sky and began thinking. There wasn't anybody in the city of Charlotte buying that much coke at one time, and seeing as how Giovanni, who was also a good friend of Pedro's, had put this together, going down on the price wouldn't hurt.

"Because my good friend Giovanni said that you're a good guy, I'll take the price down to twelve and a half, and that's non-negotiable. You gotta remember I brought this shit up I-95, plus you and I both know this is the best coke on this side of America," Pedro said, looking over at Emilio.

No matter how Emilio looked at it, 12.5 was still good, especially in these times. Acquiring coke was hard in

Charlotte, and the biggest problem Emilio had was consistency. One minute you might have something, and then the next, a drought would come from out of nowhere. A deal like this wasn't gonna come by again, and Emilio wasn't about to let it pass him by.

"Gracias, mi amigo," Emilio said, extending his hand to seal the deal. With a couple of snaps from his finger, Pedro had his boys count out and pack two hundred kilos into Emilio's vehicles. He was so sure about Emilio's money being all there that he didn't bother to count it. All Pedro wanted to do was hurry up and get the hell out of that garage. There was too much cocaine and money being transferred. Within minutes, the parking lot was cleared and everybody was on their way.

Gloria opened her eyes and looked at the clock hanging up on the wall. It was 7:18 a.m., a little less than six hours 'til the switch with the Jamaicans. She thought for a moment that she may have overslept, but she had plenty of time to do what she needed to do.

"Wake up," Gloria whispered, tapping Raymond on the shoulder.

He cracked his eyes open and smiled at the sight of Gloria. It had been a minute since he had woken up to a real woman, one that made him feel good and wanted at the same time. The sex was incredible, and he didn't just feel that way because it had been almost a year since he last indulged. Gloria really did do her thing, giving Raymond everything he was looking for.

"I gotta go," Gloria said, kissing him on his forehead.

"I know," Raymond replied in a disappointed tone. "Can we just chill for a few more minutes before you rush up out of here?"

Gloria smiled. Seeing him in this light made Gloria appreciate him more. It was as if Raymond understood her and accepted her even through her shortcomings. That was something Dillon couldn't do. She couldn't believe she was falling for him this fast. Moving on from Dillon wasn't going to be as hard as Gloria had thought it would be, having somebody like Raymond to fall back on. He had proved to nothing but loyal.

"Look, if anything happens to me, I want you to know—"

"Come on, Gloria, don't dampen the mood," Raymond cut in before she could finish. "Nothing's gonna happen to you. I thought I told you that I will protect you. That means if something happens to you, then it's gonna happen to me too."

"What's that supposed to mean?" Gloria asked.

"That wherever you're going, I'm coming with you," Raymond said, sitting up in the bed.

"Raymond, you can't come with me. Where I'm going, there might be no coming back," she said, getting out of the bed. "You are an amazing man, and I can't thank you enough for what you've done for me thus far."

The whole time Gloria was talking, Raymond was getting out of the bed and getting dressed. He wasn't trying to hear anything that was coming out of her mouth right now. It didn't matter what was going on in Gloria's life. Raymond was willing and ready to see it through, standing right by her side.

"Come here. I wanna show you something," Raymond said, leading Gloria out of the room. He walked Gloria into the bedroom across the hall that Jennifer had converted into an office.

"Help me," he said, grabbing the file cabinet that was up against the wall. "My mom is a bit of a gun freak."

Behind the cabinet, there was a safe built into the wall. When Raymond opened it, there were several guns inside and a mound of money. There had to be at least a million dollars cash inside. It was Jennifer's emergency kit in case she ever fell on hard times.

"You said that you needed a half million. Well, here it is," he said, reaching in and pulling out a stack of hundred-dollar bills.

Gloria had her eyes on a .357 SIG Sauer automatic that was inside the safe. She reached in and grabbed it, cocking it back slightly to make sure there was a bullet in the chamber.

"All we gotta do is scrape the serial numbers off the guns so they can't be linked back to my mother," Raymond said, passing Gloria the twin to the gun she had in her hand.

Raymond then pulled out a Glock .40-cal, cocking a bullet into the chamber and placing it in his back pocket before closing the safe.

Gloria looked at him and could tell by the expression on his face that her words about him not being able to go with her went through one ear and came out the other. There wasn't anything she could do to convince Raymond not to travel down this road with her, and after showering and getting dressed, Gloria and Raymond headed out the front door.

Emilio didn't even entertain driving back to the house with Carmine and a car full of cocaine. Instead, he got into a cab. He had other things to attend to. There wasn't a second that went by that Emilio didn't think about Agnis and her killing machine, Gloria. The police were still on a manhunt to find Gloria, which meant that she was still out there. And as long as she was still out there, Emilio wasn't going to be able to sleep comfortably.

When Emilio got to the Jamaican hideout, Travis and Sam were there, cleaning and loading up their guns. He must have walked in on the tail end of a joke, because Sam was still laughing. It irritated Emilio, because it didn't seem like the Jamaicans were taking the situation seriously. They acted as if Gloria was just some regular dude out there in the streets. Emilio knew that she was much more than that.

"Look, y'all can leave. I'll take care of this," Emilio said, referring to Agnis, who was on her last leg.

"The bitch called. We supposed to meet up in a couple of hours," Travis said, holding up Agnis's phone.

Emilio walked over and took the phone from Travis. It was good news, but again, Travis wasn't taking it seriously. Emilio didn't know if Travis thought that Gloria was sweet, but he was about to give him a reality check.

"When you see her, kill her. If you don't, she's gonna kill you. I promise you that," Emilio told the Jamaicans before stepping outside to get some air.

Chapter 20

Gloria and Raymond did a little recon work, traveling up to the Plateau and getting good ideas for entry and exit strategies. They even had emergency routes to take in the event that something went wrong. It was like second nature for Gloria to be as thorough and on point as she was. The only thing left to be done was executing her plan.

"You ready?" Raymond asked, walking out onto the balcony where Gloria stood, looking out into the city.

He wrapped his arms around her waist and took in the view as well. It was simply breathtaking, and the calm of the night seemed to be more relaxing than anything.

"Yeah, I'm ready," Gloria answered, throwing back the last bit of scotch she had in her glass.

"Raymond, I know you have a gun, but are you willing to use it? Are you willing to kill somebody?" Gloria turned around and asked him. "As you can see, this is not a game. These people want to kill me, and they will go to any length to do it."

"Wait, what do you mean kill you? I thought we were just paying the ransom and that was it."

"I know who I'm dealing with, and Emilio don't want money. He has plenty of it. He wants to tie up some loose ends," Gloria told Raymond. She'd had plenty of time to think about the totality of the circumstances, and this was the only thing that made sense. "I guess it's my intuition kicking in."

Raymond could see the stress in her eyes. He knew for sure that her way of life was deeper than what he could wrap his mind around. It didn't change the way he felt about her, and if anything, it made him want to be with her even more. If he had to put his life on the line to stand by her side, then that's what it was going to be.

"If I have to kill somebody, I can do it for you," Raymond looked into her eyes and told her. He was dead serious and was ready to cross that bridge when they got there. It was ride or die, and Gloria was feeling every minute of it.

"Come on, let's go and get your friend back," he said, kissing her and then turning around and heading back inside.

Detective Santiago and about four other detectives pulled up in front of Raymond's house and wasted little to no time kicking his door in. Santiago didn't have enough evidence to charge him, but there was enough there to get a warrant to search his home for any evidence that could link him to any of the murders Gloria had committed.

"Turn this place upside down," he said as he flipped Raymond's couch over.

Every bedroom was tossed, including two bathrooms, the linen closet, the attic, the basement, the back patio, the front porch, the kitchen, the living room, dining room, driveway, and the two-car garage. Everything was searched. The smartest move Raymond made was getting rid of the car he was driving the night Doug crashed into him. He got it out of his garage about a week ago and had cleaned meticulously, so there weren't any traces of the car ever being there.

"The bedrooms are clear," one of the detectives said, walking into the garage where Santiago was standing.

Santiago was about to say something, but his cell began to ring. Frustrated because he could not find anything, he answered his phone with a bit of an attitude.

"Santiago."

"Dillon stopped by his brother's house to check on the kids and then he left. We're following him now," one of the on-duty detectives said, phone to his ear while he switched lane after lane.

After listening to the detective that was assigned to tailing Dillon, he found out that Dillon frequented his brother's house. Then it hit him. Dillon was probably using his brother's house as the designated spot for Gloria to see the kids. It was perfect.

"Turn around and go back to the house. I think Gloria might be there with the kids," Santiago instructed the other detective, who stopped following Dillon, turned around, and headed back to Terry's house.

Santiago took a couple of guys and did the same, hoping that his gut feeling was true. If it was, he didn't want to miss out on the opportunity to catch up to the cop killer.

Gloria drove the black Ford Taurus she had stolen, and Raymond followed behind her in a stolen Nissan Maxima. Raymond was wearing the extra vest that Gloria gave him as he drove down the highway. He cocked back the Glock to be sure that there was one in the chamber. He was a little scared, but at this point, it really didn't matter. He was knee deep. Raymond picked up his phone to call Gloria.

"Do you got the vest on?" she asked when she answered the phone.

"Yeah, so what now?" he shot back, looking in his rearview.

"Look, I'm about to get off on this exit coming up, so stay with me. The Plateau is less than a mile away. Follow the road until you get to the Plateau's parking lot. I'm going to pull into it, but I want you to keep going a little bit further down the road and park. Make sure you can see the entrance of the parking lot from where you are, and keep your car running," Gloria instructed.

Raymond did exactly what she told him, stopping about twenty yards away from the entrance. So he wouldn't look suspicious, he stepped out of his car and lifted the hood like something was wrong with his car. He kept his gun tucked into his back waist.

Gloria pulled into the parking lot and drove toward the back. There were a couple of cars there, but two more pulled in right behind her. She made sure that the safety was on and tucked her gun under her vest. She then pulled out her phone to call Emilio's cell. Travis answered immediately.

"Get out of the car and lift your shirt up," Travis instructed, wanting to make sure Gloria didn't have a gun.

Gloria got out of the car and did what she was told, showing Travis that she only had a vest on.

"A'ight, now where's Agnis?" Gloria snapped, looking around the parking lot to see only four cars there.

"Where's the fucking money?" Travis yelled back.

Gloria reached into the car and pulled out the small duffel bag, lifting it into the air to show that she had it. She still didn't know which car Travis was in, but kept her eyes on all four of them.

"Bring the money over to the white car," Travis told her. "Walk slow and keep your hands where I can see them."

With the bag in her hand, Gloria approached the white car. She couldn't see who was in it at first, but when she looked inside, she realized that there wasn't anybody in the car. She went to go turn around and head back to her car, but when she turned, Travis was standing a mere five feet away from her with a gun pointed at her chest.

Without warning, Travis fired three shots directly at Gloria's chest. She fell to the ground, dropping the bag right beside her. Remembering that she had on a vest, Travis walked over, stood over Gloria, and pointed the gun at her head. When he pulled the trigger, Gloria saw her whole life pass by. She knew for sure that she was dead. She wasn't sure if she was supposed to hear the shot before she died, but in that instant, she didn't hear anything.

Gloria looked up and saw Travis trying to cock the gun back. The bullet had gotten jammed in the chamber, and he couldn't fix it. He waved at a gray Pathfinder across the Plateau, the same one that pulled in behind Gloria when she first came into the parking lot. It pulled up and stopped right beside her. When the back door opened up, Gloria could see Agnis on the floor with her mouth and wrists duct-taped. Travis went to get into the car, and as he did, Gloria reached under her vest to retrieve her gun. She fired the first shot, hitting Travis in his back. She followed it up with several more shots to the back of Travis's head, hitting him in his dread locs.

Sam watched Travis fall to the ground, and he was stuck in shock. By the time he came to, Gloria was on her feet. She didn't give Sam a chance to do anything, firing a couple of shots at him as well. Still a little dazed from the bullets she took to her vest, Gloria's aim was a little off, and she missed Sam. He stepped on the gas and almost ran Gloria over. It was too late to call Raymond to tell him to block off the exit, and it was too risky firing at the back of Sam's car with Agnis still in the back. Gloria ran to her car, hoping to catch up with him.

Sam was on his way out of the parking lot when all of a sudden, Raymond came from out of nowhere, crashing into Sam's car head on and at a high speed. The impact from the crash deployed Raymond's airbags, knocking his head up against the headrest. Sam's car was disabled to the point that it couldn't move.

Gloria ditched her car and bolted on foot toward the crash. When she got there, Raymond was getting out of the car. He was shaken up. Agnis was still on the floor, and Sam was still dazed from the crash.

"Can you go and get my car?" Gloria asked Raymond, who nodded in the affirmative.

Gloria pulled Sam out of the car and started pistol-whipping him and kicking him in his ribs. She was beating Sam so bad that she didn't even hear Raymond pulling up next to her with the car.

"Gloria!" he yelled out, smacking the side of the door to get her attention.

"Hit the trunk," Gloria told Raymond as she grabbed Sam, dragged him to the back, and put him inside. She ran back over to get Agnis and saw that there was blood all over. Agnis's eyes were swollen shut, and she had what appeared to be cuts and burns all over her half-naked body. Agnis was hurt pretty bad, and Gloria didn't know if she was dead or alive. All she knew was that she had to get her to the nearest hospital.

"Search warrant!" Santiago yelled out before kicking in Terry's door. He didn't care that it was one o'clock in the morning and that there were a few small children in the house. Santiago had one thing on his mind, and that was to find Gloria.

"What da hell are y'all doing in my house?" Terry yelled out, jumping up from the couch and seeing all the police running through his house like wild dogs with guns out.

Santiago didn't have a warrant to search Terry's house, but he, along with the other detective that was with him, didn't care. Gloria was a cop killer, and they would go to great lengths to catch her, even if that meant doing something illegal. If Santiago had it his way, he was going to put a bullet in her head as soon as he caught up with her.

When Raymond got onto the expressway, Gloria felt a burning sensation under her vest. Afraid to look at it, she took her shirt off and pulled the vest over her head. One of the three bullets that were fired at her had gone through her vest, hitting her in the side. Blood was leaking from her wound, dripping down onto her pants.

"I'm hit," Gloria said, taking her shirt and applying pressure to the wound. "I think it went in and out, but I'm not sure. You gotta take me to my friend's house," she told Raymond.

He looked at her like she was crazy. This was the second time this week she had been shot and wasn't trying to go to the hospital. It was thuggish and also somewhat of a turn-on to see how strong Gloria was, but Raymond was concerned about whether the bullet was still inside of her and what damage it had done.

"Gloria, we gotta get you to a hospital," Raymond told her.

"No hospital. I'll go to jail if you take me to the hospital," she shot back, reaching around to feel if the bullet went out, squinting from the pain. "It did go out," she said, feeling the hole a few inches from the entry wound.

She quickly grabbed another shirt and leaned back in the seat, pressing it against the wound. It was too risky to go to the hospital, and even though Raymond wanted to take her anyway, he wasn't going to take that chance and end up losing her to the police.

"Is that your phone?" Raymond asked, hearing a faint ringing sound. "Yeah, that's you."

"Wassup," Gloria answered, looking down at her phone.

"Bloodclaat bitch. Next time you shoot a man, make sure him dead," Travis said into the phone. Gloria was shocked that he survived, seeing as how she shot him in the back of his head. The full head of thick dreads saved his life, not to mention the vest that had caught the bullets to his back. Travis had God on his side.

"Baby," a male voice said into the phone, getting Gloria's attention. He didn't have to say another word. Gloria knew her ex-husband's voice anywhere. "He said that he's gonna kill me."

"Give him back the phone," Gloria said in a frustrated manner.

"You didn't think I would come all the way out there without an insurance policy, did you?" Travis told her.

"You dumb, funny-talking muthafucka. You think I give a flying fuck about you kidnapping my ex-husband? You had a better chance if you told me that you had my Louis Vuitton bikini." Gloria laughed onto the phone. "You can keep him. He's not worth a damn. I got what I came for," Gloria said, then hung up the phone.

"They got Dillon?" Raymond inquired, looking over at Gloria with his face balled up. "I know you're not just gonna leave him," Raymond asked, looking at Gloria with disapproving eyes.

Gloria sat there silently, looking out the window at the highway lights. It was a little harsh, but that was the way she felt at the moment.

Raymond wasn't feeling it. "That's the father of your children, Gloria. You can't just leave him out there like that. Look at me, Gloria," Raymond demanded as he looked from the road to her. "I know you hate him for cheating on you, but you need to think about ya kids right now. It's not about him. Do you really want your kids to grow up without their father? Are you really as heartless as he said you were . . . ?

"I'm going to say something, and you might not like what you hear, but I don't care. Dillon wouldn't be in this position if it wasn't for you. This was the life you chose to live, not him. Is this the way you would treat me if we were together?" He grabbed hold of her hand.

"Come on, Raymond. That's not fair," Gloria responded. She started to feel bad, because the things Raymond said were the truth. Dillon didn't have anything to do with what was going on, and Gloria always vowed to make sure that no matter what, she wouldn't let her way of living affect her family. Not only would Dillon be affected by it, but now the kids would be in harm's way, if they weren't already.

Gloria picked up the phone and called Travis back. He answered it as though he had been expecting the call.

"What do you want?" Gloria calmly asked.

"Bring me my brother and the money. The real money," Travis said, looking into the bag with nothing but cut-up newspaper in it. "You play games this time, and I will kill him and then find your kids and kill them too."

"Where and when?"

"Stay by the phone," Travis said, then hung up.

Gloria dropped the phone in her lap, then looked down at her wound. She was starting to feel chills all over her body, and her eyes were starting to feel heavy. She looked over at Raymond and placed her hands on his lap. He looked over at her and saw that she was in bad shape. He placed his hand over hers and told Gloria to hang in there. That was when Gloria said the only words she could think of before she passed out:

"Please don't let me die.

Chapter 21

After the deal with the Cubans yesterday, Emilio was now was getting ready for the meeting he had set up with Tank to call a truce to the war, which was at a deadlock. Neither side was making money, and the only one that was benefitting from it all were the local funeral homes that had to bury all the dead.

"Boss, we got about an hour before we meet," Carmine spoke as Emilio finished up his dinner. "I got some guys en route to the bowling alley to make sure everything looks okay. I don't trust Tank as far as I can throw him," Carmine told him.

Emilio didn't trust Tank either, and that was why he came to the conclusion that today was going to be the day that he either got eat or was eaten, was prey or the predator, went hard or went home . . . and if he went home, it was going to be in a body bag. Emilio wanted to end it permanently, not just with Tank, but also with Gloria. Although she was on the run for killing a cop, she was still more dangerous than anybody. In fact, she was more of a threat now than ever. She had nothing else to lose, so why not finish what she started?

"Look, when we get there, I'm gonna take care of Tank myself," Emilio said, wiping his mouth with the rag. "This shit is personal. He killed some good friends of mine, and before he dies, he needs to know that it was me who killed him."

Carmine looked at the frustration in Emilio's eyes. Emilio had never gotten this up close and personal in war before. He normally sent his henchmen to do his dirty work. Carmine didn't feel right about it, but Emilio was the boss, and Carmine knew that there were no options once Emilio's mind was set on something. All he could do was follow orders, grab some men, and head to the bowling alley like he was told. Before Carmine left, he spoke.

"Boss, whatever happens, know for sure that I'ma stand by you until they put me in the grave," Carmine promised, then walked out the door.

Raymond adjusted his rearview mirror, wanting to get a better look at the unmarked cop car behind him. It had been following him from the moment he came out of the Rev. Index building. It seemed as if the detectives wanted him to know that they were tailing him, because they pretty much mimicked his every move, dipping in and out of traffic, right turn here, left turn there, and at one point, they were so bold to have pulled up right next to his car at a red light on Broad Street. Raymond couldn't afford to play the cat-and-mouse game with the detectives. Gloria was in bad shape, and the medical supplies he had on the passenger's side seat were the only things that could save her life. Time was of the essence, and it definitely wasn't on her side.

"Fuck it," Raymond mumbled, pulling over and parking by the Olney bus terminal. He figured he'd ditch the car, grab the medical supplies, and take local transportation to get back to Gloria. His chances of shaking the detectives were better this way, so he thought.

They pulled in right behind him before he could exit the vehicle. Detective Santiago calmly got out of the driver's side then walked over to Raymond. He tapped on the window so he would roll it down. The second detective got out and walked around to the passenger's side door.

"What can I do for you, Detective?" Raymond said when he rolled his window down.

Santiago was blunt and didn't have time to play games either. "Where's your girlfriend? If you freakin' lie to me, I will lock ya ass up right now for harboring a fugitive," Santiago threatened. He looked over and saw the medical supplies on the seat, and it was like Santiago had tasted blood. He nodded toward the bag and asked, "Is that for her?"

"No. Now, can you please move ya car? I got places to go," Raymond said with an attitude.

Santiago wasn't convinced by a long shot. He had a gut feeling Raymond was up to something, and he wasn't going to let up. "Step out of the car," Santiago commanded as he reached for the door.

Raymond locked it before he could pull the handle, then he rolled his window back up, almost smashing Santiago's fingers in the process. He stepped back and placed his hand on his gun and demanded Raymond shut the engine off. Raymond was uncompliant and threw the car in drive, prompting Santiago and the other detective to draw their weapons.

"Turn the fucking car off! I will shoot you!" Santiago yelled.

Both of the detectives' guns were pointed at him. The loud commotion also caught the attention of a group of people standing at the bus stop. Santiago couldn't have cared less. If Raymond attempted to run him over, he was going to shoot him.

"Don't do this to yourself. Get out of the car!" Santiago continued yelling.

All Raymond could think about was getting back to Gloria. The only thing that was standing in the way of that was Santiago. Thoughts of just running him over raced through his mind, but since that was equivalent to him committing suicide, Raymond decided against it. He realized that he would be no good to her or to anybody else if he were dead. The best thing for him to do at this point was surrender, which he did.

Santiago wasted no time placing handcuffs on him as soon as he got out of the car. Not only was he taken into custody, but Santiago also took the medical bag as evidence. He was going to make it his business to find Gloria and bring her in, dead or alive. If he had to apply pressure on Raymond to get what he wanted, Santiago was going to go as hard as the law would allow him to.

Carmine pulled up to the bowling alley, three cars deep, with four men in each car. Everyone got out, brandishing fully automatic weapons equipped with extended magazines. For it to be a peaceful meeting, it sure looked like a war was about to ensue. Standing outside of the bowling alley were a couple of Tank's guys, and from the way they stood with their hands on their hips, Carmine knew that they were strapped too. One of the men pulled out his phone to call Tank to let him know that they were there. Carmine's men spread out, scanning the area to see if anything looked crazy.

"You must be Carmine," Tank said, coming to the door of the building with Butch and YB standing next to him. Guns were visibly resting on their waists.

"Yeah," Carmine replied, trying his best to suppress the anger he felt inside for them trying to kill him.

"So, where's Emilio?" Tank asked, looking over his shoulder.

"He's coming. I think it would be proper that we both come in and check the place out first."

Tank nodded his head in compliance, stood to the side, and allowed for Carmine to enter the building with two of his men. Tank was right behind him with Butch and YB.

Off the bat, Carmine noticed that the bowling alley was spacious and completely empty. This was a neutral spot, so neither of the men knew how the inside looked. Immediately, Carmine and Tank's men took post, some by the exit door in the back, others taking positions throughout the bowling alley, and Tank made sure he had two men standing at the front door.

"Make sure nobody leaves this place," Tank leaned in and whispered to one of his men, who was heading for the door. Tank was well aware of how things could go south in a New York minute.

"A'ight, everything looks good to me. Now, where's ya boss?" Tank asked Carmine.

"He'll be here," Carmine shot back. "If it makes you uncomfortable, you can bring some more men inside, or I can make a couple of my guys leave."

Tank was becoming impatient.

"He's here," Carmine said, looking down at his phone at the text that had just come through. "The quicker you two can hash things out, the quicker we can all go home."

Tank was in agreement, except on everybody going home. He wasn't planning on letting Emilio go anywhere but to his grave.

Detective Santiago walked into the interrogation room where Raymond was sitting at the table, talking to the company's lawyer. She had informed Raymond not to say anything and that she would be there in twenty minutes. Raymond knew the rules of engagement, so he didn't plan on saying anything anyway.

"For now, you're charged with obstruction of justice, and more than likely other charges will come shortly, as soon as we find ya girlfriend," Santiago said, coming into the room. "If there's any time you would want to help yourself, the time is now."

Raymond shook his head and chuckled at Santiago's weak tactic. It sounded textbook.

"I know you might think that this is a game, Raymond, but it's not. You're in some serious trouble right now."

"Is that right?" Raymond shot back.

"Yeah, and I know more than you think I know," Santiago responded.

Raymond sat up in his seat, curious as to what the detective was talking about. Up to this point, he was sure that nothing could lead back to him. Fortunately for him, that was true. It was unfortunate that Santiago was talking about another issue, one that was sure to get Raymond's full and undivided attention.

He began pulling the contents from the medical bag out onto the table, spreading it out so everything was visible. Having been shot before, along with watching others fall victim to the bullet, Santiago was very familiar with the wounds bullets inflict and what kinds do the most damage.

"From the looks of what you got here, your girlfriend seems to be wounded pretty bad," Santiago said, picking up the large pack.

"You got the works here: penicillin, sewing kit, alcohol, bandages, and just about every type of over-the-counter painkiller."

The thought of Gloria lying in bed with her wounds smacked Raymond like a freight train He hadn't thought about that until now. Messing around with Santiago, he had forgotten all about her. Santiago could see the scared look in his eyes, and knew that he was knocking on the right door.

"I gotta get out of here," Raymond frantically expressed, getting up from his chair. "You can't keep me here."

"Actually, I can keep you here. You've been charged with a crime, so you'll have to go through the process just like everybody else."

The process of formally being charged, running the paperwork through the system, and finally seeing the judge for a bail hearing could take up to 48 hours. It could take even longer depending on how fast the precinct moved, or if Santiago decided to make up some new charges. He would do something like that in order to hold onto Raymond for as long as he could. Santiago knew what he was doing, and he had plans on applying the right amount of pressure to make Raymond crack.

"The way I see it, you only have a couple of options. You can tell me where Gloria is so I can go and arrest her, or I can see to it that it will be at least five days until you see a judge for a bail. From my experience and from what I see sitting here on this table, Gloria's gonna bleed out and die before you get a chance to get back to her. I doubt that she'll last that long," Santiago explained.

Before Raymond could say a word, there was a knock on the door, grabbing their attention.

Dorothy from Rev. Index's legal team had walked in, and without acknowledging or greeting Santiago, she instructed Raymond not to say anything. Santiago instantly became frustrated, but he quickly realized that he had already made the desired impact on Raymond that he had set out for. It was written all over his face.

When Emilio pulled up to the bowling alley, they were met by two of Emilio's men. They were escorted from the car to the front doors with heavy security. It looked like Emilio was the President of the United States. He was dressed in an all-white Tom Ford suit, and on his feet were a pair of cream-colored crocodile loafers. He looked like the Mob, raw and uncut.

"I was hoping you'd come," Tank said, extending his hand as soon as Emilio entered the building.

"Not just yet," Emilio replied, looking down at Tank's hand. Emilio never shook it, then signaled for Carmine to check the place out again before the meeting was conducted. Seeing as how Emilio and Tank were going to be at the table alone, the agreement was that both men could not be armed and had to undergo a search. It was done relatively quickly.

"So, here we are, finally face to face," Tank said, taking a seat at the table. "I called this meeting because I wanted to look into the eyes of the man I envy. You are a smart man, Emilio, when it comes to war, and I respect that, but this whole thing could have been avoided if you just would have given me the bitch who killed my nephew. Speaking of which, is she here now?"

Emilio smiled and shook his head. "I couldn't find her. But know that my men are looking for her as we speak. She'll be dead before the week is out. And look, kid, since we're here, I'll be real with you. Your nephew was treading in deep waters when he came to my side of the city and bought up a property that belonged to me. He thought that he could make millions of dollars without paying taxes. You just don't come into a man's house and start eating out of his refrigerator without asking first. That would be rude. Your nephew was being rude, so I offered to buy him out, and when he declined, I had to make him leave."

Hearing the confession boldly being stated had Tank hot under the collar. He smiled to keep from showing his anger. "And what about my brother? What did he have to do with anything?" Tank asked. "And don't lie to me, 'cause I know—"

"You didn't call this meeting to call a truce, did you?" Emilio asked.

Tank shook his head with an evil grin on his face. "Know for sure that this war will never be over. Even after I kill you," Tank told him.

Emilio gave Tank the same sinister grin, then allowed a butterfly knife to slide down his sleeve and into his hand under the table.

"Kid, you were dead from the moment I walked through those doors. You just didn't know it," Emilio spoke.

Tank looked up to the window on the second floor and nodded his head. A cold chill passed over Emilio's body as he clutched the knife in his hand. A muffled shot was fired from the window, striking Emilio in his left arm. Not for one second did it stop him from lunging forward out of his seat and stabbing Tank in his eye. Another shot was fired, but Emilio took the knife and jammed it into Tank's neck before Tank could roll out of the chair.

Tank tried screaming at the top of his lungs, but began choking on his own blood. Carmine and his boys opened fire on Tank's crew. The shooter on the second floor wasn't able to get another shot off after being hit himself.

It was total chaos. Everybody who had a gun was letting it rip. Men were shooting at each other at close range, emptying out whole clips with ease. Emilio hit the floor in search of his man. Bullets flew over his head as he crawled over to Tank, who was still on the ground, holding his eye. Another bullet struck Emilio, this time in his leg, but it was as if he didn't feel it. he continued crawling until he was on top of Tank. Emilio's eyes were bloodshot red because of anger, and there was nothing in this world that could save Tank except God.

"Look at me," Emilio told Tank with the knife clutched tightly in his hand. "Look at me!" he yelled, squeezing Tank's cheeks and turning his face toward him.

Tank looked up through his one good eye. Emilio's face was the last thing that he saw before the sharp piece of steel dug into his gut. Blood filled Tank's lungs instantly. Emilio kept stabbing him until his arm got weak.

"Emilio, we gotta get out of here!" Carmine yelled out as he continued shooting at Butch, who was taking cover behind one of the vending machines. "Emilio, let's go!"

Emilio stood up, towering over Tank's dead body with the knife still in his hand. His white suit was covered in blood, and he had the look of death in his eyes. Emilio's mayhem was far from over. He was going to make sure that here was where it all ended.

"Kill every last one of them. Nobody leaves!" Emilio shouted out to Carmine and his men.

On hearing the command, Emilio's boys turned it up. The men from Tank's crew were dropping like flies. Butch ran out of bullets, and it was inevitable for him to soon be staring down the barrel of Carmine's gun. He sat behind the vending machine, listening and watching as his crew was getting slaughtered.

Oblivious to where Carmine was at, Butch flinched when he felt the barrel of the gun being pressed up against the back of his head. He turned around slowly, and before he could plead for his life, Carmine blew his head off. Particles from Butch's head splattered on the vending machine.

Turning around to leave, Carmine was now in the same predicament Butch was just in. Morrisa stood there with her gun pointed at Carmine's face, only a few feet away. Tears filled her eyes as she glanced over at Tank's dead body.

Carmine could see that Morrisa had been shot and was already weakened by the bruises to her chest. Hoping her reflexes weren't as good as his, Carmine attempted to raise his gun. He wasn't able to lift it past his waist when

Morrisa squeezed the trigger. The first bullet entered Carmine's face right below his left eye. Then several more projectiles hit the top of his head. Carmine fell face first to the floor.

"Noooo!" Emilio yelled, seeing Carmine get murdered.

Having lost a lot of blood, Morrisa fell to the ground too.

"Cops! We got cops!" Frank, one of Emilio's boys, yelled out, running into the building.

Emilio wanted to run over and make sure Morrisa was dead, but he was out of time. If he stayed any longer, he was going to jail, and Frank wasn't having that. He grabbed Emilio and rushed him out the back door, right in the nick of time. No more than a minute went by before uniformed cops pulled up in front of the bowling alley.

Raymond sat in the interrogation room with his lawyer by his side, hoping that he made the right choice pertaining to Gloria. He was so in love with her and wanted nothing but the best for her. He didn't want to lose her in any way, shape, or form, but the longer he was being detained, the slimmer Gloria's chances of survival were. Detective Santiago stood firm on his word of making sure that Raymond wasn't going to be able to leave the building. It was eating at him, too. He felt like the decision he made was selfish and ultimately was about to cost Gloria her life. This was by far the hardest thing he had ever had to do, and as he looked up at the clock on the wall. he regretted it with every minute that went by. The only thing left for him to do was to pray that Gloria was still alive.

***

"This might hurt a little," Emilio's personal physician said as he dug the tweezers into his arm. Emilio didn't budge nor make a sound while the doctor did his thing. Aside from the multiple painkillers he took, Emilio was thoroughly numb from the events that had taken place earlier that day. He'd never been in the trenches so deep before. Seeing Carmine fall was the worst part of it. Emilio had seen death plenty of times, but Carmine's was just a little more personal. He was like a son to Emilio, and although the war was officially over, the bitterness of losing Carmine far outweighed the joy of victory.

Gloria

Something was not right. I could feel it, and I'm not just talking about the bullet wound in my gut and the fact that I was bleeding internally and externally. Raymond should have been back hours ago, and my senses were telling me I needed to get up and get out of this house. I asked God to give me strength.

Urghhhhh. *Damn, I couldn't move. This wound was killing me. I tried again.* Urghhhh! Oh my fuckin' goodness. *Every time I tried, the pain knocked me right back down. I knew one thing: I refused to let this bed be my final resting place.*

Oh, shit. *I thought I heard somebody coming.*

Gloria let out a sigh of relief when Raymond opened the bedroom door. Her body was getting weaker by the minute, and she didn't know how much longer she was going to last.

"W-where have you been?" Gloria whispered through her dry mouth.

Raymond walked over and sat next to her on the bed. His eyes began to water instantly, looking down at the blood-soaked patch covering her wound.

Gloria couldn't help but to notice that he was empty handed, no medical supplies of any sort. She looked up at him with a confused look on her face. Raymond could barely look at her, wiping the couple of tears that rolled down his face.

"I'm sorry," he said, putting his head down.

Those were the only words he could get out before Detective Santiago walked into the room with his gun in his hand. Gloria looked at him then glanced back at Raymond, who immediately got up from the bed. He couldn't stand to be in her presence any longer, feeling like he had betrayed her.

Gloria

Damn, I couldn't believe Raymond gave me up to the cops That shit hurt more than the bullet wound, and to be honest, I would have preferred for him to have left me there to die instead of sending me to jail. And to think that I was falling in love with him. I thought we had a connection. I thought that he was going to be the one. I swear I never saw this one coming. Not from him, anyway. Something told me that it was too good to be true, but I let my guard down anyway.

I looked at the cop standing over me like he wanted to do something to me. Can you believe the nerve of this guy, telling me that I was gonna burn in hell? I already knew that the doors of heaven had been closed on me, but the difference between me and Santiago was: I didn't give a fuck. I killed more men in my lifetime than he'd probably put in prison, and if it was time for me to pay for all of my crimes against humanity, then so be it. I was not complaining. Just know that at the end of the day, when it was all said and done, there would never be another contract killer like me.

Chapter 22

Raymond

I knew Gloria must have been thinking the worst of me, seeing how things looked with her lying in a hospital, handcuffed to the bed. At times, even I felt like I betrayed her, and from the looks of things, it seemed like she was on her way to prison to remain there forever, or possibly be put to death for the nature of her crimes. Killing a cop in just about any state is a capital offense, punishable by death. With Charlotte's District Attorney Lynne Walsh on Gloria's case, death by lethal injection was almost inevitable.

Not on my watch, though. The truth was, I was not about to let her be subject to that type of persecution, especially if I had the ability to do something about it. If it meant me putting my life on the line for her, then that was what had to be done. She did it for me before, so why not return the favor? She had plenty of opportunities to kill me, but she didn't. She didn't do it, and it was probably for the same reasons why I was sitting there, pushing bullet after bullet into a clip. She fell in love with me, and after all that we had been through, I realized that I, too, allowed my heart to open up for her. If you think for one second that I was not about to fight for her, then you are sadly mistaken. Whatever happened, fuck it. They were gonna have to dig two graves. And I knew some people might have thought that I was crazy, but just like I told you before, I was not letting my girl go to prison, nor was she gonna be put to death. And let's be clear about something: You heard me correct when I said "my girl," because that was exactly what Gloria was to me, and if anybody had something to say about it, I could easily put their name on one of these bullets.

Gloria cracked her eyes open to see Detective Santiago and two other detectives standing outside of her room. Both of her hands were handcuffed to the bed, a reminder that she had been caught. Her thoughts were interrupted by Santiago, who had walked back over to her after seeing Gloria's eyes open. He calmly took a seat next to her bed, and before he said or did anything else, he read Gloria her rights.

"I was gonna wait to do this, but it seems as though you're gonna be here for a few more days," Santiago said, pulling out his small notepad and pen.

Gloria cut her groggy eyes over at the detective. She thought that he would have had a little respect for her by now. Whether it be in a hospital or in a jail cell, Gloria wasn't doing any talking. She really didn't have much to say. Everything that happened was either eyewitnessed or caught on tape. Lying and trying to talk her way out of it wasn't going to do her any good.

"I wanna talk to you about the murder of Carmen at the TGI Friday's restaurant a few days ago. Was that personal, or was that business?" Santiago asked, holding up a picture of Carmen's dead body slumped over on the table.

Gloria didn't say a word, nor did she look at the photo, for that matter. It only frustrated Santiago, but he kept his cool.

"Is it true that you are a hitwoman?" he asked, reaching into his folder and pulling out a couple more pictures. Again, Gloria didn't say a word. Detective Santiago continued, even though he knew he wasn't about to get any answers from her.

"What about my partner? What did she do wrong?" Santiago asked, holding up a picture of Cruz laid out in Gloria's driveway. "She had a family. She has a little girl who keeps asking when her mommy is coming home."

Gloria did feel a little bad about killing Cruz, but in her mind, she had no other choice. At that time, going to jail wasn't an option for her, and she was willing to do anything in order to get away. Cruz was just at the right place, but at the wrong time.

"Well, since you don't have anything to say, let me inform you of this. You'll be charged with two counts of murder for now, and I can guarantee beyond a shadow of a doubt that you'll be on death row before the year is out. When they stick that needle in your arm, I'll be there to watch, and I hope God doesn't have any mercy on your soul," Santiago finished. He looked into Gloria's eyes and could see nothing but emptiness. "Heartless" was the only word that came to mind.

Gloria cleared the phlegm from her throat and finally said her peace. They weren't the words Santiago wanted to hear, but they were the only ones she could come up with. "I stand in any and everything that I do," Gloria spoke, then turned her head in the opposite direction.

Santiago wanted to jump up onto her bed and strangle Gloria, and the only thing that probably stopped him was the thought of him being no better than Gloria if he acted out in a violent way. He wanted to be nothing like her, and that was the only reason he reconsidered killing her. All that was left for Santiago to do was suck it up, probably one of the hardest things he had to do in his career.

Raymond felt a hand on his shoulder, and when he picked up his head, Agnis was sitting up in her bed. She started removing the IV from her arm. She was beat up pretty badly, but Agnis was a battle horse, and it was going to take more than what she had been through to keep her down.

"Where is she?" Agnis asked, looking around the room for her clothes.

She didn't have to say her name for Raymond to know who she was talking about. It was just a little difficult giving Agnis the bad news, knowing how close she and Gloria were.

"She's downstairs on the fourth floor," Raymond answered.

"All right, let's go get her and get the hell out of here," she told him, getting up and limping toward her clothes. Sheer will and determination gave Agnis the strength to move around the way she was.

Raymond remained seated and wasn't in a rush to do anything. He had done his homework in advance. "Homicide detectives have her room blocked off. They officially charged her with two counts of murder and a slew of other charges. The cop killing trumps everything," he explained.

Agnis threw her head back and let out a loud sigh. Hearing that piece of news forced her to walk back over and take a seat on the bed. This was the first time she got wind of the cop shooting, and it was the last thing she expected to hear. At the same time, it wasn't that much of a surprise considering who Gloria was.

"A'ight, we can get her back," Agnis said as her thoughts went into overdrive. "We just need to figure out how she's going—"

"Gloria has about two days before they take her to the county jail," Raymond explained. "Here at the hospital will be our only window of opportunity."

He was already five steps ahead of Agnis and had been contemplating how he was going to take Gloria back from the detectives. His plan was so vicious he wasn't even sure that he could go through with it.

The look that he had in his eyes convinced Agnis that whatever he had up his sleeve, he was going to go through with it. It was mind-blowing, and Agnis couldn't believe what she was witnessing. Raymond went from being the one person they were about to kill, to being the only person who was willing to risk his life in saving Gloria. Agnis missed a lot during the time she was held by the Jamaicans, but the one thing that she could see clearly was the love he had for Gloria. It practically poured out of his eyes, and if Agnis knew anything about love, she knew that it had a unique way of bringing out the best in somebody, but also the worst.

"Can you let me go now?" Dillon pleaded, looking over at the rugged, dreadhead Jamaican sitting on the couch, smoking weed. "My wife is locked up. There's nothing she can do to you or for you. Come on, man. I got kids," Dillon pleaded, hoping he would get some type of response. His words went through deaf ears, and all Dillon could think about was the horrible death he would face at the hands of Travis. Thus far, he'd been beaten repeatedly, yelled at often, and was bound wrist and ankle for the past three days. The only thing Dillon was fed was a chicken-flavored ramen noodle soup.

"I have money. I can give you money. I got 100k," Dillon offered. He had forgotten that he offered this to Travis before, but Travis had turned it down.

"I don't want ya money. Your wife knows where my brother is at. If he come back alive, I'll let you go. But if he's dead . . ." Travis sucked his teeth. "If he's dead, I'm gonna kill you and your kids."

Dillon snapped. He began kicking and screaming at the top of his lungs, but unfortunately, nobody was able to hear him. He was at Travis's mercy and didn't know how it was going to end. At times, he prayed to God and asked Him to get him out of this situation, but there was no answer from the one above at this time. Just another long day and a restless night to look forward to. There was only one person Dillon knew that could save him, and she was lying in a hospital bed, waiting to be taken to jail. Hopes of Sam popping up alive and well were also something Dillon held on to. That was pretty much all he had at this point.

As bad as Detective Santiago wanted to stay behind and watch Gloria, he had to go home, check in with his family, and get some rest. He'd been awake for well over 48 hours, aside from the twenty-minute cat nap he took while Gloria was in surgery. Though there weren't any apparent threats on Gloria's life, her room was under constant watch by several police officers. That was expected with a case so high profile. Santiago made sure that the people that were watching her were individuals who he either knew for an extended amount of time, or who he had worked with personally during his time as a cop.

"Don't worry. She'll still be here when you get back," one of the detectives assured Santiago as they both stood in the doorway, looking over at the heavily sedated Gloria. They pretty much had the whole wing blocked off, and only a select few nurses and doctors were allowed access to the floor in order to treat other patients who occupied the same wing. Other than that, there was nobody in and nobody out without flashing the proper ID. Even still, Santiago felt the sense of unease.

"I want somebody checking in with me every ninety minutes. Keep this crazy chick here at all times. I wouldn't care if she needed an emergency operation. This girl better not leave this room," Santiago told everyone, then turned around and walked off down the hallway toward the elevator.

A part of Santiago wanted Gloria to die right there in her bed, but another part of him wanted to stick his gun into Gloria's mouth and blow a hole through the back of her head himself. The fact was, the criminal justice system was going to have the final say in what happened to Gloria, and that was the only thing that eased Santiago's heart a little.

When Santiago exited the hospital, the media frenzy began. News cameras from every station were pointed at him, and questions concerning Gloria were yelled out in different forms.

"Will you be attending Detective Cruz's funeral on Sunday?" one of the reporters yelled out.

This whole ordeal seemed unreal, and at times it was hard for Santiago to accept the reality that his partner was gone. Santiago desperately required some rest. He was going to need it, because the process of justice had only just begun.

Jennifer couldn't respond right away, but once the sharp pain passed, she reached into her desk drawer and pulled out a bottle of medication. It felt like she was about to have a heart attack, and considering her health issues, it would only take one to put her in her final resting place. Raymond and all of his drama would surely be the thing that would give her more than enough stress to send her over the edge.

"Now, considering the recent events, I'm going to put James at the top of my beneficiary list," Jennifer said, throwing back a couple of pills.

"Mother, don't do that. You know how irresponsible he—"

Jennifer cut Raymond off before he could get another word out. She was so disgusted with his actions. She couldn't stand him being in her presence, and she definitely let him know it.

"Get da hell out of my office," she snapped without even looking at him.

Raymond's heart dropped to the pit of his stomach, hearing his mother talk to him in that manner. He went to say something, but she stood up out of her chair and pointed to the door.

"Out!" she yelled with a mean look on her face.

Raymond slowly got up with tears in his eyes, and as he crossed the threshold of her office, Jennifer slammed the door behind him. He was hurt, angry, disappointed, and confused, all rolled up in one.

Emilio lifted his head up from his desk when Frank knocked on his door. Emilio waved him in and then closed the black folder he was writing in.

"So, what's going on?" Emilio asked, wanting to know how the streets looked.

"Everything looks good. Business looks to be picking back up in the city. We have a few new allies in Delaware who are eager to do some business," Frank happily reported.

With Tank and his crew out of the way, the streets of the south side were wide open for the taking, and there wasn't a soul ready or willing to try to fill Tank's shoes, at least for now.

"So, what about you? How are you holding up?" Frank asked Emilio.

Frank was Carmine's youngest and only brother. He had taken the news of his brother's death pretty bad, but he managed to pull through. He was tough in that regard.

"I'm doing better."

Emilio's office phone began to ring, and seeing as how he was waiting on an important phone call, he excused himself to answer it.

"Yeah," he answered. Frank took a seat. "*Who is this?*" Emilio yelled into the phone after nobody said anything. He was just about to hang up when a familiar voice put the fear of God in him.

"You dumb, fat fucker. Did you really think you could kill me?" Agnis spoke as she took a puff of her joint.

This wasn't the phone call Emilio was waiting for. In fact, it was the opposite. He hadn't heard from Travis or Sam for a few days, and he was hoping that this was one of them calling to tell him that Agnis was at the bottom of the river.

"I assume you'll be giving my family back home a call. That's if you already haven't," Emilio spoke into the phone. He was trying his best to play it cool, as though he wasn't scared to death of what the Castellano family would do to him once they found out what he'd done. Emilio didn't have permission from the higher-ups to kill Agnis, so that was a guaranteed death sentence, especially since the victim here was Agnis, who was deeply loved. She still had strong ties with the family.

"Nah, Emilio. No phone calls from me. This thing between me and you is personal," Agnis spoke. "I'm gonna kill you myself."

"Well, come and fuckin' try, you stupid bitch," Emilio snapped. He wasn't too pleased about his life being threatened.

Agnis chuckled at his outburst. "You see, Emilio, it's easy for me to send somebody over there to kill you. That would be too easy. I think I'm gonna let you sweat for a little while. But trust me, you're gonna die. Just when I want you to die, though, not when you're expecting it. I want you to live in fear and wake up every day wondering if today will be the day that Agnis decides to put a bullet in your head," she told Emilio, taking another puff of her joint.

Emilio just sat there listening, thinking about how torturous that could be. He would constantly have to look over his shoulder while he was out and about, and having to sleep with one eye open when he was at home. He knew how vicious Agnis could be, even with Gloria being out of the game.

"How much?" Emilio asked, hoping to strike a deal with Agnis for his life. "How much?" he asked again when she didn't say anything.

Emilio looked down at the screen and saw that Agnis had hung up the phone. He slammed the receiver, then pushed the phone off his desk. Just when he thought that all his problems were over and things were starting to look up, the devil had appeared, and she was out for blood.

Raymond stepped into the elevator, and before the doors closed, James stuck his hand out to stop them. He stepped into the car with a sick smile on his face, which pissed Raymond off.

"You know, the funny thing is, I don't have to kill you anymore." James looked over and smiled. "Now all I have to do is kill your mom, and then the whole company will be mine. Ya li'l spoiled ass will be out on the streets, too."

Raymond stood there with a blank look on his face. Without warning, he reached for the gun that was on his waist, pulling it out, and pointed at James's face. He lined his body up with James's, then he stepped forward and pressed the gun up against James's forehead.

James showed no signs of fear. "Pull the trigger," he dared, seeing the look in Raymond's eyes that told him he wasn't going to do it. He didn't think Raymond was built for a murder. "I didn't think so," James said, turning his back on him.

Once the elevator stopped on the ground floor, James walked out of the car. Raymond wanted to shoot him so bad, but he couldn't bring himself to do it; not here, and not now anyway. Too many witnesses were around, and Raymond would be guaranteed a one-way trip to prison.

Raymond leaned his back up against the elevator and looked to the ceiling. He was mad at himself for doing what needed to be done. He felt somewhat weak and powerless, and it was at that moment that something inside of him changed. He tucked the gun back in his waist and got off the elevator. He had much to think about. His financial future was looking dark

Gloria's nurse enter the room but was watched closely by the detectives in and around the room. As she was changing Gloria's IV bag, she looked down at her to see if she could get her to make eye contact. Gloria wouldn't look up, though.

"He said that he loves you," the nurse mumbled very low, so it was only Gloria who heard her.

She finally looked up at the nurse, and in return, she cracked a little smile to let her know that she heard her.

Raymond had seen the nurse yesterday in the cafeteria and asked if she could deliver that message to Gloria for him if she was able to do it without getting in trouble. The story Raymond told the nurse about how they met and how he fell in love with Gloria moved the nurse enough for her to get Gloria the message. Unfortunately, she couldn't stick around long enough to hear Gloria's response. One of the detectives had gotten up from his seat and walked over to Gloria's bedside. He was checking out the nurse and making sure she wasn't doing any funny stuff.

After she changed Gloria's IV, wrote down her vitals on a chart, and changed her colostomy bag, she left without saying another word. Nothing else needed to be said.

Raymond pulled up to Shelby's Diner, a low-key eatery in downtown Charlotte. He and Sally were to meet up in order to take care of some serious business. When he got out of the car, two females who were walking by the diner took in the sight of Raymond. He had on a blue-and-white striped button-up Polo shirt, some blue Seven For All Mankind jeans, and on his feet were a pair of blue Balenciaga sneakers. He had a fresh haircut showing off his deep waved hair, and on his face were some Ray Ban sunglasses. He was as handsome as they came.

"It's crazy we had to go through these extreme measures in order for me to get my lunch date," Sally joked, standing up to give Raymond a hug and a kiss when he walked over to the table.

He smiled and had a joke of his own. "You play ya cards right, there might be a happy ending for you."

They both shared a laugh, but then got right to business.

"Did you bring it?" Raymond asked, taking a seat in the booth.

The information Raymond was asking for didn't come cheap. The cream Tumi duffle bag he brought in with him had one hundred and fifty grand inside, and when Sally affirmed that she had the information, he kicked the bag over to her under the table.

"You know that what I'm about to give you can cost me my job. Hell, more than likely I'll be put in prison for a very long time," she said, reaching into her bag and pulling out a piece of paper.

"I know, Sally, and I'm sorry I'm asking you to do this, but just like I told you before, nobody's gonna get hurt and nobody will ever know that you did this for me," Raymond assured.

Handing over the information on the small piece of paper was equivalent to Sally committing treason. It was sensitive information from the police department, and though Raymond promised that nobody was going to get hurt, this whole situation could end up turning into a violent act. Sally's job and a prison sentence were the least of her problems if the government got wind of what she had done.

"I gotta ask you something, Raymond," Sally said, wanting to know some truth about what was going on. The question had been plaguing her from the very moment Raymond asked for her help.

"Do you love this girl? I mean, is she worth risking everything for? Think about it, Raymond," Sally said with a concerned look on her face.

Raymond sat there and thought about it for a minute. Before he could be truthful with anybody else, he had to be honest with himself. It was rare in this day and age that someone could fall in love at first sight. Not only that, but taking into consideration the totality of the circumstances of how they met and all that he and Gloria had been through over the past few weeks, Raymond was sure of his answer.

"Sally, I wouldn't be here if I didn't love her," Raymond said, taking the piece of paper and putting it into his shirt pocket. He got up from the table, leaned in, and kissed Sally on the forehead, then turned to leave. He wished he had more time to sit and talk, but time was of the essence, and though he had some concrete intel about Gloria's future movements, Raymond still had to come up with a foolproof plan to get Gloria out.

Detective Santiago went home, ate a good meal, took a shower, and got several hours of some much-needed rest. When he finally woke up, it was to his wife slowly riding him, rocking her hips back and forth while holding onto the headboards. He got right into the game, wiping the sleep from his eyes and gripping her waist. Maria had that good stuff, and too much of one position could lead to Santiago prematurely ejaculating. He had to get her off top.

"Come here, mami," he said, gently turning her over onto her back. She was a little on the chunky side, but she still had the face of an angel, and her sex drive was strong.

"You know I love you, papi," she whispered as Santiago continued stroking.

"I love you too," he replied as his strokes began to speed up.

The pleasure in Maria's eyes made him want to cum. She had already cum once before Santiago even woke up, and now she was working on number two. She stuck her tongue in his mouth as her volcano started to erupt. Her walls tightened up around his dick, and she could feel it coming from her gut. Santiago also was at the point of no return. The sound of his cell ringing on the nightstand didn't stop the show. It only enhanced it, causing Santiago to stroke faster, deeper, and harder until he splashed off inside of her.

"Yes, papi," Maria yelled out, feeling his warm cum along with her honey inside of her. She gasped and let out a frustrated sigh at the phone as it continued to ring. She knew it had to be his job.

Santiago felt her frustration but knew that he had to answer the call. "Santiago," he answered, holding the phone up to his ear while sitting on the edge of the bed.

"Doc said she needs to go back into surgery," the detective said as the doctors and nurse were gathered around Gloria's bed.

"I'm on my way," Santiago replied, then hung up the phone.

Maria had high hopes for her husband to be able to lay up with her for a few more hours before he headed back to work, but those hopes quickly diminished when he jumped out of bed.

"Will you be home for dinner?" Maria yelled out to him in the bathroom as she began to change the sheets on the bed.

He came out of the bathroom within a minute, almost fully dressed. "I don't know, babe. We could be moving this girl any day now, and I need to make sure that I'm there when it happens."

Santiago was going to make it his business that when Gloria was transported to jail, it was done in his car, and with Cruz's handcuffs on her wrist.

"Well, I want you to be careful out there," Maria said, walking up to Santiago while he fixed his clothes in the mirror. "I don't know what I'd do if I lose you."

Santiago turned around, hearing the concern in his wife's voice. His family meant everything to him, and the last thing he wanted to do was make her a widow and his kids fatherless. Detective Cruz was a constant reminder of how ugly things could get out there in the streets. He could understand the concern of his wife, but at the same time, he had a job to do.

"How about you call me when dinner is done? I'll come home for a couple of hours and put you and the kids to bed," Santiago told her, grabbing Maria by the waist and pulling her body closer to his.

His words provided some comfort to Maria, and though she didn't feel one hundred percent confident that the worst couldn't happen to him, she was glad that he would at least try his best to make it home for dinner.

Raymond pulled into the junkyard just as the sun was starting to go down. It was quiet, aside from the two dogs barking at the gate of the auto body shop next door. When Raymond got out of the car, Agnis was nowhere in sight, like she said she'd be.

"Come on wit' the bullshit," Raymond mumbled to himself.

He pulled out his phone and began to dial her number as he walked toward the two trailer homes in the back of the yard. Agnis's phone went straight to voicemail, which made him even more frustrated. He stopped, turned, and looked at his car sitting at the front of the junkyard. It was dusty, along with the clothes he had on, from being in the junkyard.

When Raymond tried to call Agnis a second time, the phone went to voicemail yet again. He decided to leave in hopes that she would contact him later. As he was about to head back to his car, the hairs on the back of his neck stood up. He could feel the presence of somebody standing behind him. It was too late for him to draw his weapon, because in a flash, the barrel of a gun was pressed up against his back.

"Turn around slowly," a male voice spoke.

Raymond did as he was told, turning around to see a white man dressed in a suit standing a few feet away.

"I'm here to see Agnis," Raymond said, holding his hands in the air.

The man cocked the hammer back, then pointed the gun in Raymond's face. Seconds seemed like hours, and at that point, Raymond was scared to death. He didn't know what he walked into, and had thought that Agnis was going to finish the job Gloria had started.

In an act of desperation, Raymond went for his gun. The man standing in front of him pulled the trigger before Raymond's hand got to his waist.

CLICK!

Raymond closed his eyes but then quickly opened them, seeing that he was still alive.

"If he'd had bullets in his gun, you'd be dead. Your brains would be all over that Buick," Agnis said, coming out of one of the trailers. She nodded for the gunman to step back, but he didn't go too far.

"What the fuck is wrong with you?" Raymond snapped, wanting to punch Agnis in her face for scaring him like that.

"Do you really think you have what it takes to get her back? Do you?" she yelled, walking up to Raymond. "You think they're going to hand her over to you on a silver platter? This ain't no fuckin' game!" she yelled. "You ever kill anybody? Answer the fuckin' question!"

"No," he replied in a low voice with his head down.

It seemed like Agnis was about to walk off, but then she spun around and backhanded Raymond across the face. The guy who was with her stood between them.

Raymond grabbed his face, tasting the blood in his mouth. He looked at her like she was crazy. The Italian man then punched Raymond, and this time Raymond fell to the ground. He walked over to him and grabbed Raymond by the ankle and began dragging him through rocks and dirt toward the trailer. Raymond struggled, trying his best to get to his gun, which was still on his waist.

A brief stop at the bottom of the trailer steps gave Raymond the opportunity to grab the .45 automatic from off his side. The Italian reached down with both his hands, gripped Raymond by his chest, and lifted him to his feet. He didn't notice that Raymond had the gun in his hand, but Agnis did. She watched as Raymond pointed it at the Italian's face.

"Yeah, that's it. Now all you gotta do is squeeze the trigger," Agnis said, walking up to Raymond. The Italian didn't budge or look like he was scared at all.

Raymond gritted his teeth, then gripped the gun tighter. Agnis provoked him even more.

"Shoot. *Shoot!*" she yelled.

The thought of the guy punching him in the mouth ran through Raymond's thoughts. He could still taste the blood in his mouth and feel the cuts on his back from being dragged across the yard. That, along with so many other things going on in his life, caused him to snap. He squeezed the trigger, but the gun didn't discharge. He kept squeezing, pushing the gun into the Italian's face, but the bullets wouldn't come out. By the time he realized that the gun safety was on, Agnis had snatched it out of his hand. To Raymond's surprise, she cracked a smile, then put the gun back in his hand.

"If you have any hope of getting our girl back, you gotta be willing and ready to kill at the drop of a dime. Anything can happen, and if it ever came down to either taking somebody else's life or losing your own, your choice better be to live instead of dying." Agnis looked into Raymond's eyes and spoke with every sincere bone in her body. "Now, come on, we got a lot of work to do," she told him, then turned around and walked up the stairs of the trailer.

Raymond looked down at his gun then around the jun yard, still trying to process everything that just happened. Just two minutes ago, he was ready to kill Agnis, but now all he wanted to do was follow her inside the trailer. He didn't know it yet, but this was only the beginning of his journey, and as he walked up the steps of the trailer, he could feel that his life was about to change.

Everything was quiet at the hospital by the time Santiago got there. The nurses were prepping Gloria for her final surgery, in which they planned on removing her spleen. Doctors predicted that she was going to be at the hospital for more than a few days, and that depended on how well her body recovered. She was a cop killer, but the doctors weren't going to jeopardize the integrity of the hospital by fixing Gloria up halfway and kicking her out. She would die shortly after that without proper care, and her doctor was well aware of that.

"Look, I don't care how long we gotta be here. I want this wing secured at all times," Detective Santiago told the uniformed cops.

Santiago couldn't put his finger on it, but something seemed off. He didn't want to take any chances, and that's why he was so concerned about security and wanting two or three sets of eyes on her at all times. He didn't think that anybody was stupid enough to run up in the hospital and try to do something crazy, but just in case they did, Santiago wanted to be prepared for it. He made it his business to see to it that Gloria would stand before the court of law for the many crimes that she committed. And nothing was going to get in his way of making that happen.

Chapter 23

Raymond was going to show up at work that day but decided against it. He went down to the Index building to try and speak with her about the argument they had the other day. He was hoping that she had cooled down by now and was willing to listen to him. He didn't know what the outcome of what he was about to do would bring him, but if things went south on this mission, he didn't want the last conversation he had with his mother to have been an argument.

"Is she here?" Raymond asked his mother's secretary, who was sitting outside of her office.

"Yeah, and I think she was expecting you," the woman answered.

Raymond tapped on the door a couple of times before he entered. An instant wave of relief came over him when he saw that his mother had a smile on her face when she lifted her head from her computer. She got up and out of her chair, walking over to her son with open arms. She quickly noticed the bruise on his face that resembled a fist print.

"Are you okay? What happened to your face?" she asked, examining his face like she was a doctor.

Raymond didn't want to lie to her, but at the same time, she would flip out and have a heart attack if he told her the truth about Agnis trying to turn him into a killer. A small bar scuffle sounded a little less dramatic and believable.

"I'm sorry, Mother," Raymond said, wrapping his arms around her. He did feel bad that he hurt her with all the mess he had gotten into. In all actuality, Jennifer was getting past that.

"There's no need to apologize, son, and you don't have to explain to me what's going on. I'm sure, and I trust that whatever happened with that situation, you used good judgment and did what you did for a reason," Jennifer said as she held him.

"Mother, I just want us to be good. I don't wanna fight."

"No, baby. No more fighting," she replied, looking up into his eyes.

"Mom, I really need to talk to you about James—" Raymond said, but he was cut off.

"Don't worry about that. What I said to you was out of anger. He will never run this company as long as you're still alive and breathing. I brought him in here earlier and explained that to him."

Jennifer was so naïve about what was going on with her brother, and though James wasn't to be trusted, Jennifer never thought that he would be so crazy as to bring her or Raymond any harm. On the contrary, Raymond was well aware of what money, greed, and power could do to a man like his uncle. He wasn't going to quit until he became the owner of Jennifer's distribution company. James's reckless behavior made him a liability, and before Raymond allowed him to tear apart what family he did have and run his mother's business to the ground, Raymond was going to have a nice long talk with his mother. Depending on how James would act, it would ultimately determine his fate. One way or another, James was going to get some act-right, and it was going to be in the near future.

Gloria

My eyes were closed, but I could still hear what was going on around me. From the conversation Detective

Santiago and another detective were having inside of my room, it looked like I'd be getting shipped out of there after the weekend. That shit was crazy. The government was gonna fry me, and there was nothing I could do about it. I definitely wasn't supposed to go out like this. I always pictured it being in a blaze of glory. It's funny how life takes us in the opposite direction than the one we set out for.

Believe it or not, when I was a kid, I wanted to be a movie star. I wanted to be on TV with some of the good actors like Al Pacino, Danny Glover, Samuel Jackson, and Joe Pesci. I wanted to be in an action movie with me playing the bad girl. Yeah, that was when I was a kid. It's crazy when one starts to think about the more innocent times in life.

Here I was, at the end of my road. I couldn't even say that I had that much of a good life while I was on this earth. Aside from the kids I really didn't want, the husband who turned out to be a cheater, and owning my own home, I really didn't do much. I mean, I had been to a few places, though: Miami, Jamaica, Mexico, the Bahamas, Las Vegas, and to Disney World with the family. Other than that, it had been nothing but work, work, work. I was taking jobs left and right, so much so that the only real time I spent with my family was during those vacations that I just mentioned.

Speaking of family, I wondered how the kids were doing. And whatever happened to Dillon? The last I could remember was the dumb-ass Jamaican calling my phone, telling me that he had him. Oh, well. Forget him. I hoped he cut Dillon's head off. That's what he got for cheating on me.

What was I talking about? That was the father of my kids. I was dead wrong. I hoped he was all right. Fuck it—no, I didn't. Man, I was confused like shit. I think the

*morphine was making me go crazy. I was going back
to sleep. My body hurt like hell, and my thoughts were
everywhere.*

It was official. Rev. Index was going to open up another
distribution company overseas. Within a few days of
her decision, Jennifer had multi-millionaires wanting
to invest in her idea of becoming a worldwide business.
Even Wall Street inquired about whether Rev. Index
would become a stock option.

"Jenny, it's me, your little brother. Trust me, I can
handle it," James pleaded as he followed behind her. He
wanted to be the one who ran the new company in China,
but Jennifer already had plans on sending Raymond over
there to get things up and running.

"Look, you can stay over here with me, and if you prove
yourself, maybe I'll consider making you president,"
Jennifer said, stopping at the fire exit door. "Now, if
you'll excuse me, my ride is waiting for me," she said,
opening the door.

James continued following behind her as she made her
way down the steps. He pleaded one more time for the
opportunity to go overseas, but he was shot down again.
James was infuriated. He hated the fact that his sister
treated him the way that she did and how she was putting
all this trust in Raymond, even after he was implicated in
a cop killing.

"Are you sure about this?" James asked, looking at
Jennifer's back as she walked down the steps.

"Yes, little brother. I'm sure about it," she replied,
unaware of what was about to happen.

There were at least two more flights of stairs to go
down before they made it to the parking garage, but at
Jennifer's old age, coupled with her health issues, it was

only going to take a fall from one flight of steps to cause severe damage, and hopefully death.

"Sorry, sister," James said before raising his foot up and kicking her in the back.

It was more than enough force for her to go airborne, barreling head first down the remainder of the steps. Jennifer tumbled like clothes in a dryer, hitting just about every step on her way down. She finally crashed at the landing at the bottom of the steps. Blood immediately leaked from the side of her head, and there were no visible signs of life coming from her. James heartlessly walked down the rest of the steps until he stood over his sister's motionless body. The guilt only lasted for a minute before dollar signs danced around in his head. And without giving Jennifer a second glance, James walked back upstairs and headed to his office.

"Check mate," Agnis announced, then started fixing the pieces back on the chess board.

Raymond knew how to play chess, but he wasn't as good as Agnis. Yet, he still continued to play, getting better with every game. He didn't see the logic for it, but Agnis did. She wanted to make Raymond think before he reacted, and to strategize as opposed to moving out of impulse.

For the past couple of days, she'd been putting Raymond through all sorts of scenarios. She saw and recorded all his reactions in order to improve upon them. Chess was simply another one of Agnis's mental tests.

"Make sure that every move you make is for a reason," Agnis explained as she watched Raymond move his pieces across the board. "You have to defend, but at the same time, you have to attack with precision."

Raymond kept his eyes on the board, and the more Agnis spoke, the more he started to see the game in a new light. It was as if he began to anticipate where Agnis's pieces would land, and in other areas of the game, he envisioned ways to capitalize off of her thirst to check mate him.

Agnis was making him think. She was making him sharper, and Raymond didn't know it right now, but she was turning him into a killer. Not just any killer, but one of the elite. That's what she did, and she did it well. For countless men, and even for Gloria, she turned the average person off the streets into a silent killer. Raymond was next on deck. He had so much potential. Agnis couldn't help herself, and took the challenge head on.

"Check!" Raymond yelled out, putting Agnis's king in danger.

Agnis paused, looking at the board attentively. Raymond's cell going off broke the silence in the room. He picked the phone up off the table and noticed that it was his mother's office number that popped up on the screen.

"Hey, Mother," he answered with a smile on his face. His smile turned into a frown when his mother's voice wasn't the one on the other end of the phone.

"Raymond, your mother had an accident," Jennifer's secretary spoke into the phone.

He jumped up from his chair. "What happened?" he asked with a panicked look on his face.

The secretary broke down all the information she had thus far, which wasn't much except that Jennifer had fallen down the steps. She was in the hospital's ICU.

She couldn't get another word out before Raymond hung up the phone. Agnis looked up at him as he scrambled around for his things.

"What's going on?" she asked, thinking that something had happened to Gloria

"It's my mom," Raymond said, then headed for the door.

The first thing that came to Raymond's mind was his uncle, who had recently made the threat on his mother. He thought that James had made good on his promise, and if it turned out to be true, Raymond was going to make good on his promise as well.

"Yes, son. I'll will be home soon," Dillon told Anthony before telling him to put his uncle on the phone.

"Dillon, what's going on, bro?" Terry asked.

"I'm good, bro. I should be home in a day or two," Dillon replied, looking over at Travis, who was sitting on the couch staring at him. "I love you too, bro," Dillon said, then hung up the phone.

He got up from the floor and passed Travis his phone. Raymond had to practically beg Travis for that phone call. It was a must that he checked on his kids, especially not knowing how all this was going to end.

"You know what your girlfriend said to me when I—"

"Wife. That's my wife," Dillon corrected.

"That's even worse. You know your wife told me to kill you?"

"No, she didn't," Dillon replied. "She wouldn't say that."

"I don't believe in God, but if I did, I would swear to him. Your wife is a piece of shit, and even if she wasn't going to jail, she wouldn't come for you," Travis said. "I would never leave my wife behind. I don't care what the circumstance is."

Dillon got quiet thinking about what Travis said. He didn't want to believe it, but being as though Gloria caught him cheating on her, the statement she made to Travis about killing him could very well be true. It was something he definitely was going to think about, and hopefully by the grace of God, Travis wouldn't go through with taking Dillon's life.

Raymond sprinted through the hospital hallways until he reached the nurse's station of the ICU. Mindy was there waiting for him, and within minutes, a doctor came out to explain Jennifer's situation.

"Your mother suffered significant brain damage during the fall, along with several broken bones. She's unable to breathe on her own, and her heart has stopped twice since she arrived," the female doctor explained.

Raymond broke into tears hearing all she had said was wrong with his mother. It sounded bad, and the doctor didn't hesitate in telling Raymond that the chances of his mother making it through the night were slim. That caused him to break down even more.

Mindy quickly wrapped Raymond up in her arms, trying her best to console him in this horrible time.

"I wanna see her. I wanna see my mom," Raymond cried out to the doctor.

"Take a few minutes to get yourself together, and then I'll have somebody take you back there to see her," the doctor told him before turning around and walking off.

"I think ya wife killed my brother," Travis spoke out to Dillon, who was still in the shower. "He's not coming back."

Travis stood at the bathroom door, waiting while Dillon took a quick shower. He didn't trust him enough to give him privacy, plus the window up by the ceiling was large enough for Dillon to fit through in the event he wanted to get happy feet. A two-story drop into some bushes and Dillon was free.

"I'm starting to think that your wife killed my brother," Travis said again as Dillon was coming out of the shower. "You know, I'm getting tired of waiting."

The only reason Dillon wasn't dead by now was that Sam was kidnapped instead of being killed on the spot. Gloria was going to let Sam live for some odd reason, and that alone was enough for Travis to pump the brakes on killing Dillon. His patience was running thin, though, and with Gloria sitting in the hospital with multiple police watching her every moment attentively, Travis was finding it hard to hold onto hope.

"Trust me. If your brother was dead, you would know," Dillon told Travis. "If I could make a suggestion, I would say you allow me to go to the hospital and try to gain access to my wife and find out what she did with him."

"Bloodclaat. You must be mad. You think I'm stupid?" Travis said, pointing at him with his gun. "I'm not stupid."

"I'm not saying that you're stupid. I'm just trying to get your brother back to you so I can get back home to my kids," Dillon shot back. "Look, I know my wife. She probably has your brother tied up in a basement in the middle of nowhere so nobody can hear him."

Travis walked over to Dillon and punched him in his mouth. He didn't like what he heard, but in all actuality, what Dillon said may have been true. Still, Travis wasn't willing to let Dillon leave the house, and he definitely wasn't going to kill him. Not yet anyway. He needed to be one hundred percent sure that Sam was dead before he made that decision. Until then, Dillon was going to remain in his custody, and other methods of figuring out what happened to Sam were going to be used.

Raymond thought that he was strong enough to see his mother, but when he walked into her room, he immediately broke down in tears as he sat next to her. Her face was badly bruised and disfigured from the fall. Raymond could barely tell that it was her. She was hooked up to all kinds of tubes and cables, which was the only thing that keeping her alive at this point.

"Damn," Raymond snapped, walking away from the bed. "How did this happen?" he asked Dorothy as he was unable to hold back his tears. It was only a matter of time before James made his guest appearance, and when he did, he put on a show.

"Oh, God, no!" James yelled out when he walked into the room. He put both his hands on his head and managed to muster up a few tears.

Raymond wasn't buying it at all and wanted nothing more than for him to leave. "What are you doing here?" Raymond said coldly, walking up to James.

"What are you talking about? This is my sister," James shot back.

Raymond hadn't gotten all the facts about the incident yet, but a "fall" down the steps had James's name written all over it. Knowing how slimy he was, Raymond decided to pry.

"And where were you when she fell?" Raymond asked, examining James's body language at the same time.

"I was in my office," he replied.

"Yeah? And you're just now getting down here?" Raymond's P.I. skills started to kick in.

James wasn't feeling his line of questioning, and made it known when he walked up on him. "Are you trying to imply something, Raymond?" James said with an angry look on his face.

He was faking well, but Raymond wasn't buying it. It was about to be the Clash of the Titans right there in the room.

As soon as Raymond was about to flip out, Jennifer's heart monitor flat-lined. He looked over at his mom, and as he rushed over to her bedside, several doctors and nurses ran into the room, pushing James and Raymond out of the room. They watched from outside as the hospital staff worked on her, doing everything they could to revive her. Raymond couldn't stand the sight of it, and had to walk off down the hallway by himself.

James and Dorothy stood next to each other outside of the room.

"You're vicious," Dorothy whispered to James while she continued to stare at Jennifer being worked on. She was well aware of everything James had set out to accomplish. After seeing him follow Jennifer down the stairwell, rather than go to the police, she had decided to capitalize on the situation. She had gone up to James's office right after the ambulance took Jennifer away. She asked for a check to keep her mouth shut and a better position within the company if he became the owner. James agreed. For insurance purposes, Dorothy got him to cut her a check, just in case things didn't go as planned. James gave her everything that he had, which was a little more the one hundred thousand dollars. He did it without a second thought.

Gloria felt something tapping her forehead, waking her from her sleep. When she opened her eyes, Santiago was standing over her with a stupid-looking smile on his face.

"Do you even go home?" Gloria said in her groggy voice.

Santiago plucked Gloria on her head again. "I'll go home just as soon as I get you nice and tucked in at the county jail."

"Good, 'cause I wanna see all my friend, and guess what else?" Gloria chuckled. "I'll never have to pay rent again," she joked with a painful laugh.

Santiago laughed, too, but not at her joke. "Your surgery was a big success. It seems like you'll be seeing your friends as soon as tomorrow," Santiago told her.

Gloria's body took to the surgery better than the doctors had expected. She had already begun the healing process, and after running a few tests, the doctor deemed Gloria capable of being discharged. That meant she was stable enough to be taken to the county jail.

Detective Santiago was ecstatic, wanting to hurry up and get this show on the road. Every moment he sat around Gloria and thought about the day Cruz died in his arms, Santiago wanted to take matters into his own hands. Getting Gloria to the jail was probably the safest thing for her right now.

Miraculously, Jennifer didn't die, but the doctor knew that it was impossible for her to survive if her heart stopped beating again. They explained in detail his mother's condition and left it up to him whether to keep her on life support and allow her to continue to suffer from her injuries until she could no longer survive, or to pull the plug. It was a difficult decision for him to make, especially with vultures like James around, waiting to get a piece of the company.

"Raymond, I gotta go home, but I'll be back in the morning," Dorothy said, pretty much exhausted from the events that had taken place that day.

James had gone home an hour ago, so that left Raymond there with his mom all by himself. He didn't want to leave, and he wasn't going to. Jennifer was going to have to die on her own, because he wasn't going to pull the plug on her and wasn't going to let anybody else do it either.

He got comfortable in the chair right next to her. Several hours had gone by before Raymond finally fell asleep in the chair.

He was awakened by the presence of somebody else coming into the room. He cracked his eyes open to see Agnis pulling up a chair next to him, then taking a seat in it. Raymond was surprised that she had come by, especially at two o'clock in the morning. She sat there for a moment without saying a word, only looking over at Jennifer. She had only known Raymond on a personal level for a few days, but she had a great deal of respect for him. She could see why Gloria couldn't pull the trigger. He had strong morals and the heart of a lion when it came down to it. Respect was due to Jennifer, where all those qualities came from.

"My dad died from cancer when I was a kid," Raymond began to speak. "My mom loved him so much. She used to tell me that I acted just like him."

"I've got a great deal of respect for your mother. This might sound a little messed up, but I'm glad Gloria didn't kill you," she looked over and told Raymond.

It did sound a little crazy, but looking back on it, Raymond was happy she didn't kill him too.

They both just sat there for a few more minutes in silence, looking over at Jennifer. However, Agnis was there for a reason, and it wasn't just to pay her respects to Jennifer. She had gotten the word from her people down at the police station that Gloria was being moved tomorrow to Montgomery County Jail. If they were going to make a move to get her back, they needed to get on the ball right now.

Agnis reached over and patted Raymond on his leg three times before getting up from her chair. "They're gonna move her tomorrow," were the only words she said before leaving the room.

Raymond sat there looking at his mother. After about ten minutes, he got up, leaned over, and kissed Jennifer on her bruised cheek; then he grabbed his things and walked out of the room. As badly as he wanted to stay there with her through the night, there was unfinished business he needed to take care of, and it wasn't going to get done sitting there in the hospital. All Raymond could do was pray that his mother would still be alive by the time he came back tomorrow afternoon. And if she weren't, then at least he didn't have to watch her die. At least that's how he felt.

Chapter 24

Dillon shook the radiator that he was handcuffed to, trying his best to get it to fall over, but it was way too heavy, and it was bolted to the floor extremely well. Travis had gone out to get some more food and weed and had been gone for the past hour. Dillon couldn't even take advantage of the situation. He thought about yelling out, but that strategy hadn't worked yet, plus he didn't want Travis to come back and catch him trying to escape. That would mean a sure death.

"Come on," he said, trying to shake the radiator again. Nothing. Then, out of nowhere, keys could be heard jingling in the door. Travis had come back, taking a large amount of hope away from Dillon. He heard the door open and close, and then heavy steps coming up the stairs. Dillon look around in a last-minute attempt to see if he could find some type of weapon to use if he got the chance. There was nothing. At least nothing he could reach.

"I got a cheesesteak, pizza, chicken wings, and some french fries," Travis said, walking into the room with the food in his hand.

Up until now, Dillon wasn't really that hungry. When Travis put the food on the floor in front of him, Dillon attacked it like an animal. This was so much better than the ramen noodles he was being fed since he'd been there.

Why is this dude being so nice? Dillon thought to himself.

Yeah, Travis was being nice today, but it wasn't for the reasons Dillon thought it might have been for. Today was probably Dillon's last days on Earth, so Travis figured that his last meal should be a good one. He liked him enough to do that. The truth was, Travis didn't have any more use for Dillon now that Sam was almost definitely dead, and he quickly came to his senses and realized it. He knew that if given the opportunity, Dillon would go to the cops, despite the fact that Dillon said he wouldn't do so. Travis just couldn't take the risk. For him, it was a no-brainer.

Four uniformed officers, along with Detective Santiago and Detective Young, were selected to transport Gloria to the county jail. The high-profile case attracted a lot of media, and for reasons unknown, news stations got the word that the transfer was going to happen that day. Fox News, along with several other news vans, were parked outside of the hospital, reporting live, with hopes of getting a shot of Gloria before she was put into the cop cars.

"These are my partner's cuffs," Detective Santiago said as he put them on Gloria's wrists.

"How sentimental. It's really not that deep," Gloria said, looking up at Santiago from her wheelchair.

Her smart remarks were quickly answered by Santiago spitting in her face. Gloria wanted to spit back on him, but her mouth was too dry, and her insides were killing her. She simply wiped the spit from her face and put it onto Santiago's sleeve, then responded with a fresh set of offensive words.

"You're a coward. Under no other circumstances would you ever even consider doing something like that to me," Gloria told him. Her words held a lot of truth.

"Get this piece of shit out of here," Santiago commanded one of the uniformed officers who was standing by the door of her room.

Instead of taking Gloria out the front door, Santiago took a different route. They went through the back way. Santiago's unmarked car was waiting in the back by the docking station.

"Take in a deep breath, because this will be the last time you smell freedom," Detective Young told her when he opened the back door.

He wasn't gentle at all in shoving her into the back seat, and because Cruz was dear to him as well, the ride to the county jail was going to be rough.

Gloria

Damn, I was on my way to jail, and it was such a beautiful day out. Clear skies, the sun was shining bright, and everybody seemed to be outside enjoying themselves. I would probably have been out with the kids that day. I think Anthony had a football game.

Damn, I was gonna miss being free. I should have bought a motorcycle. I would have been riding it that day if I had one. Hell, what was I talking about? I couldn't ride no motorcycle.

Get it together, Gloria. It's over. *These people were about to kill me, and there was nothing nobody could do about it.*

Detective Santiago looked down at his phone as it began to ring. The screen showed that it was his house number, so he knew that it had to be his wife.

"Yes, mami?" he answered while keeping his eyes on the road ahead of him.

"Baby, I need you to listen to me," Maria said in a scared voice.

"What's wrong?" Santiago asked, hearing something in the background.

"Somebody is here, and she wants you to pull over and let the girl you are transporting go," Maria said.

Santiago quickly put his phone on speaker so Detective Young could hear what was going on.

"Say that again, Maria."

"You have to let her go!" she yelled into the phone before Agnis snatched it away from her.

Detective Young pulled out his phone to try to get a few units over to Santiago's house, but he stopped once he heard his name being called out next.

"Detective Young, your son is in daycare right now, and your wife is at the doctor's office getting a checkup. She's pregnant. Am I right?"

Young looked shocked.

"I could have both of them killed right now, just as easily as I can brutally murder Detective Santiago's whole family right now."

"I'm not letting her go," Santiago said, but he was slapped on the arm by Detective Young, who wasn't willing to risk his family's life in order to keep Gloria in custody.

Agnis made even more sense of the matter as she continued to speak. "Before you make this life-changing decision, I want you to think about this: You might lose your badges for letting a suspect go, but at least you'll have your families to come home to," Agnis said. "At the same time, I wanna make this clear to you: If you don't pull over and let her go in the next sixty seconds, I'm gonna execute everybody in this house, including your two-year-old daughter. The same will happen to your family as well, Detective Young." Agnis spoke with total conviction.

Silence took over the car. They both sat there in deep thought. Santiago looked in the rearview mirror at Gloria, who was sitting in the back seat with a smile on her face. She recognized Agnis's voice and was happy to hear her good friend coming to her aid.

"*Por favor,*" Maria cried out. "*Mi hijo, mi hija.*"

"Thirty seconds," Agnis spoke, reminding them of the time.

A gun being cocked could be heard over the phone, and if anybody knew that Agnis was serious about killing Santiago's family, it was Gloria.

"Just let me go. You caught me once, and I'm sure you'll do it again," Gloria said to the detectives.

"Ten seconds!" Agnis yelled out again, this time pointing the gun at the two-year-old's head.

Maria yelled out, begging Agnis not to do it.

"Don't shoot!" Gloria yelled out from the back seat, stopping the brutal murder that was about to take place. "They're pulling over right now."

Santiago took in a deep breath then exhaled. He looked over at Detective Young, who gave him the nod of approval. Reluctantly, Santiago put on his right turn signal and pulled over to the side of the highway. The patrol cars accompanying them pulled over too. From one of the other cars, an officer rolled the window down to see what was going on.

"You guys go ahead of us. I'm gonna rough her up a little bit before I take her in," Santiago said, waving the squad car ahead. Seeing as how Gloria killed his partner, the uniformed cops didn't even question it.

"Get a couple licks in for me," the young cop told Santiago before they pulled off into traffic. The other cruiser pulled up next to them, and Santiago explained the same thing to them. They, too, proceeded into traffic.

Santiago waited for a minute until the cop cars were a little bit farther down the highway, then he unlocked the door and got out of the car. Detective Young followed him, securing the perimeter.

"You know that the next time I see you, you won't be going to jail," Santiago threatened as he took Gloria out of the car. It was a clear indication that he was going to kill Gloria. She was well aware of that. A man's family is not to be played with nor threatened with death. Gloria simply nodded her head in respect for his words.

"So, now what?" Santiago spoke into the phone while looking at the heavy flow of traffic passing by.

"Now get in your car and drive off. I will leave your home without any further incident once she's secured."

Santiago tucked his phone in his back pocket, then took the handcuffs off of Gloria. He and Young got back into their car and pulled off into traffic.

Gloria stood there, but she was becoming weak. She couldn't stand much longer, and just when she was about to sit down, a black SUV pulled up and stopped right beside her. It was a sight for sore eyes when Raymond opened the door and got out of the driver's side. He ran over to her, and in his hands were two Glock .40s, and over his face was a mask.

"Here," he said, passing Gloria one of the guns as he helped her get into the car. Gloria was still in shock that it was him who came.

"Can you see the car from here?" Santiago asked, looking into his rearview mirror.

"Yeah, a black SUV. They got her," Young answered, seeing somebody help Gloria into the vehicle.

Due to the distance, he was unable to see who was helping her. Santiago immediately pulled out his phone and called his house. Maria picked up the phone, yelling and crying hysterically.

"Did she leave?"

"Yes," Maria cried into the phone. "Please come home."

"'Listen, baby. Take the kids upstairs, grab the gun out of our closet, and wait for uniformed officers to get there," Santiago instructed. He was trying to calm her down, because without a cool head, she was no good to herself or the kids.

Detective Young was on the phone also, checking up on his wife and also his son at the daycare center. They both wanted to make sure that their families were secure, and once they were, Santiago pulled over onto the shoulder of the highway.

"Tell me when you see them," Santiago said, throwing the car in reverse and slamming on the gas.

Young was on his phone, calling for backup, and then out of the midst of traffic, he saw the black SUV approaching.

"Oh, shit," Raymond said, seeing the Crown Victoria backing up in traffic and coming their way. He pulled over into the opposite lane, slowing down traffic in the process. Detectives Santiago and Young were a mere twenty-five yards away. When Raymond came to a complete stop, he looked at Gloria, then pulled the ski mask back down over his face. Gloria was in awe watching as Raymond exited the car with both hands wrapped around the Glock. Without warning, he let the bullets fly. *POP! POP! POP! POP! POP!*

Santiago lost control of the wheel as several bullets crashed through his back window. He ended up crashing into an oncoming car that was trying to get out of his way. He and Detective Young exited the car with their guns drawn. Raymond forced them to take cover as he continued unleashing havoc. *POP! POP! POP! POP!*

Bullets struck the trunk, the driver's side window, the tire, and the back window. Traffic continued passing by while Raymond fired down on the detectives from across the highway.

To avoid civilian casualties, the detectives hesitated firing back. When they did finally lift their heads up from behind the car, the black SUV had gone through the median and was going in the opposite direction on the highway. The front and back tires of the Crown Victoria were blown out, so Santiago was unable to pursue them. They could only call out over their phones the direction the SUV was going in. Santiago was pissed.

Dillon sat in silence, looking over at Travis, who was sitting on the bed. He was looking at the TV screen but wasn't really watching anything the whole time. He gave off a different vibe than the one he had before, and from that, Dillon knew that something was wrong.

"Is everything cool?" Dillon asked, adjusting his hands around the radiator to get a little more comfortable.

"Yeah, mon. Everything is good," he replied, getting up from the bed. Travis stepped out of the room for a moment, and when he came back in, he had something that looked like a tarp in his hands, rolling it out onto the floor right next to Dillon.

"Damn. Come on, man, don't do this," Dillon began to plead. He knew that this could only mean one thing. "Please, man, I got kids," he said, hoping Travis would understand.

Travis didn't understand, because he didn't have any children, and at that point, he felt that he had no other choice but to kill Dillon.

"This is not personal," Travis said, pulling the automatic weapon from his back pocket.

Dillon began to cry and begged Travis not to do it. Nothing but God could save him now, and in a split second, it seemed like Dillon's prayers were answered.

He glanced over at the TV and saw a picture of Gloria on the screen. It made Travis look over, and when he saw Gloria's picture, he froze.

"Bloodclaat," he mumbled under his breath as he listened to the news anchor explain the situation.

"A brazen escape took place on I-95, where a suspected cop killer got away from detectives on a busy highway. Witnesses said that a man jumped out of a black SUV and began firing multiple shots at an unmarked cop car," the anchor said, pointing to Detective Santiago's vehicle.

"The SUV fled northbound by way of this median, with suspected cop killer Gloria Parker inside. She's expected to be armed and dangerous, so please, by no means do you approach her if you see her. Call the police immediately," the news anchor reported before the news switched to another topic.

Dillon and Travis sat there stunned by what they had just heard. Dillon was especially happy that Gloria had gotten away, and in a sense, his life was spared because of it. Hearing the news about her escape gave Travis another round of hope that his brother Sam may still be alive. Killing Dillon could now prove to be detrimental, and if anything, he was going to be used as a bargaining tool, like Travis had set out to do from the beginning. Travis had no doubt in his mind that once Gloria found out that Dillon had been missing for the past few days, she was going to come looking for him. If Sam wasn't alive, he was going to lure Gloria in with Dillon, then kill both of them.

"I guess you live to see another day," Travis said, stuffing the gun back into his back pocket. He turned around and walked out of the room, leaving Dillon to breathe a sigh of relief.

***

"You gotta be fuckin' kidding me," Emilio said as he listened to the news reporter on the TV reporting about Gloria's escape. He was shocked, nervous, and scared to death, all wrapped up in one. Emilio damn near pissed his pants thinking about what was going to happen to him once Gloria got her hands on him. It was so unreal right now, and all Emilio could do was stare at the TV in awe. He was sick, and at this point, he didn't know what to do. The one thing that he did know was that waiting on Gloria to come to him was out of the question. Until she was either apprehended or ended up in the morgue, Emilio was getting the hell out of the city with his family. The more he thought about it, getting out of the country sounded even better.

"Allahu Akbar, Allahu Akbar."

Gloria didn't know where it was coming from, nor did she know where she was, but just by listening to the call to prayer, Gloria's body aches went away for that moment. That was odd, because that never happened before. After further looking around the room, she laid her eyes on Raymond, who was sitting in a chair by the window, fast asleep with his gun in his lap. He looked so peaceful that Gloria didn't want to wake him.

She didn't have to, because Raymond woke up on his own, hearing the ocean water outside of his window. He looked over at Gloria and smiled.

"Hey, beautiful," he greeted.

Gloria couldn't find the right words to say to him. Her gratitude for Raymond doing what he did was beyond a mere "thank you."

"One of your staples came out yesterday. I stitched it up the best I could," Raymond said, walking over and taking a seat next to her on the bed.

Gloria moved the sheet away from her stomach and could see that Raymond had definitely played doctor on her last night. She looked like Frankenstein with how many staples she had running up her stomach.

"Damn," was all she could say.

"Yeah, I know, but the good thing is, you're going to live," Raymond said with a huge smile on his face. "Now, I know you might have a lot of questions, but they will have to wait. I have to go down to the hospital to check up on my mom," he told her. He paused, remembering that Gloria was unaware of Jennifer's fall. "That's another story in itself," he said, hopping up from the bed and heading for the bathroom.

Gloria's mind told her to try to sit up, but her body had other plans. The pain from her injuries knocked her back down. It shot through her whole body, making her think twice about doing anything. The bullet did some significant damage to her insides, and Gloria could vividly remember the doctor telling Santiago that she was going to be in severe pain for a couple of days after surgery. The doctor wasn't lying.

"So, listen, Agnis will be here in a couple of hours, and I should be back later on tonight," Raymond said, walking over and taking a seat next to her again. He leaned over and kissed her dry lips. "You're safe now. I got you," he told her before hopping back up and walking toward the door.

He stopped, turned around, and couldn't help but to confess his feeling towards her. "I love you," Raymond said, then left the room before Gloria even had a chance to respond.

She sat there, letting the words marinate in her brain.

Detective Santiago sat in Jennifer's room, watching as the nurses tended to her, and at the same time hoping that Raymond would show up. After yesterday, Santiago had still managed to hold on to his gun and badge, but Internal Affairs did take him off the case. His superiors were told to keep him on desk duty while they finished doing their investigation on how Gloria, the cop killer, got away from them.

"Excuse me, nurse. When was the last time her son was here to see her?" Santiago asked about Raymond.

"He's been here every day, only going home for a couple of hours at a time. He should be here any minute now."

"What about yesterday? Was he here around two o'clock in the afternoon?" Santiago questioned, trying to pinpoint Raymond's whereabouts during the escape.

The nurse wasn't able to say, seeing as how she hadn't been at work the day before. Even though he was off the case, he was still trying his best to piece things together. He was obsessed with this case, and there was nothing or nobody that could stop him from closing it.

Raymond felt tension from the very moment he got off the elevator and onto the ICU floor. Not to his surprise, once he got to his mother's room, Detective Santiago was sitting there, waiting. He looked like he'd been through the wringer. He clearly hadn't slept in a couple of days. His eyes had bags under them, and on his head were a couple of scratches. Raymond knew that it had to come from him taking cover yesterday when he was being shot at.

"Where is she?" Santiago asked in an aggressive tone as he jumped up from his chair. "And you better not lie."

Raymond kept his cool, not wanting to seem suspicious.

"Yes, I saw the news this morning, but no, I haven't seen her," Raymond replied, walking over and pulling up a chair next to his mother's bed.

Santiago didn't believe a word he said. Thoughts of wrapping his hands around Raymond's throat and choking him until he confessed ran through his mind. He was treading on thin ice with Internal Affairs, and at this point, any misconduct could get him kicked off the force.

"Where were you at yesterday?" Santiago continued.

Raymond was well versed in the law, and he knew not to incriminate himself by talking. "If you have any question, you can contact my lawyer, who is on call seven days a week. Now, if you don't mind, I'm trying to spend some time with my mother," Raymond told the detective.

Santiago gritted his teeth, mad that Raymond wasn't cooperating. One thing he felt deep within his heart was that Raymond had something to do with Gloria's escape. He had too much invested in her, and Santiago knew that. He regretted not locking Raymond up the first time he attempted to help Gloria, and if it wasn't for the DA making the deal with his lawyer, giving him immunity as long as he gave up Gloria, jail was exactly where Raymond would have been by now.

Gloria could smell the strong scent of a lit cigar, causing her to open her eyes. Her vision was a little blurry at first, but Gloria already knew who was blessing the room with her presence.

"And the old woman lives." Gloria chuckled, clearing her eyes to see Agnis sitting at her bedside. "You look like shit."

Agnis laughed, looking at her still badly bruised face in the mirror up against the wall.

"Yeah, so imagine what you look like," Agnis teased.

The amount of respect and love they had for each other didn't require any words of gratitude. Them saving each other's lives was more than enough.

"I guess you didn't hear anything about Dillon?" Agnis asked, thinking about the conversation she and Raymond had had about the night they came and took him.

"Nah, I didn't hear anything yet. Once I get up enough strength to get up and move around, I'll figure out what's going on," Gloria assured. There was so much unfinished business that needed to be taken care of, and there wasn't a lot of time to get it done.

Emilio was still out there, and Agnis was getting concerned. She thought that he would either skip town or find somebody else to finish the job so he wouldn't have to worry about living in fear. Agnis knew that at least one of the Jamaicans was still out there as well, and it wasn't a mystery how brutal Travis could be.

"I don't know how you feel about it, but I think ya boyfriend might be ready," Agnis said, referring to Raymond.

"No, no, no, Agnis. This way of life isn't for him. I told you, just give me a couple of days and I'll be up and moving again. I'll take care of the Jamaicans. I'll take care of Emilio, and then I'm out," Gloria spoke through the pain in her gut.

Agnis reached over and pulled the sheet away from Gloria's stomach. The colostomy bag was filling up, and the bullet wound looked beyond painful. There was no way Gloria was going to be up and walking around in a couple of days. Then again, Gloria wasn't like most women. She was a warrior and had the will and determination to do anything she set her mind to. She reminded Agnis of herself in so many ways. If anybody was capable of recovering from this type of injury, it would surely be somebody like Gloria.

James had all the executive staff in the conference room to have an emergency meeting to vote on who was more capable of running the company in his sister's absence. With enough support, James could manipulate the system and take over the company.

"I just don't think that's legally possible," Dorothy spoke out while pulling some papers from her briefcase. "The insurance policy states that everything was to go to Raymond if she were to die or become incapable of running the company for any reason." Dorothy would be able to contest any judgment they made today. In any court of law, she would win.

"Do you really think that it would be wise to allow Raymond to run this company? He barely makes it to work on time, not to mention the fact that he is suspected of aiding and abetting a cop killer," Steve from finances spoke freely.

A lot of the executive staff was in agreement with Steve, not wanting to leave a multimillion-dollar business in the hands of someone who they felt was irresponsible.

"I'm sorry, but there's only one way James will be able to run this company in Jennifer's absence—" Dorothy said, but she was cut off.

"That's if I'm dead." A voice spoke from the door of the conference room. Raymond was standing there, and he had been for a decent portion of the conversation. He wasn't too thrilled at all. "You know, this isn't the first time somebody has spoken about my death," he said, walking into the room. "I know some of you would love to see me dead."

James looked on while Raymond slowly walked around the long marble conference table, looking over the shoulders of his mother's employees.

"Get up," he told Jake from HR. Raymond stood on his chair, then climbed onto the table.

James threw his hands in the air. "This is exactly what I'm talking about," he said, looking around the room at everybody.

Raymond stood in the middle of the table, rocking a pair of black Balenciaga jeans, a white-and-black Balenciaga shirt, and some black Ferragamo sneakers.

"Effective immediately, James will no longer be an employee at Rev. Index," Raymond announced.

James tried to cut him off, but Raymond continued on his war path. "Effective immediately, Steven Strasberg will no longer be employed at Rev. Index. Along with you, you, you, and you," Raymond said, pointing out several other staff members who he had caught agreeing with Steve and James when they made their comments.

"You don't have the power to fire anybody. My sister is the only—"

"My mother passed away at nine twenty-eight this morning. She died from the injuries she sustained from her 'accidental' fall," Raymond said, using sarcastic finger quotes. "As of right now, I am the owner, CEO, President, and Vice President of this company. So, in a nutshell, I can fire whoever I want."

On hearing that, James grabbed his things, and so did everybody else Raymond had fired, and they all headed for the door.

James stopped and stood at the head of the table with his face as red as a cherry. "I don't think you're understanding what you're getting yourself into."

With a snap of the finger, two Rev. Index security guards walked into the room. They walked behind James and began leading him out of the room. For a second, it looked like he was about to flip out, but one look at the overly muscular security guards and James decided to take the easy way out.

Raymond looked around the room at the remainder of his staff. "Is there anybody else here that wants to oppose my new position?"

Everyone remained quiet, and on that note, Raymond walked over, climbed down off the table, and took his seat at the head of the table, exactly where he belonged.

Chapter 25

The manhunt for Gloria was underway, and the Charlotte Police wasted little to no time kicking in doors. They pulled over vehicles randomly, shook down drug dealers in Gloria's old neighborhood, and both state and federal informants were working around the clock trying to find out where Gloria possibly could be.

"Do you really think that she's here?" Detective Young asked Santiago as he pulled up to the street were Gloria and Dillon lived. "Chances of her coming back here are slim to none"

"Yeah, well, we gotta be sure of that," Santiago replied, waving for Young to pull the car over.

Santiago knew that they didn't have that much time before police units would be there, so they moved fast, running down the street with their guns out by their sides.

The house was pitch black. Santiago hesitated the least, kicking the door in with force. With his flashlight and gun in hand, he entered the house. Young was right behind him.

While Detective Young skulked downstairs, Santiago headed up the steps. His whole motive was to kill Gloria on sight, whether she was armed or not. Young didn't know that bit of information, and Santiago was going to do everything in his power to prevent Young from seeing him brutally execute Gloria.

In a matter of minutes, the entire house was searched and cleared. Just as they were leaving, several police cars were pulling up to Gloria's house. Among them was Detective Shields, the lead detective who was assigned to Gloria's case.

"Is she in there?" Shields asked when he walked up the driveway.

Santiago shook his head. Shields gave him a frustrated look, disapproving of him still trying to work the case.

"I understand how you feel, but you gotta let me do my job," Shields told Santiago. "Trust me, we're gonna catch this girl."

"Yeah, I know," Santiago said, holstering his weapon.

If Shields reported this incident to his superiors, Santiago would be facing reprimand and possibly termination. Shields wasn't going to report it, and in a sense, he did need Santiago to catch Gloria. Santiago knew this case better than anybody, and he had somewhat of an understanding of how Gloria thought. As Shields could see, Santiago was already a step in front of him, and that was all fine and dandy as long as Santiago played fair. Working together was definitely better than working apart. Wires could easily get twisted, and somebody could end up getting hurt.

Raymond had to admit that when he left the Rev. Index building yesterday, he was a little nervous. He expected for James to pop up out of nowhere and blow his head off for the stunt that he had pulled in the meeting. He could see the fury in his eyes as he was leaving the conference room, and it was at that moment Raymond knew what he had to do.

It took Raymond every bit of two hours to get to the beach house where Gloria was staying. He had to make sure that nobody was following him, so he took the long way. He understood that the possibility of Santiago following him was high. He had learned a few things from Gloria, switching his car and then taking public transportation before getting into a cab to get to Gloria. Raymond felt a little more confident that he wasn't being followed once he could see that there weren't any cars behind the cab on the dark highway.

Gloria was sitting up in the bed when he walked into the room. She'd been trying to get up and walk all day, but sitting up in the bed was the best she could for now. Her face was covered in sweat, and it looked like one of her staples had come out.

"I see you must like pain." Raymond chuckled, walking around to the side of the bed closest to her. "It's way too early for you to be trying to walk around."

Gloria had things to do, and lying up in bed wasn't going to get the job done. "Whatever happened to Dillon?" Gloria asked. "Is he dead?"

"I'm not sure, but I think I know where we can find out. Come on," he said, leaning over and wrapping Gloria's arm around his neck to carefully lift her out of the bed. "You wanna walk? Then let me help you."

On the count of three, they both heaved Gloria off the bed and onto her feet. It seemed like her body weight shifted to her bullet wound, and for a second, she was ready to sit back down. She didn't do it, though, and instead, she dug deep and took the first step. She took another step, and then another, and then another, all the while with Raymond holding on to her.

"Are you okay?" he asked as they got closer to the bedroom door.

If she wanted to stop, now would have been a good time to do it, because the hallway that led to the other bedrooms was very long. Gloria thought about it, looking down the hallway. She wasn't going to stop. She pushed through it and continued walking slowly.

"Did you really mean what you said earlier?" Gloria asked.

Raymond already knew what she was talking about.

"I meant every letter of the word," he said as he continued walking her down the hall.

It was somewhat of a relief, because Gloria had felt the same about him, but she wasn't sure how to tell him. She never thought that it would be possible to fall in love with somebody after Dillon, but here she was, falling for someone who she started out trying to kill. She had to admit, all these feelings and emotions were happening all too fast.

"I want to tell you that I love you too, Raymond, but I'm afraid to. I have to be sure that what I'm feeling is love. I care about you very much and . . . and . . ." Gloria spoke through her heavy breathing.

Raymond smiled. "You don't have to explain. I understand, Gloria."

She was tired as hell from walking down that hallway, and it looked as though she had a long way to go. Fortunately for her, Raymond stopped at one of the bedroom doors in the middle of the hallway and picked her up. He opened the door, and the foul stench of Sam's body almost knocked both of them down.

"Oh, shit," Gloria said, looking down at Sam on the floor. He was hog-tied, gagged, and chained to several hooks on the floor.

"Who did this?" Gloria asked, curious as to who in their right mind had though of something like this. It didn't matter what Sam did or how long he tried it for, he wasn't getting out of those restraints.

"I learned a few things while I was in Texas with my cousins," Raymond confessed. "At first I didn't know why I kept him alive after you got locked up, and trust me, there were a couple of times I came in this room about to put a bullet in his head. Then I thought about Dillon, and I figured that if things didn't work out with me getting you back, I would try to trade him for your husband. If that didn't work, I was gonna kill him."

"Damn, you would do that for me?" Gloria asked.

"For you, I'd do just about anything. And even though I know you're mad at Dillon, I know you don't want your kids growing up without a father."

These were the reasons why Gloria fell for him so fast. He was so thoughtful and caring, and he showed that he would move a mountain for her with his actions.

She stood there for a few seconds, soaking up all the love, but in a heartbeat, it was time for her to switch gears and go back to beast mode.

"A'ight muthafucka, it's time to wake up."

Travis paced back and forth across the room with his phone in his hand, waiting for it to ring. If Sam was alive and Gloria wanted Dillon back, he knew that he'd be getting a phone call. When it finally did start ringing, Travis stopped in his tracks, looked at the screen, and saw that the number was blocked.

"G'wan. Who's this?" Travis answered.

"You see that our problem is back out on the streets," Emilio spoke, also pacing back and forth across his living room.

"Yeah, so what you wanna do?"

"I say that she's not gonna stop until both of us are dead. Do you still got her husband?" he asked, hoping Travis hadn't killed him yet.

"Yeah, I still got 'im, and he's alive and well," Travis told him, looking over at Dillon on the floor, asleep.

"Good, 'cause we're gonna need him. I can be—"

"We," Travis said, cutting him off. "Are you forgetting about my brother? If he's still alive, I'm gonna trade this bloodclaat for him, and that's it. I don't need ya money, so don't try to—"

"All right, all right, all right, calm down, Dread. I understand how you feel, and if your brother is still alive, then we're gonna get him back. Just give me a couple of hours to find out if he's in the city. If he is, then we'll negotiate. Is that all right with you?" Emilio asked, trying to come to some type of understanding.

Travis agreed, but in all actuality, Emilio couldn't care less about Travis and his brother. Right now, it was all about self-preservation, and having Dillon as a bargaining chip to better Emilio's chance of survival just a little more.

Chapter 26

Gloria watched as Raymond walked across the room with only a towel wrapped around his body. He had just gotten out of the shower and was drying off. He was so sexy and handsome. His innocence was pure, and Gloria felt bad that she had exposed him to her way of life. He didn't deserve to be caught up or be a part of something that was so sinister. The feelings that she had for Raymond were becoming deeper and deeper as the days were going by, and at this point, she was more concerned about his well-being, not just the physical portion of it, but also the mental. Hurting people could take a toll, and she didn't want him to lose himself in the process of it all. If anybody knew how fast a soul could get lost in this way of life, it was Gloria.

Gloria struggled once again to get out of bed, but she managed to rise to her feet by herself this time. She wasn't quite ready to walk on her own, so Raymond quickly got up to help her.

"You should be trying to get some rest," Raymond advised as he got up under Gloria's arm. "And where are you going anyway?"

"It's round two," she said, referring to Sam.

Gloria came up empty-handed in her first round of questioning, and that may have been due to her weak physical assaults. She barely got anything out of him concerning Travis and Dillon's whereabouts. Sam literally didn't say a word, only smiling at Gloria the whole time.

"Babe, be careful," Raymond said as they slowly made their way down the hallway. He was more worried about Gloria bleeding internally.

"I'll be fine. I just don't have time on my side right now. If Dillon's still alive, it won't be for long."

Gloria stopped Raymond at the door before she entered the room where Sam was. "Why don't you go back into the room? This is about to get ugly in here, and I don't think you would want to see this," Gloria said, leaning up against the wall.

"I'm not leaving you in this room by yourself with him," Raymond shot back with a concerned look on his face. He thought that Gloria might hurt herself in the process of trying to hurt Sam. Her protest was pointless, because Raymond wasn't leaving her side.

Gloria cracked the door opened and led the way. Sam was lying down on the floor when she walked in. He had the same dumb smile on his face from the previous interrogation. Gloria was pissed off already. She leaned over and whispered something in Raymond's ear. He had a strange look on his face when he heard the request she had made, but without further delay, he walked out of the room.

"You might not wanna talk now, but eventually you're gonna tell me what I wanna know," she said, slowly taking a seat on the bed next to where Sam was on the floor.

His body odor brought water to Gloria's eyes, but in a few minutes, that smell was about to get even worse. Gloria just sat there on the bed, smiling back at Sam. He had stopped smiling out of fear of what was about to happen to him. Some clear and unequivocal understanding was about to be reached, or Sam was about to die the most horrific death imaginable.

Detective Santiago sat in his cubical, looking up at the many pictures he had pinned to his bulletin board.

Most of them were pictures of murder victims who had been killed in or around the Charlotte area, in Raleigh, Greensville, and Bucks County. To the naked eye, all of these unsolved murders would seem coincidental, but for Santiago, he saw something more.

"What are you looking at?" Detective Young asked, walking over with his chair and taking a seat next to Santiago.

There had to be at least twenty-five pictures posted, including the most recent murders like Dion, Carmen, and Detective Cruz. Until Carmen's murder, every last victim had something in common pertaining to the way they were murdered.

"She did it, and it was done quietly," Santiago said, pointing to Dion's picture. "Other than that, it was done somewhere secluded, in somebody's home or in the middle of the night when no one was around," Santiago explained. "You wanna know the crazy part? Everyone died from a hollow point bullet. Drug dealers, gun smugglers, white collar criminals, and two rapists all died in the same fashion: several shots to the body, and two to the head to make sure her victims were dead."

"You think Parker did all of this?" Young asked, looking up at the bulletin board at all the pictures.

Detective Santiago wasn't just sure of it; he knew beyond a shadow of a doubt that this was all Gloria's work. It was too easy in making the connection. She didn't kill for fun. She was paid to do the job, which meant she had a boss, and if Santiago could find the person she was working for, that person could lead him to Gloria. Santiago needed a break in the case, because as of right now, the city of Charlotte had hit a brick wall with trying to find Gloria. One thing was for sure: Santiago wasn't going to get a good night's rest until he found her and the people who held his family hostage in Gloria's escape.

"Aaarrrgghhhh," Jamaican Sam yelled out, forcing Raymond to put the gag back in his mouth. Sam was breathing heavy through the socks in his mouth, looking down at the skin on his chest melting off with the scalding hot grease Gloria had poured on him. The scent of his flesh frying almost made Raymond vomit. With a nod from Gloria, Raymond walked over with a bucket of ice water and poured it onto his chest.

Gloria thought that the sight of Sam's chest would bother Raymond, but it didn't. He stayed cool, calm, and collected.

"Now are you ready to talk?" Gloria asked in her normal tone, looking at Sam with the frying pan still in her hand.

Sam just gave Gloria the mean mug—not exactly the best thing he could have done.

"Do it again," Gloria instructed Raymond, passing him the frying pan.

He took it and left the room.

"After I'm done burning your chest, I'm going to work on your face, and . . ." she said, looking down toward Sam's crotch area.

Sam continued breathing heavily through his gag. Ten to fifteen minutes went by before Raymond came back up the steps with another frying pan full of hot grease. It was so hot you could see the smoke coming off the pan. Gloria reached for the pan, but Raymond pulled it back.

"Let me try something," he said, placing the pan on the floor.

Gloria looked on curiously, trying to figure out what he was up to. He started to pull off Sam's boxers until his dick and balls were fully exposed.

"Oh, shit!" Gloria chuckled, seeing his vicious vision had aligned with her own.

Sam looked at Raymond and then back to Gloria, who simply shrugged her shoulders. Raymond picked up the pan and stood over Sam.

"I promise you, you will never be able to use it again," Raymond said, dripping just a little bit of grease on Sam's thigh.

The hot grease burned his thigh, and a small drop actually hit his balls. He started screaming through the gag, nodding his head hysterically. He wanted to talk now, thinking about how excruciating the pain was going to be. Even if he was going to die, he didn't want it to be like this.

"I'll tell you what you wanna know," Sam yelled out when Raymond took the gag out of his mouth

A knock at the door caught Travis's attention. He cocked a bullet into the chamber of the .45 and headed to the door. Travis had agreed to meet with Emilio so they could come up with the best strategy in order to exchange Dillon for Sam. Emilio informed Travis that he had gotten in contact with Agnis, and she was supposed to be calling him back with the logistics.

"This place was hard as hell to find," Emilio said when he entered the house. "I came alone," Emilio assured, seeing Travis looking over his shoulder.

"I don't trust nobody right now," Travis said, closing the door behind Emilio.

Dillon was bound by his wrists and ankles, lying on the floor next to the couch in the living room. Travis walked past Emilio, tucking his gun into his back waist, then he sat on the arm of the couch.

"So, you must be Gloria's husband," Emilio said, walking over and kneeling down next to him.

He confirmed with a nod. His face was a little bruised, and Emilio could see that he had been doing some crying.

Right at the moment when Travis and Emilio were about to talk, Travis's phone started to ring. Sam's cell number popped up on the screen.

"Yo, Star," Travis answered, getting up and walking off.

Sam started to speak in Jamaican Patois, but Gloria snatched the phone away from him.

"Where is he?" Gloria asked off top.

If Dillon wasn't alive, there wasn't going to be any need for further conversation. Travis walked over to Dillon and put the phone on his ear.

"Yeah, I'm here," Dillon spoke in a low voice.

"Dillon?" Gloria asked, wanting to make sure that it was him.

"Yes, Gloria, it's me," he managed to say before Travis pulled the phone away from his ear.

"Tell me how you wanna do this," Travis spoke.

Unexpectedly, when Travis turned around, a large caliber revolver was pointed at his face, and standing behind it was Emilio.

Gloria was saying something, but Travis couldn't hear her. His focus was on Emilio, and when he went to question what Emilio was doing, he saw a flash. *POP!* The bullet hit Travis right in the center of his head, knocking him backward onto the ground.

Gloria pulled the phone away from her ear after hearing the blast, and for a second she thought that Travis had killed Dillon.

"Hello?" Gloria yelled into the phone, grabbing the gun off the bed and pointing it at Sam.

A few seconds went by before Emilio picked Travis's phone off the ground.

"This must be Gloria," Emilio said into the phone as he looked down at Travis's body lying on the ground.

"Who da fuck is this, and where's the fuckin' dread-head?"

"Ahh. Travis is no longer in charge. You have to deal with me now," Emilio said. "We're gonna do this my way. I want you to kill Agnis, pay me five million for your husband, and give me your word that you'll never come after me." Emilio tried to negotiate.

Gloria hung up the phone in his ear without responding. Emilio looked at the phone, then looked over at Dillon.

"Your wife doesn't seem to care about you that much," he told Dillon.

Dillon was getting tired of hearing that from people, and he was even more crushed when he realized how true that may have been. His life meant nothing to her, and she constantly showed him that time and time again, to the point where Dillon was losing hope that he would make it out of this alive.

"Dumb bitch," he mumbled under his breath.

Emilio heard what he said but didn't say anything. The phone ringing in his hand prompted him to answer it. He knew that it had to be Gloria calling him back.

"Called to reconsider?" Emilio answered.

"This is a one-time offer, so you better make the right choice," Gloria spoke. "Let Dillon go, and I give you my word that I will not kill you. Whatever you and Agnis got going on, that's between y'all. I won't get involved. But let something happen to him, and I will guarantee that everyone that you care about, everybody you love, and everybody that's a part of your organization will perish, and then I will kill you," Gloria promised.

It was no secret to Emilio that Gloria was capable of doing everything she said she would do, and for all purposes rendered, the objective of saving his own life was met, despite the fact that he had to deal with Agnis on his own. His chances were a whole lot better with Gloria out of the way. The offer that Gloria made was one that Emilio couldn't refuse.

"He'll be in a cab before the night is out," Emilio said, then hung up the phone.

"So, now what?" Raymond asked when Gloria hung up the phone. She sat on the bed and went into deep thought for a minute.

"Right now, I need you to go to work and act as normal as possible. Detective Santiago will be watching your movements closely, and I don't want you drawing any unnecessary attention to yourself," Gloria explained, not wanting him to get caught up.

He understood clearly, plus there were a lot things he had to get established at Rev. Index. His undivided attention was going to be required, especially with James up to no good. James was a problem within himself, and though his situation urgently needed to be dealt with, there were other things of importance that Raymond had to deal with. One of them was doing all he could do to stay true to his mother's dream of turning her company into a billion-dollar industry.

"So, what about him?" Raymond asked, nodding at Jamaican Sam.

Now that Travis was dead and Dillon was being released, they had no purpose for Sam. Gloria definitely wasn't going to let him go free so he could come back and kill her. That was out of the question, and Raymond got a sense of that when Gloria looked down at the gun she had clutched in her hand.

"You might wanna step out of the room," Gloria told him.

Raymond shocked Gloria once again when he walked over and sat next to her on the bed. He wanted to watch, and at first Gloria was hesitant, but then she realized that this wasn't going to be the first time he'd seen her kill somebody.

She raised the gun up and aimed it at Sam's face. What happened next threw her for a loop. Raymond reached out for the gun before Gloria had the chance to pull the trigger.

"Let me do it," he said with a straight face.

On hearing that, Gloria immediately pulled the trigger, sending a single bullet into the direction of Sam's face. He died on impact, and without saying another word, Gloria got up from the bed on her own and slowly hobbled out of the room. When Raymond tried to get up and help her, she pushed him away. It was evident that she was mad about something, and Raymond hoped that it wasn't something he said or did. Until Gloria cooled down, he surely wasn't about to find out what it was.

Dillon waved down a cab on 17th Street, where Emilio had dropped him off. He thought that he would have been happier being released by his captor, but the truth was, he was sick and hurt about the way Gloria had treated him. No matter what happened in the future, Dillon wasn't going to forget this mind-blowing experience and all that had taken place.

Chapter 27

Santiago's family was safe, staying with other family members in another state, which gave him more time to focus on the case and piece everything together. Every murder had some type of motive, and the only thing Santiago could think of was the money. Some kill for other reasons: political, or personal, and some kill to balance out the scale of power. None of those stereotypes seemed to fit Gloria. She was a different type of breed, plus she lived a more luxurious lifestyle.

"Money trail," Santiago mumbled to himself, looking up at the pictures on the bulletin board.

The richest person up there was Raymond. He wasn't killed by Gloria, although she did have a contract on him. Santiago thought that his case was worth digging into. He went online to find out more about Rev. Index and how much money the company was worth. A half billion dollars was a nice piece of money, and seeing that Jennifer, the owner, had passed away recently, Santiago continued to dig.

"Jennifer Green fell to her death," Santiago said, looking at his computer screen.

Santiago read that Raymond was the only child and had taken over the company after her death. Santiago sat back in his chair, processing the information he just read. His thoughts raced, and the first concrete thought that came to his mind was that Raymond was meant to be killed by someone in the company, someone who would benefit from it. But who?

Santiago kept researching the company and all those who would be next in line to take over the company. There was another, and that was Jennifer's only sibling, James. Santiago was getting somewhere, and he could feel it. There were a lot of variables to consider.

Detective Young walked in just as Santiago was in thought. He, too, had been doing some research and come up with something interesting.

"You're not gonna believe where this homicide took place," Young said, laying the pictures out on Santiago's desk. It was pictures of Agnis's shop.

Santiago reached down and grabbed the photos while Young explained.

"This is Agnis's Beauty Salon, and that's not even the best part," Young said, inserting a flash drive into his computer.

The surveillance from the restaurant clearly showed the two Jamaicans killing Tish and kidnapping Agnis.

"Now, going back a couple of days earlier, look who comes into the salon and walks to the back with Agnis," Young pointed out.

Santiago sat there in awe. "Anything on this Agnis chick?" he asked.

"Yeah, she had checked into Presbyterian Hospital around the same time we were there watching Gloria. She checked right out the next day," Young explained.

Even more puzzled than he was before, Santiago sat back in his chair and looked to the ceiling. This whole ordeal was getting even more confusing with every day that went by, but Santiago was eager to see this thing through to the end.

"Let's go have a word with Agnis," Santiago said then got up from his chair, grabbed his blazer, and headed for the door.

***

"Raymond, there's two detectives out here waiting to speak to you," Mindy, Raymond's secretary spoke through the intercom on his office phone.

Raymond exhaled in a frustrated manner, got up from his desk with an attitude, and walked out to see what the problem was. When he got there, two new detectives were standing by his secretary's desk. One was holding a briefcase. He figured Santiago sent them to see if they could crack him.

"I already gave Detective Santiago my statement. If y'all have any further questions about the case, you need to speak to my lawyer," Raymond demanded. He was about to walk off.

"Sir, I don't mean no disrespect at all, but I don't know Detective Santiago, nor do I know what case you're talking about. We're here on account of your mother," the young female detective stated, holding up her briefcase.

Raymond looked at both of the detectives, then nodded for them to follow him back to his office. He didn't know what business he had concerning his mother, but he didn't want everybody in his business either.

"What's this all about?" Raymond asked when they all got into his office.

"We're investigating your mother's death, and we were wondering if you thought there was anybody who would want to kill your mother."

The first and only person who came to mind was James, but Raymond didn't mention it. "No, not at all," he replied. "Why would you ask me that? The fall was accidental."

The female detective began to remove some photos from her briefcase and lay them out on Raymond's desk. There were photos of Jennifer's clothing, and more specifically, the blazer that emergency staff removed once she showed up at the hospital. Raymond noticed the foul play from the very moment he laid eyes on the photos. There was half of a footprint embedded on the back of his mother's blazer, indicating to Raymond that somebody had kicked her down the steps or stepped on her back when she was down. The former sounded more feasible to Raymond.

Just the thought of it brought Raymond to tears, but he maintained his composure in front of the detectives. They asked him a few more questions about his mother, and though they knew how crazy it might have sounded to Raymond, they had to question his whereabouts in order to rule him out as a suspect. Raymond said that he was out with a friend.

Seeing that he was apparently hurt about the information they had given him, the detectives ended the conversation and left Raymond with their card in case he came across some information that could help out in the investigation. At one point, Raymond did want to mention his uncle's name, but then came to the final conclusion that he could no longer prolong the inevitable. James being put down was long overdue, and this incident was pretty much the straw that broke the camel's back.

Gloria

I dozed off for a minute, but then I was awakened by the beautiful sound of that chant I'd heard the other day.

"Allahu Akbar, Allahu Akbar . . ."

I got out of the bed as fast as I could, but when I got to the window, I couldn't see anybody. I could still hear the chant, so I kept looking around until I spotted a man in all white, with a white hat on his head, standing at his back door with his hands up to his ear, chanting that sound.

"Allahu Akbar, Allahu Akbar . . ."
I wanted to give him a round of applause, but I thought that might have been a little too much. Instead, I opted to be a little more awkward and try to catch him before he went back into the house. I swear I can't explain what was drawing me to that chant, but I felt compelled to meet this man and see what he was about.

Thankfully, the bedroom Gloria was in had been on the first floor, because anything besides that, she wouldn't have been able to get around the house. When she finally made it to the back door, the man who was calling the chant was gone, but since she came this far, she decided not to turn back around, but to wait a few minutes to see if the guy would come back outside. About fifteen minutes later, he did, taking a seat on his back patio. Gloria slowly made her way outside, disregarding the fact that she was the most wanted person in Charlotte right now.

The man watched as Gloria crossed the lawn and walked up his steps. Gloria was tired and out of breath and could hardly get her words out.

"I'm sorry for bothering you, but I couldn't help but to tell you how beautiful those words you were singing sounded," Gloria said, looking around to check out the area.

The man smiled and got up from his seat. He didn't help Gloria, though she looked like she was struggling to get up onto his patio. "That's how we call the people to prayer. By the way, my name is Simair," he greeted.

Gloria extended her hand out for a shake, but he didn't take it. She thought that was rude, until Simair explained.

"It is not permissible for me to touch you. You are a woman that is not my wife."

"So what? That goes against—"

"The religion of Islam," Simair cut off.

"Oh, so you like one of those Muslims?"

"Yes. I am a Muslim. Have a seat," Simair offered, pulling out a chair from the table under the large green umbrella. "You must be Gloria," he said, shocking the hell out of her. "I noticed you from the news—oh, and Raymond asked me to keep an eye out on you." He smiled. "By no means do you have to worry about me calling the police."

Gloria was starting to regret even coming over there.

"Do you believe in God?" Simair asked, then grabbed the Quran he had on the table.

"Yeah, I believe in God, but I don't think that He's happy with me right now," Gloria answered, putting her head down in shame. "I was brought up as a Christian, but as I got older, I started to see that the church was one big scam to make money."

"Well, Gloria, in the religion of Islam, we believe that there's only one God. No fathers, no sons, and no Holy Spirits. Just one God who deserves all acts of worship."

Gloria put her curious face on, and was dying to ask a Muslim this question. "Why are your Muslim brothers killing innocent people overseas? I mean no disrespect, but ISIS is some cold-hearted muthafu—" Gloria caught herself, feeling that her language was inappropriate.

"What you see on TV—that's not true Islam. But the media makes us all out to be the same. That's like calling all Christians and Catholics child molesters because one priest was tried and convicted of having sexual relations with a minor. If ISIS is running around killing people unjustly, then that's on them. They'll have to bear that burden when they stand before God on the Day of Judgment. But let me be the one to tell you that they don't represent what true Islam stand for, and that's peace."

Gloria sat there for a moment, soaking up all the information Simair was giving her. "What if I killed somebody? Do you think Allah will forgive me for that?" Gloria asked in a sincere manner.

Simair opened the Quran and began to speak in the Arabic language. His recitation of the Quran sounded even better than the call to prayer.

"Allah says in His book: 'And do not kill anyone whom Allah has forbidden, except for a just cause.'"

Gloria let out a sad sigh, thinking that she was doomed in this religion as well.

"But to answer your question, Allah says in His book in Surah An-Nisa 'Verily, Allah forgives not that partners should be set up with him in worship, but He forgives except that, anything else, to whom He pleases,'" Simair explained, making Gloria feel a little better.

She sat there and talked to him about the religion, and even though Gloria didn't think that Islam was the religion for her, she still sat there and listened. It gave her a better outlook and understanding.

"You know, Gloria, you are welcome to come over anytime," Simair said. "I think you are a good person, despite some of the horrible things you may have committed. We all have done wrong before. No one is perfect, except Allah, but let me leave you with this to think about: When you become Muslim and testify that there's no deity worthy of worship except Allah, and that the Prophet Muhammad is the messenger of Allah, all of your past sins will be forgiven, as long as you don't go back to committing those sins while you're Muslim. You will not be held accountable for those sins on the day of Judgment. It will be as if your slate is clean and a new life has begun."

"You mean, whatever I've done in my life before I was Muslim, God won't punish me for it?" Gloria asked with enthusiasm.

Simair closed the Quran, looked Gloria dead in her eyes, and with all sincerity, uttered some words that touched Gloria. "You becoming Muslim and believing in Allah far outweigh anything you could have ever done in your previous life," Simair said, then got up and gathered his things to head inside. "See you here tomorrow at the same time," he said before disappearing into the house.

Gloria smiled then wobbled her way back across the lawn.

Dillon picked up Alisha and kissed her fat cheeks, causing her to laugh uncontrollably. She tried to get away, but Dillon held her tight in his arms, enjoying the laughter and joy he felt being home with his kids. They missed him too, and Anthony had a million and one questions as to where he had been. Anthony also surprised Dillon when he asked for his mother. He obviously missed her, too.

Terry wasn't helping the situation much when he started talking crazy about Gloria and how the cops had run up in his house looking for her.

"Yo, shut up, bro. Not in front of my kids," Dillon snapped. "Come here, Anthony," Dillon said, taking a seat on the floor. He wrapped his arms around him and pulled him in close. Dillon kissed the top of his big head. "I know you want your mom, and I'm sure she's gonna come home soon. But guess what?" Dillon asked, pulling Anthony's head back.

Anthony looked up at his dad with the sad eyes.

"I'm here now, son." Dillon smiled. "And if you start crying, then I'm gonna start crying. You don't wanna see your dad cry now, do you?" Dillon chuckled as he began to tickle him.

Anthony started laughing and trying to protect his sides. Before it was all said and done, he hugged and kissed his dad, and although he missed the hell out of his mom, Dillon being there was going to do for now.

Chapter 28

Agnis had just gotten out of the shower when she heard her doorbell ring, and seeing as how only a couple of people knew where she lived, she immediately walked over to her closet where the security monitors were.

She stood there drying off her hair, looking at Detective Santiago and Detective Young standing out front. Agnis wasn't worried about their presence. If they were there to arrest her, they would have come harder than this.

"Can I help you?" Agnis greeted when she opened the door.

Immediately, Santiago noticed the injuries from where Travis had melted her eyelid shut were still somewhat fresh. Santiago and Young identified themselves, then asked if they could come in to talk to her. Agnis declined, but gave them permission to speak freely from the porch.

"According to the surveillance footage from your salon, one of your employees was killed in cold blood, and then you yourself were knocked out and kidnapped by the same two men," Santiago said. "You checked into the Presbyterian Hospital a few days later."

"Look, I'm gonna tell you guys just like I told the other suits when they interviewed me: my place was robbed. The two guys took me to my place in Raleigh and took fifty grand from me. That's it. That's the end of the story," Agnis told them. "Is there anything else I can help you with?"

"As a matter of fact, there is," Santiago said, pulling out a large photo of Gloria.

"Do you know this woman?" he asked, holding the photo up so Agnis could get a good look at it.

This wasn't Agnis's first ride around the block, and she knew that nine times out of ten, if they were asking this question, they already had the answer to it. Agnis was a little smarter than your average bear.

"Yeah, she comes to my shop to get her hair done. Mainly on the weekends. I think her name is Gloria or something like that. Why? Do you think this woman had something to do with my place being targeted?" Agnis shot back.

"I'm not sure. Have you ever had a conversation with her before, of any sort?" Santiago asked, looking into Agnis's eyes to see if she was lying.

"No, I never had like a full-on conversation with the girl. Like I said, she only just started coming to the shop," Agnis lied, trying to downplay her relationship with Gloria. Agnis and Santiago held eye contact for a moment. It was awkward, but they both wanted to see what the other may be thinking.

"Will that be all?" she asked, rushing the detectives off.

Santiago could feel the negative vibe, but he didn't want to show his hand to Agnis. He cracked a smile, nodded his head, then tapped Detective Young on his arm to let him know that they were leaving.

Santiago felt that he had heard enough lies anyway. He knew everything that came out of Agnis's mouth was a lie, especially when it came down to knowing Gloria. The video surveillance clearly showed Gloria coming into the salon and walking straight to the back with Agnis. They were back there for a while. It looked as though there was some laughter and play before Gloria went to the back, and it also looked like some of the people in the salon knew her. There was no way in the world Santiago was going to fall for that, and just like a lion on a fresh water buffalo carcass, he could taste blood.

Raymond cleared the mound of paperwork from his desk, finally bringing his long day to an end. It was a wonder that he was able to focus considering the information he'd gotten from the detectives that day.

Visions of James kicking his mother down the flight of stairs invaded his mind. Retribution was within in reach. He could see that some of the things Agnis taught him had manifested in his actions, because without Agnis's advice, Raymond would have acted on impulse and probably would have been in prison right now for shooting James in his face in the middle of the factory for everyone to see. Now things were different, and Raymond had all day to figure out the perfect murder.

"Okay, Mindy, I'm on my way home," Raymond said, walking out of his office. As he was walking toward the elevator, he stopped and decided to take the emergency exit; the same one that his mother had taken the day she was murdered.

The blood and all the medical supplies had been cleaned up from the scene, but Raymond could smell death in the air. He pictured how his mother was laid out on the floor with blood coming from her head and his psychotic uncle standing over her. Raymond pushed through the exit door, needing some fresh air. It was raining cats and dogs by the time he got to the parking lot, and as he headed toward his car, a black SUV drove around the ramp and came onto his level. Raymond's hand went for the gun on his waist, and at that point, the SUV had about five seconds before he opened fire on it. Somebody needed to identify themselves, and they needed to do it now, but they didn't.

The car pulled up next to him, causing Raymond to draw his weapon. He aimed it at the driver's side window and was about to let it go. The window rolled down. Raymond hugged the trigger, waiting for any false moves.

Agnis poked her head out and cracked a smile. "Get in," she said with a nod of her head.

Raymond's heart was still pumping when he got into the Dodge Durango. He thought that this was another one of his uncle's attempts to get him out of the way.

"I almost shot you."

"Yeah, I know," Agnis said as she pulled off down the ramp.

"What's going on?" he asked, looking at the rain fall down the window.

"You'll see when we get there," Agnis told him.

She pulled out of the garage and into the heavy flow of traffic. "You know, some detectives came by my house asking me a bunch of questions. They were following me for a while, but then I lost them by switching cars," Agnis said.

Raymond knew all too well how it felt shaking a police tail. He had to do it every day, and every day was a different tactic.

About twenty minutes into the ride, Raymond began to recognize the area they were in. When Agnis pulled up and parked three blocks away from James's house, Raymond looked over at her with curiosity written all over his face. Agnis shut the car off, and the only thing that could be heard was the raindrops hitting the hood of the car.

Agnis looked over at Raymond, who was still staring at her. "I think you know what needs to be done."

***

Detective Santiago contacted Detective Shields and convinced him with the surveillance footage of the salon and the conversation he'd had with Agnis today to get a warrant to search Agnis's home, because Gloria may have been in the house. The affidavit for probable cause to search was signed by a judge in a matter of minutes, and Agnis's door was kicked in shortly afterward. The detectives and the local police ripped her place to shreds, checking every nook and cranny for Gloria or anything that could lead them to her. Though Gloria, nor any evidence pertaining to her, was found, police did find a large amount of cash and confiscated several guns, including hollow point bullets.

"I'm telling you, this girl knows more than what she's telling me," Santiago told Shields.

Their conversation was interrupted by a federal agent who had walked over to them.

"This girl that you're talking about is vicious. People in the Mob call her Agnis," the federal agent spoke.

"The Mob?" Shields asked, giving the agent his full and undivided attention.

Being very familiar with Agnis and the family she was raised under, Special Agent Daniel Grey gave Shields and Santiago a history lesson on the Gambino family that ran the streets of New Jersey back in the late '70s and early '80s. He explained how most of the family was either dead or in prison serving life sentences. Agnis had beaten the Feds twice in two separate indictments. Agent Grey really got their attention when he started telling them about how Agnis was a hitwoman for the family before she moved up in rank and became something like a boss. The Feds knew that she was a major player and still had ties to different Mob families all over the United States and in Italy.

"Some say that nobody was bold enough to tell on her during her reign because of fear, and others say it was out of respect. Whatever the case may have been, she never went to jail, and she stayed under the radar up until now."

Armed with that information, Detective Santiago was now more sure than ever that he was barking up the right tree. Things were definitely becoming clearer now.

"Stay here," Raymond told Agnis as he exited the car. He looked around and then threw his hood over his head and proceeded to walk down the dark street. It wasn't raining as heavily as it had been earlier, but it was still coming down hard enough that Raymond had to keep wiping his face.

Agnis had given him an old .38 revolver so he could take care of his business. Raymond remembered from a long time ago that his mother told him that James had an emergency set of keys hidden in a small box, buried by the corner of the house under a flower pot. He prayed that it was still there, and after creeping up to the house and checking two of the four corner flower pots, Raymond found the extra set of keys. His heart was racing as he looked around nervously. He wanted to make sure that the neighbors didn't see him. The coast looked clear.

"Come on, Raymond. Don't bitch up now," he mumbled to himself, heading up the front steps.

He stuck the key in the door, unlocked it, and pushed the door open. Seeing that the silent alarm went off, Raymond pulled the .38 from his pocket and proceeded to run through the downstairs, gun cocked, aimed, and ready to shoot. The house phone began to ring throughout the house, and Raymond knew that he didn't have much time left.

He darted up the steps and ran right into the bedroom where James slept. There he was, reaching over for the phone on the nightstand. He looked over right before he was about to answer it and saw Raymond standing there with a gun pointed at his face.

"Answer the phone and tell them that everything is fine. Any words outside of that, and I'll shoot you before you can utter them," Raymond said in a threatening tone.

James did as he was told, answering the phone and telling the operator that he couldn't get to his keypad fast enough. He had to give up his code word, along with a number, in order for the operator to believe that he was the owner of the house.

"What is this all about?" James asked Raymond as he hung up the phone. "So, what, you're gonna shoot me now?"

Raymond pulled the wet hood off of his head so James could see him clearly. "How could you kill my mother? How could you kill your own sister?" Raymond fumed, walking closer to the bed. "You ain't shit."

"I don't know what you're talking about," James tried to lie.

Raymond explained everything that the detective had told him about the foot mark on Jennifer's back and how she suffered for days until she passed away. James broke down and began to cry, thinking about what he had done. His conscience had been beating him up ever since it happened.

"I'm sorry, Raymond. I didn't mean for this to happen. I tried to tell her what was best for the company, but she wouldn't listen to me," James cried out.

Raymond had heard more than enough, walking closer to James and pointing the gun at his forehead. "Open your mouth," he told him, pressing the barrel up against James's lips. James opened up and was scared to death, praying that Raymond was only trying to scare him.

"Look at me. *Look at me*," Raymond screamed, thinking about his mother lying dead.

James looked up at him and saw nothing but the devil in his eyes. Without blinking or shedding a single tear, Raymond pulled the trigger, blowing a hole straight through the back of James's head. Brain fragments splattered all over the headboard and onto the blankets.

He stood there for a minute in shock. He couldn't believe he had just killed his uncle. He wiped the gun off with the sheet, then laid it on the bed next to James's body. He felt nothing as he turned around and walked out of the room, throwing his hood back over his head before leaving the house.

Chapter 29

Black Gucci shades, black-with-gold-trim Seven Jeans, a black button-down, and some black Louis Vuitton sneakers. That's what Raymond wore to his mother's funeral. There had to be at least three hundred people who decided to show up to the viewing to show their respect. Raymond, along with other selected family members, sat in the front row. Until now, he hadn't known that he had so many relatives on his mother's side of the family. They came out of the woodwork. Most of them were there only to see if they could get a piece of the millions of dollars Jennifer left behind. Her life insurance policy was worth five million dollars alone, and that wasn't to include what she had left in her last will and testament.

"Have you seen my dad?" Linda, James's older daughter asked Raymond.

"No, I haven't seen Uncle James," he responded. "Did you try calling him?"

"Yeah, but he's not answering his cell or the house phone."

"Don't worry. I'm sure he'll be here any minute. He took my mom's death pretty hard, so this might be a little difficult for him."

"You're right. He's probably somewhere getting drunk." Linda sighed before going back to reading the obituary.

In Raymond's eyes, James didn't deserve to be at his mother's funeral anyway. He was exactly where he should have been.

Raymond felt a little bad at first, but then his heart became like stone, to the point where he had zero remorse for killing his uncle. James took away the most important person in Raymond's life, and the pain from that outweighed everything else. Raymond wished that he could have brought James back to life just so he could kill him again.

The more he sat there and thought about it, the tears he had held back all day found their way to falling from his eyes. He missed his mother, and there were going to be some very rough nights ahead of him.

Gloria was sitting out on the back balcony talking to Simair, and she had been for the past hour. Simair was telling her about some of the things he'd been through when he was back home in Syria. Come to find out, he, too, had his fair share of bloodshed. The most interesting to Gloria was the story he told pertaining to a man who killed one hundred people but was admitted to heaven when he died. It was a story from the days of old, but it was still relevant now.

When it came to Gloria's life and her believing in God and the hereafter, she knew that there was going to come a time when she had to answer for all the people she had killed. In a sense, she was trying to find some peace with her Lord, hoping that His punishment would be lighter. The things Simair was saying about Allah and how forgiving He was sounded too good to be true.

"So, that's your lesson for the day." Simair smiled, standing up from his chair. "Now, if you don't mind, I have to go and tend to my wife," he told Gloria as he collected his cups and books from the table.

"Wife?" Gloria asked with a confused look on her face. "Man, you can't have a wife." Gloria chuckled, not believing him. Since Gloria had been staying next door, she hadn't seen a woman coming in or leaving Simair's house. The only person that she ever saw was him.

"Just because you've never seen her doesn't mean that she doesn't exist."

"Why haven't I seen her then?" Gloria asked jokingly.

Simair stopped, put his books back down on the table, and took a seat. He became serious; not in the form of him being mad or upset, but rather to show the importance of what he was about to say. "Am I supposed to share my wife's beauty with the world?" Simair began. "Am I supposed to entice men with her looks so they can lust off of her? Her beauty is for my eyes only. I safeguard her, myself, from men who don't know any better."

"But I'm a woman. Does that make a difference?"

"We have male neighbors who come outside often just to sit around. My wife is so modest she only wants to be seen outside if it is necessary, and even when she does come outside, she's covered up in the traditional Islamic garments. This is a command from God for women to cover themselves, especially out in the public eye. . . . Now, how do you think Raymond would feel if I was trying to have sex with you?"

Gloria's face got serious.

"Now, imagine you actually fell for my charm and we ended up having sex. Who do you think it's going to hurt the most? It would hurt Raymond. But yet, you sit in front of me with your figure showing through your clothes, with that enticing baby face and lustful eyes. Now, if you were covered up, I wouldn't be able to see you in that light."

"Are you trying to say—?" Gloria questioned him, in shock.

"Not at all," Simair said, cutting her off. "Like I told you, I'm married. I love my wife, and I would never allow myself to see another woman in that light."

"Wow, that's deep."

Gloria thought about it and could understand where Simair was coming from. She knew all too well from first-hand experience. Dillon showed her just how a woman's beauty could entice a man to commit adultery. There were now two lessons Gloria got from Simair today, and they were two well-needed ones, for that matter.

Raymond was the last person to stand at his mother's burial site. Everyone else had dispersed and gone back to their normal lives. For Raymond, nothing was ever going to be normal. He stood there while men poured dirt over her casket, and in his peripheral vision, he could see a shadow approaching from the side. It was Agnis, dressed in a black Tom Ford suit and a pair of pumps. The scent of Acqua Di Gio blended with her cigar smoke as she puffed along.

"We still have work to do," Agnis said, blowing out the smoke.

Raymond stood there, staring at his mother's grave as she continued to talk.

"There's one more threat we need to get rid of," she continued.

"Can't you see that I'm burying my mother?" he shot back.

"Yeah, I can see that, but if you don't hear what I'm trying to tell you, that could be me, you, and Gloria who these guys are pouring dirt over," Agnis told him. "This is the only favor I will ever ask you for."

"Why me?"

"If I didn't think that you were capable of doing it, I wouldn't ask you. Plus, Gloria is not healthy, and sending her would be like committing suicide."

Agnis knew that Gloria was a weak spot for him, and she planned to use that to her advantage. Raymond stood there in silence for a moment, watching the last of the dirt being put on his mother's grave. He really wasn't in the mood to talk, but he decided to hear Agnis out.

"I'm listening," he said, kneeling down and placing a single rose on top of the dirt.

Agnis passed him the folder she had in her hand, which Raymond immediately opened. It was a picture of an older white guy standing in front of a restaurant.

"Who the hell is this?" Raymond asked, staring at the picture.

"That's Emilio, the guy who tried to kill all of us. He knows entirely too much information about us, and he's not gonna stop until he sees to it that we all die. He still has ties with the Mob, so you gotta expect that everyone is on his payroll," Agnis explained.

Also in the folder were several names of businesses he owned and frequented throughout the course of the week. In order to kill Emilio, Raymond was going to have to do his homework.

"I'll take care of it," Raymond said as if he were going to get this done relatively easily.

Not having to say another word, Agnis took another puff of her cigar then walked off, leaving Raymond to finish mourning. Several minutes later, Raymond left the cemetery as well. He wasn't trying to waste any more time with the Emilio hit, so jumping all over this was the plan.

"Did you see that?" Detective Santiago asked Detective Young, as they sat in a different section of the cemetery, watching Raymond. They had had the whole funeral under surveillance, trying to see everyone who showed up. Neither one of the detectives could have guessed that Agnis would be one of them.

Santiago was dying to see what was in the folder Agnis just gave Raymond, and he was almost tempted to blow his cover to do so. Detective Young had to remind him of all that had been accomplished thus far in the case. Santiago ultimately decided against it, but he was going to stay hot on Raymond's tail to find out what he and Agnis were up to.

Rev. Index was closed due to Jennifer's funeral, but Raymond decided to stop by his office to get a jump on the building contracts for the overseas project. They needed to be done by Monday, so there was a little urgency behind it. After that, he planned on checking out Emilio's establishment too.

When Raymond got into the building, there was nobody there but the cleaning crew; at least that's what Raymond thought when he got onto the elevator and headed to the third floor. It was only by mere chance he stepped off the elevator car and saw Dorothy and a well-dressed white man in one of the conference rooms with a bunch of papers scattered about on the table. More than curious about what was going on, Raymond headed for the room.

Both of them were startled when he opened the door.

"Am I interrupting something?" Raymond asked when he walked in.

Dorothy had a dumbfounded look on her face, but she quickly tried to clean it up. "No, we were just going over some paperwork pertaining to your uncle's assets," Dorothy explained.

"My uncle's assets?" Raymond asked with a curious look on his face. "And who is this?" he asked, pointing to the well-dressed man sitting with her.

"I'm sorry, my name is Detective Shields. I'm with the Darby Homicide Unit," Shields introduced, extending his hand for a shake.

Raymond ignored his hand, still confused as to what was going on. "Like I asked before, why are you looking into James's assets?"

"You're telling me you don't know?" Dorothy asked, looking from Raymond to the detective. "James was found dead in his bedroom this morning," Dorothy informed him, not knowing that Raymond was well-aware of his uncle's death.

He had to play it off, falling into one of the conference room chairs. Raymond couldn't muster up a tear to make it look like he was hurt. That's how much he hated James. What he did do was stare off into space as though he were in total shock.

Detective Shields wasn't buying it. He knew all too well how vicious families with wealth could be. From the paperwork he had read thus far, Raymond was inheriting a lot from both his mother's death and his uncle's.

Shields took Detective Santiago's advice to follow the money trail, and it eventually led him to find out that in the event of Jennifer's death, the company would be divided by two people, James and Raymond, with Raymond owning 85 percent and James owning 15 percent. In the event that one of the two died, the other would gain full control of the company.

Detective Shields didn't get a chance to read all of the paperwork, but as it stood, Raymond was in full control of the company, not to mention the large sum of insurance policy money from the deceased. For all Detective Shields knew, Raymond could have killed his mother and his uncle. It was nearly impossible to prove with the lack of evidence in both cases, but Shields had his money on Raymond being at the head of the ship. Hell, he'd been sitting there for the last five minutes, and Raymond didn't even ask how James died. It really showed how concerned he was about his family.

Instead of attacking him and badgering Raymond with a million and one questions, Shields opted to make a speedy exit without tipping everybody off to what he was up to or where his investigation was leading him.

"Well, I have to get back to my office. I will let you know if any new information comes up in your uncle's case," Detective Shields said before excusing himself.

Terry yelled out from upstairs for somebody to answer the house phone that kept ringing downstairs in the living room.

"I'll get it," Dillon yelled back as he walked to the kitchen. "Hello?" he answered. It was silent on the other end, and then a voice spoke to him.

"How are you?" Gloria asked as she stood in a phone booth inside of the bus station.

Dillon's heart began to race at the sound of her voice. He held back his tears, though he felt like crying. "I'm doing better," he answered, taking a seat at the kitchen table. "What about you? Are you okay?

"Yeah, I'm good. I know this phone is probably tapped, and the police are more than likely listening to this call. I just wanted to let you know that I'm sorry things worked out the way they did."

Dillon couldn't hold back his tears. The way Gloria was talking sounded like it was going to be the last time he was going to hear from her.

"For what it's worth, I did love you, and a part of me still does. Whatever happens from here on out, I needed you to know that. I needed you to know that I loved our kids very much too. You know that, right?" Gloria asked, looking around the bus station.

"Yeah, I know, Gloria," he replied, wiping the tears from his eyes.

"And, Gloria . . .?"

The phone was silent, and Dillon was taken by surprise. Gloria had hung up right before Dillon had the chance to truly apologize to her for everything that he did. After careful thought about the whole ordeal, he realized that cheating on her played a major part in everything that went on up until this point. It was selfish of him and uncalled for, especially since he knew and accepted the lifestyle Gloria was living. Dillon had so many "what if" or "should have" regrets constantly running through his mind. The thing was, it was a little too late. The damage was done, and he had to live with it, just as much as Gloria had to live with the choices she made.

Dorothy pulled into Agnis's driveway late that evening. She couldn't wait to tell her about the events that had taken place earlier that day. Agnis was in the house directing the cleaning crew she assembled to put her house back together after the police ripped it apart.

"Hey, baby," Dorothy greeted, walking up behind Agnis and wrapping her arms around her waist. She turned around and smiled before kissing her.

"Damn, you sexy as hell," Dorothy said, looking into Agnis's eyes.

"Tell me something good," Agnis said, turning back around to watch the cleaners.

"A detective stopped by the salon today. He was snooping around, trying to find a motive, I guess," Dorothy explained. "I think he's focused on Raymond more than anything," she said, taking a seat on the couch. "He walked in on us while we were going over James's assets and the percentages divided after Jennifer died."

Agnis walked over to the couch with a confused look on her face. Dorothy eased her worries, though.

"Don't worry. He didn't see it," Dorothy said as she unstrapped her heels.

Thus far, things were going according to plan. It just needed to speed up in order for Agnis's plan to work. Agnis dug into her robe and pulled out her phone and began to dial a number. She couldn't help but notice Dorothy removing some of her clothes in an attempt to get a little more comfortable.

"Are you going to send your workers away so we can have some alone time?" Dorothy asked. "I have something special for you," she teased with lust-filled eyes.

As bad as Agnis wanted to indulge in some of Dorothy's sweetness, she had to make this phone call. It was one she should have already made. She looked down at the screen as the phone started to ring. Then, when Emilio answered the phone, Agnis got up and walked into the other room, not wanting Dorothy to hear the conversation. What she had to say wasn't for all ears to hear.

Gloria was standing in the mirror, looking at her colostomy bag and trying her best to make it look a little less noticeable. She looked for a back brace. She found one with Velcro on the ends, which fit perfectly around her stomach and concealed the bag, all while giving it a little room to function. The bullet wound itself wasn't hurting that much. Sixteen hundred milligrams of Motrin kept the pain at bay. Her challenge tomorrow was going to be walking up and down the steps by herself.

"It's about time," she mumbled to herself when she heard Raymond's car coming up the driveway.

As soon as he walked into the house, she could see from the look on his face that something was wrong. He got no further than the couch before dropping to his knees. Tears poured out of his eyes, and for a second Gloria was expecting for the police to come running into the house to haul her back off to jail. She even walked over to the window to check. But there was nobody outside.

She walked back over to Raymond, who was on the floor, crying his eyes out. With all the strength she had, she reached down and grabbed him by the arm.

"Come on," she said, lifting him to his feet. They walked back to the bedroom, and once there, Gloria sat him on the bed.

"What happened?" she asked.

"My uncle killed my mother," he began, wiping the tears from his face. "He was the one who kicked her down the steps.

Gloria put her head down and let out a sigh of frustration. "Don't worry about it. I'll take care of it," Gloria assured.

Raymond wiped the remaining tears from his face, then looked over at Gloria with an empty stare. Gloria knew that look all too well.

"What did you do, Raymond?" she asked, only to see him putting his head down. She knew right then and there that he had killed him. This was the very thing she wanted to protect him from, but he was hardheaded. He thought that it was going to be easy taking somebody's life, but it wasn't. It was something that he was going to have to live with for the rest of his natural life.

"Damn, I wish you would have let me take care of that for you," Gloria said.

Raymond looked up and could see the sincerity and concern in her eyes. He couldn't explain or understand why, but Gloria was turning him on right now. The love practically poured out of her eyes and into Raymond's heart. He leaned his head up against her and snuck in a kiss. He kissed her again and again, and before he knew it, Gloria was kissing him back.

Raymond smiled, pulling his head back from her. Even with a colostomy bag on, Gloria was ready to go.

"You better stop," Raymond chuckled. "Trust me; when you heal up, I'm gonna give you everything you're looking for."

"Yeah, and I'll be waiting," Gloria responded, then kissed him. Even through the pain of having her spleen removed, she still desired to have him. Raymond was going to make her wait, because messing around with him and how horny he was, Gloria would end up having to be worked on by Anisa from how hard Raymond would give it to her.

Detectives Santiago, Young, and Shields sat in one of the interrogation rooms, going over all the intel they had uncovered so far, which happened to be a lot. Getting the news about James being murdered in his home today, accompanied by his theory about what he thought was going on at Rev. Index, were huge breaks in the case. There were still some things that were unclear about the whole ordeal, but for the most part, Shields had the bulk of the story mapped out. He knew about Gloria working for Agnis as a hitwoman, and that some of the murders in the recent past had similarities that equaled up to the M.O. of Gloria. He knew about Dillon cheating on Gloria and it being the reason why Gloria killed Carmen in TGI Friday's. He knew about Agnis being kidnapped by the Jamaicans and how one of the bodies was found in a studio apartment on top of an old garage on the South side of Charlotte. He eyewitnessed Gloria shooting and killing his partner, and he also knew that somewhere down the line, Gloria, too, was shot. It ultimately led to her getting caught.

Raymond's role in this was relevant and became more serious when he decided to help her. Santiago still believed that Raymond had something to do with the escape, but lack of evidence made it hard to prove. Not only that, but Santiago knew that Raymond had knowledge of Gloria's whereabouts but wasn't going to say a word. However, the chain of events was only a reaction to something that was much bigger.

When Detective Santiago told Detective Shields to find the money trail, it opened up another set of doors that gave them a better understanding as to why all this violence and death was taking place. Rev. Index was worth a little more than a half billion dollars. The throne was up for grabs for the immediate family member who could stay alive. The motive was clear, but some things were still a bit fuzzy. The one thing that all the detectives could agree on was that Raymond was at the center of it all. He held the key, and Santiago felt that if they squeezed hard enough, Raymond would crack. They just had to find out what would it take for him to let his guard down.

Chapter 30

Raymond got to work early, and he could now see why his mother did this every morning. So much work needed to be done in order to run this company, and most of the work landed smack on the owner's desk.

"Breakfast of champions," Raymond mumbled to himself, reaching in his mother's drawer for her stash of scotch. She kept a couple of bottles at hand's reach for those stressful days she underwent.

"Raymond, can I get you anything?" Mindy asked, peeking her head into his office. "There's coffee brewing in the staff lounge."

"No, I'm fine, but what you can do is tell Dorothy I need to speak to her the moment she walks through the door," Raymond said, pouring himself a glass of scotch.

Because of the discovery of his uncle's body that day, Ray was unable to check Dorothy about allowing the detective to snoop through James's financial business, especially without a warrant. She should have known better, seeing as how she was a lawyer and all. Depending on how she responded to the admonishment, it was going to determine whether she kept her job. Raymond had low tolerance for foolishness.

A couple of hours went by before Raymond picked his head up from his desk. He had to sign off on at least one hundred deliveries, read over several contracts, and take a look at proposed stock options, and this wasn't even the tip of the iceberg. There was so much more work that needed to be done by day's end, and from the look of Mindy standing at his door with the "you got a guest" look on her face, Raymond wasn't about to get much done.

"Who is it?" Raymond asked, taking off his glasses and rubbing the corners of his eyes.

Mindy couldn't even get the woman's name out of her mouth before District Attorney Gladice Turner made her way into the office. Mindy started to snap on her, but Raymond raised his hand up to stop her. He knew exactly who Ms. Turner was.

"To what do I owe this visit?" Raymond smiled, standing up to shake her hand.

Turner unbuttoned her blazer and took a seat in the chair in front of Raymond's desk. "Raymond, I'm gonna be honest with you. I have two detectives waiting outside of your door, and if you don't come clean with me about what's going on, I'm taking you to jail today. Now, the only reason why you're not already in jail is out of respect for your mother, but I promise you, if you're not straight with me, you're gonna lose everything your mother worked so hard to build," Turner said without holding any punches.

She gave Raymond something to think about off the bat. The last thing he wanted to do was lose his mother's company by being put in jail, but at the same time, he didn't know what Turner was looking for.

"My mother probably did this the first time you contacted her," Raymond said, reaching for a bottle of scotch. He pulled out two plastic cups and poured two shots.

"I think you might end up needing this," Raymond said, pushing the cup across his desk. "So, what do you wanna know?"

"Everything," the DA said, taking the scotch and throwing it back.

Raymond threw back his shot as well, then sat there in thought for a moment before speaking.

"My uncle tried to have me murdered so he could take over this company when my mother died," Raymond began. "He hired a hitwoman to do it. For a couple of weeks, I drove around with her in my car thinking that she was somebody else."

Raymond told Turner about them finding that Gloria's husband had cheated on her. Raymond denied being present when Gloria killed Carmen at TGI Friday's, but stated he had a feeling that she was going to do it. He broke down the situation about Agnis being kidnapped, and how Gloria asked him to help get her back. He admitted to being at the Plateau when they got Agnis back. He also told Turner that was when Gloria had been shot. He admitted to trying to help her with getting medical supplies for her bullet wound, but then that's when Santiago caught her.

"I know you're probably wondering why I would help her," Raymond said. "But she saved my life."

Raymond told her about the time Doug was going to kill him, and right before Doug could do so, Gloria shot him. Raymond said he felt obligated to help.

"And your uncle?" Turner asked.

Raymond took in a deep breath. "Aside from the fact that I think he killed my mother, I honestly don't know what happened to him. I know he owed a lot of people money. That's why he wanted to take over my mother's company so bad," Raymond explained.

DA Turner sat up in her chair. The look she had on her face became more serious. "Did you help Gloria Parker escape custody?"

"Oh God, no. I may have done some messed up things in my life, but—"

"Where is she?" Turner asked, cutting him off.

"I don't know," he shot back.

"Where is she?" Turner snapped, smacking her hand on the desk. "Don't lie to me, Raymond."

"I swear I'm not lying. I haven't heard from her."

Not in a million years would he be willing to give Gloria up again. He had been through too much with her, and that's where his loyalty stood. The DA didn't know that Raymond was in love with Gloria, and when he loved, he was the type to love hard. It was gonna take a lot more than some yelling and banging on the table for him to change how he felt.

"That's it. I told you everything," Raymond said with a sincere look in his eyes.

Fortunately for Raymond, DA Turner believed most of what Raymond had told her, and it was just enough for her not to haul him off to jail.

"Stick to the distribution business and leave the thugs alone," Turner said, then rose to her feet.

When she finally walked out of the office, Raymond let out a sigh of relief, then laid his forehead on the table. He held his own, but DA Turner was a beast, and she definitely wasn't the one to be played with.

Gloria rested her hands on her head once she got to the top of the steps. This was her third trip up the steps, and she was good and tired. Sheer determination was what had her working so hard. She knew that getting out of the United States wasn't going to be that easy, and she needed her strength and good health to do it.

"Come on, Gloria. Two more times." She spoke out loud to herself. She took in a deep breath before going back down the steps. The moment her foot hit the last step, she could sense that something was wrong. It didn't feel right, and without second-guessing her intuition, Gloria pulled the compact .45 from her sweat pants.

With both hands gripping it tightly, she aimed the gun in front of her and began walking slowly through the house. She cleared the living room and moved onto the dining room, and right before she made it to the kitchen, she felt the need to turn around. She spun around, but it was too late. She turned right into a Glock .40 that rested up against her cheek. She froze, looking at the bulky-looking slide on the gun.

"You're dead," Agnis said, then lowered her gun from Gloria's face.

"What da fuck, Agnis?" Gloria said, letting out a deep sigh. For a second, she had thought that her life was over. "I gotta go change my freakin' colostomy bag," she said, walking off to the bedroom.

Agnis got a good laugh out of that, following behind Gloria. She laughed even harder when she saw that Gloria was serious.

"So, look, I got a way for you to get out of the country," Agnis said, lighting up her cigar.

"Good, 'cause I can't wait to leave," Gloria replied.

"I got some guys in Philadelphia who said they can have you in Africa within three weeks."

Gloria turned and looked at Agnis with one eyebrow up. "What do you mean?"

"You know, the freight boats. You'll be stuck in one of those huge containers the whole time, but you'll have food, water, a TV, and a phone. The thing is, it's a guaranteed ticket out of here. That is what you want, right?" Agnis asked.

Gloria definitely wanted out. Staying in the States wasn't an option if she wanted to stay alive and out of prison. She wasn't too enthused about being in a container for three weeks, but at the end of the day, it was well worth it.

"Since you're here, we might as well talk about the Emilio situation," Gloria said while clamping on a new bag. "I think I can take care of that before I leave."

"Nah, don't worry about Emilio. I'm already in the process of taking care of that. Let's just worry about getting you out of here."

Agnis walked up to Gloria and lightly tapped the side of her face several times. "I lost your dad, and I'm not gonna lose you too," she said with a sincere look on her face.

"A'ight, Agnis, I hear you," Gloria replied with understanding.

On that, Agnis left, leaving Gloria in her thoughts about her dad. She knew Agnis cared about him deeply and wanted the best for him, so anything Agnis asked her to do would be in her best interest. Gloria felt lucky to have somebody like Agnis in her corner.

Dorothy damn near jumped out of her skin when her office door slammed shut. She lifted her head up from the computer and saw that it was Raymond standing there.

"Boy, you startled me." Dorothy smiled, taking off her glasses.

Raymond wasn't smiling, though. "Like I did when I walked in on you and that detective going through my uncle's business? Tell me, Dorothy, what's really going on around here that I don't know about." Raymond could feel that there was more going on than was on the surface. He just couldn't pinpoint exactly what it was.

"Nothing is really going on. That day with the detect—"

"Cut the bullshit, Dorothy. Don't end up on the wrong side of the playing field. You know I don't have a problem putting you out on your ass," Raymond threatened.

Dorothy didn't take too kindly to Raymond talking to her the way he was. It was as if he was trying to belittle Dorothy, which caused her to have an instant attitude. She was about to play right into Raymond's hands.

"You don't have a clue about what's going on in this company, do you?" Dorothy spoke in a more arrogant tone. "Did you really think that you were capable of running one of the largest distribution companies on the East Coast while you run around playing P.I.?" Dorothy said, leaning back in her chair.

"What da fuck is going on?" Raymond snapped, getting tired of Dorothy's riddles. "Tell me now, or you can consider this your last day working here."

Dorothy laughed. "You couldn't fire me if you wanted to. I don't work for you."

"What are you talking about? I own this company."

"You think you own this company. See, while you were off trying to rid the world of cheating spouses, your uncle was selling parts of your company to the Mob," Dorothy mischievously informed.

Raymond stood there in shock, listening to how James got into debt with the Mob. What was even more of a shock was to hear that James had gotten his mother to sign over thirty percent of the company to him. In return, he was using it to clear his debt with the Mob. He cut them in 15 percent of the company. It was mind-blowing, but it made total sense to him. If James had succeeded with getting Raymond out of the way, he would have had a whopping 85 percent of the company to himself. He still would have been a multimillionaire.

"You know I'm not gonna let the Mob have any parts of my mother's company," Raymond assured. He had it set in his mind to kill any and every Mob member who had something to do with the conspiracy.

"And, yeah, I know what you're thinking," Dorothy said, gathering some things from her desk. "But I can assure you that the Mob is probably thinking the same thing," she said, then headed out the door.

She didn't tell Raymond right then and there, but the rules of ownership still applied, which meant that if Raymond would have died, his portion of the company would go to the Mob, and vice versa. His only problem lay where he had no idea who and what Mob members owned the 15 percent, and until he found out who it was, he wasn't going to be able to kill anybody. The person who was in possession of the documents pertaining to that issue was walking out the door.

In Raymond's eyes, Dorothy was playing for the other team, and that meant she was liable to get the same treatment.

"So, are you going to charge him with something?" Santiago asked DA Turner when he walked into her office.

"I can charge him with aiding and abetting, but what's that gonna do? He'll bail out, and his attorneys will make a big deal about the delay in prosecution, plus the previous deal we had with them for immunity covered what he had confessed to already. And nine times out of ten, the judge will side with them if we tried to challenge or take back the deal," she told Santiago.

"But he knows where she's at," Santiago protested, thinking that putting Raymond in jail would make him crack.

The DA disagreed and wasn't going to waste the court's time with a case she wasn't certain of. There was a lot going on with that situation, and though it seemed as though Raymond was pulling all the strings in a battle over the company, Gloria was the only person they desperately wanted to get off the streets, and they had plenty of evidence to do so.

"I know you might not want to hear this, Detective, but you're gonna have to be patient in bringing in Ms. Parker. One thing I'm sure of is that she'll slip up. In the meantime, keep your eyes on Raymond. I noticed something about him while I was interviewing him, and that's the fact that he actually loves this girl. And if I know anything about love, it's a guarantee they won't be able to stay apart," DA Turner advised. She wasn't slow or dumb by a long shot, and she'd been in the criminal justice system long enough to know that people like Gloria always got caught. It was only a matter of time, and the charge of murder in North Carolina didn't have a statute of limitations. Even if she got away for now, Gloria would be running for the rest of her life.

Chapter 31

It had been a couple of days since Raymond had been to work. He'd been laying up with Gloria, trying to spend as much time with her as he could. Not knowing how things were about to play out concerning the Mob and the company, one thing he was fixed on was not allowing the Mob to have any parts in something his mother bled, sweated, and cried over building. He would kill everything moving or burn it to the ground before he let that happen.

"I need to talk to you about something," Raymond said, looking down at Gloria resting her head on his chest.

"Yeah, what is it?"

Raymond hesitated, and then decided not to speak about what was going on. He didn't want to make Gloria upset, plus she wasn't in the best of health to be able to help him with it.

"I was thinking. How would you like to work with me at Rev. Index? You said you wished you could live a normal life."

"How would I look working for you?" Gloria chuckled. "You know I don't like to be bossed around, especially by my man."

"You must didn't hear what I just said," he went on, sitting up in the bed. "I said I want you to work with me, not for me. I want you to be my partner, not just as my woman, but in everything that I do," Raymond expressed. "I'm starting another company in China, and I want you to be the face of it while I continue to run our United States branch."

He was itching to tell her about the Mob trying to take parts of the company. He really didn't feel completely safe unless he had Gloria riding with him on this one. When her health was at 100 percent, there wasn't anybody in the Mob who would be stupid enough to play games with Gloria. She killed professionally and did it at an all-time high.

"Listen, baby, you will always have me in your corner, but the thing is, you gotta be able to walk on your own two feet without the help of others. You're good at that. That's one of the many reasons why I fell for you the way I did. Look at me, Raymond," Gloria said, turning his chin so he faced her. "You're probably the smartest guy I know, and from being around you, I know for sure you don't need my help."

Raymond sat there and was upset on one hand that she didn't take him up on his offer, but on the other hand, he was flattered that she had so much confidence in him. It actually made Raymond want to believe that himself.

Detective Santiago heard everything DA Turner said about being patient, but being patient wasn't his thing. He needed to put pressure on Gloria so she'd show her face once more. The only thing Santiago thought that would get her to do that was if he threatened the people she loved the most. That's what led Santiago to Dillon's house. He could hear kids playing around inside when he stepped onto the porch.

Dillon answered the door, still smiling from play wrestling with Anthony on the living room floor. His smile turned into a frown when he saw that Santiago was standing there.

"She's not here," he said, shaking his head. "If you really feel the need to check—"

"No, I know she's not stupid enough to be here," Santiago interrupted. "But I need you to give her a message for me the next time she contacts you."

Just then, little Anthony walked up and stood next to Dillon at the door. Santiago looked down at him and smiled, then looked back up at Dillon.

"Tell her if she don't contact me in the next day or two, I'm gonna start taking it out on you and your family," Santiago said, looking down at Anthony. "Tell her not to force my hand."

"Are you threatening me and my kids?" Dillon asked, pushing little Anthony back into the house. "You might wanna be careful of what you ask for. You know when Gloria comes, there's no talking involved." Dillon was implying that Gloria wasn't the one Santiago wanted to mess around with.

"Did you forget who you was dealing with? I'm the police, and if anybody could make your life difficult, it will be me. I'm not fucking around with your wife anymore. Make sure you give her my info," Santiago said, passing Dillon one of his cards.

Dillon looked down at it and wasn't about to take it, but Santiago threw it at his feet, then turned around and walked off.

Dillon stood at the door and watched him get into his car. Eventually, after Santiago pulled off, he reached down and picked up the card. He was hoping that Gloria would call so he could tell her what Santiago said. When it came down to her family, Gloria never had a problem addressing any issues that arose. It was a guarantee that Santiago wasn't going to like it when he did get what he was looking for.

Dorothy took one last look in the mirror to make sure her outfit looked okay. She was about to head to the Rev. Index building to grab a few things, and then she was off to meet up with Agnis for lunch. Her whole day was planned out, and at the end of it, she was hoping to be in a better position concerning the company. A lot of promises were made to her for her services, and cashing in on them was at the top of her agenda.

"Damn, you still got it," Dorothy said, blowing herself a kiss before leaving out of her bedroom. When she opened the front door to leave, Raymond was standing there with the screen door open and with a gun pointed at her. Dorothy tried to slam the door, but Raymond stopped it with his feet, then barged his way in.

"You really must have a death wish," Raymond said, raising the gun up to Dorothy's face.

She raised her hands, trying to hide behind them. Raymond backhanded her with the gun, knocking her to the ground. The blow instantly put blood in her mouth. Dorothy barely got a word out before Raymond cracked her again.

"Please don't kill me!" Dorothy yelled as she spit blood from her mouth.

Raymond stood over her with the gun in his hand. "I want a name. Who is it my uncle sold parts of my mother's company to?" Raymond snapped.

Dorothy spit out more blood then looked up at Raymond. "I need your word that you're not gonna kill me," she pleaded, trying to negotiate for her life.

"I'm not promising you shit. Tell me or die," Raymond said, taking the safety off of the gun.

Telling him what he wanted to know would only improve her chances of staying alive. "It's a guy named Emilio Castillo. People call him Emilio," Dorothy began. "Now, I told you what you wanted to know, so please let me go," she begged. "The paperwork is right over there in that briefcase."

Raymond saw the case sitting on the side of the couch. He walked over and grabbed it. Its content were exactly what he thought it was. His mother's will, life insurance policies, and the papers James got Jennifer to sign when they heard about Raymond's involvement in the cop shooting. Raymond didn't have time to sit and go through every page, but as long as he was in possession of them, he would get around to them. Right now, there were more pressing issues that needed to be dealt with, and it started with Dorothy.

"Oh God, no!" she cried out, watching Raymond walk back over to her. Raymond let off a single shot, hitting Dorothy in her chest. The bullet blasted through her chest and out her back. With the briefcase in hand, Raymond stepped over her dead body and walked out of the house, but through the back way.

"*Assalamu aklaikum*," Gloria greeted, walking across the lawn to Simair's house. Gloria did know that much about Islam.

"*Wa alaikum assalaam*," Simair returned.

Gloria was about to take a seat in the beach chair, but Simair stopped her. "Let's go inside," he offered, opening the back door for her.

This would be the first time Gloria had been inside his house. It was beautiful inside. "Are these yours?" she asked, pointing to the mantel. There were several plaques and trophies on it.

"Nah, those are my wife's," Simair said in a proud manner. She's a doctor. Come on. Let me show you something." Simair led Gloria down the basement steps to a plush activity room, equipped with a pool table, big screen TV, and a section that looked like it was for praying only.

"This is my man cave," Simair announced, spinning around with his hands in the air. This wasn't even the best part about it. Simair walked over and punched in some numbers on the keypad up against the wall. It didn't look like anything at first, but then the wall shifted over a little. It was a room within a room, and inside was several shelves of handguns, assault rifles, and more. There were small .22-caliber Dillingers, .50-caliber Desert Eagles, AR-15s, and AK-47s. Simair had scopes, beams, and bulletproof vests, and it looked like he was ready to take on a small army.

"Now, these are my babies," he said, taking one of the AR-15s off the shelf. The whole basement was soundproof, and he even had a little firing range where he fired his weapons on a daily basis.

"You sure you're not some kind of terrorist?" Gloria joked, reaching for her favorite gun, which was the Glock .40

Simair laughed. "I'm positive I'm not a terrorist," he shot back. "Now, follow me. I wanna see how you shoot."

He led Gloria to the back of the basement for what he called play time. This was something Simair loved to do, and Gloria was about to see just how good he was at it.

Emilio wasn't at six out of the ten places Agnis had listed in the folder she gave Raymond. The last of them was a meat market on the south side, where Raymond had just pulled over to watch. He was a good block away with his car facing the establishment, and through a pair of binoculars he watched attentively. He also watched Detective Santiago and Detective Young out of his rear-view mirror. He knew they were following him ever since he picked up his car at Rev. Index's parking garage about an hour ago.

"You might as well walk up, knock on my window, and let me know that you're following me," Raymond mumbled. He was about to have fun with them and go around the block a few times, but then two black Tahoes pulled around the back of the meat market. Raymond leaned back in his seat with the binoculars.

It was obvious who Emilio was when he got out of the front passenger's side of the Tahoe. Raymond didn't even have to look at his picture to know that it was him. His security gave it away when they surrounded him as he made his way to the back door.

Raymond's cell phone ringing diverted his attention for a minute. "Yeah," Raymond answered, putting Agnis on speaker.

"I think our friend is making rounds," she said.

"I'm already on top of that. I'll give you call tonight," Raymond said, then hung up the phone.

Emilio disappeared inside but not before Raymond marked the time he arrived. He also got the make and model of the vehicles he came in, and how many men he had with him. If it weren't for the fact that Santiago and Young were watching him, Raymond would have made a strong effort to get this done now. It would have to be another day. Right now, Raymond had to shake the detectives before they got too nosey. He gave Emilio less than twenty-four hours to live, and not a minute over.

"What in the hell is he doing?" Detective Santiago asked, watching Raymond's car just sitting there. "Is he watching us?"

"I doubt it. He's probably just waiting for somebody," Young said.

"Oh, shit. He's on the move," Santiago alerted. He threw his car into drive and pulled off into traffic. He followed behind Raymond at what he thought was a safe distance, but Young knew that Santiago was too far behind.

"Don't lose him," Young told Santiago, feeling that the fun and games were about to start.

They'd been trying to follow Raymond home every night to see where he was resting his head, and every night he evaded them, using a different route. This time wasn't any different. Within minutes, Santiago lost Raymond's car in traffic and damn near got himself lost in the process. He ended up in Greensborough somewhere. Raymond was good. So good that Santiago decided tomorrow, he was going to have multiple units following him. That was the only chance Santiago would have in finding out where Raymond rested his head. If he could find out where Raymond went every night, Santiago hoped it would lead them to Gloria.

Agnis drove over to Dorothy's house to see why she didn't make it to meet her earlier. Several police cars and the coroner were sitting out in front of her house. Nosey neighbors were talking to police officers and detectives on the scene. Before she rode completely past the house, she saw the coroner rolling a body out the front door.

"What in the world?" she mumbled to herself. For fear of being asked a bunch of questions she didn't feel like answering, Agnis kept driving, getting as far away as possible. All kinds of thoughts ran through her head, but there was only one that made sense. Raymond must have found out Dorothy had something to do with the possible takeover of his mother's company. Just thinking about it made Agnis a little nervous. She wondered how much information Raymond knew. Was he aware of her involvement, and would Agnis be next on his list? She had made it this far and was close to obtaining the objective. A bullet in her head would really put a dent in Agnis's plans. It was time for her to press the issue a little harder.

Gloria lay on the pool table with a towel covering her face so she wouldn't have to see what was going on. Simair's wife had examined Gloria and found that the colostomy bag could have been taken off, even though it was still a little early. It took her every bit of three minutes to pull the long tube out of Gloria's intestines, and it took another five minutes to stitch her up. After she finished, Simair's wife went back upstairs to let Simair know that she was done. It was like nothing never happened. Simair waited until Gloria got fully dressed before coming back downstairs to talk to her.

"How do you feel?" Simair asked, passing Gloria two painkillers. "This is the good stuff, too." He smiled.

She sat up on the pool table, took the two pills, then reached down and lightly rubbed her fingers across the stitches. "Damn, she's good," Gloria said, barely able to see the incision. It may have been a little bit early for the bag to come off, but Gloria's body was healing rather fast. She was getting stronger with every day that passed, and though she wasn't nearly at 100 percent, she definitely was a lot more mobile than before.

"I really appreciate this, Simair," she told him. "I've only known you for a few days, and you have already been a better friend to me than most of the people I've known my whole life.

"It's nothing," Simair said in a modest tone.

"Nah, it is something, and I hope one day I'll be able to return the favor," Gloria added.

Simair smiled. He understood Gloria and what she was going through. Samir also had his fair share of wrongdoing and wasn't proud of it. He could see the same sincerity he found in his own heart inside of Gloria's eyes every time she spoke. Her constant inquiring about whether God would forgive her showed him that Gloria was remorseful. In Simair's eyes, a person who had a heart like that always had the ability to change, and at this point, that was all Samair hoped for with Gloria: a change for the better.

Chapter 32

Raymond sat on the back patio with Gloria, but he knew that his time with her was going to be limited today. There was a major staff meeting at the company to go over the new contracts with china to lease out one of their factories and an office building. He also had to make the decision on who to send over there to oversee the new company.

"You sure you don't wanna do it?" Raymond asked as he rubbed Gloria's bullet wound lightly. He thought he would try one more time before he appointed somebody else to do it.

Gloria chuckled at the thought. "I don't wanna work for ya bossy ass. You gon' drive me crazy. It's bad enough I'll have to deal with you on an everyday basis."

"I'm not bossy," Raymond said, smacking her leg. "A'ight it's cool, but bae, I want you to know that whatever you decide to do with the rest of your life, I'm gonna back you. Anything I got is yours," he assured her.

Gloria was certain Raymond had love for her, but she was the type of woman who made it on her own. It was true that she killed for a living, but besides that, she was very intelligent and book smart. She could have done anything she put her mind to, and that included running a multimillion dollar company if she wanted to.

"You know I love you, right?" she said, slowly rolling on top of him.

"Do you really?" he shot back, looking up into her eyes.

Gloria didn't just say it because she thought it was the right thing to say at the time. She really did love Raymond and couldn't begin to explain how he had broken her guard down so fast.

"Yes, I love you," she said, leaning in to kiss him.

Raymond gently rolled her onto her back and pulled at her boy shorts with a seductive smirk on his face. It seemed like in a blink of an eye, the hairs on Gloria's back had stood up, and her heart began to race.

"Something's wrong."

When she lifted up, silence settled throughout the whole house. Gloria got up from the bed and walked over to the bedroom door. Raymond looked on, trying to figure out what was going on.

"Get up and get dressed," Gloria whispered, reaching for the gun on the nightstand.

Raymond got up and was dressed in record-breaking time, then grabbed his gun from the floor. "What's wrong?" he whispered back, walking over to the window to see if anybody was outside. Raymond immediately noticed the black SUV sitting in front of the house. They were Emilio's men. There was a man leaning up against the driver's side door, with his hand rested on his hip like he was holding onto a gun. A second SUV was in the middle of the block, also with a man standing out in front of it.

"I think it's the cops," he said, prompting Gloria to walk over to the window.

Gloria knew how the cops would come, and this wouldn't have been the way. She walked back over to the bedroom door, and that's when all hell broke loose.

POP POP POP POP POP POP POP POP! Bullets nearly missed Gloria's head as she dropped to the ground. Raymond dipped behind the dresser, cocking a bullet into the chamber. He reached around and let off multiple shots into the hallway. *TA TA TA TA TA TA TA TA TA TA TA TA TA TA TA !!*

The gunman who was in the hallway let bullets fly, knocking chunks of wood off the door frame, blowing holes in the walls the size of tennis balls, shattering the vanity mirror and taking out the flat screen TV on the wall. This definitely wasn't the cops.

A brief pause in the shooting gave Gloria time to get to her feet. She came out of the room firing, hitting the first gunman she encountered at the top of the steps. The second gunman slipped into the hallway bathroom before Gloria could get the shot off.

Raymond came out of the room, firing at the walls of the bathroom from the hallway. Chips of sheet rock flung into the air. Gloria headed for the steps with her gun aimed in front of her. Shockingly, the gunman who Gloria shot wasn't at the bottom of the steps. Looking around, she could see a man running across the lawn toward the SUV.

Gloria ran to the door but was met with heavy gunfire. She dropped to the floor, backing away from the front door on her butt. The engine of the SUV could be heard roaring as it sped away.

"Gloria!" Raymond yelled out from upstairs.

Her adrenaline pumping rapidly made it easy for Gloria to run up the stairs to Raymond's aid. He was coming out of the bathroom with his gun in his hand.

"I got 'im. He's dead," Raymond said, walking up to her. The sound of sirens could be heard in the distance, and they were coming their way.

"We gotta get out of here," Gloria said, walking back into the bathroom to get something.

"I can't leave," Raymond said, standing at the door.

"What do you mean?" Gloria shot back with a confused look on her face.

This was Raymond's father's house, and when the police got there, they were going to be asking a lot of questions. Raymond needed to be there to answer them, especially with a dead body to explain. He knew that it would fall back on him anyway.

"A'ight, you stay here," Gloria agreed, throwing the small duffle bag over her shoulder. I'll be in Raleigh at the Fox Manor Hotel, under the name Marcia Green." She kissed him then headed for the steps.

"I love you," was all Raymond could say before Gloria was gone. He walked down the steps, sat at the front door, and waited for the cops to get there, which was only seconds after Gloria left. He already had his story mapped out, and with the back door broken into, bullet holes all around the house, and one of the dead gunmen there, an attempted abduction sounded believable.

The Camden County homicide detectives had Raymond down at the police station for well over three hours, questioning him about what happened in the house. The story that he gave was a little shaky and didn't fully add up to all the evidence that was in the house. The detectives were insisting that someone else had to have been there with him, considering all the different shell casings that were found. Without any further evidence to support the detectives' claim, nor any evidence to charge Raymond with anything, they had to let him go.

"Mindy, we're gonna have to reschedule the meeting," Raymond said when he was finally driving back to Charlotte.

"Mr. Green, everybody is still here, plus you have some people from the bank here that really want to speak to you," Mindy spoke. "Look, Raymond," she said, getting on a more personal level with him. "Whether you like it or not, you're the boss. and if you even think about walking in your mother's shoes, you need to make yourself available for the important things," Mindy sincerely advised.

Raymond couldn't deny the fact that she was right in every word that she spoke. "Thanks, Mindy, and please let everybody know that I will be there in about a half hour," Raymond told her as he came up on a red light.

Raymond kept Mindy on the line to go over the agenda for the meeting, and what exactly the bank wanted to talk to him about. When the light turned green, Raymond stepped on the gas. As he was crossing the intersection, a car ran the red light and ended up crashing into the front passenger's side fender, spinning Raymond's car 180 degrees until his front driver's side fender smashed into the car that was behind him. His airbags deployed instantly, busting him in the face so hard that it knocked him out cold. He was almost ejected from the car, but thankfully, he had his seatbelt on.

People got out of their cars to try to help him, prying Raymond's door open to get him out. He wasn't dead but knocked unconscious, and he would remain that way until the ambulance got there.

Gloria put her aviators and her fitted cap on before she walked into the bus station to use the pay phone. It was pretty crowded, so the chances of anybody noticing her would be slim. She picked up the phone and dialed Dillon's number. She knew that his calls were still being monitored by the law, so it was in her best interest to talk fast.

When Dillon picked up the phone, Alisha's loud cries soared through the receiver. "Hello," Dillon answered with distress in his voice.

"Dillon, it's me. I need you to stop whatever it is that you're doing."

"Gloria, that cop came by here threatening to do something to me and the kids if you don't contact him," Dillon yelled into the phone. "I really don't want to leave the house right now. I don't know what he got planned."

"Dillon, calm down," Gloria told him. "Listen to me. Do you remember where our backup money is?"

"I think so. I mean, yeah, I know where it's at," Dillon replied.

Gloria was so pissed she had to move the phone away from her ear. She inhaled and then exhaled before getting back on the phone. "A'ight, take that money and go somewhere far away. Don't even tell me where you're going. Just got now, and don't waste another minute," Gloria said in a serious tone.

"Okay, okay," Dillon said, getting up from the couch. Dillon tried to say something else, but the phone went dead. Gloria had hung up before he could get a word out. She stormed off, mad as hell that Detective Santiago crossed the lines by threatening her family. She knew that it was a setup move, and she was trying so hard not to fall for it. Though her and Dillon weren't together right now, her kids were still the most important people in her life. For them, Gloria was willing to go as hard as she needed to, and she didn't care about the consequences. Santiago was playing with fire, and had better pray that Gloria had mercy on him whenever she caught up to him.

"How da fuck did you miss him?" Emilio yelled out at his crew while they stood lined up in his living room.

Emilio smacked one of his men damn near across the room, then turned and mugged another. He was pissed that they had missed the opportunity, and Emilio knew that it would take nothing less than a miracle for another opportunity like that to present itself.

"I want you to find that bitch and that fuckin' muli and kill both of them," Emilio snapped. Just when Emilio was about to smack another one of his men, Frank walked in from the other room with that miracle Emilio was hoping for. One of the guys in the SUV saw Raymond's car crashed up by the Mint Bridge.

"He's in Presbyterian Hospital right now, but there's no signs of her," Frank informed him.

Emilio stood there in thought. At this point, and with a new offer on the table to take his business to another level, Emilio wanted Raymond and Gloria dead at any cost. Not only that, but his life depended on it. With that being at stake, he was willing to raise the bar a little higher.

"I got a million on his head, and two million for Gloria's. I don't care what it takes. Just get it done," Emilio said, then walked off.

His boys wasted little time dispersing, all wanting to get the easy target, which was Raymond. Gloria was like a ghost at this point and couldn't be found, so it was pointless going after her. On the other hand, there was Raymond, in one of the city's most unsecured hospitals. Raymond wasn't safe at all. He had a cold million dollars on his head, and with a group of up-and-coming gangsters coming after him, Raymond was as good as dead.

Chapter 33

Detective Santiago casually walked through the bus station wearing civilian clothes to try to blend in. Gloria was right about Dillon's phone being tapped. Santiago was able to get a trace on the call, which led back to the bus station.

It had been a few hours since the initial phone call, so Santiago wasn't too convinced that Gloria was still there, but in the event that she was, he was locked, loaded, and ready to go. After making his rounds, Santiago determined that she wasn't there.

"Excuse me. I'm with Charlotte Police Department, and I was wondering if you recognized this woman being here today," Santiago said, showing the cashier a picture of Gloria. She couldn't remember her, but called out for another cashier to come over. That cashier didn't notice Gloria either. Santiago was getting frustrated.

"Do the surveillance cameras work?" Santiago asked.

Santiago needed clearance from the manager in order to see them, and when he did finally gain access to the footage, he recognized Gloria immediately, standing at the phone booth by the bathroom area. Even through the glasses and the hat, he knew it was her.

"Where is she going?" Santiago asked, pointing to Gloria on the monitor.

One of the security guards quickly went out and grabbed the female cashier to figure it out.

"Oh, I can tell you exactly where she's going," the young female looked into the monitor and said. She remembered Gloria because she thought that she was cute and had made a joke to her about all the beautiful women leaving the city. The cashier paused. "I'm gay, just in case you were wondering," she told Santiago in a joking manner. "She bought a one-way ticket to Atlanta. That bus left about an hour ago."

Santiago wanted to make sure Gloria was indeed on the bus before he pursued it. Being about an hour out, the bus had to be close to South Carolina, and it was about to make a quick stop in Charleston.

"Wait, where did she go?" Santiago asked, looking at Gloria in the monitor, walking out of one of the doors.

"Oh, that's the doors that lead to the bus terminal," the cashier answered. "She's definitely on that bus."

On hearing that, Santiago took out his notepad and wrote down all the bus's information: the identification number, the license plate number, how many people were currently on the bus, and the driver's full name. After doing so, Santiago bolted for the door in hot pursuit of the bus. It didn't matter where Gloria had plans on going, Santiago was going to follow behind her until the end of time, and he hoped that he caught up to her before some other police agency did.

Raymond woke up with a banging headache and knew from the way his side was hurting that at least one of his ribs were broken. He couldn't see the knot that was on the side of his head, but he could feel that bruise, too, along with the black eye from the airbag busting him in his face.

"Ahh, I see you have awakened," the male nurse said.

"How long have I been out?" Raymond asked, trying to sit up in the bed.

"A couple of hours. Aside from the two broken ribs you sustained, you had a slight concussion," the nurse reported.

"I gotta get out of here," Raymond said, pulling the IV needle out of his hand. "Where's my clothes?" he asked, looking around the room.

The nurse rushed over to him, not wanting Raymond to hurt himself by trying to get up and walk. "Whoa, whoa. The doctor is waiting for the results of the CT scan to come back to make sure you didn't have any major head trauma. That and your blood work should be back any minute."

Raymond felt like shit, but he didn't want to stay there knowing that he had other important things to take care of.

"He should be right here," a loud voice said from the door of Raymond's room. Mindy and her girlfriend walked right into the room without knocking.

"Oh my God, are you okay?" Mindy asked, walking up and giving Raymond a soft hug. When she heard the accident happening over the phone, she immediately left the Rev. Index building in search of where the accident occurred. It took her all the way up until now to find Raymond.

"I don't know what happened. One minute I was at the light, and then the next minute, boom!" Raymond said.

The nurse told them that the police said it was a drunk driver. That was helpful, because Raymond thought for a moment that it might have been one of Emilio's boys.

"I gotta get out of here," Raymond leaned over and told Mindy. He had to make sure that Gloria got to her destination. Raymond knew that she was liable to go off and take care of that Emilio situation on her own. As much as she was capable of doing it, he wanted to be by her side to make sure that it got done and she made it out alive. First things first, and that was getting out of the hospital. It had to be done before the night was out. The notion didn't look promising, considering the look the doctor had on his face when he walked into Raymond's room.

Detective Santiago finally caught up to the bus, but just as he thought, Gloria wasn't on it when it made the stop in Charleston. It was a waste of time and energy, and Santiago could only blame himself for not giving Gloria a little more credit.

"Damn, damn, damn!" Santiago yelled, smacking his steering wheel while he drove down the highway. He was tired of Gloria being one step ahead of him, and it was a sure thing that Santiago was going to have one of those frustrating nights. He was going home feeling defeated once again, and he wasn't going to get any rest behind it. He was never going to sleep well until this whole ordeal was over with. Gloria had become more than just a criminal to Santiago. She had become an obsession, one that wasn't going to be kicked easily.

Chapter 34

All heads turned in the Rev. Index building when eight men all dressed in tailor-made suits got off the elevator and walked down the hallway toward the conference room where the party was about to begin. Leading the group of men to the victory of taking over the company,was none other than Agnis, a woman everybody was about to get to know.

"Good morning, everyone," Agnis announced when she walked into the room. The meeting Raymond was supposed to have the other day was postponed until today, and though doctors didn't want to release him until his second CT scan came back, Raymond decided to participate in the meeting via Skype.

"Look at this. My seat is already reserved," Agnis joked, tapping one of her men. She took a seat at the head of the table and pushed the TV screen to the side.

"And who are you?" Jeff from accounting asked with his face twisted up.

The men that Agnis came with had positioned themselves around the table. Agnis lifted her briefcase onto the marble table and popped it open. "I am now officially part owner of Rev. Index," she said, sliding a copy of the updated paperwork establishing percentages of the company to certain persons in the event death was to occur.

Everyone began reading through the forms, even the new lawyer, Salina Vasquez, whom Raymond recently hired. Agnis also had her attorney there, just in case anybody tried to dispute her claim.

"This is some bullshit," Jeff spoke out. "This can't be right," he said, looking at Salina for answers.

Mindy jumped right on her phone to call Raymond to let him know what was going on. She got up and walked up to the TV screen so she could get Raymond in on the conversation.

"You know, you people are so fuckin' dramatic. I tell you, there's gonna be a lot of changes around here," she said, pulling out a cigar.

Mindy turned the TV around so everybody could see Raymond when his face popped up on the screen.

"Is this really happening?" Agnis joked, looking at Raymond on the screen.

"What's going on, Agnis?" Raymond asked with his face frowned up.

Agnis sat back in her chair, taking a pull of the cigar, then blowing the smoke at the TV. "It's the takeover, Raymond, and you know I really do like you," she said, pointing her cigar at him. "The thing is, I like other things too. Things like money, power, and respect. This company provides me with all of the above."

"Agnis, you must have lost your mind. What makes you think you can have parts of my company?"

Salina cut in before Agnis could respond. "According to these documents, your uncle and mother made a very specific agreement in the event of your mother's death." Salina continued reading the paper. "If these documents are authentic, which I can see that they are, Agnis here is now part owner of the company," Salina said, tossing the papers back onto the table.

Raymond wanted to jump through his computer screen and wrap his hands around Agnis's neck. "Everyody out of the office!" Raymond demanded, wanting to speak to Agnis alone. "Now!" he yelled when everybody was moving sluggishly.

Agnis sat in her chair, laughing as everybody was leaving. She was so arrogant and disrespectful, but she was married to the Mob. After remembering that, Raymond wasn't surprised anymore. This is how the Mob moved when they cut in on somebody. They find the weak link, and in this case, it was James. They gave him enough rope to hang himself, and that's exactly what he did. James turned a half-million-dollar gambling debt into what was happening right now.

"You know I'm not gonna allow you to have any parts of my company," Raymond told Agnis.

"I really don't think you have a choice in the matter."

"You was playing me this whole time," Raymond shot back.

"From the very beginning. I'm an Italian. This is what we do and have been doing for centuries," Agnis told him.

Except for being kidnapped by the Jamaicans on behalf of Emilio, everything Agnis did up to this point was for the purposes of taking control of Rev. Index. When James got in deep with the bookies, Agnis took on the debt for millions of dollars, but with ulterior motives. She did her homework on the company and gained access to some of the most important and intricate details pertaining to ownership.

First, Agnis thought about trying to buy the company, but when James informed her that it would be impossible, Agnis saw another opportunity. She convinced James to get Jennifer to sign over a portion of the company to him in the event that she died, and in return, after Jennifer's death, James was going to make Agnis a partner, giving her a small percentage of Rev. Index. That's exactly what had taken place thus far. It was all a game. Agnis was vicious, and she did nothing but pull strings like a puppet. James killed his own sister, Raymond killed his uncle, and now, Raymond was next. It was unfortunate that Gloria fell in love with Raymond, because the whole family would have been gone by now. With everybody out of the way, Agnis could claim full ownership of Rev. Index, having held onto the percentage she owned. It was pure genius, except that Agnis underestimated the very monster she had created in Raymond.

"Agnis, you know I'm going to kill you, right?" Raymond threatened, looking into the screen with promising eyes.

Agnis remained calm, taking another pull of her cigar. His words sounded so sincere, and in any other circumstances, she probably would have believed him, seeing as how she taught him everything he knew about killing. As of right now, Agnis wasn't sweating it. In fact, Agnis had something brewing right now, and if Raymond didn't get his mind right, he was truly in for a rude awakening.

"It's unfortunate that you won't even be alive to go through with your threats," Agnis said, reaching over and turning off the TV. She sat there, leaning back in her chair with the cigar in her mouth. The company was already starting to feel like hers as she kicked her feet up on the table and plucked her ashes on the floor. Not only was Agnis arrogant, but she was also confident that by the end of the day, Raymond would be lying on the coroner's table, and she would be renovating her new office at Rev. Index.

Detective Santiago woke up to the sounds of the afternoon trash truck stopping in front of his house. He jumped up out of bed, remembering that he forgot to put the trash out. With only a pair of jeans on, he ran down to the kitchen, grabbed the trash, and shot out the front door.

"Hold up!" he yelled, stopping the truck before it got too far down the street.

After throwing his trash in the truck, he headed back toward the house. He stopped at the bottom of his steps, noticing a dark blue Ford sitting up the street. It looked like the engine was running, but he wasn't sure. The windows were tinted, so he couldn't see inside. Instead of drawing attention to himself, Santiago played it off, waving at one on the neighbors as though he didn't notice the car. He turned around to go into the house so he could grab his gun.

He darted up the steps to his bedroom, and at the very moment he crossed the threshold of his room. Gloria came from out of nowhere, clobbering him upside the head with a plaque she had taken off the wall.

"Stay down!" Gloria instructed, tossing the plaque on the floor right next to him. She then pulled out her gun and pointed it at him.

Santiago lay on the ground, rubbing the side of his head and squirming a little. When he finally shook off the pain and looked up, anger filled his veins when he saw that it was Gloria standing over him.

"Get up and take a seat on the bed," Gloria told him.

Santiago slowly got up from the floor and followed instructions. What he really wanted to do was rush Gloria, take the gun from her, and shoot her with it. The distance Gloria had between them, plus the knowledge of Gloria being able to kill without remorse, prevented Santiago from trying his hand.

When he sat on the bed, Gloria leaned up against the dresser and lowered her gun. They both silently stared at each other before Gloria decided to break the silence.

"You've been busy for the past week," she said, looking around the room at the few pictures of Santiago and his family hanging up. "You flipped my old neighborhood upside down, harassed innocent people concerning my whereabouts, and then you go on TV calling me a coward." Gloria smiled and then got serious again. "You see, when you threaten my family, I take that personal."

"Yeah, well, so do I," Santiago shot back, referring to his family being held at gunpoint during Gloria's escape from custody.

"I had no idea that was going to happen. And whether you believe me or not, I didn't mean to kill your partner."

Santiago was furious at this point. "If you're gonna shoot me, then do it," he said, wanting to get it over with.

Gloria looked at Santiago, then leaned off the dresser. "Truth is, I didn't come here to kill you," Gloria said, walking over and grabbing one of the pictures frames from the window.

Santiago had enough. He quickly reached under his pillow for his gun while Gloria had turned her back, but the gun wasn't there. He looked over, and it was sticking out of Gloria's back pocket.

"I came here to give you a warning, and I swear by God that this is a one-shot deal. Leave my family alone, or I will kill you and everybody in this picture," she said, tossing the frame onto the bed. "You can chase me down. Hunt for me as long as you want, but if you threaten them again, there will be nothing else to discuss or negotiate."

Santiago looked down at the picture of his wife and two kids and almost cried at the thought of losing them. By the time he picked his head back up, Gloria was standing a mere foot away from him with the gun pointed at his face again.

"Am I clear?" she asked, looking to get eye contact with Santiago. He simply nodded his head, but that wasn't enough for Gloria.

"I wanna hear you say it," she said, pointing the gun at Santiago's temple. If he didn't say it, Gloria was going to take that as a sign that Santiago was going to be a danger to her family, and the answer she had for that was to blow his head off. As angry as Santiago was, he really didn't want to die, and in some crazy way, he could understand how Gloria felt about her family.

"I give you my word that I won't bother your family again," Santiago promised. "But you know I'm never gonna stop chasing you, right?"

Gloria lowered the gun from his head and jammed it into her back pocket. "Yeah, I know," she replied, cocking her fist back and landing a bone-chilling punch to Santiago's jaw. The punch knocked him clean out, so much that a light snore could be heard coming from his nose. Gloria took Santiago's gun from her other back pocket, popped the clip out, ejected the bullet from the chamber, then tossed the gun onto the bed next to him before leaving.

Disregarding the doctor's orders to stay until his second CT scan results came back, Raymond got out of bed and got dressed as quickly as he could. He really needed to bring Gloria on board with what was going on, not so she could try to rectify the situation, but rather to let her know what he was about to do. Now that everything was out on the table, it was time to deal with it accordingly.

"Sir, you can't leave yet," the male nurse said when he walked back into Raymond's room and saw him getting dressed.

There was nothing anybody could do or say to keep him in the hospital. "Look, I don't have time for this," Raymond said, grabbing his bag and heading out the door. The nurse followed behind him the whole way to the elevator, trying to explain the potential risk of him leaving. He was about to ask the police officer they had passed to stop him, but it was against the hospital policies to hold patients against their will.

"I'll see my personal physician sometime tomorrow," Raymond assured the nurse as he smacked the elevator button.

When the car got up to the floor and the doors opened, a man with a hood draped over his head caught Raymond's eyes immediately. As two other people were getting off, the hooded man pulled a chrome automatic from his waste. Raymond didn't have time to do too much of anything, and it seemed like everything went in slow motion. The gunman looked Raymond right in his eyes and then pointed the gun at him. The elevator door began to close, and that's when he let off the shot. *POP!*

The bullet hit Raymond on the top of his shoulder, knocking him backward to the floor. The male nurse covered Raymond as the gunman got off another shot before the doors closed.

It was intended for Raymond's face, but it hit the nurse in the back. Staff and civilians began yelling after hearing the shots, and it took seconds for a uniformed officer to run down the hallway with his gun drawn.

"Shit, shit, shit," Raymond said, feeling the burning sensation in his shoulder. The nurse that lay over him was motionless, and just when Raymond thought the worst was over with, the elevator doors opened back up.

"Drop the gun!" the police officer yelled, but he was met with gunfire. *POP POP POP POP POP!*

Raymond wiggled from under the lifeless nurse, then scrambled to his feet while the officer and the gunman exchanged bullets at close range,

POP POP POP POW POW POW POP POP POW!

The police officer hit the gunman at least twice, but he wasn't budging, only firing back as he exited the elevator. He aimed for Raymond's back as he ran down the hallway ,but the cop fired his weapon again, this time hitting the gunman in his neck. He spun around and returned fire.

As he backpedaled into the elevator, holding his neck, the cop shot him one more time, striking the gunman in his chest.

Doctors and nurses were afraid to come out of hiding, but when they did, Raymond was lying in the middle of the hallway, waiting on them.

"I need somebody down here!" the officer yelled as he stood over the nurse, while also guarding the elevator doors in case the gunman came back. It was a bloody mess, and Raymond didn't have to be a rocket scientist to know that the gunman who just tried to kill him was either a product of Agnis's camp or one of Emilio's guys. Not that it wasn't already serious, but now, shit just got even deeper. Once Gloria got wind of this attempted assassination plot against her man, she was going to snap. Whoever did it was going to regret the fact that Raymond dodged yet another bullet.

Detective Santiago woke up about ten minutes later and could tell by the pain all over his face that his jaw was broken. It hurt like hell, too, but Santiago still managed to find enough strength to call Young to let him know what just happened. He was still in such a daze that he ended up calling his very own house phone. Noticing it, he shook his head.

"Damn, this shit hurt," Santiago mumbled under his breath. He couldn't lie, from the moment he opened his eyes, he had an epiphany. All this chasing Gloria around like a madman, just wasn't working. The intrusion, along with a sure death threat to his family, really took a lot of the fight out of him. Gloria made it look too easy. If she did want to go through with her death threats, there was nothing he was going to be able to do. How could he protect his family when he couldn't even protect himself? He was thankful they weren't home at the time.

"Yeah, I'm done," Santiago said to himself. He reached over and grabbed the picture of his wife and kids and made a vow that he would no longer go after Gloria. There were plenty of young detectives looking to leave their mark in the department, so for the most part, Gloria would always be hunted until she was either caught or killed. It just wasn't going to be done by Santiago. He was done, at least with this case.

At least one police cruiser was sitting outside of Raymond's beach house when Gloria got back. She got out of her car and walked down the block, knowing that the chances were slim to none that the police in this town knew who she was. She walked right by the cruiser and even waved at the cop as if she were one of the neighbors and was happy he was there.

"*Assalamu aklaikum*, brother," Gloria greeted when Simair opened the door. Simair smiled.

"*Wa alaikum assalaam*," he returned, then stepped to the side so she could enter. "I had a feeling you were going to come here. I'm sorry about Raymond," he said, leading her to the basement.

"What are you talking about? What happened to Raymond?" she asked with a concerned look on her face.

Simair walked over and grabbed the remote control off the pool table. "You didn't know? It's been all over the news all day," he said, turning on the TV. He flicked through the channels, trying to find a news station that was reporting, but at the same time began to explain what he did know.

"Simair, I need your help," Gloria requested. Simair was more than willing to lend a hand.

"Oh, here it goes right here," Simair said, pointing to the TV. The news anchor was reporting live from Presbyterian, explaining the shooting.

"An officer that was on the scene killed the gunman. A male patient was shot but is in stable condition. A male nurse was also shot and is in critical condition, with multiple gunshot wounds to the back and head," the anchor explained.

It blew Gloria's mind hearing what went down. Simair walked over to his gun closet and opened it up. Gloria's face was glued to the TV, until a commercial came on. When she turned around, Simair was holding a baby Desert Eagle by the barrel and extending it to her.

"You take whatever you need. Just don't bring them back."

Gloria took the gun from Simair and tucked it in her waist, then went gun shopping.

"Take your time. I'll be upstairs getting permission from my wife to go outside and play." Simair chuckled then headed for the stairs, leaving Gloria alone to pick her weapon of choice. It was about to go down in a major way.

Agnis paced back and forth in her living room with her cell up to her ear. She'd been trying to call Gloria all day, needing to speak to her before Raymond did. Gloria wasn't answering the phone, though, which started to make Agnis a little nervous.

"Antonio wants to speak to you," one of Agnis's men said when he walked into the kitchen with a phone in his hand. Agnis took it from him, then waved him off so she could speak to him alone.

"Yeah, I know," Agnis answered, already knowing what he was calling for.

"You have to make this right," Antonio said, seeing that the plan to take full control of Rev. Index was going down the drain. Antonio was a good lawyer, but even he couldn't put up a good fight with Jennifer's last will and testament. He would look like a fool in any courtroom trying to contest it. Without Raymond being dead, everything that they'd done up until now would be futile.

"I'll do it myself," Agnis assured, then hung up the phone. She'd had just about enough and was going to bring this thing to a close. If Agnis couldn't kill Raymond, then nobody could.

Raymond

Damn, this shit hurt. I'd never been shot before. Now I saw how Gloria felt. I got hit in my upper shoulder, but I could feel the pain shooting down the whole right side of my body. I knew one thing: I had to get the hell up out of there before these people let me get killed. Why da fuck was it so easy for somebody to walk into a hospital with a gun anyway?

I couldn't believe Agnis did this to me. And I had the nerve to think that she was good people. It was only because of Gloria I thought that way. Agnis wasn't shit, and I couldn't wait to tell Gloria about her so-called friend. I hoped she would cut her head off with a rusty butter knife. Damn, a rusty butter knife. I was vicious. No I was not. I was a normal human being. No, I was not. I was lion. Ha ha ha. Man, I was trippin' out. I think the morphine was kicking in. I felt high as a giraffe's ass. Shit, that was high. And why in the hell was the room getting dark? Who turned down the lights? Wasn't nobody getting no booty.

Ha ha ha ha. I should take a nap now, *I thought.*

Chapter 35

Raymond woke up to some commotion in front of his door. He could hear someone saying that only immediate family could see him. Listening closer to the voice, he recognized it as being Simair.

"Excuse me, detective," Raymond called out to get his attention. The black detective turned his head.

"Can you please let him in? He's family," Raymond lied.

Simair looked mad as hell with his kufi tilted halfway off his head and his garments wrinkled up pretty good from the authorities pushing him away. His angered face quickly turned into a smile once he saw Raymond.

"*Assalaam alaikum*," Raymond greeted.

Simair walked up and stood next to his bed and greeted him back.

"I wouldn't have let you up in here neither, looking like you about to blow some stuff up," he joked, wanting to get a laugh out of Simair, which he did.

"How do you feel?" Simair asked, reaching under his garments to grab his cell phone.

Raymond gave him a quick rundown on how the bullet ripped through his shoulder blade and how doctors said he would have some nerve damage in the future.

"Hold on. He's right here," Simair said, then passed Raymond the phone.

"I love you," Raymond said, already knowing who it was.

"I love you too, handsome. Are you okay? And don't lie."

"Yes, babe, I'm good, just as long as they keep the morphine in my IV," Raymond chuckled. "But no, I'm good, though. I should be able to leave in a couple of days," he told her.

Hearing his voice was one thing, but to see him in person was Gloria's desire. With all the police presence and the fact that Gloria's face was still all over the news, she wasn't going to take the chance.

"Babe, I need to tell you something," Raymond said, wanting to let Gloria know about Agnis.

As soon as he was about to get into it, one of the detectives walked into the room and took a seat in the chair up against the wall. The detective still didn't trust Simair, plus he just wanted to be nosey.

"But I'll let you know another time," Raymond said, indicating that he couldn't talk.

"So, now what?" he asked in a low voice, wanting to know Gloria's next move. "And don't lie to me." He smiled, copying her words.

"I'm gonna finish this shit, something I should have done a long time ago," Gloria told him.

They both became quiet and were probably thinking the same thing, because at the same time Gloria said "I'll be all right," Raymond said, "Be careful."

They both knew that in this murder game, life wasn't promised to anybody. Just as fast as Gloria could take somebody's life, her life could also be taken away from her, and if she were to die, Raymond didn't know what he would do.

"Listen, Raymond, I want you to know that after this, I'm done. I don't want to live like this anymore. All I wanna do is live the rest of my life making you happy and putting a smile on ya face every day you wake up. I want to be with you and you alone, and who knows, maybe we could start our own family one day."

Raymond smiled at the notion.

"I changed the way I look at life, and for that, I wanna give you the best of me," Gloria spoke in a tone which he'd never heard before.

"Go take care of what you need to do so we can get on with our lives," Raymond said before giving the phone back to Simair.

Simair looked over at Raymond and said something that he already knew. "Shc's gonna be all right," Simair said.

Raymond nodded his head.

"Look, I'll be back to see you tomorrow, if God wills," Simair said, shaking Raymond's hand, then leaving the room.

Seeing as how the police presence was so heavy around his room right now, Raymond decided to get some rest, something he definitely was going to need.

"Tear this fuckin' place apart!" Agnis demanded when she walked through the broken front door of Raymond's house. The group of guys she had with her wasted no time turning the house upside down. They were in search of Jennifer's last will and testament. It was the one thing that could ruin Agnis's plan to take over the company, and it would strip her from having any percentage of the company at all. Without it, she was dead in the water.

Gloria

Damn, I hadn't been back in the hood for a minute. It still looked the same, though, with the exception of a few new stores. Being back on Pine Street brought back so many memories, both in a good and bad way. I remembered my dad used to be the talk of my neighborhood, especially when he pulled up to the house in a different car every other month. He dressed nice, too, and most people thought that he sold drugs. He did show a lot of love to people, so the hood had love for him. That was probably why nobody ever tried to rob or hurt him.

I also met Dillon on the corner of this block. Those definitely were the good times. I remembered him and his girlfriend were visiting a freak chick named Barbra, who did hair real good. Dillon went in with am afro and came out with the best-looking braids I'd ever seen. He looked handsome, too. Young and thuggin', just how I used to like 'em back then. I knew I was going to give him some cookies the first time I saw him.

Before that, I remembered my homegirl Anita got jumped by some crazy bitches from the east side. I jumped in and helped her. We both got our asses kicked that day, but it was cool, 'cause the hood respected up. Our whole four years in high school, we never had a problem with anybody. I was sick when Anita got murdered. I thought she was going to be the one who made it in life. She was so smart and was cute to death. I ended up killing the guy who did it once I got into the contract killing business. There was actually a war behind that whole situation. The thing was, nobody knew that I did it, so neighborhoods were going to war about it for a couple of months. They tore the city apart. Damn, I missed my girl.

Shit, I missed my mother even more. I lost her to the streets as well. She overdosed on heroin when I was like twelve years old. She was one of the many people who believed in me and always showed her love through actions. She was the best mom in the world. I tried to find the man who sold her the bad batch of heroin, but by the time I got older, he was dead and gone. Trust me, if I could have, I would have killed him. He brought that

*heroin all the way from Philadelphia, some stuff called
fee fee dope. It was a monster and took the lives of about
twenty other people in my neighborhood around that
time. At one point, I did place the blame on my mother
for being a dope fiend, but at the end of the day, she was
still my mother.*

*As I sat there and thought about it, I was glad I made
it out the hood. Don't get me wrong, I still had love for
my city, but I just didn't miss it like I used to. Shit, I was
standing on the corner of my old block right now, and
it didn't look like much had changed. Dudes were still
outside on the corner selling drugs, dope boys riding
down the street with bid boy rims on their cars, and just
about every female that walked past me had close to
nothing covering their bodies. Yeah, this definitely was
still Pine Street, and I couldn't wait to hurry up, do what
I had to do, and get the hell out of there.*

"Let's arrest her," Detective Grant suggested, watching
Agnis and her boys coming out of Raymond's house.

Agnis should have known that Raymond's house was
going to be under surveillance. Her desperation clouded
her judgment and made her unaware of the police sitting
about a block away.

"We gotta move now," Grant said as he attempted to
get out of the car. Detective Young grabbed a hold of his
arm before he could. Grant was now the new detective on
the case since Detective Santiago was assigned to another
case.

"No, no, let's wait to see what they do next. This case is
a lot bigger than a breaking and entering charge," Young
said. "Look at these guys. Do it look like they'll spend a
day in jail for this?"

Detective Grant looked at all the men who were dressed in suits and casual clothes.

"This here's the Mob, and that right there is Agnis," Detective Young explained to the rookie he had along with him for the day.

"Yeah, but I thought we were looking for Parker," Grant said, not really sure how the Mob tied into the case.

"We're out looking for Gloria, but if we keep our eyes on these guys, they should lead us right to them," Young told him.

He tried to hide his frustration, but Grant could tell that he was beginning to wear out his welcome with all the questions. It was moments like this when Detective Young wished he had Santiago with him, but due to the events that had taken place at his house with Gloria, Santiago really did remove himself from the case. Detective Young and Shields were heading the investigation now. Though Young understood Santiago's decision in the matter, his presence was missed dearly.

The whole Charlotte Police Department was still looking for Gloria, but that didn't stop her from roaming her old neighborhood looking for Maliah. They had been friends since second grade, and she was probably the only person that was true in friendship, at least in the hood. Maliah was in the streets and was probably the baddest chick in the hood. Finding her without drawing attention to herself was the only problem Gloria had.

"Come on, girl," Gloria mumbled to herself walking around 5th Avenue to the Chinese store where Maliah use to be at. Gloria cracked a smile when she heard a familiar voice yelling out from the center of a crowd of people emerged in a craps game.

"Boy, don't play yaself!" Maliah yelled out from within the crowd of men.Somebody was always trying to run game on Maliah to get in her panties, but most failed.

"Damn, shorty with da fat ass!" Gloria yelled, making her way through the crowd. She walked up and took the hood off her head so Maliah could see who it was.

Maliah smiled when she saw that it was Gloria standing there. The crowd of men also looked at Gloria, seeing that she was pretty as all outdoors as well. "Now, that's how you bag a bad bitch," Maliah said, looking around at all the men standing there. The crowd went up in arms seeing Maliah wrap her arm around Gloria's shoulder and walk off.

"They got ya face all over the news, and plus you got a bounty on ya head from the Italians for two million dollars," Maliah said, stopping and giving Gloria a hug.

"Yeah, I know. Things got crazy," Gloria responded, shaking her head.

Maliah could tell by the look in her eyes that Gloria was there for a reason other than to catch up on old times. Maliah stopped in front of her 2015 Impala and leaned up against the door.

"What do you need?" she asked. If Gloria could depend on anybody to be there for her during her time of need, it was Maliah. It didn't matter what it was, or how much Gloria needed her to do, Maliah was there.

"I need you to help me take care of a situation," Gloria said in a serious manner. The look she gave Maliah spoke volumes, and without any further words, Maliah nodded her head, then leaned in for another hug.

"Whatever you need, I got you," she promised, giving her a wink of the eye.

This was why Gloria had the amount of respect for her girl. And just like that, Gloria had someone backing her that she could not only trust, but who would go as hard as her.

Raymond lay in the bed, trying to figure out a way to get out of the hospital without the police making a big deal out of it. The doctor did inform the uniformed police officers that he needed to run a few more tests before Raymond could leave. The surgery was over, and he was patched up with his arm in a sling, so there was no other reason Raymond felt he should be there.

"I guess you think you got this whole thing planned out, don't you?" a voice said, causing Raymond to look up.

Agnis had walked into his room unannounced. Raymond had a confused look on his face, wondering why the officers didn't approach her like they did Simair.

"I know people everywhere, especially in Raleigh," Agnis said, answering the question she knew Raymond wanted to ask.

"What do you want, Agnis? There's nothing left for us to talk about," Raymond said, sitting up in the bed.

"I came with a final offer," Agnis replied, walking closer to his bed. "We both can run Rev. Index. You overseas and me in the States. There's more than enough money for both of us to live comfortably. And at the end of the day, nobody has to die."

Raymond looked at Agnis like she was crazy. After all that had been done, she was still trying to run her old game. "You must have bumped ya fuckin' head if you think I'm about to agree to that. Go fuck yourself, you fake-ass gangster."

Agnis smiled at his insult. She looked over her shoulder to see where the police were, then she turned back to face Raymond. "Last chance," she offered. then began to reach into her blazer pocket.

Raymond came from under the sheet with a compact eight-shot .45 automatic he had sitting on his lap. He set it on his thigh, with his finger snug around the trigger, and it was pointing right at Agnis.

"I know people too," he said.

Agnis definitely wasn't prepared for this. She only had a butterfly knife to work with. She looked at Raymond and smiled again, easing her hand from her pocket, leaving nothing in it when it came out.

"Just like I said, you can go fuck yourself, Agnis," Raymond told her again.

She didn't show it, but she was mad as hell. Every time she thought she had Raymond trapped, he always managed to come out on top. It was frustrating. Agnis never found it this difficult to kill somebody, and definitely not the average Joe. She was almost ready to test his hand, but the thought of those bullets penetrating her body was more than enough for her to think twice about it. Instead, she decided to go another route, one that was sure to get Raymond's juices flowing.

"Let's see if you can save her too," Agnis said with a crooked smile on her face. She didn't even give Raymond a chance to respond before she walked out of the room.

Raymond wanted to shoot her in the back for threatening Gloria's life, but at this point, the only thing Raymond could do was figure out a way to leave the hospital and hope that he got to Gloria in time to let her know what was going on. Up until this point, Gloria was still in the dark about Agnis and her plot. Now, Gloria's head was added to the list of Agnis's madness, and the bad part about it was, Gloria wouldn't even see it coming.

Gloria sat in her car in the middle of Tasker Avenue, strapping a bulletproof vest on and then checking her

weapon to make sure she was locked and loaded. Emilio
pretty much owned the north side when it came to the
drug trading business, and it was certain corners and
establishments that made him the most money. In order
to find out what she wanted to know, Gloria was going to
have to ruffle a few feathers, which could easily become
dangerous for her.

"You good?" Maliah asked when she pulled up next to
Gloria's car.

"Yeah, I'm straight. Let's get to it," Gloria shot back
before getting out of her car and jumping into Maliah's.

They pulled down to 14th Street and pulled over a
nice distance from where Emilio's main stash house was.
To Gloria's surprise, there were a bunch of little kids
standing out in front of the building. They had to be no
older than fifteen. Looking a little closer, Gloria could see
that they were selling drugs and they were packing heat.
She and Maliah sat there and waited, watching the flow
of traffic and seeing how the young crew was moving.

"This gotta be Emilio's shit," Gloria said, seeing all the
traffic coming and going. She tried to wait for the perfect
time to strike, but there wasn't one. Gloria was just
gonna have to go hard, which she had no problem doing.

She tapped Maliah to let her know it was on. They both
got out of the car and headed down the block. Maliah
walked ahead of her. It was broad daylight, but that
wasn't going to stop Gloria from doing what she had to
do.

She walked up on the kid that was doing the most selling, then pulled her gun from her waist. The youngster
peeped the move, but his reflexes were too slow. Gloria
grabbed his arm before he could grab his gun, then
jammed the baby Desert Eagle into his gut.

"Listen to me, little boy. This is not for you," Gloria said,
trying to calm him down.

The two lookouts across the street saw what was going on and tried to come to the rescue. They both froze once they got across the street and saw Maliah come from out of nowhere with an AR-15 in her hands. The long magazine sticking out of it had them shook by itself.

"You know who shit this is? This Emilio's corner," the youngster yelled out. He was under the impression that the corner was getting robbed.

"Little boy, if I wanted to rob you, I would have been done it. I'm trying to see if you wanna make some real money," Gloria said. "Look, I'ma lower my gun, and I'ma tell my friend to lower her gun too, so we can talk. Is that cool?" Gloria asked, looking into his young eyes. Gloria really didn't want to kill any of these kids, but she would if they jumped out there like they were men.

The kid looked at his boys and gave them the nod. The two lookouts lowered their guns.

"What's your name?

"Rico. Why? What you talkin' bout?" he asked, wanting to hear what Gloria had to say.

Gloria lowered her gun too, looking around to make sure they hadn't drawn any attention to themselves. "Check it out. I need you to take me around the city and show me some of Emilio's stash houses and businesses. You do that, and I'll give you fifty grand," Gloria said, pulling out a thick wad of money.

"Why would I do that to somebody who feeds me?"

"'Cause your boss won't be alive by tomorrow, and after he's dead and gone, you're gonna need some money to fall back on. Hell, with fifty grand and a corner like this all to yourself, you should be ahead of the game the next time I see you. I'm telling you, big things can happen for you."

Rico thought about it and came to the conclusion that fifty grand didn't sound too bad. Plus, from the sincerity

in her eyes, he knew that Gloria was serious about Emilio
not living to see tomorrow.

"Yeah, well, I'm still gonna need a connect. Fifty grand
is only good if I can flip it," Rico said, trying to negotiate.

Gloria liked the hustle in this kid. "Yo that's my girl
over there," Gloria said, pointing to Maliah. "Whatever
you need, she got you, and that's my word. There's no
better person to get you connected than her," Gloria told
him.

Rico looked over at Maliah and then down at the
money in Gloria's hand. He grabbed the money, looked
at Gloria, and stuck his hand out to shake on it. It didn't
matter how much money it took for Gloria to shut Emilio
down; she was going to pay it, and truth be told, if Rico
had asked for more, Gloria would have given it to him.

Raymond had his whole legal team come down to
the hospital to help with getting him discharged. They
stormed down the hallway four deep, suited and booted.
When they walked up to Raymond's door, he began to
unhook himself from the IV.

The two uniformed officers stopped Salina and the rest
of the legal team at the door. Salina immediately went to
work, asking the officers if Raymond was being arrested.
The officer said that he wasn't, and that they were only
there for his safety. Salina didn't go for that, writing
down both of the officers' badge numbers.

"Now, you can move out of the way, or I can guarantee
that you won't be a cop by tomorrow," Salina threatened.

The two cops didn't know who Salina was and what
she was capable of, but seeing as how Raymond wasn't
being detained for a crime, there was nothing they could
do. They both stood down, but not before checking with
Raymond to make sure he was okay with leaving with her

"Damn, Salina, remind me to give you a bonus," Raymond said, while one of his other employees helped him get dressed.

"I'm just doing my job. Oh, and I guess this would be the best time to tell you that your company is safe. I have a copy of your mother's last will and testament, and there is nothing the Mob can do as far as taking any sort of ownership pertaining to Rev. Index."

It was a relief for Raymond to know that his mother's company was safe, but Raymond had other concerns and needed to get out of there before he ended up losing the person he loved the most. No amount of money nor success would be able to make him happy if he couldn't have Gloria in his life. Just the thought of it gave Raymond an extra boost of energy, and in a matter of a few minutes, he was up on his feet and ready to get the hell out of the hospital.

"They have the last will and testament from Jennifer," Antonio told Agnis as they rode in the back seat of Agnis's car. Agnis gazed out of the window, watching other cars pass hers. "This still can work if we just get rid of the son," Antonio said.

"I can get rid of him right now," Agnis responded. "Gloria is the key to all of this. That's the only way we can get to him," Agnis said, struggling with the thought that she might have to kill Gloria in order to pull Raymond out into the open. Gloria was like a daughter to her, and this was something Agnis couldn't grasp.

"Well, do you know where she is?" Antonio asked, looking over at Agnis.

She knew exactly where Gloria was headed. She knew her all too well, and knew that Emilio was now her new target. It was a no-brainer.

"I'ma drop you off. I gotta go and handle this myself," Agnis told Antonio. This wasn't just some random person in the streets that Agnis was speaking about. If she did have to kill Gloria, it was going to be between the two of them. She had way too much love and respect for Gloria for her to do anything less.

Gloria had Maliah on another mission while she took care of the small stuff with Rico.

"First things first," Rico said from the back seat. "I'm only showing you these stash spots. Don't expect me to be running up in these spots with you. You're on ya own. Second, I gotta drop this money off in case you have second thoughts and decide to rob me too. And third, if you get killed while you're on this mission, I don't know you, so I don't have anything to give your family."

Gloria chuckled a little at Rico's words. "A'ight, li'l homie, you got yourself a deal," Gloria agreed. "Now, where do we go first?"

"A'ight, Emilio got one stash house where he keeps the bulk of his drugs. Packages normally get picked up by runners, then brought to corner boys like me. On some real shit, that spot might be a little too much for you. Emilio be there a lot, and the security is like Fort Knox. When you get about five or six more men and some bigger guns, you just might be able to make it through the front door," Rico said, not too enthused about Maliah and the guns that they had. "You can turn right here. I'll take you to a spot that's a little more your speed."

When Gloria pulled up to the 5th Street projects, there were dope fiends everywhere. They were coming from all angles. The house that Rico pointed out had constant traffic running in and out of it. It was like a fast food restaurant.

"I'll be right back," Gloria told Rico before she exited the car. There were so many types of dope fiends around, it was nothing for Gloria to blend in with the crowd. She got inside the house and scoped the whole scene out while buying some goods. A female came from out of nowhere, asking Gloria if she wanted to have a good time upstairs in one of the rooms, which Gloria quickly declined. She went into the basement with the rest of the fiends who were smoking and using.

"You shooting in here, or are you leaving?" the dealer asked when he came down into the basement.

Gloria saw her opportunity and took it, pulling her gun from her waist as the dealer turned his back to head back upstairs. She put the man in a chokehold with her left arm, then jammed the gun into his back with the right hand as soon as they got to the top of the steps.

"Act stupid and I'ma leave you here," Gloria said, pushing the guy into the kitchen.

Dope fiends were knocking on the door, but Gloria had her man. A quick pat-down revealed a gun that was taken from him. When a second dealer walked into the kitchen unexpectedly, Gloria spun around and shot him in his chest, knocking him into the kitchen door. The fiends who were sitting in the back of the kitchen saw everything, but they were too high off the dope to yell or scream. *POP!*

Gloria shot a dope fiend, too.

"Aw, shit, please don't kill me," the dealer pleaded.

"Shut da fuck up. Where's the rest of the shit?" Gloria quizzed, walking up to him.

The dealer didn't care if it was Emilio's dope or not. He wasn't trying to die for it. He slowly reached up into one of the cabinets and pulled down a small backpack.

"This is it," he said, walking it over to Gloria. She didn't even check the contents of the bag. "Come on, baby girl,

I gave you what you want," the dealer said with a crying look in his eyes. Fortunately for him, Gloria needed somebody to live in order to tell the story to Emilio. There was a method to Gloria's madness, and she predicted that by the end of the day, she was going to have Emilio's full and undivided attention. On that, Gloria made the dealer lay down with his face to the ground, and then she walked out of the house.

Raymond was in no condition to drive, so he had Mindy play chauffeur. After leaving the hospital, he went straight to Simair's house. Anisa came to the door but didn't open it.

"*Assalaam alaikum*, Anisa," Raymond greeted.

"*Wa alaikum assalaam*. Simair isn't here," she spoke through the door. For a Muslim sister, Anisa was well aware of her boundaries with interacting with men besides her husband. "He left about twenty minutes ago, and please don't ask me where he went. Are you in pain?" she asked, seeing the sling holding Raymond's arm up. "I'll get you something for it. Just hold on."

Raymond was in pain, but he sucked it up for the most part. His thoughts were somewhere else right now, and he knew that time wasn't on his side. "I hate to ask you this, but can you call Simair for me? I really need to speak to him," Raymond said as Anisa passed him two painkillers through the mail slot.

Anisa knew that it was about Gloria and wanted to help out as much as she could. As soon as Anisa was about to retrieve her phone from the kitchen, Simair was pulling up to the house. Raymond was more than happy to see him, but he didn't like the look he had on his face when he got out of the car.

"Where is she?" Raymond asked with a concerned look. "I honestly don't know. I left her about twenty minutes ago. When I tried to call her phone to let her know to call me if she needed me, the phone went straight to voicemail."

Raymond leaned up against the banister and looked to the sky. At the moment, he didn't know what else to do, or even if it was possible to save Gloria before something bad happened to her. It was as if his hands were tied behind his back, and right at the moment when he was about to give up, one more idea popped up in Raymond's head. It was far-fetched, but it was worth a shot. At this point, he really didn't have many options to choose from.

"Simair, let me see your phone."

Chapter 36

Rico drove around with Gloria all day, showing her the most lucrative trap spots Emilio had, all of which Gloria robbed. She had dropped Maliah off earlier and asked her to scrape up a few important items. Gloria had pretty much set the north side on fire, along with a few spots on the south side, which included a car dealership, two numbers houses, and a restaurant Emilio sold grams of cocaine out of. Gloria moved like a ghost in the night and left behind a path of destruction for Emilio to see.

"So, what are you gonna do about the main stash spot?" Rico asked, still counting up all the money and drugs Gloria gave him from the robbery. There was no doubt as to what Gloria was about to do next, and from the stern look she had in her eyes, things were about to turn up.

"I'm going to burn it down and whoever else is in there," Gloria said.

Rico glanced over at her, then went back to doing what he was doing. "Well, I guess this is where we part ways," Rico said, putting all the cash and drugs into a small duffle bag. "I tell you one thing: you're going on a suicide mission, and as much as I would like to stick around and watch the show, I gotta get the fuck out of here," he concluded, and then got out of the car with the duffle over his shoulder. Rico was all the way on the other side of the city, but he didn't care. He just wanted to get as far away from Gloria as he could.

"Let me call him," Gloria mumbled to herself, picking up her phone from the center console and turning it back on. She wanted to call and make sure Dillon was home and safe. When the phone turned back on, there were at least fifteen missed calls. It began ringing in her hand, with an unknown number popping up on the screen.

"Yeah," Gloria answered as she started her car.

"Hey, kid, what's goin' on?" Agnis spoke.

"I'm about to go and take care of that situation," Gloria replied.

"Have you spoken to Raymond? He was trying to get a hold of you," Agnis said, trying to check Gloria's temperature.

"Nah I haven't heard from him. I'll get in touch with him later."

"Well, before you do anything, I need to see you," Agnis said as she took a puff of her cigar. "Can you meet me at the old restaurant?"

Gloria looked down at her watch, not wanting to allow Emilio to live another minute. "Yeah, but it's gotta be quick," Gloria replied.

Agnis watched as the smoke she blew out clouded the lamp at the table where she was sitting. She had fought with herself over this decision over and over again, but this needed to be done. Agnis couldn't take the risk of Gloria believing Raymond's words over hers, and the fact that love was part of the equation didn't give Agnis too much confidence that Gloria would choose her over Raymond.

"I'll be here waiting on you, and don't worry, I'm gonna get you in and out of here in no time," Agnis said, looking down at the Glock .40 sitting on the table.

"Sally, thank you so much," Raymond spoke into the phone as he and Mindy were driving back over the bridge on their way back to Charlotte. He had an idea where Gloria was heading, but he had to make sure before he took a shot at it.

"What's going on, and what are you about to do?" Mindy asked, not sure what she was getting herself into.

"It's best that I don't answer that question. Just make sure the new paperwork and contracts are complete and secured," Raymond directed, taking his gun from the glove compartment and placing it in the sling with his arm.

Mindy knew that something was going on but didn't want to comment on it at first. She thought that it might be better that she didn't know anything. Getting Raymond back to the city was her only task; then after that, she was done.

Gloria met back up with Maliah, hoping that she had what she was looking for.

"Damn, girl. This shit was hard to get," Maliah said, pulling the two grenades from her hood pocket. "And these muthafuckas cost me fifteen hundred apiece."

"You couldn't get any more?" Gloria asked, looking at the merchandise.

"Nah, that's it, girl. You gon' have to work with that."

Holding the grenades in her hand made Gloria want to go and put the work in right now. Agnis was going to have to hold on.

"Yeah, I appreciate everything, girl, and I'm not gonna ask you to go where I'm about to go. Shit, a bitch might not make back from this ride," Gloria said in a joking but serious manner.

Maliah looked at her like she was crazy. It was somewhat of an insult. "Yeah, I can tell you ain't been in the hood for a while. You got me fucked up if you think I'm about to let you roll out by yourself," Maliah shot back, then walked around and got into the passenger's side of Gloria's car.

Gloria smiled, remembering how good of a friend Maliah was. More than grateful to have her by her side, Gloria got into the car and pulled off into traffic.

Emilio

I'd been sitting there all day watching the news, and just about every anchor was reporting live from one of my establishments. In every instance, somebody was either shot or killed. It got to the point where my people down at the police station weren't even trying to talk to me. I knew it was that muthafuckin' bitch Gloria burning my shit down, and that dumb bitch Agnis was letting her. I should have killed both of those bitches when I had the chance.

"Are you good, boss?" Frank asked, walking into the living room.

"Yeah, I'm good. Just make sure the guys are all on point tonight."

Aside from living in a gated community and having round-the-clock security guards patrolling the premises, Emilio had a few of his own guys watching his home at night while he was there. Jake and Tito were at the front of the house, while Jimmy and Mike were at the rear. Emilio wasn't sure if Gloria would be brazen enough to come to his house, or even knew where he lived, for that matter, but he wasn't trying to take any chances. He got on the phone and called more of his men over to the house.

"Look, Jesse and the rest of the guys are on their way over. Keep a close lookout until they get here," Emilio told Frank when he got off the phone.

It was a waiting game, and until Gloria got caught by the authorities or shot dead in the streets, Emilio wasn't going to get a wink of rest.

Gloria cocked back the .45 ACP to make sure she had a round in the chamber before screwing on the custom silencer. Thirteen in the magazine, and one in the head, plus two extra magazines were all she really needed. Maliah, on the other hand, cocked a round into an AR-15 and had a forty-two round magazine. She wasn't about to play any games at all.

"Let's get it," Gloria said, then exited the car.

Maliah was right behind her. A quiet suburban neighborhood provided the perfect cover they needed, walking down two whole blocks with guns out. It was 2 a.m., so everybody was either sleeping or getting ready to go to sleep.

Gloria put her hand up to stop Maliah while she took care of the man in the security booth. Another guard stood outside of the booth. Gloria concealed her weapon, stuffing it into her back pocket as she approached the guard. A smile and a wave of the hand gave the armed guard the impression that Gloria was a harmless civilian. But as soon as Gloria appeared to be walking past him, she spun around and punched him across his face with an overhand right hook. By the time the guard shook off the punch, Gloria had pulled her weapon from her back pocket and pointed it at his head. She looked at the guard in the booth, who immediately put his hands in the air. Gloria secured both men inside the booth, removing any way of them communicating to anybody for help. She then locked them inside and waved Maliah over.

"Watch the front gate. Nobody in and nobody out," Gloria told Maliah.

She already knew where Emilio lived, so there was no need for her to check the books. She walked right through the smaller gate on the side and entered the community.

"You want me to put it in ya ass tonight?" Jake spoke on the phone while walking up and down the driveway. "Nah I want you to suck it after." He laughed, grabbing a handful of his crotch.

Tito shook his head, listening to Jake talk dirty to one of his female friends. He waved his hand in front of Jake to get his attention, to let him know that he was about to walk around the property. When he turned around and headed for the side of the house, Gloria came from out of the dark. Before Tito got a chance to yell out or say anything, a silent flash, followed by a bullet to the head, put him down.

Jake heard the chirping sound, and when he looked up, Gloria was coming across the lawn with her gun aimed at him. He dropped his phone, dipped behind one of the cars, and drew his weapon. Jake fired two wild shots in the direction Gloria was coming from, but he hit nothing. When Jake looked up, Gloria was coming around the back end of the car, letting her bullets fly. Jake was submerged in gunfire, getting hit at least seven times before he could get another shot off.

"Check on it! Check on it!" Emilio yelled from the top of the stairs.

Frank ran across the dining room, into the living room, with his gun aimed at the door. Out of nowhere, something came crashing through the window and landed on the floor by the couch. Frank and Jimmy looked at it and couldn't believe it was a grenade. They both took off. Jimmy ran back up the steps, and Frank ran out the front door.

BOOOOOMMM! The grenade went off, rocking the whole house and blowing a huge hole inside the living room floor. Emilio's ears were ringing, Jimmy's ears were ringing, and unfortunately for Frank, who was outside, lying in the grass, his ears were ringing too. He was unable to hear Gloria walk up, stand over him, and fire a shot into the back of his head.

"You two play it cool," Maliah told the two guards in the booth when the explosion went off. The whole gated community heard the explosion and got up out of their beds to see what was going on. No more than a minute went by after the blast, and two SUVs pulled up to the gate. Maliah faded to around the back of the station but kept her gun pointed at the guards.

"Don't let them in," Maliah instructed, not caring who they were.

The sounds of shots being fired in the community could be heard out by the front gates, which riled up the occupants of the SUV. Smoke coming from the direction of Emilio's house could also be seen.

"Open the freakin' gate!" one of the occupants of the SUV yelled, getting out of the SUV with his gun pointed at the guards.

Two other men jumped out to join, while the other SUV tried to ram the gate. Maliah came from behind the station opening fire on the men. *DA DA DA DA DA DA*

DA DA DA DA! All of the men scattered, taking cover behind the SUVs.

DA DA DA DA DA DA DA DA DA! Maliah was relentless, trying to hit everything moving. Copper-jacketed projectiles peeled through the SUVs with high velocity impact. The two security guards dove to the ground for cover, scared by the sound of the large assault rifle.

DA DA DA DA DA DA DA DA! Emilio's boys couldn't even get off a shot, and with every round of shots being fired, they started to drop like flies.

Gloria ejected the empty clip, then popped a fresh one in as she entered the house. She kept her gun clutched in both of her hands in front of her, walking around the huge hole in the floor. The smoke was heavy in the house, and a small fire had started in the living room from the blast.

As Gloria made her way up the steps, she could see Mickey coming out of one of the bedrooms in the back. He fired on Gloria, striking her in the chest, just about knocking her backward down the steps. She caught herself, though, firing back and hitting Mike in his back before he got a chance to dip back into his room.

Gloria walked up to him before Mike could grab his gun that fell. For shooting her in her vest, Gloria gave him the rest of the clip, filling his body up with hot lead balls.

Silence filled the night and not one soul was moving from behind the two SUVs. Even if there was somebody alive back there, they damn sure weren't about to come out. Maliah wanted to be sure of it. She held the AR-15 in her hands while looking under the SUVs for movement.

The sounds of sirens in the distance quickly caught her attention. She looked up and down the street before running back over and emptying the rest of her clip into the two SUVs. As she was walking off, she reached in her jacket pocket, pulled the grenade, snatched the pin out, and threw it into the back window of one of the SUVs. She took off running back to the car, and right before she got to it, *BOOOOOOMMM!*

Gloria heard the blast outside, indicating that she didn't have long before the cops got there. She ejected the clip and popped in her last one. Gloria cleared every room upstairs with tactical precision, until she got to the master bedroom. She opened the door slowly, and there, sitting in a chair across the room, was Emilio. He had a gun in his hand, pointed right at Gloria.

"The woman of the hour," Emilio said, looking into the eyes of Gloria for the first time.

"Emilio," Gloria acknowledged, knowing who he was.

"You know, things could have been a lot different if you would have come to work for me. Now you gotta die," Emilio said, squeezing off the first shot.

Gloria spun off, firing several shots of her own. She sidestepped across the room until she found cover behind the partition. Emilio stood up out of his chair and tried to chase Gloria down with multiple bullets that hit almost everything in the room.

"Kid, let's talk it out," Emilio said in a deceitful tone as he stood in the middle of the room.

Gloria popped her clip out to see how many bullets she had left in it. There were four, and she wanted to make every last one count. Unscrewing the silencer off for better a better effect, she jumped up from behind the partition, getting off one shot before Emilio let her have it. *POP POP POP POP POP!*

Three bullets hit Gloria in her chest, one of which penetrated the vest on the right side. The fourth bullet hit her in the thigh, dropping Gloria. The fifth bullet just missed her head. The impact to her chest alone almost knocked her out. She was dazed pretty good but came to in a couple of seconds. By then, Emilio was standing over her with an evil look in his eyes. Blood from the bullet wound Gloria gave him leaked from the top of his arm, but Emilio didn't feel any pain.

"You had a good run, kid. And I gotta admit you got a big pussy thinking you could take Emilio out." Emilio leaned in to shoot Gloria point blank in the head when all of a sudden, a hammer being cocked in front of him caught his attention. When Emilio looked up to see Raymond standing there with a gun pointed at his head, he smiled.

Raymond wasted no time pulling the trigger. *POW!* The .357 revolver almost knocked Emilio's whole head off.

The shock effect caused Emilio to squeeze the trigger, sending his last and final bullet right at Gloria's face. Luckily, Gloria was already in the process of moving her face when the gun went off. The bullet grazed her cheek, then struck the floor. Emilio's body slumped over to the side of Gloria, with a hole in the center of his head the size of a golf ball.

Gloria had never been so happy to see Raymond. "How did you find me?" she asked, slowly sitting up on the floor.

"Once Sally pinpointed your cell phone from the tower and saw that you were in this area, I pretty much put it together. We gotta get out of here. The cops should be about to clear the main gate," Raymond said, helping Gloria to her feet.

The small fire downstairs had started to grow, and it wasn't going to be long before the whole house would be engulfed in flames. They had to get out fast, and as they headed for the bedroom door, Agnis came walking up the stairs. Fire could be seen coming from downstairs behind her, and the smoke was starting to rise.

Gloria and Raymond looked at her walking toward the bedroom with a gun in her hand.

"Agnis," Gloria said, happy to see her. "Come on, we gotta get out of here," she said as she limped toward her.

Raymond pulled the tail of Gloria's shirt, stopping her midstride. He knew that Agnis was up to no good.

Gloria could sense the tension between Raymond and Agnis, looking back and forth from him to her.

"All you had to do was kill him," Agnis said, shaking her head. "The money, the company, and the power could have been ours for the taking.

Gloria looked at Agnis with a confused look on her face. She still didn't understand what Agnis was talking about.

"It could still be ours," Agnis said, raising the gun and pointing it at Raymond's chest.

Instinctively, Gloria stood in front of Raymond, shielding his body with hers. "No, Agnis, not him," Gloria said with a stern look in her eyes.

Agnis put her head down and let out a sigh. She regretted having to do it, but at this point, she didn't have any other choice.

"Damn, kid," Agnis said, closing her eyes and squeezing the trigger. *POP!*

The bullet hit Gloria in her chest, knocking her backward. As she fell into Raymond, he caught her, while also taking the revolver he had in his hand and aiming it at Agnis. He fired as they both fell to the ground. *POP POP! CLICK CLICK!*

Raymond fired, but he missed Agnis. He was all out of bullets, but Agnis was all over him, walking up and pointing the gun at him and Gloria on the ground. She kicked the revolver across the room, then stood over them, looking down on them with emptiness in her eyes.

Right at the moment she was about to finish them off, a shadow appeared in Agnis's peripheral view. When she turned to see who it was, the blast from the Mossberg pump knocked half of Agnis's face off. Her body fell to the ground in the hallway, right at the feet of Maliah, who was still holding the shotgun in her hands. She quickly entered the room, got Gloria and Raymond to their feet, and led the way out of the now burning house, barely missing the many police officers who finally made it to the scene.

Gloria

I could hear Raymond yelling out for me to stay awake while Anisa worked on me. I couldn't stay awake for more than one or two seconds at a time, and now it felt like somebody had turned the air conditioner on. I knew I was dying. I could feel it, but the crazy thing was, all I wanted was a glass of water. Damn, that shit hurt like a bitch. Some people say that you see the light of God right before you die, and now I was getting really scared, because all I could see was darkness. I wanted to wake up. I'd rather be alive and in pain than deal with what God had in store for me in the hereafter. One thing

*I did know was that I was not ready to face God with all
the evil I had on my plate.*
    Oh God, *I prayed,* if you can hear me, please let me
wake up. Please give me another chance.

    After Anisa removed the bullet from her chest and
another that was lodged in her thigh, Gloria was out
for a couple of days. The surgery was a success, but it
remained to be seen how long, or even if she would
recover fully from her injuries. Having recently being
shot, her body wasn't strong enough to take another
bullet. It was a waiting game.
    Raymond Greeted Anisa when she opened the door.
    She stepped to the side so Raymond could enter.
"She's doing better. She squeezed Simair's hand this
morning," Anisa reported. "We also made it a little more
comfortable for her.
    When Raymond walked down into the basement, the
pool table was pretty much converted into a hospital bed.
Several soft comforters lined the table beneath Gloria,
along with a couple of pillows that inclined her upper
body slightly. They even had an IV hanging from the
ceiling, providing constant fluids to her.
    "Thank you so much," Raymond said before Anisa
headed back upstairs. If it weren't for her, Gloria would
surely be dead by now.
    Before Raymond sat down in the chair, he leaned over
and kissed Gloria on her forehead. Gloria's body jumped
a little, and it appeared as though she was trying to open
her eyes. Raymond stood there watching as she continued to struggle. Her eyes opened and then closed again,
and she did that several times before finally coming to.

Raymond almost started to cry when she looked up at him. He held it back, though, wanting to look strong for her.

"Hey, beautiful," he greeted with a smile.

Gloria tried to speak, but her mouth was too dry.

"You're gonna be all right," he said, trying to comfort her. "And I'm gonna be all right too," he said when Gloria looked over and saw the bullet wound to his shoulder.

"You know, you're not good at lying," Gloria spoke through her scratchy voice.

"It looks worse than it is." That was another lie, because at the time it happened, Anisa didn't know how he survived after losing so much blood.

They sat there looking at each other without saying anything for a moment. The silence was broken when Simair came down the steps to check on everybody. Raymond quickly wiped the single tear that fell down his face before Simair could see it.

"*Salam.*" Simair walked up to the side of the pool table. "The word *Salam* actually means peace," he clarified to Raymond. "It's truly a blessing from Allah that you are awake right now."

Gloria didn't know why, but whenever Simair came around, she felt more religious, and if she had a question about the religion, Simair always seem to have an answer.

"I know that I'm dying, Simair," Gloria said, clearing her throat. "Am I going to hell?" she asked with a concerned look on her face.

"I don't know if you're going to die. Only Allah knows that. But in the event that you do, going to hell is entirely up to you at this point."

Raymond couldn't stand to hear talk about death, and when he attempted to get up and leave the room, Gloria reached out for him.

"Stay," she said, then turned her attention back to Simair.

"First you have to believe," Simair said.

"Believe in what?" Gloria asked.

"You have to believe that there's no God worthy of worship except Allah, and then you have to believe that the Prophet Muhammad is the messenger of Allah," Simair told her.

"I believe . . . I believe that there's only one God," Gloria said, as she was starting to lose consciousness. She fought to keep her eyes open. "Was this Muhammad guy trustworthy? Was he a righteous man?"

"More righteous than any man during his lifetime," Simair answered.

Gloria shut her eyes, then came back to. "If Muhammad was who he said he was, then I believe in him too," Gloria said, barely able to talk. "I want to die as a Muslim. I want God to forgive me for all of my wrongs."

"Are you sure?" Simair asked.

Gloria nodded her head, affirming her position.

"Then I need you to repeat after me," he said, taking Gloria's hand and reciting a phrase in Arabic. The words Simair said translated to mean, *I bear witness that there's no deity worthy of worship except Allah, and I bear witness that Muhammad is the messenger of Allah.*

Gloria repeated every word Simair told her to and surprisingly, so did Raymond at the same time. Gloria looked over at him and was about to say something, but she began choking on her own blood. She coughed up globs of if, spitting it out onto her chest.

Simair yelled upstairs for Anisa, who came running down the steps. Raymond stood off to the side, looking on, powerless over what was taking place, while Anisa and Simair worked on her.

The bright light Gloria referred to as the light you see before you die was shining, and as her pulse began fading away, parts of Gloria's life flashed right before her eyes—her kids, her marriage, her mother and father, even moments when she was a kid all cluttered her thoughts. It was time, and there wasn't a thing anybody could do. The Angel of Death had already entered the room with the commands from his Lord.

Raymond walked over to the pool table by Gloria's side, and right at the moment she looked up into his eyes, Gloria took her final breath. She died with her eyes open, and Raymond could hardly keep his composure. The whole room became silent, and just like that, the woman who had assassinated forty-three men and injured dozens during her lifetime, was now dead.

The End